Also by MICHAEL SCOTT CURNES

To Pay Paul
Wicked Ninnish
Coping with Ash
For the Love of Mother
Val

Simpleman

a novel

MICHAEL SCOTT CURNES

The author attests that neither *AI* nor *Chat GPT* were utilized in the creation and writing of this novel which is an original work of fiction based on events and people both real and imagined. In the interest of preserving historical accuracy, the author has made the decision to include the actual names of celebrities and politicians when these associations are already deemed to be part of the public record.

TRIGGER WARNING: This is a story about living and growing up rural and gay, and it includes aspects of adolescent sexuality, as well as instances of incest, rape and suicide that may not be suitable for all readers.

This story, while fictional, is based on actual events. In certain cases, incidents, characters, names, and time-line have been changed for dramatic purposes. Certain characters may be composites or entirely fictious. This story is created for entertainment purposes. Opinions, acts, and statements attributed to any entity, individual or individuals may have been fabricated or exaggerated for effect. The opinions and fictionalized depictions of individuals, group and entities, and any statement contained herein, are not to be relied upon in any way.

Copyright © 2025 by Michael Scott Curnes
Publisher: Down Wind Press
Cover and Interior layout by Masha Shubin, Anno Domini Creative
Edited by Andrew Durkin, Yellow Bike Press

FRONT COVER IMAGE: *"Men Through the Ages"* by Greg Dow, SFCA
24" x 36" Acrylic on Canvas, Honourable Mention - 2019 Federation of Canadian Artists Juried Exhibition "Painting on the Edge." (From the private collection of the Author)

INTERIOR IMAGES:
Five Studies for *"Men Through the Ages"* by Greg Dow, SFCA

BACK COVER AUTHOR PHOTO by Bernard Sauvé

COPYWRITTEN WORKS REFERENCED AND/OR PARAPHRASED:

Your Secret's Safe with Me
Recorded by Michael Franks,1985, from the Album, *Skin Dive*
Lyrics by © Michael Franks

Dancin' in the Street
© Motown Record Corporation
Written by Marvin Gaye, William Stevenson, and Ivy Jo Hunter as recorded/released in 1964 by Martha and the Vandellas

Howl
© by City Light Books, as written/performed in 1967 by Allen Ginsberg

Our Last Song Together
© Neil Sedaka and Howard Greenfield as recorded/performed in 1973 by Neil Sedaka on MGM Records, Inc.

Simple Man
© Ronnie Van Zant and Gary Rossington as recorded/performed in 1973 by Lynyrd Skynyrd

ISBN (paperback) 978-1-998844-04-3
ISBN (hardback) 978-1-998844-06-7
ISBN (eBook) 978-1-998844-05-0

CONTENTS

(The stages of a life fully lived as described by William Shakespeare in his play, *As You Like It*.)

Simpleman

PART I: 2025–1999

Last scene of all,

That ends this strange eventful history

UNION CONGREGATIONAL CHURCH
CRESTED BUTTE, COLORADO

March 2025

THERE WAS NO CASKET, FOR REASONS OBVIOUS TO everyone in attendance. A visibly nervous Mitchell Carson had never written or delivered a eulogy before; had never felt this compelled to do so. There was a sheen of perspiration atop his shaved head that seemed to be the bullseye on which the 80s-era track lighting of the slightly modernized sanctuary had been trained. The Simpleman family—which meant Harlan at this point—could have held the service in Gunnison, which had a nicer and larger church. But it was winter in the Rockies and asking folks to travel thirty-five miles on icy roads didn't seem practical.

A month earlier, using People Search online, it had taken Mitchell all of seven minutes to get beyond a free-trial paywall to unmask Harlan Simpleman's now unlisted phone number in San Francisco. Talking on speakerphone to the brother he'd met in person only once before and with whom he more-than-suspected he hadn't left the greatest of impressions, it had taken Mitchell less than ninety seconds to lay out his case for delivering the eulogy. After a jumbled but appreciative inquiry about the state of Harlan's hip replacement—a medical detail Harlan was surprised to learn the caller even knew about—Mitchell had to clarify that he was referring to when Harlan's new hip had popped out of its socket. This had never happened, but it had seemed pointless to correct the record, so Harlan just awkwardly played along, assuring Mitchell he was all better and good-as-new now.

To the hearing-aided ears of the last surviving Simpleman from the original Crested Butte clan, Mitchell's insistence that he be the one to deliver Ronald's eulogy almost came across as sincere, honorable . . . and very much a relief. As Harlan hadn't thought this far ahead about his younger brother's funeral service, there wasn't any need for persuasion, but he couldn't stop Mitchell from listing his reasons. Harlan had no interest in taking on the task. Not because he wouldn't know what to say and not because he was too emotional or sentimental. It was because Harlan had been feeling directly responsible for nearly six weeks now for the meddlesome provocation that had led to the accident that became the reason people needed to gather for a funeral in the first place.

Now Harlan sat in the 143-year-old sanctuary of the Union Congregational Church—which he had occasionally attended with his family as a kid but hadn't been inside since their mother's funeral in 2010—observing its distinct mustiness. Given the long buildup of candle smoke and furniture wax, the countless weddings and funerals, the body odors and perfumes and leaky diapers of the congregation's infant parishioners, and the trace scents from the Glade Plugins that he could see in the wall outlets from the front pew, Harlan couldn't tell what was making his nose itch but strongly suspected the twin floral sprays of tiger lilies, positioned either side of the pulpit, that he was informed had been special ordered and paid for by Mitchell Carson. Neither spiritual nor superstitious, Harlan felt out of place—not just in church, but in most situations generally. He had never cared whether others noticed or remembered him or if they would be talking about him now that he'd reappeared or not. He'd assumed locals had written him off and had stopped talking about him the moment he relocated to California from Crested Butte—and that was sixty-four years ago, immediately after graduating from high school.

Maybe it wasn't the lilies, and he was just allergic to being back home. This hypothesis made the most sense and rang truest. Harlan had falsely supposed that few knew or interacted with this quirky solitarian who was also his only sibling, but to his pleasant surprise, several dozen townsfolk had gathered to pay respects to Ronald Simpleman, his younger brother by three years. Ronnie and Harlan had both grown up in this pocket-size town tucked into a valleyed nook on the western slopes of the Rockies. His little brother—who was different from Harlan in almost every way and had been since the beginning—had returned to Crested Butte not even a decade after leaving. He'd claimed it was to care for their aging parents, but Harlan and their folks, and Harlan was fairly certain most of their parent's friends too, had quietly suspected Ronnie's teaching career must have blown up for him to have boomeranged so quickly. At the time, Ronald had telegraphed he had zero reservations about returning to his birthplace, whereas Harlan had resolutely refused to do so. Now that the last of his family was gone, Harlan reckoned this would be the final time he set foot in Colorado. He wouldn't be here now if it hadn't been for his brother's sudden passing.

In retrospect, which is all you have left when somebody dies, Harlan knew he should have kept his mouth shut. He hadn't needed to butt into his brother's affairs when he'd phoned him with what turned out to be not only an upsetting but apparently fatal piece of gossip. But as it had become customary for more and more months to elapse between their already infrequent telephone check-ins, Harlan needed an excuse to pick up the phone and so passing along some dirt on one of his brother's former students seemed to fit the bill. Shifting his weight now from one butt cheek to the other on the unforgivingly uncomfortable wooden pew, Harlan wished he hadn't made that call. Odd was it that this former student he'd called his brother to gossip about was there sitting next to him now in the front row of the Union Congregational Church about to eulogize his teacher and Harlan's self-cremated brother.

A decade or so earlier, Mitchell Carson had established a Google alert for *Ronald Simpleman* to keep tabs on him in the absence of regular contact. In the intervening years, Mitchell had forgotten all about the alert until he received a notification on his phone citing the Crested Butte News article that detailed the conflagration and tragic killing by fire. Previously, the terms of engagement between former student and former teacher had been roughshod and sporadic over the decades. More recently, their relationship had inarguably turned frosty on account of the dustup they had in 2017 on the heels of the publication of Mitchell's third book. The ambitious novelist had written a chapter into the story based upon his teacher and their unique relationship in far more detail than Ronald would have never in a million years been comfortable disclosing. Mitchell had insisted to Ronald, well after the novel was published and out in the world, that the names and places he'd referenced—particularly in Chapter 18—had been so heavily encoded and wouldn't have been decipherable by anyone else. Not surprisingly, his panicked former teacher had a very different take on this and felt both accused and exposed. After a few years of silent treatment, an eventual written apology arrived in the mail from the offending author with the poison pen. This peace offering achieved some measure of détente, but hackles were up that never came down, and trust between them had been the irreconcilable casualty of their relationship.

Now, as the young church pastor signaled with a nod that it was time to begin the service, Mitchell rose from the forward pew that had been reserved for family which meant him and Harlan. He walked the short distance to the pulpit that—for this day and purpose without the focal point of a casket—had been relocated under the large, round stained-glass window with its eight-petal rosette motif in the Colorado State colors of blue, yellow, white, and red glass. The scene, which would have been aesthetically pleasing to the deceased, suggested that God, Himself, was standing outside and sticking the business end of a kaleidoscope through a hole in the church's façade. Mitchell attempted to clear his throat of a sudden phlegm frog. He separated and lined up the two printed pages on the slanted surface, closed his eyes, and lowered his head for dramatic effect. Then, he began.

"I don't know you and you don't know me, but we all knew Ronald Simpleman. Mr. Simpleman was my high school teacher in the 70s when I attended Stevensville High School in Montana." Mitchell looked up at the small group of mourners. "Go Yellowjackets!" he said, jutting a fist into the air. His gaze settled on a young family of four in the front row, huddled tightly together across the aisle from Harlan Simpleman even though they had the rest of that whole front pew to themselves. The handsome, thirty-something father with a buzzcut forced a courtesy grin at the high school reference. He sat shoulder to shoulder with his wife and their young daughters in pigtails—the eldest with what looked like a first-prize blue ribbon pinned to her yellow dress. All four of them exhibited puffy red eyes and seemed to sniffle in turns.

Mitchell continued. "Stevensville was, and probably still is, a sleepy little hick town with less than a thousand people—about the size of Crested Butte, I imagine. I didn't fit in there, and neither did Ron Simpleman, but man, am I glad we were both there at the same time. Despite our fifteen-year age difference, we understood each other and recognized what made the other tick. He was geeky, fresh out of Stanford grad school, and bursting with liberal ideas—a big-city transplant plopped down in the middle of Big-Sky Nowhere. I was popular—at least with the girls—which made me a target of some of the school's biggest bullies. Mr. Simpleman, I think, recognized aspects of his younger self in me. He went out of his way to be my biggest cheerleader. His encouragement saved my life, and not just in high school."

Now that he'd started his speech and had already gotten what he came to Crested Butte to confirm—that his teacher's house and all its contents were incinerated beyond any measure of salvage or evidentiary incrimination—Mitchell paused to wager whether he could abbreviate this eulogy and perhaps catch an earlier commuter flight back home, or if he should stick to the script. He figured funerals didn't make the best stage for improvisation, especially when you didn't know and couldn't easily read your audience. He plodded on, switching to his second sheet of speaking notes with the practiced dexterity and anticipation of a concert pianist's unsung page-turner.

"Mr. Simpleman—as I called him before calling him my friend—gently exposed me to his way of thinking when it came to what he called the faults of our fathers. He showed me in a hundred different ways that it wasn't just about the dad who conceived and raised me, but about the father figures— just like Mr. Simpleman—that I would encounter on my journey. Those who would teach me and reach me, and most importantly, who would love and respect me for who I was and whatever I turned out to be. He decried the faults of the fathers who made stupid and stubborn choices not to be role models of decency, tolerance, and understanding, but who instead instilled in their kids the ideas that racism, sexism, homophobia, Islamophobia, and transphobia are somehow normal and acceptable. Ronald blamed the fathers who were bullies who had been raised by bullies and who would raise bullies of their own, trapped in a cycle they weren't sensitive or intelligent enough to break out of. Fathers, he said, have been failing their offspring and damaging our better humanity since the beginning of time, and it was because of them that too many of us hate, oppress, discriminate, demean and engage in petty scuffles and endless wars. Mr. Simpleman also told me it was the faults of our fathers for not teaching us about all the different types of birds and bees when giving their talks about the 'birds and the bees.'"

Mitchell paused to catch his breath and remind himself he was standing in a church full of people whose politics and values he did not know or even care about, delivering a message they maybe didn't want to hear. He once again thought about skipping over the next paragraph and wrapping things up before he got himself run out of town. But then he thought about what Simpleman the showman would do with this center stage moment.

He gripped the pulpit with both hands and jumped into the deep swirling whirlpool of his sermon.

"I remember Ron Simpleman feeling pretty adamant that until fathers started showing their children the Big Picture and teaching them about the queer birds and the silly bees that were a part of Nature, too, humans would stay stuck intellectually and wouldn't evolve to realize the full potential of our species. Now, that's some hefty thinking, but like I said, Mr. Simpleman was straight outta Stanford. He wanted to change thinking and improve outcomes in the lives of the young people he was teaching. That's just who he was."

Out of the corner of Mitchell's left eye, he sensed movement in the front row. He glanced up from his notes and saw the young father withdraw the arm he'd been using to hug his wife and two little girls, and tip forward, planting his elbows on his knees just as a tear dropped from the edge of one of his flooding eyes onto his light-blue suit pants.

"I don't know about your upbringings, but about the time I turned ten or eleven, my father purchased a four-volume box set of *The Life Cycle Library* and pointed to where it was wedged between the Index volume of the *Encyclopedia Britannica* and the *Reader's Digest Great World Atlas* at my eye level on the family bookshelf. That was the extent of the sex talk that I never got."

Mitchell glanced at the young pastor to check if his eyebrows were arching in consternation or if perhaps the holy water in the font at the back of the sanctuary had started boiling. The congregation seemed engaged and not the least enraged, so Mitchell continued.

"My dad never told me that some boy birds were attracted to other boy birds, that some wolves, like Mr. Simpleman, preferred to be loners, and that there are girl bees that preferred the company of other lady honey makers—and that all of these variations were okay, even completely natural. Was that because my dad didn't know this himself? Or was his ignorance the fault of his father for not teaching him? Or his father's father before that? Thankfully for me, it was Mr. Simpleman the educator who stepped in where my father and his father and his father's father had all fallen short because they'd been brainwashed too and hadn't been strong or brave or enlightened enough to break this enduring cycle of perpetual intolerance. To the fathers inside this sanctuary and everywhere beyond these walls, I implore you to teach your children better or else the faults of the fathers will continue to handicap and sabotage every generation yet to come."

Mitchell had improvised that last bit and worried that he was grand-preaching now sounding like the politician or embassy diplomat he'd once aspired to become before he'd landed on writing as the safer calling. He'd mostly made his point with his eulogy so far but there was one more piece of business he felt he needed to address, more with Ronald than with this bystanding congregation of innocents who maybe were and maybe weren't paying attention to his sermon.

"A few years into my university career, at age twenty, I learned I had cancer. I found myself stuck back in Stevensville in my parents' house, shuttling back and forth to Missoula for chemo and surgeries. Throughout this awful ordeal, Ronald—by then a good friend—kept me entertained, cerebrally engaged, and hopeful. Sitting side by side in his stuffy attic apartment, we dove with abandon into the world of foreign cinema and music. I remember him exposing me to surrealist movies by directors like Luis Buñuel and Marcel Duchamp. He had this viewing device he said he picked up in Berlin that was prone to overheating because the electrical current was of course different there. This thing was half movie projector half View-Master and he balanced this contraption on his lap on top of a Stevensville phone book so the tops of his thighs wouldn't get too hot. Aside from films, I also remember his love for Michael Franks." Mitchell's eyes squinted as a smile blossomed across his handsome face and his tear factory cranked up water wheels behind each of his green olive-colored eyes. "For those of you not familiar with Michael Franks, he is this smooth jazz musician and singer/songwriter that Ronald revered. He heralded him as the leader of the quiet storm movement in R&B radio. I guess this was around the late 70s. Michael Franks instantly became the soundtrack of that part of my life too." Mitchell used the heel of his right hand to squeegee away a burgeoning tear.

"Mr. Simpleman was my acting coach, my director, my English-Lit teacher, my mentor, my friend, and I suppose my muse. He deserves full credit for launching me into adulthood, for getting me through my cancer battle, and once I began writing seriously, he became my go-to beta reader for every one of my ten novels. I would have asked him to read my latest, but for many reasons, I'd been holding it back, rewriting whole passages, reworking the plot, letting the story ripen—unsure, and not for the first time, of what Ronald's reaction might be. Sadly . . ."

Mitchell stopped, biting his lower lip and letting loose a couple of persistent tears he'd been fighting to hold back. "Sadly, I will never know, now."

On a deep inhale, he continued.

"About the time Michael Franks released his album *Skin Dive*, in 1985, Ronald was already scratching out his post-teaching life in San Francisco. I had returned, cancer-free, to the University of New Mexico. We both raced to record stores to see which of us would be the first to review the latest from our favorite musician. Somehow, we both landed on the same song as our favorite from that album. It was the third track, 'Your Secret's Safe with Me.' This instantly became the theme song of our forty-eight-year-long friendship."

Mitchell looked up from his papers, his upwardly tilting chin directed his gaze onto the open timber-framed white ceiling of the Union Congregational Church. This movement served to redistribute his fresh tears that had been mounting a prison break over the low walls of his thickly lashed eyelids. In this pause, he filled his chest with enough oxygen and courage to get through the final part of his speech.

"In closing," he started to say just as that pesky phlegm frog hopped up from deep in his throat like it was about to croak out a protest. A quick, hand-muffled cough cleared the way. "I'd like to recite a few lines from that Michael Franks' song now, in celebration and in memory of our brother, our teacher, and our friend, Ronald Simpleman."

> *…You're searching for someone*
> *Whose got no lies to conceal…*
> *Waiting for someone*
> *Whose eyes will tell you it's real*
>
> *…Don't you know the deepest love*
> *Comes to those who wait*
> *Why be smart, hear your heart*
> *Leading you to someone who*
> *Know it's not too late*
>
> *Your secret's safe with me.*

Mitchell detected more open sobbing now, emanating mostly from the girls in the front pew as their pigtails quivered and beyond the front row heads on both sides of the sanctuary had bowed in unison. He rejoined Harlan Simpleman in the front row, the oak pew creaking almost maleficently as he sat down.

Harlan patted and squeezed Mitchell's thigh in faux appreciation, while internally, he was seething. He'd long harbored a grudge from the bit of personal history he'd had with Mitchell Carson some years ago when they'd met for the first time, but before this memorial service, Harlan had also skimmed an online synopsis of the novel Mitchell Carson's publisher was readying for release. What he read there made him highly skeptical that his dead brother's secrets were safe with this opportunist. He frowned now, watching Mitchell Carson, his performative eulogy in the can, make the hastiest of exits from the church just seconds after the pastor had blessed the thin flock with his parting benediction.

As mourners idled in the vestibule, waiting their turns to pay respects to the surviving Simpleman who stood hands clasped in front of him just inside the wedged open set of church doors, the young father from the front pew sensed a gap in the one-person receiving line and herded his young entourage toward the exit. Harlan lifted his sorrowful face in recognition.

"Junior," Harlan said, shaking the outstretched hand using both of his own. "It's so good to see you. Thank you for coming. I don't know that I have met your wife and daughters before."

Junior spread out his arms to bring the three women in his life into the circle. "Harlan, this is my wife, Sofie, and our two daughters, Madeline and Rose."

"I am delighted to meet you," Harlan said, bending to shake the hands of the two girls in matching dresses. "You've won a prize, I see."

Junior issued a nervous laugh when the blushing daughter couldn't overcome her shyness to speak for herself. "She won her class science fair," he boasted. "With a great deal of help from your brother."

"*Pepperoni* helped me win!" the freckled girl practically squealed as though someone had just pressed a button to animate her out of her shyness.

Harlan had a quizzical look on his face and Junior jumped in to translate. "From birth, really, the girls have always known your brother as *Papa Ronnie*. But when Madeline was quite young, she thought we were calling your brother *Pepperoni*."

The adults laughed as both girls, ages 12 and 10, spun into their mother's protective embrace. "Madeline insisted she be allowed to wear the ribbon to the memorial service today," Sofie added.

"Ah, I think I remember hearing something about this," Harlan confided to the parents. "You should be very proud, dear," he said to the older of the two sisters. "And I am proud to learn that my brother could contribute to your scholastic achievement in some way." Realizing he was maybe talking above her comprehension level, he added, "I am happy knowing Pepperoni could help." She swiveled her head that had been buried in her mother's skirt and flashed a delightful gap-toothed grin. Junior used his meaty hand to pull Harlan into a half hug which normally would have been against Harlan's will, but Junior had the physique of an athletic lumberjack and for Harlan it wasn't an altogether unpleasant experience. "Thank you for coming, Junior. It's lovely to meet your young family." The girls hopscotched through the doors and into the high-altitude Colorado sun, gulping in the mountain air as though they'd just broken surface after ascending from great underwater depths.

AFTER HOBBLING WITH his cane back to the pew at the front of the sanctuary—feeling he needed some time alone after the last of the respect-payers had left the premises—he sat there in a low-grade daze, taking a moment to remember his brother and their shared upbringing. Harlan hadn't been the best brother. The truth was, he hadn't tried all that hard. Their parents had harped on him since Ronald was born to be his brother's protector and to set the example of good behavior, but Harlan's mind and selfish heart hadn't seen this as his obligation, so he'd shirked it, plain and simple. If anything, he'd led his brother astray more often than he'd shown him the way. In his defense, this had been out of boredom and not maliciousness.

Still, having Ronald die first wasn't the right order of things and Harlan couldn't help fixating on that fact. He'd always figured he'd be the first one to go, since he'd had a few health issues, ranging from a chronic iron deficiency (likely due to his vegetarianism) to the irregular heartbeat he'd had since infancy. Plus, he was the eldest by three years. But the fallacy of this life-expectancy forecast was that little Ronnie had always needed to be the first at everything.

Before retreating to the abandoned sanctuary for this quiet interlude, Harlan had asked the pastor if he'd mind phoning Rocky Rides to arrange for his airport shuttle pick-up. Now, the pastor popped his head back inside the nave from his adjacent office to confirm the van was about twenty-five minutes away and that he was welcome to remain in the church until it arrived. This ETA would still give Harlan plenty of time to get to the Gunnison-Crested Butte Regional Airport for his commuter flight to Denver, where he'd connect with his redeye home to San Francisco.

In the weeks since his brother's accident, he'd become both resigned and comfortable with the realization that he no longer had any living relatives binding him to Crested Butte. Immediately listing the family acreage with the first realtor that topped his Google search, and hoping for a quick sale, he looked forward to having no property ties here, either. He'd known when he got the call from the retired fire chief, who was an old family friend, that this would be the last trip he'd make to the place where he'd grown up—the place he'd gotten the hell out of as soon as he could.

Harlan had initially brokered his deliverance from what he referred to as "redneck evil" decades ago by delegating the oversight of the family holdings to his younger brother. It was Ronald who had been given uncontested power of attorney, including medical directives for each of their parents, whose wills provided for the brothers to co-own, maintain, and dwell in the family home for as long as they both desired and needed. Given Harlan's twin requirements for culture and life at sea level, offset by his disdain for ignorance and altitude, Ronald had been instructed by his older brother to keep the home fires burning and their parents cared for until they passed. Harlan figured it was pointless to quarrel over semantics now that he'd lost his lifelong scrimmage and debating partner, but he still felt compelled to defend the proposition that *keeping the home fires burning* should not have been misconstrued to mean *burn down the home.* For fifteen years after the last of their parents had passed (their father, Paul in 2008, followed by their mother, June, in 2010) Harlan had tried to light a different fire under his brother's butt—one that would get him to sell the property and use his half of the proceeds to downsize and move anywhere he wanted to live in the world. But little Ronnie couldn't be coaxed or budged from that house. That tediously long-running campaign by Harlan the Harper, as his brother had nicknamed him, had finally ended now, and cataclysmically. Ironically, as things turned out, and in keeping with his younger brother's dramatic flair, the caretaker designate had been perfectly capable of lighting his own fire. As the fire chief's report and soon, Ronald's epitaph would read, Ronald Paul Simpleman (1946–2025) perished in a house fire that destroyed everything.

The subtext: everything except Harlan's manufactured but enduring childhood trauma.

About a week before the funeral, Junior—the newly promoted rural volunteer fire chief—had confirmed with Harlan by email that he had towed the charred hulls of the three vehicles off the property to his auto-body shop for parts and scrap. This meant that all that was left of the Simpleman legacy now was an insurance claim, a hopefully expedited real estate transaction if he was lucky, and the brief coda of Harlan's dwindling years, which he hoped would play out as undramatically as possible, in keeping with his anything-but-showy-character. Sitting alone in that church, Harlan felt oddly relieved by this catastrophic and yet tidy ending to nearly all the irritants that had been bugging him.

From the shadowed wings of the nave, the young pastor—having removed his regalia to expose either a moth-nibbled or a campfire ember-singed black turtleneck under bibbed snow pants held up by suspenders, one of which hung off a shoulder—approached the elder in the front row. He not-so-subtly jangled his keys, anxious to hit the slopes for a few downhill runs before the lifts stopped operating at 4 p.m. Hearing him approach, Harlan cane-leveraged his weight off the pew to a standing position that favored his good hip. The pastor reached out a set of neatly folded papers.

"The fellow who delivered your brother's eulogy left these notes on the pulpit. I thought you might like to keep them," he suggested in a soft whisper.

Harlan unfolded and examined the pages, gauging the value of such a keepsake. He could see that the speech had been printed on recycled paper. Printed on the back of the first page was a copy of his rental-car reservation, and on the back of the second, a Google map with driving directions from the airport near Gunnison to the rural address of the Simpleman home, or what was left of it. If the infamous writer had stopped by the ruins before the memorial service to rummage around the ashes and debris, searching for something he thought belonged to him, then Harlan hoped he had found it. Because Harlan had no intention of doing any such reconnaissance himself.

CRESTED BUTTE

January 2025

RONALD SIMPLEMAN DEVOURED THEN HELD A BREATH as he powered through severe osteoarthritis in his right shoulder to inspect and then gingerly reinsert into his anus the three hemorrhoids that he'd nicknamed Alecto, Tisiphone, and Megaera. Most days, he dispensed with formality and just referred to them as "the Furies." But sometimes, he found it necessary to single them out by name and recognize them for their outstanding achievement of turning his sunset years into a mostly miserable affair.

This was neither the high point nor the only part of the seventy-eight-year-old's morning routine, but the trio kept him company, kept him guessing, and kept him focused at least once every day. All three of the Furies had popped out this morning—perhaps hoping for an early Groundhog Day to cast their shadows.

Outside the double-paned and frosty windows of the mid-last-century three-bedroom ranch house it was minus-14 degrees in rural Gunnison County before factoring in the windchill. With three new inches of overnight snow added to the existing accumulation—the white stuff had been falling, drifting, and rearranging its aspen-leaf-speckled semblance since the first of the year, six days ago—Ronald accepted that winter had finally arrived and would likely stay until May. For the first time he could remember—amid this dire and troubling age of climate change—it had not been a white Christmas. Crested Butte Mountain Resort had still not begun lift operation, though he'd heard on KBUT radio a minute ago that this unusual dearth of snow might be remedied by the coming weekend if the current rate of accumulation continued.

His scraggily, long, grayish-blond hair and beard—neither of which had been clipped since the start of the millennium created a wet curtain that hung from his head like drab party streamers as he half squatted in the utility room shower for the requisite reinsertion. Thankfully, Ronald didn't need a visual on the worksite, so his Yeti-esque hairstyle was not the obstacle. The main reason for the oodles of lost time he experienced each morning was his ever-cramping right shoulder, which had been dislocated at least twice in his youth and was now riddled by bursitis. Each time, it had been brutishly reset by his father, an orthopaedic surgeon by training and trade, who had unapologetically body slammed him against the nearest wall. With his dad now long gone, Ronald babied the shoulder, fearing that he'd just need to let it dangle there if it ever popped out again. The other ailment he had been unable to evolve his way out of was a fused index finger that had been jinxed by calcified joints. Because of these infirmities, his probing and fumbling typically meant that the limited hot water ran cool before the reinsertion ritual could succeed.

Ronald was more than aggravated by lukewarm shower water, but living alone for the past fifteen years, he felt relegated to using the narrow shower in the middle of the home's utility room, since he could more easily brace himself against its plastic walls, thereby reducing his fall risk. The issue with the hot water supply to this shower stemmed from the camper-sized hot water tank across the room, concealed behind the gingham curtain under the laundry folding counter next to the washing machine.

Back when he was growing up, June Simpleman—Ronald's home-making mother and the only woman in the household—had insisted on washing clothes in hot water, as she felt this was the only way to temper the pungent stench she claimed only males could produce. She touted and stood by a body of evidence that Simpleman men had to be the worst. Bio-logically, Ronald fancied manly scents and had been drawn to these odor molecules ever since he was knee high to a male grasshopper's armpits. Just like an elk in rut, he could catch whiff of another male from miles away, his odiferous essence carried on the slightest breeze, such was the dialed in state of his nasal instrumentation. For Mother's Day, 1957, the stinky Simpleman men surprised June with a dedicated hot water tank that had been excised with the delicacy of a transplant organ from the father's former travel trailer, by the surgeon-father himself, after both axles snapped when the trailer got stuck in rain-eroded channels of a backcountry road during a late-season elk hunt. One night when June was on the other side of the county playing bridge with other sophisticated rural ladies, this water heating device had been secretly plumbed directly to her washing machine with a dogleg feeder hose looped under the rafters and dropped to the shower stall that had been roughly framed in with two-by-fours in the middle of the utility room without an accompanying toilet or sink. The shower—technically separate from the Mother's Day surprise—had been installed so the big game hunter could wash the deer and elk blood, bone, and tissue off the second-hand orthopaedic tools he'd brought home from the Gunnison Valley Hospital and used for dressing his seasonal kills during hunting season.

Every time Ronald stripped down and stepped inside the shower stall roughly the dimensions of an upright casket, he had to visualize high mountain meadows replete with columbines and rainbows to block out the horror show that must have played out inside that rubber-curtained box. In a matter of seconds, though, his mind couldn't help wandering, and he wondered if maybe one of his father's left-behind hospital gadgets could snip and cauterize the Furies that tortured him so. There was one nifty feature of this unusually placed shower stall and that was the molded plastic bench seat integrated into its design. This came in handy as a footstool when Ronald felt compelled to trim his thick, yellowed crop of toenails. But not today with the Furies pushing DEFCON 2, at max inflation.

Harlan—Ronald's older brother by three years, and his last living relative—would have nothing to do with the family house or Colorado in general. Harlan instead revelled in his rather Bohemian lifestyle cocooned inside San Francisco's Castro District. He would squawk during their every-so-often telephone calls that it was high time Ronnie hired in-home care if he was going to squat in their parents' house for much longer. But Ronald didn't feel he'd be there (or anywhere) much longer, so he tuned out the nagging advice, stubbornly determined to age in place and in private, like his parents before him.

The house in which the Simpleman brothers had grown up during the 50s—long before the ski resort had been developed on Mt. Crested Butte, bringing with it the "Godzilla of Tourism" as their mother had coined in reference to the onslaught of ski bums that annually invaded their quaint little pocket in the Rockies—had been locally considered an architectural achievement when it was first built. To anyone not personally directed to or attached to the place, the out-of-the-way rural address might have seemed a dilapidated oddity by 2025, but few ventured out that way, which had always suited the Simplemans just fine.

According to their mother, who liked to rail against the commercialism of the ski resort but conceded that if it hadn't been for skiing, the county probably would never have gotten around to building the new regional hospital in the 70s. With its state-of-the-art orthopaedic surgical suite, designed for and with input from their father—known outside the household as Paul Simpleman, MD, OS—this development meant their father, June's husband, and the sole bread winner no longer had to commute back and forth to Gunnison over winter roads that could often turn treacherous during the course of a long hospital shift.

This house in which Ronald "squatted"—the term was his brother's—had been left to the two of them equally by their doting folks. They were instructed to carry on the Simpleman tenancy and continue to exert their father's dominion over the seven-and-a-half acres of aspen- and ponderosa-dotted grasslands their folks had christened "Simplemans' Paradise." The young family had started out living in a different, much smaller house in town that Ronald had no memory of but that his mother recalled as having nothing redeemable worth remembering. The ortho surgeon had apparently spent a long weekend in a downtown Denver low-rise office building staring over the shoulder of the big-name architect he'd engaged to convey his napkin-sketched design into a blueprinted and buildable reality. Before, during, and long after the house was constructed over the spring and summer of 1953, Doc Simpleman had loved showing off the blueprints and drawings to his colleagues while boasting how he had over-scrutinized every detail of the 3,412 square foot, three-bedroom, three-bathroom house with its sizeable office that his wife constantly and mistakenly referred to as a den. Doc Simpleman certainly liked bragging about his custom-built home, June often remarked, but not once did he invite his colleagues to see it for themselves. She, on the other *Better Homes and Gardens* hand, entertained lady friends and hosted smoky bridge nights while her husband found excuses to be otherwise entrenched in some emergency at the hospital. The home's building site had been somewhat of a challenge, Ronald remembered, as construction needed to meet the rural zoning and structural codes of the time and materials needed to be hauled a fair distance out of town. With the arrival of Godzilla shortly after the ski resort opened in 1960, Crested Butte stretched its avenues, alleys, pavement, plumbing, telephone poles, and mountain biking paths out their way making their house not all that remote by the mid 70s.

The home's exposed timber-framed layout featured a grand living room offset by a floor-to-ceiling fireplace faced with black rocks, orange shag carpeting, and a dramatically vaulted ceiling, seemingly held aloft by a wall made entirely of glass. This special effect was formed by square, trapezoidal, and triangular fitting thick-paned windows that overlooked the vast, sloped expanse of their acreage below and the Butte's foothills in the distance—on any day that wasn't socked in like this one. The kitchen and dining area also took advantage of the impressive Butte views, while the bedrooms stacked behind it weren't anything architecturally worth mentioning, except that they were staggered along the length of a wide hallway and were interspersed with bathrooms and closets. The office, which was not a den, positioned off the other side of the living room and next to the utility room and garage, had served as the private quarters for the doctor, and was strictly off limits to the rest of the family. He claimed it housed file cabinets full of sensitive medical records. But the curious brothers discovered quite early that the file cabinet was where the doctor kept his collection of pornography.

In its initial decades, the unusual Colorado Rockies home appeared ready-made for its DeMille close-up. It should have been but was never featured in or on the cover of *Better Homes and Gardens*, despite June's regular and cleverly written photo-story submissions. The home fit the Simpleman Family like a glove. From the outside, it wasn't a log cabin, because June had always insisted they not appear like hillbillies. But the windowless walls of the living room were faced with the trimmed off sides of logs that old Joe Falsetto, running the sawmill in the 50s, said Doc could have for free, around the time the roof was going on the house. The log-textured walls turned out to be a pain to dust and keep clean, but this had been one of Ronald's earliest allowance-incentivized chores once he topped out at six feet, around grade ten. By then, he could reach another three or four logs higher when he balanced on tiptoes. His mother, quite possibly stoned on Lemon Pledge fumes, loathed that living room wall finishing from the get-go; often referring to the feature as her "Clampett compromise." She wore her fingers to the bone creating a multitude of macramé hangings—several including pots of hearty philodendrons—to soften what was clearly an assault on her *Better Homes and Gardens*-informed sensibilities.

The family abode had been crudely modified several times in the 80s, after the young Simplemans had shuffled off to different California universities to start their new lives. The necessary upgrades were mostly on the exterior approaches, to accommodate the wheelchair that their by then diagnosed MS-stricken mother would need for the rest of her life. Now that Ronald was a senior citizen with his own suite of hunched-over ailments, he was well-served by the ramps, railings, grab bars, lowered kitchen counters, and widened passageways.

Topping the chart of Ronald's afflictions, at least for the moment, had to be Alecto. This hemorrhoid was the largest and most stubborn of the Furies. It's not that he saved her for last by choice; it was that the other two irregularly blooming nodules needed to first be parked off to one side of the garage before the voluminous, unrelenting goddess of vengeance could be accommodated in the bay that was his bottom. Adding futility to defeat, he knew his valet parking arrangement was only temporary. But if it was a good day, he could keep her tucked in through lunch.

An English teacher and a literary scholar by education and vocation, Ronald was painfully aware that the original Furies only punished the wicked. He wasn't about to wiggle out of that judgement. He couldn't plead innocence or expect probation given his proclivities and the unspeakable acts—some of omission—that he'd committed back when he should have damn well known better. In hindsight, given that he'd lived through the Harvey Milk and George Moscone assassinations in San Francisco in the late 70s, he might have deployed a "Twinkie defense," as it was called in trial law. But Ronald's transgressions had nothing to do with junk food and everything to do with a certain twink—which he understood was the urban vernacular these days for a male classified as underage—with whom he'd tangoed, also in the late 70s. Thus far into his twilight years, he'd avoided arrest and having to take the stand in his own defense and since he had no alibi and no excuse, his testimony would have been disastrous. Instead, he'd voluntarily skipped town and expeditiously got himself out of state, and at least for the past fifteen years since his parents died, he had been remorsefully serving out his self-imposed punishment in solitary confinement.

Rectal baggage stowed, Ronald towel-dried the spots he could reach, and air-dried the rest, shuffling buck-naked with his butt cheeks clenched through the house to tend the fire he'd restarted roughly ninety minutes earlier, when he'd climbed shivering out of bed. He deduced from the sound and smell that there must have been a hefty raft of cedar in the last few cords of firewood. Ronald had this acute nasal knack for isolating and discerning scents and odor molecules. He'd easily combusted several tons of fuel in that fireplace over the decades and his nose could note the differences between cedar, aspen, alder and ponderosa. His mother thought he should have been either a perfumer or sommelier—depending of course on which paid better since both her boys had ruled out medicine but still needed to make a living. He'd strategically stocked up the shed and under the roof overhangs three weeks before the holidays and before the eventually beckoning ski hill would steal away Junior—his athletic skier friend, auto mechanic and firewood supplier—for the rest of fireplace season. The mouth of the black stone fireplace popped and creaked and snapped and hissed like demons back at him as the flames grabbed hold and steamed the bejesus out of the split logs.

Each polished rock in that floor-to-ceiling fireplace had been hand-selected, using child labor, from the banks of the nearby Slate River. Under the watchful eye of the commandant—their father—whose own hands were the money-makers that kept the family flush and therefore could not be subjected to domestic injury (or so he'd insisted), the Simpleman boys toiled in backbreaking conscription every weekend for a month while the family home was being finished.

Oddly, their father denied the equivalency between rock gathering and his annual elk hunts, which even to a seven- and ten-year-old seemed more fraught and dangerous than hauling flat rocks up from the riverbank. Ronald still remembered his father shouting down at them from his watchtower—that is, the lawn chair he constantly realigned with the sun's short march across the sky between mountain peaks, so that he could tan his face and upper body. Every time the boys paused to watch a fish, skip a rock, or try to catch a tadpole, he'd yell at them to get back to work, claiming this would build their characters and grow the muscles they would need to carry them through life.

The Simpleman brothers didn't build many muscles, but they became quite adept at recognizing platitudes—in other words, their father's bullshit. Their toil and sacrifice eventually paid off, as the final touches of the family home came together around the imposing masonry fireplace, which became the centerpiece of the log-paneled "great room."

Years later, this ebony monolith was adorned by the taxidermized head of a Rocky Mountain elk that had antlers a good four feet tall and as many feet wide. The elk head ruled the living room space like an overlord. This remarkable specimen of *Cervus canadensis nelsoni* had been the surgeon hunter's final victim. Harlan had been the one to name it "Bruce." A length of cobwebby silver-and-gold Christmas garland and a dozen or so teal ornaments that adorned and dangled from Bruce's impressive rack had been left up there when the last Simpleman went off to college. Apparently, it had been too risky for the surgeon to be up a ladder, with his moneymaking hands and all. Ever since Ronald had returned home, the prodigal son made it his practice to give Bruce an all-knowing wink every time he entered the room. After both his parents passed, Bruce was the only creature to converse with, and Ronald often thought he caught Bruce winking back at him. Such were the haunts, mirages, and illusions of living in isolation.

Ronald scoot-limped his plantar-fasciitis-riddled heels through the kitchen and down the darkened hallway. Several of the seams on the wallpaper were peeling back, but even in the absence of natural light, he could make out the viny and leafy peony pattern each time he transited to or from his bedroom. His bedroom, the largest in the house, had been his parents' room until fifteen years ago, when the last of the pair slipped the surly bonds of earth. As a literary scholar, Ronald knew the credit for that evocative line—slipped the surely bonds of earth—belonged to John Gillespie Macgee Jr. from his 1941 poem *High Flight*, even though Ronald Reagan seemed to want the masses to believe he came up with the line all by himself when he addressed the nation following the explosion of the Space Shuttle Challenger in 1986.

Ronald sluggishly got himself dressed in the same clothes he'd worn since the first of the year. It was a habit of convenience, since he always kept the previous day's uniform slung over the back of a vanity chair situated across from the bed, where it practically begged to be donned again. Consisting of threadbare sweatpants with a timid drawstring that kept retreating inside the waistband where it couldn't easily be fished out, topped by a somewhat matching faded pink Stanford hoodie, this uniform sometimes included socks and underwear but generally didn't unless his crack was slathered in Preparation H, like it was today.

Ronald returned to a whistling tea kettle on the stove in the kitchen without so much as straightening his bed or fully pulling up the gray logger socks with the red heels and red double ankle stripes. He'd managed to hook the ends of his feet into the sock openings without having to bend over, knowing full well the Furies would take advantage of any such movement to jack-in-the-box their way out of cramped quarters. He scooted each of his socks further onto his feet during the first few steps down the carpeted hallway, knowing this might be as *on* as his socks would get that whole day.

Armed with his second mug of sweetened Sanka, the seventy-eight-year-old, self-identified geezer, feeling worn out though it was only 9:30 a.m., perched half-cheek on a ratty tasselled barstool he'd scooted to the kitchen window to watch the snow falling. He adjusted himself inside the crotch of his sweatpants and scooted an inch forward. When he sat just right, he'd learned through trial and error, Alecto couldn't pull her usual escape-artist routine.

He was thinking he should phone his brother and wish him a Happy New Year, but he also knew he wouldn't. He was always the one doing the calling. To drive that point home, he had decided to see how long it would take Harlan to make the effort. The problem with this test was that Ronald couldn't exactly remember when it began. He thought maybe it stretched back as far as Thanksgiving when he and his brother last spoke, but he couldn't pinpoint if that chat had been this year or last. There might have been an email forward of a magazine article or book review, or an e-card exchanged somewhere in that period, but the brothers certainly hadn't *spoken*.

And maybe it was no wonder. Ronald usually harped on getting Harlan to move back to Colorado with such frequency that they'd both tired of playing the same broken record. This could be avoided, they'd learned, by not turning the stereo on in the first place. Harlan couldn't be talked into leaving the Castro, and his brother knew it, which made his senseless campaign more irritating for both. Easily the more cosmopolitan of the two, Harlan was not ashamed to profess that he was a hillbilly reformed. The summer smells of aspen sap and high mountain blossoms wafting down the draw behind the family house was not his notion of utopia. Not then. Not now. Not ever. And the idea of padding around on orange shag carpet with his geriatric brother until one of them died just couldn't compete with taking in the Film Noir Festival, "accidentally" cutting through the Folsom

Street Fair on his way to an out-of-the-way market, or spending the better part of any morning at the Conservatory of Flowers.

In not-so-secret fashion since he'd mentioned it nearly every time they spoke, Harlan had wanted to sell their parents' Colorado property after their mother had passed, as his perpetually dwindling bank account could have used the cash injection. Harlan Simpleman had dabbled in interior design, did some off-and-on acting and voiceover gigs for regionally produced commercials, and even wrote and published a vegetarian cookbook at one point. But he never accumulated wealth sufficient to see him through his end years—which had certainly arrived by now, as he would be turning eighty-two in the spring.

Harlan been the first to leave home for college and hadn't looked back. Why or how could he, since the eldest was supposed to be the one to strike out and conquer the world? The youngest was not; some unwritten hogwash established it was the unnegotiable duty of the youngest to nurse the ailing parents that had brought them into existence. That's how it felt to Ronald, anyway. Mr. and Mrs. Simpleman had long deployed a strategy of *keep your relatives close but your biologically assigned caregiver closer*. It was as though they could decide to snatch away Ronald's otherwise meaningless life and trivial pursuits when their need for caregiving arrived. And when that moment came, they didn't even bother asking Harlan what he was up to and whether—whatever his mystery career at the time happened to be—he could perform it remotely from their Rocky Mountain home. Why would they? He wasn't the youngest.

Despite a three-year age difference and their common bloodline, the brothers had always behaved like they were forced allies. This was another symptom of rural living, perhaps. There had been no free or natural selection involved in the choosing of playmates or co-conspirators. You either played with your brother, or you played by yourself. In practice, the Simpleman nuclear family may have been more radioactive than most—though they managed to publicly fake harmony.

And sure, the affluence and socio-economic status provided by their father's medical career helped them keep up appearances. When it came to having the latest cars and fashion or masking the quirks and personality traits that would have stuck out as peculiar had they been middle-class or poor, the Simplemans rather elegantly floated above the fray. But there was something odd—almost alien—about the doctor's children. Something that didn't sit right with the handful of locals who bothered to pay attention. Their teachers and classmates also took note. The revolving door of Union Congregational Church pastors sent up silent prayers to their God to heal the boys' common affliction.

What all the fuss boiled down to was this: the Simpleman boys did not ski. This abomination seemed to eclipse if not overshadow the usual smalltown suspicions and aspersions that might have been more accessibly obvious, like why the boys never had girlfriends and why they appeared to have been born without tendons in their limp wrists.

The brothers were not in fact, theory, or practice, interested in any sports. Neither did they, at any age, display romantic interests or leanings toward girls. And though the surgeon had tried his darndest to imprint his free-wheeling frontier love of the outdoors on his offspring, he had been forced to accept early on that fowl and game hunting (big or small) was regarded by his boys as a cruel and detestable pursuit. This was one rite of passage, one campaign for manhood that was destined to jam and backfire in the surgeon's hands. Not only did hunting repulse his boys—the more he tried to push it on them, the more they threatened to become rabid, foaming-at-the-mouth, anti-hunt pacifists. And in the Rockies, that and being non-skiers could get *them* targeted. Doc Simpleman backed off.

But as far as anyone outside the family was concerned, the boys' aversion to field and court sports, girls, and guns were among the lesser failings of Dr. Simpleman's fatherhood. What offended the highbrow Crested Butte chionophile set the most, was that the boys—never mind their parents—were not skiers. Of course, nobody needed to whisper their concern into Mr. or Mrs. Simpleman's ears after Christmas Eve church service, or stage a cautionary intervention in the frozen foods section at Clark's Market. The senior Simplemans were educated people who already suspected theirs were not normal Rocky Mountain children. But they shrewdly calculated they had enough civic standing and the means to either fend off or ignore any ostracization that came their way.

The boys grew into awkward, straight-A-earning lanky teens; then into serious, cerebral, collegiate men. But the twin sour cherries on top of their father's colossal sundae of disappointments was that neither of his apparent brainiacs showed any interest in pursuing medicine, marrying, or producing offspring that would carry on the rather rare Simpleman family name. Once again, not to be defeated or deterred, Paul and June jutted their privileged chins high into the mountain air and choked down their expectations before pivoting to a new stratagem. In their eyes, their post-graduate boy-men were now available to serve them as their indentured porters and wheelchair pushers on the worldwide expeditions the doctor's income afforded them. The adult brothers in their twenties, thirties, forties, and fifties were—shamelessly, opportunistically and unapologetically—still accompanying Mommy and Daddy abroad, all expenses paid, to Transylvania, Malaysia, India, Morocco, Buenos Aires, Cappadocia. The elders were well into their seventies before they buckled their old-style suitcases for the last time.

Ronald had taken on far more than Harlan—more than toting luggage and wheelchairs, certainly. He'd become his parents' nurse, companion, diaper changer, pharmacist—really, their only adult friend in their final decades. He'd relished being useful and having a purpose, but it had come with costs that made it difficult to reconcile his life's balance sheet, what with his jettisoned teaching career and especially now that his folks were gone and it seemed too late to make up the lost opportunities. Ronald realized with a start—or was it a leg cramp—that he'd become melancholic and mesmerized by memories again. At the same time, as he swiveled there on that barstool in quarter turns back and forth, he willed himself to become hypnotized by the heavily falling snow into believing he was living in some different reality where he could make a change, be decisive, take action. But the steam had long since left the gritty Sanka that he slurried around in the bottom of his enamelware mug, just as the excitement had long ago evaporated from his life.

He'd loved traveling both with and without the family, and while he was reticent to admit he was now grounded permanently, Ronald was well aware he genetically lacked his parents' endurance and stamina. These were traits he would have found useful in this elder phase, but they seemed to have leapfrogged his generation, since Harlan had become rather sedentary, too. It was easier—it had always been easier—for Harlan. He had broken free from the family more than six decades ago and now lived in a city oozing with conveniences. Ronald, in contrast, hadn't spotted another human since the start of the new year and was twenty minutes away from the nearest grocery store, on a country road that often, like today, was the last to get plowed.

He hardly had the stamina for more than a half day's drive in any direction. It made no difference which of the three vehicles he chose to take; it was always a lottery to see which one would turn over and they were all currently buried under a good yard of snow anyway. One of his rides was a tarped green VW bug with most of its floorboard rusted away. He'd been meaning to restore it but hadn't bothered ordering the parts yet. Next to that was the '77 Ford pickup with the musty camper on its back that he hadn't used since the start of this century. The most reliable of the three was the other, slightly newer Ford pickup with a shell canopy that was missing one of its side slider windows, though the screen portion was still intact.

The act of driving anywhere had lost its appeal. Whether it was his bursitis-ridden right shoulder (an affliction originally stemmed from a jousting mishap during a high school performance of *Twelfth Night*), his spinal stenosis and overactive sciatica, his plantar fasciitis, or the Furies—whether throbbing in tandem or isolation—his physical state was just no longer conducive to road trips, rail travel, or flying coach. Getting that skeleton of his to town and back every other week for groceries and other errands was the only travel he could endure anymore. And even then, just barely.

All three vehicles ran, but each in their season. This was only thanks and credit to his dashing young mechanic friend (and formerly mentioned firewood supplier) Junior Cavaletti, who lived out that way with his wife, Sofie, and their two pre-teen daughters, Madeline and Rose, to whom Ronald was a reluctant godfather. The young parents, who were Catholic, had asked Ronald, who wasn't, to take on this role and attend each of their christenings in this capacity. He'd first declined, worried that he could be named their legal guardian if anything happened to their parents. Junior, who had also recently been minted as the local volunteer fire chief, came off as a daredevil and risk taker, both on the slopes and on his snowmobile, and the odds spooked Ronald, who proclaimed he wouldn't know the first thing about raising girls.

But Junior had assured him the role was mostly ceremonial and all he was expected to do was to support the girls in their early development and feed their spiritual growth. This seemed more palatable—like an acting role Ronald could pull off, perhaps even convincingly. Indeed, he had long acted like Junior's second father. In the end, godparenting came more naturally than he might have predicted. Over the past decade, Ronald had risen to the task which turned out to be a joy, heaping more attention and love on those girls than their own grandparents could manage given their frailties—both before Franco Cavaletti Sr. passed, but especially afterwards when his widow, their grandma, began losing her faculties.

For two generations now, *Crested Butte Auto Body & Towing* serviced everything from Subarus to Ski-Doos to motorbikes to ski hill snow grooming equipment. It was the only automotive game in town. Junior's father, Franco, son of Sicilian immigrants, had been the founding mechanic—with whom Ronald had his own history—rest his gentle soul. Ronald affectionately remembered him like a second dad, picking up the surgeon's slack whenever Doc Simpleman had been too busy—which, in Ronald's formative years, had seemed like always.

Now that Ronald was seventy-eight, he had the knowledge and experience to recognize and understand the reoccurring pattern of his life. It had started with Franco Sr., who had loomed large in Ronald's adolescence as a father figure. Franco hadn't been old enough to be Ronald's dad, but neither had he been young enough to act as the caring, mentoring, and protective eldest brother he never had, despite Harlan. He might have passed as a younger uncle, except Ronald didn't see Franco as a relation at all. Confused and infatuated, Ronald had idolized the auto mechanic and manifested him into a crush, his first. Predictably, and awash with teenage angst, this played out unrequited for Ronald.

That same inconvenient fifteen-year age gap was to show up again years later after Ronald had moved on from Franco Cavaletti, Sr. and far away from Crested Butte, this time crushing on a prized student of his—fifteen-and-a-half years younger—named Mitch Carson. In a casting twist, Ronald found himself reprising Franco's role as a father figure to Mitch. While his feelings for the student were certainly casual and professional at first, this innocence began to mutate and gradually morphed into a climactic three-act tragedy. Ronald struggled both ethically and epically to hold the professional line and dutifully played that part until his one-time student ruthlessly brought the curtains and lighting grid down on top of him. Ronald, with his broken heart hemorrhaging all over his sleeve, eventually slinked back to Crested Butte which seemed the nearest he could get to the oblivion he felt he deserved. He supposed he had been licking his wounds ever since but as the decades mounted, he'd succeeded in mostly convincing himself that he must be in the clear by now, that any statutory threads had either been snipped by the passing of time or yanked out from the seams that had held the patchwork of his guilt together. As he was complacently resting on this vindication, along sauntered by his latest infatuation. The predestined father figure dormant in Ronald had been aroused to active duty, to mentor—if not humor—Franco's only son and namesake, Junior.

From the time Junior was a teenager, raising that curly haired, classic chiselled Cavaletti head of his from out of the weeds, he had Ronald frozen at the knees and immobilized in his coveralls. His elder by forty-three years and ancient enough to be his grandfather, Ronald once again had no resistance and no choice but to frantically weed another overgrown garden in order to tend another crop of his not-so-secret crushes.

When he heard the familiar sound of the diesel tow truck that always announced Junior's arrival with rolling thunder that jiggled the glassware in the cupboards, Ronald had just been thinking, as snowflakes continued swirling down from an obscure sky outside the kitchen window, how much Junior was the spitting image of his own father who was headlong handsome in his day, just as Junior was in his.

The driver of that truck pulling up outside was hands-down Ronald's favorite human being this side of the Rocky Mountains. With his pulse accelerating, Ronald wondered if he should make himself more presentable but followed up this thought with a silent reminder that *this was as good as it got*. At the kitchen sink, he refilled and then put the kettle back on the stove and shuffled down the carpeted peony-lined pathway for a quick pee in the bathroom. Standing rather crooked in front of the mirror above the set of double sinks, he finger-combed his unruly long hair and gathered the edges of his long beard in a chin ponytail he held in his fist for a count of five. He could hear and feel the exhilarating scrape of the snow-plow blade as Junior cleared half of the rectangle of cement at the culmination of the mile-long driveway. The other half he'd dispatch in the ditch on his way back out—after a requisite visit and instant-coffee warmup, of course.

When the truck shifted into neutral but was still running, that was Ronald's cue to wedge open the heavy, wood-carved front door. He tried to affect a younger, casual lean against the timber door frame, but in truth, he could no longer stand without support. The badly worn and peeling wallpaper, all along both sides of the hallway, was evidence of this—that Ronald had to feel his way through the house multiple times each day.

The flannel-clad driver climbed down from his rig and ambled Ronald's way. Big grins that hurt teeth in the subzero air were exchanged just as a gust of snowy wind blew the ballcap right off Junior's freshly crewcut head and sent it cartwheeling up and over the newly created snowbank. The tall, spry and athletically put-together man plucked the cap with a telescopic stretch of his arm, taking less than three strides out of his way in snow-pant-covered legs. Ronald much preferred the summer visits, when Junior would show up, usually unannounced, in surfer shorts and a tank top, or without any shirt at all. Ronald knew this was just to tease him, but any visit from Junior was welcomed.

"Say, what's with the buzz cut?" Ronald barked, not sure he liked the new cut. "What happened to all your wavy hair?"

Junior gave the old man his trademark side hug with a single back pat. The two had grown closer since the funeral of Junior's father in 2009. Tragically, Franco Sr., who'd been seventy-six at the time, had skied out of bounds and fallen into a tree well where he was knocked unconscious, and then buried and suffocated by a cave-in of snow. It had been a jarring blow for such a small town, but with public relations folks who could frost any disaster into fluffy méringue, the lifts kept running, the skiers kept coming, and the slopes remained open every year in the sixteen years since. Well, every year except this one, so far—though with the snow currently falling, opening day was likely just hours if not minutes away.

"What?" Junior asked, stomping his boots on the welcome mat. "My haircut?"

Ronald lifted the wet lid of Junior's purple Colorado Rockies baseball cap with one hand, rubbing the short stubble on the mechanic's handsome head with his other. "What happened?" he asked a second time. "Is this some requirement for rural firefighters, so the helmets fit better?"

One corner of Junior's mouth lifted into a Cheshire smile, revealing his two rows of perfectly aligned teeth—except for that one front tooth, slightly chipped from a snowboarding tumble. He'd never bothered to get it fixed because he said it gave him character.

"Take your coat?" Ronald said, already lifting the insulated flannel jacket off one shoulder. Junior pivoted a quarter turn so that the outer layer slipped off his chiselled frame as he shook his muscled arms free of the sleeves. He pinned the heel of each rubber boot to the tiled floor with his opposite foot, pulled them off in turn, and then led the way in his bulky, insulated logger socks down the peony path to the great room. Ronald limped after him.

"Heya, Bruce!" Junior greeted the stuffed elk hung high on the black-slate fireplace with his usual military salute, though he'd never been a soldier or even a reservist. "As you were," he added with mock formality, before addressing Ronald's earlier inquiry. "Madeline has this science fair project she's doing with human hair. She's in the process of collecting as many different specimens as she can. That's the main reason I came by—though you needed plowing out if you were thinking of heading into town." The thirty-six-year-old leaned on the back of one of the sofas closest to the crackling fireplace, sniffling his runny nose. "I know it sounds gross, but she's really into hair at the moment. I told her you would never in a thousand years cut off your hair or beard, but she sent me over here anyway because—and these were her words—she doesn't have any 'really old man hair yet.'"

"Thanks," Ronald said sarcastically, "but you're right. My hair is like that chipped front tooth of yours. It's the only thing that gives me any character at all. Sanka?"

The mechanic nodded and then grabbed the poker to make room on the fireplace's wrought-iron grate for more cedar. It cracked and popped when he added it, but after a minute or two, it settled down some.

"Must have a gallon of Red Bull sitting on my bladder," Junior said. "Been plowing one end of Creation to the other since before dawn. I need to take one mighty piss. Be right back." And down the hall he went.

"Aim, please," Ron hollered after him.

"Yeah, yeah." Junior's words ricocheted back, bouncing off the bashful peonies.

The truth was that Ronald had grown his hair and beard out so that he could not be easily pegged as his former, younger, offending self. The initial *P* of his middle name was for *Paul*—after his father—and not for *paranoia*. But his persecution complex had ripened over the past fifty years, practically rotting him from the inside out, and Paul or paranoia had become interchangeable. He unconditionally adored Junior, and by extension, his wife and their young daughters too, and there probably wasn't anything he wouldn't do for them. But shearing off his disguise would be too much. Ronald freshened his Sanka and held out a steaming cup for Junior, who now returned from the bathroom, the troublesome gurgling refill of the toilet audible all the way in the kitchen.

"You know, Ronnie, you should get that toilet looked at."

Gingerly—on account of the Furies—Ronald sat on the couch opposite the matching sofa where his young mechanic friend had just plopped down. He recited his excuse for not tending to the toilet. "They will just tell me that tree roots have grown into the septic tank again. Damn aspens!"

Junior tried to suppress a grin, having heard this same delay tactic from

Ronald so many times before. "Yes, damn to Hell their shared root systems!" He raised his coffee cup in affected solidarity.

"How's your mom?" Ronald said, launching into the pleasantries that usually preceded their talk about cars or town gossip.

"About the same. She doesn't remember the girls' names and she's convinced that Sofie is the girl I'm dating and not the wife I've been married to for fifteen years."

"So sad, that dementia," Ronald said into his coffee cup mid-slurp.

"Heard from your brother yet?" Junior looked over the top of his cup with his father's light-blue eyes, raising his almost jet-black eyebrows as the steam licked at his equally dark eyelashes. Ronald shook his head, then Junior laughed, joking, "Harlan's probably too busy being his usual whore-dog-self in the Castro."

"I seriously doubt that," Ronald squawked. "That dog is eighty-one now, but that's in human years. I have no idea what that would be in dog years," Ronald admitted.

"I don't know about that. You Simpleman men are lifelong studs, both of you Eveready Bunnies meant for mating."

"Really? Where'd ya read that?" Ronald was sure he was blushing.

"Read it? I'm the one who wrote it—permanent marker—on the bathroom stall down at the auto body shop. Oh, and above the middle urinal at the ski lodge."

"Lordy, you look just like your dad." Ronald was desperate, as always, to shift attention away from himself.

"Dead? You mean, I look dead?" Junior balked. Ronald knew that Junior knew what he'd meant, having heard other people make this comparison all the time. "I haven't slept much since this snow started falling. Maybe this haircut makes me look older," Junior stated more than questioned. He brushed the top of his head. "Who knows?"

"I meant when he was your age and especially with that flattop," Ronald said, though he didn't need to clarify this. "Cut back on your *Red Bull* intake—maybe you'd sleep better. Caffeine's a killer. I keep telling you that." He raised his decaffeinated cup o' neutered instant joe.

Junior uncrossed his snow-panted legs that Ronald imagined had to be cooking that close to the fireplace. The tow truck driver checked his iPhone as if looking for an excuse to head back out again. He was a shark that way; couldn't stop moving or he'd perish as Ronald often compared his traits to different animals in the wild kingdom. When Junior had awakened the sleeping cellphone, it sounded with a text alert. "No rest for the wicked," he announced. "I'm needed up at CBMR." He was texting a response as he stood back up. "Seems they're thinking they will open the East River and Teocalli lifts by noon today." He added an ETA to his message. "They're having issues with one of their snow groomers. Not my speciality, but I should be able to find a way to rig it."

"I swear, Junior, you can fix anything," Ronald said. He was afraid he sounded patronizing, but he meant it.

"Well, I can't fix my mom's dementia. And apparently, I can't talk you into buzzing off your beard and hair for a good cause." Junior crossed the room, rinsing his mug in the sink and leaving it upside-down on the counter like always, before ambling down the hallway. "I have the electric clippers out in the rig. I could leave them with you in case you change your mind." He picked up the quilted flannel jacket off the boot bench at the front door and bundled up. "Or I could bring Madeline by in the next day or two and you could look into that adorable twelve-year-old freckled face and explain to her why you can't bring yourself to help her with her science project." Ronald playfully shoved Junior in the shoulder as he followed him down the hall. He would have kept following him right off a cliff; such was the affection he had for this, his only friend in the world.

"Stay safe out there," Ronald said, sounding like a dad—or maybe a mother.

Junior extended an arm for their goodbye hug and single back pat. "Be sure you start all three of your cars sometime today," he lectured. "'Don't want those batteries to seize in these temperatures." He opened the massive wooden door and all of winter seemed poised to barrel its way inside. "And call your brother, Ronnie."

Ronald leaned against the doorway to wave goodbye. Each inhale he drew in through his nose quick-sealed his nostrils together. "Hey," he hollered loud enough to be heard above the wind. "Why don't you leave me those clippers? I'll give it some thought."

Junior's face broke into a gigantic Hollywood smile beneath the bill of his purple ballcap. He reached up into the truck, extracted a shiny black vinyl kit containing the clippers and various guards, and jogged it back to the house. "You're a good man, Simpleman. I don't care what everyone says."

On one hand, Ronald was certain he lacked the nerves and bravery to reveal his true, un-coiffed appearance to the prying, outside world but on the other hand he wagered that even expressing he would consider this act of selflessness might earn him an extra hug, and it did, with two pats on the back this time. Junior returned to his diesel truck, and it roared into gear and chugged its way down the long driveway, disappearing within seconds into the gullet of a whiteout.

ALONE AGAIN WITH his overactive brain, toing and froing between what he would and would not do, Ronald stashed the vinyl shaving kit on top of the whining toilet tank in the bathroom on his way back to the kitchen to resume his storm watch. Sure, he'd start up the car and trucks once he'd thawed out. He'd been chilled to the bone standing in the doorway in the subzero weather, like an abandoned lover.

But he would not call his brother, and he would not shave or trim his head or beard. It was winter. You didn't have to be a shepherd to know you didn't shear a sheep in winter and expect the animal to survive the bitter temperatures.

He chuckled at his flimsy rationale. It could not be disputed that Ronald Simpleman had been hirsute his entire teen-to-adult life. Hair covered the front of his torso, head, face, legs, arms, feet, knuckles, and butt crack. Even his ass cheeks were fuzzy. If he dyed all his body hair orange, happened to be naked, and collapsed dead on the living room shag carpet, his lifeless body might go undetected. He had been the first in his junior high PE class to sprout a grove of pubic hair. He'd had a full bush and thicket complex down there before his older brother had detectable peach fuzz. It had been one of the many points of contention between them. It was as though Sasquatch himself had ambled down the ravine from the mountains to impregnate their mother while infant Harlan napped in his crib and the young surgeon father had been sawing and hammering away at the hospital.

Even in adulthood, his brother Harlan nurtured a certain jealousy, having never cultivated all that much body hair. The poor guy couldn't grow decent sideburns or a moustache, despite those being requisite in San Francisco in the 70s when he first popped on the scene. Ronald didn't remember their father having a hairy chest either. Both his grandfathers had passed long before Ronald's interest in the subject had piqued so he'd been unable to inspect those bare or furry branches of his immediate family tree. By the time Ronald was darting in and out of the gymnasium showers at age thirteen or fourteen, inexplicably looking like the Burt Reynolds of the Rockies, he'd become a bit of a show-off about it, further punctuated with an exclamation point by his other endowment. This only fueled the locker room rumor mill that Ronnie Simpleman had to have been held back a grade or two in elementary school. And that was the other attribute that had rubbed Harlan the wrong way. Back then, a little person figured out who he was and how he was different or even special by measuring up to the others around him. When you lived rural, like the Simpleman brothers had, the comparative sampling was geographically limiting at best and border-line incestuous at worst. For the longest time, Ronald figured these were the reasons why his older brother had this mean streak about him and treated his only sibling like they weren't even related. Now, he'd come around to believing that Harlan had always been and so would always stay jealous and bitter that he had drawn the short straw.

Neither brother inherited their father's thick, slick, almost leading-man hairline. Throughout high school and his teens, Ronald's dark swoopy head of hair—no longer the brownish blonde of his adolescence—had much darkened and lacked any follicle enthusiasm that might lend body, self-assurance or character. He'd had no choice but to naturally let it part on the side but then lobbed the rest over the crown with a single brush stroke giving his hairstyle the appearance of a wind-formed cornice at the end of a brown snow drift. Aggravating his general pelt unease, his mane became even more untameable during his university years once the ragged hairline began prematurely receding. But by then, he'd discovered other things to obsess over, like avoiding the Vietnam draft and bilking his parents for ever more tuition and living expenses. For the next decade or two, his hair just went along for the ride, but come the start of the new Millennium, Ronald stopped intervening and decided to just let it and his facial hair grow; the best non-grooming decision of his life.

So, he couldn't cut off his hair now.

Or could he? Setting parameters, defending boundaries, protecting his anonymity, and staying vigilant for the bounty hunters that might be, but probably weren't still hot on his trail, had been the four pillars of his survival strategy for over half a century. Hiding in general, concealing his identity, disenfranchising himself from his past—these tactics had all become second nature. In his paranoid mind, the known universe would come crashing down if even one of these supports went off kilter even slightly. Truth was, even Ronald couldn't remember what he looked like under all that scraggle. So, there was that mystery to maintain—or not.

At the same time, all the nice and silly things he'd done for Junior and his family over the years always made him happy, perhaps providing him his only true joy. He was always looking for opportunities to shine in Junior's estimation, and this seemed like an easy win. Plus, the hair would grow back—although maybe now that he was in his twilight, there wouldn't be enough enzymes, proteins, or time left to achieve the impressive, grizzled lengths he currently had. But what did that matter? It wasn't like he'd be competing for any octogenarian hairdressing titles any time soon.

With the snow falling with even more rigor now on the other side of the glass and another winter season to further cover his tracks, Ronald Simpleman was starting to think he could let his guard down. The potency of his lifelong-festering secrets had surely lost most of their statutory venom by now. Nobody, so far, and no bounty hunter had tracked him down. There was an outside chance that nobody had been truly harmed by his actions or inactions or cared enough to look for him in the first place, but that wasn't something he could bank on and so the made-believe fugitive continued to evade capture, and by doing so, his redemption.

"That's it!" he proclaimed his decision out loud to Bruce overhead, as he cut through the great room. "It's a new year, my friend. If Junior can go for a new look, so can I."

Once in the bathroom, he squinted into the mirror and issued a long groan meant to ground and focus his spastic mind. With a grunt, he stretched the sweatshirt sleeves off each shoulder turning the garment inside-out as he began to address his emancipation from his questionable past. If he was going to sheer his head and face, why stop there, he logically asked himself. He lowered the untied sweatpants to the floor and because he generally lived commando, the task of hair removal at first glance presented as gargantuan. Using the full-length mirror behind the bathroom door, he further appraised the sizeable swath of real estate slated for sudden depilation. Standing there naked, he saw how he might be mistaken—by child or throwback hippie—as Papa Smurf, or even worse, a troll doll. He scrunched up his bearded face and backhanded what he viewed as a deformed penis, contorted into its crescent moon curvature by Peyronie's a decade or so ago. Once the dangling pride of his many show-and-tell escapades, his former exclamation point had become as rarely used as an Oxford comma these days.

He pulled back the crusty zipper of the black shaving bag and extracted the weighty device with its long cord. Cognizant of where the clippers might have been, Ronald raised its oiled blades to his nose for a good whiff. He imagined Junior using this very appliance to manscape the privates of his taut, youthful, and mostly hairless body, from what he'd seen of it. He plugged in the shaver and spread out the assortment of differently sized length guards on the adjacent toilet lid. From the middle linen shelf behind his left shoulder he thought to snatch an ancient pink flat sheet for clippings catchment and mostly covered the linoleum floor with it, stretching out the badly frayed ends with his hairy foot. In determining which length guard he should snap on the clippers, Ronald was thinking he didn't really mind Junior's buzzcut once the initial shock had diminished and so Ronald thought he'd try to mimic Junior's look.

He spun the wall dial activating the antique heat lamp embedded in the bathroom's ceiling. Squinting again at the raised fine print on the plastic guards, he selected the quarter-inch guard, clipped it to the blades, and clicked the beast into vibrating action. He decided that keeping his head hair and facial hair separated would aid Madeline's scientific analysis. He'd start with his head hair.

The corners of his bearded mouth raised into a slyly determined grin that vanished the second the clippers grabbed their first clump of hair, jamming the works and flipping the breaker.

"Ouch!" he squealed in the darkness, following the electrical cord with his free hand to yank the plug from the outlet he couldn't see. He felt his way to the bathroom door and opened it, letting some winter daylight from the hallway into the windowless space. Shuffling to the utility room where the electrical panel was located trailing the long electrical cord, he tried to withdraw the weapon as he went, but the long hair had gotten bound up in the cutting mechanism. The more he tugged, the more it felt like he was getting scalped, so he stopped, holding the clippers against his head until he could restore power and see what he was doing.

It had been a while since he'd tripped a breaker and so he had forgotten what bad shape the panel cover was in, with its top hinge bent and the bottom one rusting from some unknown moisture source. He traced an arthritic finger up one column and a quarter of the way down the other before locating the problem fuse. He flipped it back on, and thankfully, it held.

He returned to the bathroom. Now that he could see again, he opened the mirrored medicine cabinet, scanning the shelves for a pair of his dead mother's blunt-ended bangs scissors. Spotting them in a plastic sleeve behind the bottles of aspirin, his prescriptions, and the sleeping pills his mother had referred to as her "judies"—a nod to Judy Garland's barbiturate crutch—he used them to snip the clippers free. He rubbed the lingering pain from his forehead with his palm and detected the smallest amount of blood on his fingertips. In the mirror, he saw there was a clipper-wide notch in his hairline. So, he was committed now.

Having learned from his trial by error, he began hacking off the hair with the scissors as a preliminary pass. It had grown long enough in some places to stretch to his belly button. He sawed through the clumps until his index finger became sore, laying out each bushel on the lid of the toilet. He swapped the inch guard onto the clippers and tried to even out the mess he'd made.

When he was moderately satisfied with his progress, he went to the kitchen for a box of large Ziploc bags—the kind he normally used for freezing plums, cherries, and apples from the small orchard down by the duck pond. He grabbed a black Sharpie out of the stuffed pottery cup sitting on top of a notepad under the wall telephone and returned to the bathroom. He labeled the first bag *Pepperoni's Head Hair*, stuffing the bounty from the top of the toilet lid inside. He sniffed the bag's contents as he sealed the plastic zipper. He didn't know why he did that except by habit he smelled and mentally catalogued scents without actively thinking about it, just as he always had. His keen nose registered plastic, a hint of Irish Spring and a few notes of residual clipper oil.

Ronald inspected his handiwork in the mirror. He could faintly make out an earlier version of himself, and that sent a fright through his body like the breaker he'd just tripped. His scraggily long beard was next. Once he had a second Ziploc labeled and sealed with Pepperoni's facial hair, he switched to the quarter-inch guard and trimmed his beard down. He goofed up a sideburn and the only way to fix it was to take the rest of his head hair down to that same quarter-inch length so it would match his face.

The more grayish hair he removed, the younger he thought he looked. He decided to shave his face completely. Instead of switching to a handheld disposable razor—he wasn't even certain he still possessed one, since he hadn't shaved in decades—he took the guard off the clipper and began mowing his face. He kept nicking his skin, and soon his face was bleeding in at least a half dozen places. He'd been enjoying the vibration of the clippers until the machine began smearing the blood around in unflattering streaks. For somebody who'd been a Chia Pet pretty much since his testicles dropped, Ronald felt like he could time travel backwards the more hair he removed. The transformation thus far, slapped him in the shaved face, and in that moment, he realized he didn't know what his own body looked like underneath the welcome mat.

So next he used the clippers, sans guard, to deforest the lower countryside. Multi-colored tufts of body and pubic hair became airborne, joined forces, and rolled like tumbleweeds around his feet. Shorn hair accumulated like the snow outside, and soon large swaths of the faded pink sheet were no longer visible. When Ronald turned around from the sink, he gasped as he didn't recognize the stranger's body in the full-length mirror.

His bursitis limited the clippers' reach, but he managed to clearcut the fronts of his shoulders, upper pectorals, and biceps. In a moment of over-confidence, he clipped his left nipple, drawing a bead of blood that stung, then itched. He was more cautious and nimbler with the device—which he could feel was overheating—as he deforested the right one. With each row he clipped, he revealed whole constellations of moles and freckles he'd never seen before.

Fascinated, Ronald became obsessed with excavating down to the original canvas. He didn't think he had that much hair on his back, though he had a lower saddle above his fuzzy butt cheeks, and this bothered him. He might have to get up the nerve to ask Junior if he'd mind helping him with the parts he couldn't reach. He nicked himself again while driving the clippers around his innie belly button, an anatomical feature he couldn't recall examining properly since he was a kid. He placed the running clippers on the sink edge to probe his newly excavated navel with a pinky, and the device quickly vibrated off the rim, creating quite the cacophony in the sink bowl before he could wrangle it back into submission. He turned the clippers off. This provided him a break to bag and label his body hair—not that this had been requested or required for Madeline's project—but he liked accounting for his yield by the number of Ziplock pillows filled during harvest.

All that was left were his underarms, his legs, and his pubic hair. He reduced the pom poms beneath each of his arms to stubble, and because he thought his legs had always looked scrawny, he left that hair alone, thinking it added bulk, creating an illusion that his twigs could be trunks. Unable to resist his curiosity in wanting to experience the sensation of the vibration near his privates, he used the clippers to joyride around his manhood, which began to respond with the fulsomeness of a waxing crescent moon; crescent on account of its age-rendered curvature. His hair down there was distinct from the other samples—more like a Brillo-pad texture—and so deserving of its own Ziploc. He scribbled beneath the label, *not for Madeline.*

This time, when he turned around from the sink, the stranger staring back at him from the full-length mirror on the back of the bathroom door gave him a second startle that made his weak legs even weaker. He could see, even without his glasses, that he had just shaved decades from his appearance. He felt he looked so much younger, in fact, that a flush of panic drained the blood from his shorn head. He felt queasy, suspecting he would be instantly recognized by anyone familiar with his previous transgressions and lapses in judgement. Even if he could bring himself to leave the Butte, with this new old look of his, he would be foolish to visit any of his earlier haunts, where ghosts from his past possibly kept a look out for him still. Already wondering how long it would take to grow it all back, Ronald Simpleman trembled, second guessing what he had just done. The sudden click of the heat lamp going off nearly made him jump out of his exposed skin. He knew he needed to pull himself together, before the chills set in. He couldn't keep standing there, staring at his naked truth.

He rinsed the guards, brushed the hairs from the clipping mechanism, coiled the cord, and packed the clippers with their implements back inside the carrying bag. Slipping his mother's special scissors back inside their protective plastic sleeve and returning them to the medicine cabinet, Ronald spotted a disposable lady's pink razor that hadn't been disposed and that he hadn't remembered seeing before. Leaving the sheet on the bathroom floor, he gathered up his four fleece-filled Ziplocs, the shaving kit, and the pink razor, and headed for the winter-darkened kitchen. If the Furies were behaving during his evening shower, he thought he might use the pink razor to clean up his pelvic area, just like he'd done a couple times in college, when he'd been sexually more active and aware of his appearance and the preferences of others.

As he placed the items on the kitchen counter, the wall phone began ringing, and echoed in the other areas of the house that had phone extensions. There wasn't time to pull on clothes, so he perched nude on the edge of the barstool positioned in front of the blizzard still in progress. He lifted the phone to his ear, but with his head and facial hair gone, he miscalculated the distance and inadvertently clunked his noggin. He answered with an "Ow!"

The gravelly voice on the other end was familiar.

"Ronnie?"

It was his brother. "Well, hello there, Harlan."

"Happy New Year, Ronnie."

"And Merry Christmas to you, too." It was hard not sounding bitter, so he didn't bother masking his perennial disappointment over the short shrift he'd always gotten in the brotherly love department. "Happy Thanksgiving, too," he added sarcastically to drive home the infrequency with which the brothers spoke.

Harlan didn't trade in sarcasm and so wasted no energy in getting right to the point of his call. "Listen, I came across something on the Internet today that you might want to look into or at least be aware of."

As a former English teacher, Ronald was peeved whenever someone ended a sentence with a preposition. Harlan had a fancy PhD in something or another and should have known better.

"Oh, yeah?" Ronald faked attentiveness, but he was double-tasking. He extracted one of the few remaining plastic grocery bags out of the bottom hole of the recycling cylinder that lived under the kitchen sink. It was a vintage Clark's Market sack that had to have pre-dated 2018, when the single use plastic ban came down from the town council. He put the hair trimming kit and the labeled Ziplocs in the bag and stretched the phone cord as far as he could down the peony path to set the bag on the side table near the front door, certain that Junior would stop by to check on him tomorrow.

"It's concerning Mitchell Carson and his new tell-all book."

The detonation of this atomic bombshell stopped hairless Ronald in his barefoot tracks. Looking aghast amid the peonies, he was as petrified as he was certain the authorities would be coming after him now if Mitch Carson was truly telling all. The realization hit Ronald like a plank to the side of his crewcut head. The other shoe had finally dropped. They'd hunt him down at last, and they'd likely find him too, now that he'd just become easier to recognize. "What do you mean by tell-all," Ronald demanded to know in a tone that sounded clearly panicked. "Is that your terminology or the way Mitch Carson is promoting the thing?"

His brother's heavy breathing into the mouthpiece prompted Harlan to try watering down the severity of whatever his brother's past entanglements and calamities might have entailed. "Well, it was billed online as the author's memoir. Don't you tell all in a memoir?" Harlan asked rhetorically. "Anyway, I'm sure it can't be that bad," he said. "When was the last time you even saw Mitchell?" Harlan asked not because it mattered or because he cared, but because he too had experienced an unsettling run-in with the author in the past—not that he'd ever confided this with his brother—so the subject gave the brothers something tangentially in common and an excuse for Harlan to pick up the phone. He could already tell by his brother's reaction, though, that the news had not only struck a match but tossed it on the tinder dry brush pile that was his brother's paranoia. He hadn't intended for this call to be that incendiary or to last any longer than it needed to, but, at the very least, he did want to ensure that he got credit for making some effort to stay in touch.

"The hot springs at Ouray. 1997." Ronald still hadn't moved, his brain pinballing off imaginary bumpers that sustained the chaos. Even though he'd made believe all these years that he and his former student were bound by confidentiality, that they had this unspoken loyalty and a shared imperative to conceal the truth of their early relationship, Ronald realized now, on a raft of hindsight rapidly taking on water, that he should have either formalized their pact in light of the life-altering and potentially life-ending consequences or he should have turned himself in decades ago, facing the music no matter how ear-splitting and discordant the melody. Because in the back of his reasoning mind, if he were being honest with himself—contrary to his dishonesty with others—Ronald had always suspected his secret would not be safe with the younger man forever. Why else would he have spent forty-six years in hiding?

"There," Harlan interjected. "You see? That was almost thirty years ago and nothing bad, or even good, seems to have happened between you two ever since. Add that to what—another twenty years since you first met the kid?" Harlan realized he needed to be more careful with what he knew, with what Mitchell Carson had once told him, or else he'd have to explain why he knew all this time and why he didn't say so. "You've gotten this far in life with your dignity still intact as far as I can tell. You'll get past this rough patch, too, if that's what this even turns out to be. A lot will depend on whether this book takes off. I haven't read it. You haven't seen it. It may not be all that explicit and maybe it doesn't even mention you in the first place."

Ronald exhaled with a whoosh into the mouthpiece, starting to wonder what his brother maybe knew that he didn't. "Thanks for the heads up,

Harlan. You're probably right." But he spoke with little conviction. Then the call was over, and Ronald was left confused as to whether his brother had hung up, or if the ferocity of the snowstorm had knocked out the lines. The phone didn't ring again but still he checked for a dial tone to confirm it wasn't the storm. He allowed the loose coil of the phone cord to reel him back to the kitchen where he placed the handset receiver in its cradle.

The fire snapped, prompting him to pad across the great room to stir and stoke the embers, rearranging what was left of the logs that were half on and half off the grate. He added more fuel. Everything felt different to him without hair—without his mask, his disguise. Heat reached his skin much quicker. So did chills and drafts. So might the authorities.

What had he done? He examined his scruffy face and torso with fingers and eyes in the growing light of a reconstituting blaze. What did he need to do now and what was coming next? His brain was on fire, seemingly in competition with the black slate fireplace. He was besieged by a legion of doubts.

Evidence! It struck him like the thud of a cast-iron fire poker to the side of his head. He needed to destroy all evidence.

With rekindled purpose, he shuffled down the hall to his bedroom to force open the warped and finnicky oak drawer closest to the headboard. But it pulled at an angle that wedged it stuck. "Not now," he grunted, ignoring his bursitis to give it an adrenalin-fueled tug. The momentum and torque yanked the drawer completely out of the bed pedestal and onto his foot. Pain radiated up his leg, shocking his already racing heart. He held his breath in agony, massaging his throbbing, wounded toes. He began breathing rapidly—alarmingly so. Now he snatched the rudimentarily machine-sewn denim bookbag from the disembowelled drawer and hobbled with it back to the hillbilly-log-adorned living room, eerily illuminated orange by the restoked fire.

The bulging bookbag's contents had been meticulously catalogued in his memory, but not so organized in the bag itself. Still, he didn't need his glasses to scrutinize the treasures within. He had them memorized. Ronald lowered the bag to the edge of the orange carpet where it came up against the slate hearth in front of the ferocious firebox. Using the end of one of the sofas for support, he bent his creaking knees until their caps met the shag. He scooted the bag closer to him and pulled the looped straps open. He'd fawned over these mementos from the only great love affair of his life so often—and occasionally for corporeal self-gratification—that many of his favorite photos had become inadvertently cemented together. Up until this moment, Ronald had coveted this evidence, his only proof—incriminating or vindicating—to remind himself that he had been in love once—that he was capable of loving, and that perhaps he could love again, except now he was closer to being out of time. And there was enough evidence in this bag to put him away for the rest of his life which had seemed a colossal length of time back then, though with not so many more seasons left in him now, a more rationally thinking Ronald might have been more open to the inevitability of come what may.

But he was panicked.

He'd lost track of the times Mitch had at first casually asked for, then fervently demanded he surrender this secret stash to him. He had every right to make this demand since he'd been the sole subject of the photographs and Super 8 home movies in Ronald's collection. The eager and willing model at the time—who called his own shots, who'd been old enough to drive, owned licensed guns for hunting, and worked for a living wage—experienced an epiphany when he thought he was dying from cancer, then had a sudden change of heart when he turned 21 and officially broke off his clandestine affair with Ronald; an affair that the boy had been the one to start. Ever since, Mitch had relentlessly campaigned for the return of the photos, negatives and short films under the principles these images were of him and so belonged to him and would be safer with him, by which Ronald suspected he meant, destroyed, not safer. He didn't refuse to turn over the goods just to exert some passive-aggressive power trip over the kid. He protected this collection with his life for self-preservation because he feared under cross-examination the very first question anybody would ask was: *Who was behind the camera?* And in the response, Ronald's fate and criminal indictment would have been sealed. Then, just as now, he would have had no defense in any courtroom in America but to point out the lover who made him do it.

His brown eyes welled with an onslaught of emotions as he knelt to feed the flames.

Celluloid film stock and photographs burned fastest. Letter-stuffed envelopes took longer until he learned to empty the crinkled contents dispatching one page at a time. In the mix were several out-of-focus black and white photos of him in the nude with his head chopped off that had been taken by Mitch. Next came the cartridge of eighteen developed polaroids that had been threaded back inside their original black plastic cartridge for safekeeping by Mitch, the self-photographer. One at a time, his thumbs scooted each salacious image out of the felt-lined flap, imitating the grinding mechanisms of the instant camera that had ejected them out into the world in the first place. Trace chemicals inside the raised pouch of each card made the flames behave differently, showcasing new colors that fizzled and popped like fireworks before his widened eyes.

At least seven seasons of Mitch's Christmas Photo cards, a rubber-banded series of mimeographed programs from theatrical productions that had starred the object of his lifelong obsession were next to get fed into the roaring furnace. The papers were so degraded that they lifted into flight as they disintegrated. Ronald extracted a ratty stage beard from the book bag, delicately animating it in his fingers, trying to see which end was up. The fragile filaments had been married together by ancient clumps of spirit gum. This adhesive residue exploded with a blinding flash when introduced to the dancing flames and suddenly, Ronald's olfactory sensors weren't only smelling cedar.

HIGH ABOVE WHERE Ronald was frantically shoveling his memories into the mouth of the abyss, an errant fragment of his past had floated undetected out of the fireplace, rising on the thermals before coming to rest, orange-hot, on one of the tripled strands of jute macramé rope that had secured Bruce—the elk trophy—to the black slate stone fireplace for more than sixty years. Hoisted and hung there by Ronald's father, on a crucifixion-sized nail that had been plunged deep into the still setting mortar, Bruce had a front-row seat to a chunk of human history that had been neither earthshattering nor entertaining—until now.

In that hissing, sizzling, crackling moment, Bruce exacted his revenge on the Simpleman family by freefalling and smashing Ronald's head, knocking him out cold against the hearth before the elk's mange-ridden pelt detonated into flames on top of him. Forked tongues of fire lashed out in all directions, alighting the faux-log-cabin walls, which launched flaming splinters onto the orange shag carpeting made from acrylic, nylon and polyester filaments synthesized from petroleum origins.

With that head start, the unstoppable conflagration next spread to the four corners of the great room and began licking the peony motif wallpaper in the hallway. Fire rushed into the bedrooms raiding any and all available fuel sources. More than a decade earlier, Ronald had converted one of these—his original bedroom—into a photography darkroom and hobby editing suite, replete with blacked out windows. In here, where he'd spent hours dappling in film-editing, movie pirating, and CD/DVD copying he also had hundreds of VHS movies and Super 8 reels organized on shelves. Each of these let off like fuse-intertwined bundles of firecrackers in rapid succession. Electrical wires fizzled and fuses and components began exploding like cluster bombs, blasting the metal door off the electrical panel and sending it flying across the utility room, where it lodged in the outer plastic shower wall.

In mere minutes, the once-sturdy timber frame holding up the living room ceiling, along with its snow-laden roof, buckled and collapsed atop the lone, unconscious occupant, who had already been mostly consumed alive by the inferno. The suffocating blanket of snow deprived oxygen to portions of the rapidly spreading house fire, which had by then roared through the bedroom wing of the once-lauded architectural marvel. Other sections of roof burned and collapsed, randomly dowsing the blaze in odd nooks, like the alcove at the front door, while whooshing the blaze into crawl spaces.

IT WAS FORTY-FIVE minutes later with dusk falling on an already dark day, at the tail end of the first blizzard of the season, when the Gunnison County Volunteer Fire Brigade barrelled up the long driveway. Busting through snowdrifts in near-zero visibility, it was a shaken, white-knuckled Captain Franco Cavaletti Jr. clenching the wheel. As he set the emergency brake, a rogue tear defied his training and raced down his cheek disappearing under the collar of his turnout coat. Seeing nothing but steam and smoke with no fire left to fight, Junior looked away from the destruction and squinted through the white-out in the direction of the tree line, desperately hoping to see his goofy friend, the godfather of his two daughters emerge from under the cover of safety. But with visibility and Ronnie's chances both at or near zero, he suspected this story was not going to have a happy ending, and that he'd have to break the hearts of his daughters once he made it back home.

The scene of destruction that this ragtag crew of ski-bums-by-day encountered on that scarred hillside was puzzling. Nearly all the house structure was gone and smoldering except for the upright front door and part of the entryway behind it, somehow still intact under a cave-in of snow. It was Junior who opened that never-locked door, just as he had for most of his life. A demonic wind rushed through the breach, rustling a partially melted plastic grocery sack, its handle sticking out of the snow. Junior plucked it from its snowy insulation and his helmet light illuminated the contents, which he knew in an instant had been meant for him.

Twenty feet away, his volunteer deputy captain, the young pastor from the Union Congregational Church, made a more gruesome discovery: two charred and seemingly unrelated skulls at the base of the disarticulated stone fireplace, its tower of black river rocks still hissing and letting off steam. "It seems the fire started here," he said, shouting his findings through cupped and sound-amplifying gloved hands. With a gloved finger, he flicked thin shards of what looked like broken Christmas ornaments that were reflecting shafts of his helmet light back into his eyes. "I see at least one human fatality."

Junior—who'd been captain only since the start of the new year—dropped to his knees on what was left of Ronald Simpleman's entryway floor. He clutched the Clark's Market bag to his chest, and very un-firefighter-like, began to sob. When his deputy captain, the pastor, gave his heavily padded shoulder a firm squeeze, Junior stopped quaking long enough to confirm the unbelievable.

"Pepperoni is gone."

DENVER INTERNATIONAL AIRPORT

May 2023

RON SIMPLEMAN WAS NO NOVICE WHEN IT CAME TO adventuring. He had travelled extensively around the world—both with his family and solo. There were a few hard-and-fast rules he'd been able to distill from his experiences: 1. don't book regional airlines operating smaller aircraft, and 2. if your destination is less than 8 hours away, you're far safer taking a bus.

He'd once met a justifiably cantankerous man named Cornelius during his travels through the Baltics. The man claimed to be the sole survivor of an Aeroflot flight out of Sheremetyevo International Airport that in the '90s crashed into a mountain range in the Kuzbass region, killing the entire top-seeded local soccer team and everyone else but him on board, including the twelve crew members. Cornelius had fixed his one working blue eye to stare piercingly into Ronald's browns, and warned him, in his gravelly Slavic accent, "You must never fly regional."

He still remembered that conversation all these years later, and that's what led him to climb aboard a Bustang coach at the 4-Way stop in downtown Crested Butte at 5:15 that morning. He slept most of the bus ride arriving at Denver Union Station just before Noon. From there, he took the sleek A-line out to Denver International Airport.

Mitch Carson had been on his case for years angling for a get together so that Ronald would finally surrender the collection of compromising photos he'd snapped of Mitch when he was younger. Thinking that he'd run out of excuses—some he'd tried using more than once—Ronald had reluctantly agreed to make the trip and bring the photos to Seattle where Mitch lived. He'd even decided to surprise his former student with the set of Polaroids Mitch didn't know Ronald possessed; and that's even if Mitch remembered taking those self-portraits in the first place.

Back in the Butte, the night before climbing on the commuter bus, Ronald had extracted the old denim bookbag that contained the photos and other Mitch-related mementos from the built-in storage drawer beneath his bed. He'd tucked it inside a knapsack that he surrounded with more clean underwear, t-shirts, and socks than he'd ever possibly need for one weekend getaway. The knapsack rode on his lap through the Rockies (from the Western Slopes to the Front Range), and with this contraband dangling off one shoulder, Ronald had strolled into Denver International Airport and had gotten as far as the security checkpoint. Standing there, hyperventilating and sweating too profusely to go unnoticed by TSA workers, the seventy-five-year-old child pornography-packing mule had a panic attack just as he was about to go through security.

In the old days, before 9-11, he might have stashed the bookbag in an airport locker to retrieve on his return and then continue with his planned trip without the requested materials, anticipating he'd face the wrath of his former student on the other end. There would be nothing new about that, but he would have had time to come up with another good excuse while en route. But there were no airport lockers anymore, so he'd placed the empty gray bin back on the stack on the other side of the conveyor belt and pantomimed to an audience of nobody that he had misplaced his ticket or his medications or his flip phone or his brain. He'd shuffled out of the line and beat a hasty retreat to the voluminously peaked sailcloth ceiling of the crowded main terminal.

That was where he was still roosting now on the edge of a molded fiberglass lounge seat, rapidly tapping his foot, his long hair in a slack braid that his eight-year-old godchild had styled during her slumber party with her Pepperoni that past weekend. On the heels of COVID-19, he had already been anxious to be travelling at all—never mind the extra trepidation of seeing Mitch again and coming nose-to-nose with his checkered past. Still wary of catching the disease, Ronald adjusted his crooked face mask that had mostly been riding under his nose, as he wasn't one to miss out on a scent regardless of the attendant risks. Looking around, he noted that easily three-quarters of the passengers in transit were no longer wearing such pandemic protection. He had been in transit that day, too, until suddenly he wasn't.

He switched feet and nervously tapped the other clunky Birkenstock on the glossy mosaic tiled floor, pulling up a greyish-white sock that had gotten bunched up under the leather strap. Even though he'd arrived at the airport with plenty of time to spare, his ticketed United flight to Seattle had just left Runway 16R without him. And now he was frantic to concoct the details of another fabricated excuse that he needed to convincingly deliver by phone to Mitch Carson, who might have already been on his way to SeaTac to retrieve him for their hastily planned weekend reunion.

Ronald struggled every time he needed to interact with his one-time student, part-time lover and somewhat estranged friend. He hadn't been able to release the arthritic grip he'd held on the grudge he'd been strangling since 2017. That's when Mitch had published his third novel, with its scandalous Chapter 18, which Ronald still maintained had divulged far more truth than fiction. That revelation of secrets had been a betrayal of his trust, a confidence that Ronald felt sure they both had sworn to each other they would always keep private and safe. The rising-star novelist had defended his work as "my story to tell, too," and had even emailed a snippy rebuttal that included an all-caps quote by Albert Camus: *FICTION IS THE LIE THROUGH WHICH WE TELL THE TRUTH.* The two of them hadn't communicated after that missive for almost two years.

Carson's fourth novel—an epic tome—had been published last year and received several awards and a fair amount of critical acclaim. A hardcover edition of the same, wrapped in brown paper, had been express-mailed to Colorado, addressed to his supposed mentor and muse; an olive branch Ronald reluctantly accepted out of primal curiosity. Since he had been the author's high school English teacher, and one of his beta readers on a much earlier version of that manuscript—a review and editorial role he had dutifully played with each of Carson's earlier novels as well—he gave it a critical read and had been duly impressed.

According to the suspended giant clock in the airy Jeppesen Terminal, he'd already spent more than forty minutes fidgeting and foot tapping his ankles off after backtracking from security, all the while trying to calm himself down. The plane he was supposed to have been aboard had likely crossed into Wyoming airspace by this point. It would take the rest of the afternoon to cobble together enough nerves to make the telephone call that needed to be made, but he didn't have all afternoon if he was thinking he'd try to make it back to the Butte before bedtime. He opened his flip phone, scrolled through his few contacts to the Cs and initiated the call.

"Oh hi, Mitch." He cleared his throat. "It's Ron here."

"Ron? I thought you would have been on your flight by now." It sounded like he was on speakerphone and likely driving.

"I'm afraid something's come up and I won't be able to make it this weekend. I am so sorry. As soon as I got to the airport here in Denver, I received a message summoning me to return home at once."

For a few seconds, there was silence on the other end. "Hmm, sounds serious."

From the monotone, Ronald could tell Mitch did not believe him. He doubled down, exaggerating his fib on the fly. "It's my brother. Seems his new hip has popped out of its socket. He is awaiting follow-up surgery, and it looks like he will need to recuperate with me over the summer."

"Well, that's a shame. Give Harlan my best wishes for a speedy recovery." Again, the words were said without emotion or inflection. Mitch was peeved, Ronald could tell.

"I should get going. Let's catch up soon by phone or email or whatever."

"Sure. Whatever."

The call went silent. Whether Ronald had been believed or not, he'd been disconnected. Surely, another period of silence between the two would follow. And it did.

CRESTED BUTTE

June 2020

WHEREAS, Covid-19 is a highly contagious virus that has spread to numerous countries around the world, including the United States; and WHEREAS, on January 30, 2020, the World Health Organization declared the worldwide outbreak of COVID-19 a public health emergency of international concern, and on January 31, 2020, the United States Department of Health and Human Services declared the virus a public health emergency; and WHEREAS, on March 10, 2020, the Governor of Colorado declared a State of Emergency for the State of Colorado due to COVID-19 and the Colorado Department of Public Health and Environment has confirmed that COVID-19 continues to spread throughout the State of Colorado, and community transmission of the illness has been confirmed in Gunnison County; and WHEREAS, on March 11, 2020, the World Health Organization declared the outbreak of COVID-19 a pandemic; and WHEREAS, the Public Health Director has consulted and coordinated efforts with the Town of Crested Butte and the Gunnison Valley Watershed School District, Western Colorado University, the Towns of Mount Crested Butte, Pitkin, and Marble, the city of Gunnison, Gunnison Valley Health, the United States Forest Service, the Bureau of Land Management, National Park Service, Crested Butte & Mt. Crested Butte Chamber of Commerce, the Tourism and Prosperity Partnership (TAPP) Gunnison Country Chamber of Commerce, the State of Colorado (and its agencies and departments), the faith community, the business community and all of the residents of Gunnison County in assisting the Public Health Director in taking the steps necessary to mitigate and control the risk of COVID-19 infection, and shall continue to work with these entities and others in collaborative effort to contain the spread of this deadly virus; and WHEREAS, the Town finds that the Orders issued by the Public Health Director will control the cascading impacts on critical services by limiting spread of COVID-19 and will help hospitals, first responders, and other healthcare services continue to provide services for those who need them (along with utilities, human services, and businesses) in the coming weeks and months. Collective action can save lives and is in support of the most vulnerable in our community. NOW, THEREFORE, BE IT HEREBY RESOLVED BY THE TOWN COUNCIL OF THE TOWN OF CRESTED BUTTE THAT the Town of Crested Butte endorses and supports the orders issued by the Gunnison County Public Health Official. INTRODUCED, READ, AND ADOPTED BY THE TOWN COUNCIL THIS 15th DAY OF JUNE, 2020.

Ronald lowered the official notice that had been hand-delivered to him by Junior Cavaletti—the smartly uniformed and newest member of the Gunnison County All Volunteer Rural Fire Brigade. In addition to being the town mechanic, a young father, and now a rural fire responder, Junior was also Ronald's closest friend—and really, his only friend, since he didn't count his own brother in this category and rarely associated with anybody else.

Ronald stuck the notice on the freezer door with a colorful magnet he'd picked up in Senegal, then filled the teapot with water from the kitchen tap—though lately that water had a concerning orange tinge. He'd meant to ask Junior if his house water was orange too but had been so taken aback by the uniform, he'd forgotten to bring it up. The advance response truck had crunched up the gravelly drive shortly after the sun poked its head above the Butte before hiding behind clouds the rest of that grim news day. Junior's unusually serious and worried face was hardly recognizable behind the steamed-up shield of his visored helmet, which he declined to raise or remove since the virus was believed to be airborne. Also uncharacteristically, Junior hadn't been chatty, and he hadn't side-hugged his old friend. Instead, he had been laconic and appeared, for the first time, to either be out of his depth or scared. Ronald had only witnessed Junior's normal calmness fluctuate slightly around the birth of his first daughter, Madeline, in 2013, and then again for the birth of Rose, two years later. Though Rose had been a breech baby delivered by Caesarian, the deliveries had been fairly routine, with risks that could be anticipated and mitigated if need be. But with these lock-down, isolation orders Junior had been tasked to deliver, the younger man came across as spooked when he said he couldn't stay for coffee.

Ronald spooned three teaspoons of Sanka into his cup, waiting for the orange water to boil clear and for the sounds of the quick response fire truck to fade. Junior wasn't wrong to be scared by this COVID-19 virus, and Ronald was concerned too. According to the news, the origin was unknown, the outcomes were unpredictable (fatal for some and debilitating for others), and scientists so far didn't know how to respond. Ronald wasn't scared— yet—this being the second declared pandemic in his lifetime, after AIDS. He still got angry inside every time he was reminded how egregiously long it had taken the Reagan Administration to declare the first one. These days, there were abundances of caution and nobody seemed to be wasting precious time. He wanted to think that perhaps the scientific establishment had learned from AIDS how to better educate and protect all members of the public, but he was too cynical for that. They were likely quicker to posture for the cameras now because *this* virus was killing droves of "normal" people, and not just a shunned subset of an already marginalized sector of a very uncivilized society. He blamed the faults of the fathers for this.

He could go deep with his conspiracy theories. He just couldn't dally there for very long or the seeds of bitterness would take root again. He set his coffee mug down on the wood block counter and glanced at the framed quote he propped on a mini-easel on the kitchen counter next to the toaster so he could read it every morning, like a devotional: *In the time of your life, live—so that in that wondrous time you shall not add to the misery and sorrow of the world, but smile to the infinite delight and mystery of it.* Ronald cherished that William Saroyan line, which he got to deliver during a production of *The Time of Your Life* as an undergrad at Stanford. It grounded and calmed him still, all these years later.

He retired to the sofa though it wasn't even ten in the morning. Already, this COVID mess had triggered a stampede of repressed ponies from his past, trampling his ability to stay upright and future-focused. Isolation had become his specialization when it had been his choice. Now that it was being mandated, every cell in his being felt compelled to rebel, rushing to the frontlines of resistance.

After the quickest of catnaps, he got himself off the couch and walked his right hand along the black stone face of the fireplace, opening the double French doors to air out the old man stink that had been trapped in the great room. He squinted his seventy-two-year-old eyes and scanned the horizon for a project, something manual he could take on, to arrest his post-winter idleness and distract him from his ever-lurking demons. He didn't need to scan far. The overgrown duck pond down the slope had become so chocked with cattails and reed grass that he couldn't even make out his mother's rock pathway beyond it. He was certain that any water-seeking fowl would likely fly right past, missing the pond's original, semi-natural purpose completely.

The pond had been resuscitated for the first time, Ronald believed, during the Korean War, circa 1950. Truman had just committed US equipment and troops to fight alongside the South Koreans as they pushed back against an invasion by the North Koreans with the backing of China and the Soviet Union. While America's understanding and tolerance of communism at home and overseas had dried up faster than the Simplemans' late summer puddle of a pond, June—armed with a *Better Homes and Gardens* magazine under one arm, and a *Sunset Magazine* under the other— began mounting her own offensive in the name of peace. She did sketches and pounded stakes with colored ribbons she could spot from her kitchen window, but even more impressive, she had amassed a collection of fifty rocks, each labeled with permanent marker, that she'd hand-picked and lugged back home from their family travels. And she didn't stop until she had one from each state, including Alaska and Hawaii, claiming Lucile Ball had given her the idea. Dr. Simpleman had responded by saying he had even less patience for that sort of nonsense than Desi Arnez, but he carted the rocks back to Crested Butte anyway, sometimes in his airplane luggage. June Simpleman was always saying that that one day she would use her rocks to create a wishing well for peace. Apparently, coinciding with the start of the Korean War, that day had come.

Ronald's father hired Franco Cavaletti, to drill a hole and create a pad for the wishing well. While he was at it, Franco backhoed and enlarged, by at least twenty times, the slight depression in the lower acreage so that it would hold water in the spring even if it evaporated away over the course of the dry summers. The pond always refilled again with the autumn rains before they turned to snow and the pond to ice, giving the teenagers—and their friends if they ever had any—something to skate on all winter long. Eventually the pond was almost twice the size of a hockey rink, but by the time June declared the decade-long project completed, the teens—still friendless—had trundled off to college. That fancy water feature never produced NHL hockey players, but it did produce all-star mosquitos. June's wishing well also fell short of the hype and expectations, and never achieved its cemented, cylindrical purpose either—though the fifty stones did make a very attractive approach to the pond that she named her pathway for peace, now completely overgrown. Whether peonies or state stones, June had been awfully fond of her pathways.

So, from the French doors of his resident bubble in the midst of a deadly pandemic, appraising the ambitious, isolationist, stay-at-home opportunity that stood stagnant and overgrown before him, Ronald decided he would play the role of an undaunted archaeologist, pith helmet and all, to stealthily unearth these landscaped treasures from a happier epoch. There were weeks of pulled muscles, grass cuts to his hands, a sprained ankle from falling into the camouflaged well hole, and a burrowing tick that made significant subdermal headway before discovery. There had also been the occasional weekend mechanized assist by Junior, who enlisted all manner of machinery at his auto-body shop's disposal, to haul away the mounds of cattails that had accumulated like bushels of thatch during a medieval harvest.

Toward the end of summer, taking full advantage of Gunnison County's relaxation of COVID distancing measures, Junior brought his whole family into Ronald's bubble for a Sunday picnic, after which the girls helped the men stretch out a quarter-acre of thick, rubberized pond liner, special-ordered from the Crested Butte Ace Hardware. Ronald spent half an hour trying to teach them a nifty sing-song way to remember the state names as they hopscotched on his mother's excavated pathway for peace while the pond began to fill from the nozzle of seven end-to-end garden hoses attached to the house's hose bib. "Alaska, Arizona, Arkansas, California, COLORADO," they squealed in delight as their feet slapped onto the largest stone, which Ronald's father had long ago claimed was technically a boulder. The barefooted picnic party next changed into their bathing suits and released all their pandemic lockdown anxiety, rolling, sliding, splashing and generally tamping down the hose-wetted liner to reveal the pond's varying depths. Almost biblically, it took seven days and seven nights with the garden hose valve opened wide, to achieve a water level that was visible from the kitchen window. Then the late summer rains arrived on clouds that choked the valley sky, taking over the rest of the fill.

Even on the rainiest days, Ronald would waddle down to his mother's glistening pathway for peace to appraise with pride the rebirth of the Simpleman family waterfront. Indeed, this make-work project had returned him to a happier place, where memories tickled rather than terrorized him.

THE CASTRO, SAN FRANCISCO

September 2017

EVER SINCE HE'D ARRIVED AT HARLAN'S SOUTHWEST facing, second-floor apartment on Church Street, smack dab in the center of San Francisco's Castro District., Ronald had been an agitated and nervous nucleus of unharnessed protons. Had the older brother been able to assert more authority, he might have sent Ronald to his room or around the block to chill out. But it appeared nothing was going to rectify his sour mood or change the stance of outrage he'd adopted.

The impetus prompting this spontaneous visit to the City by his mountain-dwelling, misanthropic sibling, could be summed up in 287 pages, and especially in the dubious and offending Chapter 18. Harlan had picked up his copy of Mitchell Carson's latest novel at Fabulosa Books on his way home, after perving out at the Folsom Street Fair for the better part of last Sunday. He had mentioned this to his brother on the phone during a lull in the small talk portion of their quarterly check-in, thinking Ronald probably already knew about the book. But Ronald didn't, and sounded shocked over the phone, saying he'd drop everything—which Harlan knew meant nothing—to meet up in the City as quickly as one of his moderately unreliable vehicles could get him there. It would have been weeks before a copy of the novel could have been special ordered by Townie Books on Elk Avenue and Ronald would not have been bold enough to request the title as it would have given locals a clue about his interests which was none of their business.

Not even eighteen hours later, while Harlan was out getting the extra groceries (including a jar of Sanka coffee) he figured he'd need for Ronald's visit, Ronald had let himself into his brother's apartment using his spare key. When Harlan returned from the Rainbow Grocery Cooperative and was in the middle of putting away the groceries, Ronald bellowed from the living room, where he'd found the novel face-down on the mid-century coffee table and had been engrossed in it ever since. "I'm like four or five chapters into this, and so far, I don't see any red flags," he decreed using that bitchy, impatient tone of his that suggested he'd driven all this way for nothing.

Harlan joined him in the living room, sitting in the white chair opposite the sofa. His brother was sprawled out there on the white blanket Harlan used to camouflage the dark sofa so that it matched the other pieces and his white walls, rendering the covering untucked, which drove Harlan to prissy distraction.

"You should maybe rip the band-aid off and jump ahead to Chapter 18," Harlan advised, "because I think that's the only part where it might be interpreted that the author's referencing you." He shut his eyes, his face warmed by the last rays of the day to trespass inside his inner sanctum. He heard pages turning and braced himself for the detonation to come. In the meantime, he tried to block out the rest of the world.

"Here! Right here," Ronald said, drumming the open book with his index finger. "He mentions Stevensville, Montana right here. Everyone knows that's where I taught."

"Everyone you taught, knows you taught there," Harlan said without opening his eyes. "That's, what . . . sixty-three students, spread out over seven years? That's hardly *everyone*, Ron." In the ensuing silence that was punctuated every so often by a dramatic page turn, Harlan knew his brother was pretending he hadn't heard the last bit.

"And yes, right, yes," Ronald stammered. "You are correct that Mitch didn't use my name. But he did create a mash-up of two other faculty members—people who were actual teachers at Stevensville High when I was there."

"*Actual* teachers?" Harlan said with raised eyebrows, his eyeballs rolling behind closed lids trying to envision a class of imposters dubious enough to masquerade as fake teachers.

Ronald dismissed the jab. "You know what I mean. Whoa!" He held out his hand as if to stop traffic. "And here, he has the audacity to use the first and last names of the real students who bullied him. You know what kind of fiction this is? I'll tell you what kind. N, O, N. *That's* what kind."

Harlan could have formulated another smartass comeback, but realized it would not defuse the situation. So instead, he asked, "Care for some car-damom coffee?"

Ronald grunted something back without looking up, which Harlan could have interpreted two ways; his brother would either enjoy a cup of cardamon coffee or he might prefer a sprinkle of cardamon on top of his cup of disgustingly tasting Sanka. His brother should have figured this out by now, but Harlan was no short order barista and so his brother would get what everybody else was having. He made a quizzical face his brother didn't see as he leveraged himself out of his "babysitter." That's what he called the overstuffed recliner, which, like the sofa, was covered in a white tucked throw. He spent much of each day and night in that piece of furniture—often overnight, too—as it kept him from tumbling and injuring himself. At his age and in his condition, Harlan couldn't afford to break his left hip or de-socket his prosthetic right one that his own father had installed during the two-hour surgery that happened to be his last official procedure before retiring from orthopaedics for good.

"And here, he describes exactly how I dressed and the length of my side-burns!" Ronald's voice was loud enough for someone on the sidewalk below to hear, not to mention his brother in the kitchen about a dozen feet away.

"It was the 70s, for Krishna's sake!" Harlan said. "Everybody dressed the same and had those ridiculous sideburns." He peeled the husks off eight green cardamom pods with fingernails so discolored he was often misjudged by strangers as a lifetime smoker.

"The women didn't, so that's hardly *everybody*," Ronald sassed back, deploying his brother's penchant for technicality against him and his unhelpful generalizations. The silence from the kitchen was almost repri-manding until the coffee bean grinder whirred into a high pitched squeal. Ronald waited for the racket to wind down before delivering his next explo-sive comment. "You're kidding! He divulges my address at 305-A Charlos."

"Well, you don't live there now," Harlan mumbled as he set the teapot on the stove and fussed now more loudly than was necessary. Maybe the noise of getting teacups out of the cupboard would be an excuse for not responding, he thought, before he began grinding the cardamom seeds with his pestle and mortar.

"Right here, he says I drove a bronze Volvo sedan. I suppose you'll next tell me those were a dime a dozen in the 70s." Ronald didn't wait for a response. "Well, they weren't! And I had been assured by the dealer in Salt

Lake City that I would be driving the *only* bronze Volvo in the whole Big Sky State of Montana."

Harlan remembered that incriminating description, had expected his brother to be alarmed by it, but couldn't bring himself to rush to his brother's defense. It wasn't in his DNA. He'd read Chapter 18 several times so that he would be equipped to rebut what he had assumed would be his brother's long-distance cross examination of the plot and characters when they discussed the novel over a phone call. Being physically together involved giving off appreciative and sympathetic visual cues and so required more effort and diplomacy, so as not to come off as callous or bored—characteristics one could easily conceal on the phone.

"If memory serves," Harlan said, returning from the kitchen with the teacups and saucers, which he set on coasters that had been in place so long and had absorbed so many sticky spills that they had become affixed to the surface of the coffee table between them, "it wasn't you who drove the Volvo in this book. It was the made-up teacher, not an *actual* one."

"You're splitting hairs, Harlan. We both know who Mitch Carson is referring to with this car reference and that apartment address. It's me. That character is supposed to be me."

"Yeah, okay. But then that same character either gets a sex change or just takes up cross-dressing for fun and moves to Paris to live out his or her life as a *femme*. So, that isn't you. You didn't do these things, unless you've never shared them with me."

The tea kettle whistled, harkening Harlan back to the kitchen. He spooned the ground arabica bean coffee from the grinder into the paper filter he'd tucked inside his pour-over cone and liberally peppered the ground coffee with the crushed cardamom. He set the red plastic holder atop a wide-mouth beaker so stained it was opaque—a fact that made it difficult to know when he'd added enough boiling water. As usual with his shaking hands, Harlan overpoured, enriching the stain that momentarily flagellated like an amoeba on his originally white kitchen countertop before being wiped into the sink with an equally stained dishcloth. He padded back into the living room carrying the beaker in well-worn oven mitts. "I assume you still take milk?"

Nose buried, Ronald missed the question.

"*Milk?*" Harlan shouted as though he were a server in the dining room of a nursing home populated by the thick skulled and desperately hard of hearing.

"Sure," Ronald answered abruptly before thinking to add, "please." He closed the paperback and set it on the mid-century coffee table, face down. When he saw the author's smirking photo on the back cover, he flipped the book over, so the rather evocative cover that seemed to stare back at the reader with a bold face dare, was face up. "I think I am going to write him a strongly worded letter," he said, fuming. "Or get my lawyer to do it."

"You don't have a lawyer, brother, because you can't afford one." Harlan bit his lip in concentration as he balanced the pours from the beaker into each of the teacups before adding milk. His spectacles steamed up so he could barely see. "But I think speaking with him would be good therapy, as they say."

"*They?*"

"Pardon?" Harlan wiped the condensation from the lenses of his glasses on the shirt tail riding untucked below the hem of his moth-nibbled sweater vest.

"Who's *they?*" Ronald repeated, even though he was just being nit-picky in retaliation for Harlan's devil's advocate-like challenges to what Ronald believed was a righteous and justified outrage. Mitch had asked Ronald to be a beta-reader of this story before Mitch sent it to his publisher, but the version he'd been mailed to read had been conveniently missing this Chapter 18.

Harlan ignored the swipe as he cautiously hinged at the knees, lowered his butt, scooted it backwards into the safety of his babysitter, and habitually re-tucked the cover under the cushion on his left and then his right sides.

Ronald recognized his brother's non-answer as another unspoken reprimand and so decided to change the topic. "Hey, how's that new hip of yours doing, anyway?"

"Well, you know Dad's handiwork. I only wish he were still around so he could do the other one, though it's entirely too late now, I suppose."

Ronald took a temperature-testing slurp from his teacup. "Yes, I suppose it is, ol' man," he said. "Hmm, fancy coffee. I'll likely be up all night, since I usually only put Sanka in my tank. Delicious, though. Cheers."

"Cheers," Harlan echoed, raising his teacup off the saucer. "Say, if you don't mind driving, we could head over to Good Luck Dim Sum for a bite to eat later." Harlan had never owned a car and hadn't bothered to renew his driver's license after it expired in 1988. He considered this a badge of his ecological awareness—though Ronald knew his brother was just a cheapskate who would eagerly hop into somebody else's gas-guzzler if it got him where he needed to go, without a twitch of conscience.

"The Red Jade down the block would do, wouldn't it?" Ronald picked up the novel, re-reading its back cover. "I have to watch what I eat these days—nothing Szechuan for me."

"Oh?" Harlan asked between cardamom-laced slurps. "Why's that?"

Ronald put the book back on the coffee table. "I turned seventy last month and WHAMMO! I've got a bounty crop of hemorrhoids. I'm sitting here blowing Preparation H bubbles as we speak." This was a reference to the ointment he'd slathered between his cheeks during a rest-area pit stop earlier that morning, just this side of Sacramento.

"T.M.I.—isn't that what the kids say? Too much information?" Harlan dispatched a short chuckle into his mostly empty teacup. "And the Red Jade's fine." He topped up his cup from the beaker, before extending it to his brother to do the same. "I think I also have passes around here someplace if you felt like attending an open rehearsal of Ballet Trockadero later tonight. Apparently, the company got into town yesterday to headline the Frameline Film Festival that starts Friday. I read they'll be performing *Rebels on Pointe* at the Castro."

After filling his cup with the now lukewarm cardamom coffee concoction, Ronald said, "I'd like to try to see James at some point while I'm here. I'm not sure he'd even want to meet up—"

"James who? You mean James from my work?"

"Yes, that James," was all Ronald said. He didn't rehash how he had carried on relations with somebody he'd met from his brother's workplace, even though he and James had shared episodic history that went all the way back to Stanford.

"James died a year or two ago of AIDS-related complications," Harlan said, in his unemotional, matter-of-fact way.

This bomb stunned Ronald for several seconds. He struggled with how this news could possibly be true but in an immediate follow-up thought he more rationally wondered how James—given his early go-go dancing days with what Ronald had always deducted must have included sex work— could have survived as long as he did? His hand began to shake, jiggling the teacup in its saucer. He set it down on the coaster and worked at corralling his composure. He'd always believed he would one day find the moment to help James remember when and how the two of them had first met back in their Stanford days, decades before they'd been reintroduced and seemingly then for the first time at a Thanksgiving dinner party that Harlan hosted in 1978, and then again, only eight years later when Ronald had that stint in account payables covering for his brother at the accounting firm where he, and as it turned out, James worked too, while he subleased his brother's apartment during his 1986 sabbatical in China. Each time Ronald had seemed to kismetically cross paths with James, James appeared not to recognize or remember Ronald. Was James that forgetful or was Ronald that forgettable, was a mystery that had always dogged Ronald. At first, he elected to take this as an inside joke and thought James might only be pretending or maybe he was simply exercising discretion in the presence of others. But when James never let on, even privately, that they'd hung out and fooled around together sexually while they had been living on campus in the late 60s early 70s, Ronald had to stow his hurt feelings and play the bigger man. He didn't want to hurt or embarrass James or insult his poor memory if that were the case, so he never found that moment when it wouldn't be awkward to set the record straight.

And now, he never would.

After a few minutes in silent reflection punctuated by Harlan slurping his cardamom coffee, Ronald decided he wasn't going to put having the tough conversations off any longer. So, he leaned forward on the sofa and into the discussion he'd been meaning to have with his brother but hadn't managed to grenade-toss into any of their brief and infrequent phone calls.

"So, Harlan, you know that Mom and Dad are out there in Fairview Cemetery, north of town, in that family plot our father pre-paid with all the headstones pre-engraved?"

"Yes, brother. I was there when we buried them, I remind you." Harlan settled back in his babysitter, not at all sure where the conversation was now heading.

"Yes, of course you were there. You'll remember then that there are these headstones on either side of our parents' shared gravestone with each of our names on them, with our dates of birth and a dash for . . . you know."

"The dates we croak?"

"Exactly," Ronald said, exhaling nervously.

"And? Are you asking me to give you my date?"

His not-so-little brother (even though Ronald had shed most of the body fat he'd forklifted onto his formerly skinny frame after his teaching career had bottomed out and he'd moved back home to be subsidized and sustained by their mother's notoriously unhealthy cooking) laughed that trademark two-beat staccato *ha-ha* of his in that deep register voice. "No. You can save the date and keep me in suspense. I just wanted to know if it's your plan to, you know, be planted there in Fairview with Mom and Dad."

Harlan lowered his teacup to the saucer with a clank and then leaned sideways to deposit the jangling china set on the side table. "You can let my reservation at Fairview Cemetery go to somebody else, Ron. You go ahead and endure eternity with the rents if you want to, but I prefer to decompose by whatever means is cheapest and have my ashes scattered here, near the Bay. In fact, Mayor Newsom has already promised to walk my ashes naked down to the Presidio, where he will say a few words as he sprinkles me on the waves at Crissy Field East Beach—"

"Wait," Ronald said. "*You'll* be naked, or *Gavin Newsom* will be naked?"

"Gavin will be naked. I'll be dead."

"Then what you meant to say was that Mayor Newsom has already promised to be naked when he walks your ashes down to the Presidio." Ronald raised his eyebrows and grinned, waiting for his brother to acknowledge his misplaced modifier. "And isn't he the governor now anyway?"

"Always the English teacher, aren't you?" Harlan crossed his arms to rest on his belly. "Lieutenant Governor. But sweet Gavin Christopher will always be my personal mayor first."

"I see and thank you. Your wishes have been recorded by your only living relative. I appreciate you letting me know." Ronald wasn't sure how he felt about the family unit being desecrated by his brother's stubborn omission. But for now, he wanted to park his feelings and move on from this red herring of a curtain warmer to the main matter he actually wanted to reveal and get off his chest—that being a full throated confession before his brother—admitting at long last that he'd had a sexual relationship with a much younger student, with Mitch Carson, back in the 70s.

But his brother wasn't finished. "And what would be your wishes, Ron?" He pointed at the paperback. "Hopefully not a scheme as demanding as your writer friend's main character in that book," Harlan pointed to the paperback on the coffee table. "Who insists their ashes be divided up into film cannisters and shipped all over the world, anyway?" Harlan didn't intend to give the book's premise away, but he'd seen his brother read the back cover at least twice, and he knew that he was already several chapters in, so the beans—cremated and not baked in this case—were already spilled.

"I gave him those film cannisters, for the record," Harlan wanted this made clear, as it helped set up the confession to come. "But no, this is not my wish for what happens when I die. I am fine being interred with Mom and Dad. I have always felt this strange affinity and maybe fraternity out at Fairview Cemetery. Maybe I just like hanging out with the ghosts of those forty-six coalminers killed in the Jokerville Mine accident in 1884. They're all buried there together, in one mass grave, about fifty feet from the Simpleman Family plot. Did you know that?"

Harlan shook his head, thinking he might never figure out this brother of his. And then, in the largest non-sequitur in history, Harlan blurted out, "Say, did Dad ever touch or play with your penis?"

Ronald's eyes gaped wide. "You mean like *you* did, brother?" he asked pointedly, hoping to shut him up or knock him off this line of questioning so he could finally get to the moment he'd been building up to, albeit by painfully beating around the bush.

"Like *we* did." Harlan pointed at his brother with a finger he first had to free from the handle of his teacup. "We lived rural and frankly had no other option. It was not like the workaholic surgeon was ever going to put down his hammer and chisel for five minutes to diagram the birds and bees for his boys. Boys just figure this shit out for themselves or get somebody else to teach them. That's all *we* did. We improvised."

"Then, it's a *no*, to answer your question. I don't remember Dad ever having any interest in my anatomy." Now Ronald wondered why that question was being asked.

"Good," Harlan said, clamping his hands firmly on the arms of the chair. "That means I took the brunt of it, just like I've always suspected. Just like I'd hoped." He started to wiggle his butt out of the babysitter. "Here—I want to show you something."

With effort, Harlan was upright and heading toward the coat closet. Ronald felt he was being lulled into a cold sweat as his blood pressure began to drop. He wasn't remotely copacetic with confrontation, had never been, and so everything about this pop-up visit was beginning to feel confrontational.

When Harlan returned, he was concealing something behind his back. He paused, planting his slippered feet on the giant Persian carpet that their parents had shipped from a rug merchant they encountered while touring the Tajrish Bazaar in Tehran's District 1. Ronald had instantly recognized this rug several visits ago; Harlan had pilfered it from their father's den in the Crested Butte home without consulting him about it, sometime after both their parents had passed.

The older brother held out an unusual looking walking cane. "Take it," he commanded. Confused, Ronald did, examining the shellacked, gnarly looking stick. He held it with both hands, and then stood to try it out for length.

"Now, it may surprise you to learn what you are grasping," Harlan said, seeming to introduce a riddle. Ronald smiled, giving up before venturing a guess. Harlan pointed. "The handle part, there, is Bruce's penis, only petrified."

Harlan imagined the gears in his brother's cranium grinding to a jam.

"*Bruce?*" Ron said, at first not getting it. "The elk? *This* is the penis from Bruce the Elk, hanging on the fireplace back home?"

Harlan nodded with a devilish grin. "I was there, in the laundry room, when Dad showed it to me. He asked me to hold it, both hands, as he surgically removed it from the half-frozen carcass that he had snowmobile-dragged out of the mountains after the kill."

"Where was I? How old were you?" With his questions, Ronald was both evaluating and deciding whether he felt upset to never have been aware of this or if he felt hurt to have been left out of this father-son exchange. Harlan had said he took the brunt of it. What he didn't reveal was whether he minded taking the brunt. Something about the way this story was unfolding, informed Ronald that maybe Harlan hadn't been all that traumatized by it, then or now.

Harlan shrugged. "With this fleshy thing—Bruce's member—more or less thawing out in my hot hands, Dad made me drop my pants and underwear to show him . . . you know, to compare my size to Bruce's. God knows why, but I got an erection. That's when Dad dropped his pants to compare his erection to mine. Neither of us could hold a candle to Bruce, but that's not what Dad was interested in holding anyway."

Harlan returned to his recliner, folding his hands over his lap in shame.

Ronald was stuck imagining the gruesomeness of the scene . . . the blood . . . the dissection . . . and oh, the smells. He was feeling a bit dizzy but could come up with nothing even remotely arousing about the situation being described. This only helped him further confirm what odd ducks he'd always thought his father and dad to be, but then he seized on the visual of the two of them standing in the utility room with their pants and underwear down, and his own seventy-year-old penis begun to twitch involuntarily. Ronald had seen his brother erect—which had been no big deal at the time, since his older brother had been short shrifted in that department, but he didn't remember ever seeing their father naked, never mind with an erection. He sort of envied Harlan's knowledge of their father that way—carnally disturbing though it was. Because of his affinity and soft spot for Bruce, Ronald also secretly coveted Bruce's petrified penis. He was already trying to finagle the circumstances by which he could make this talisman his; perhaps by covertly lifting this as recompense for the Persian rug that Harlan had pilfered from their father's den.

"Well, that's quite the story," was all Ronald could think of to say in the moment.

"Dad presented me with the cane in the recovery room after he'd replaced my left hip, and as I was coming out of sedation. He told me he'd had it made special and was waiting for the right moment to gift it to me."

"And he announced his retirement a week later, didn't he?" Ronald said.

"That's right—but remember, I was home at the time and spent three months in their house rehabilitating . . . using that cane, which he insisted I graduate to when he felt I was depending too heavily on the walker. Even as an adult, I was always embarrassed using that cane in front of Mom. Dad's lecherous look every time I used it didn't help either."

"Golly, Harlan. I don't know what to say."

"Golly is right, brother. How about you say that we grab some Chinese?"

CONUNDRUM CREEK, COLORADO

June 2014

ALONG WITH THE INHERITED TRUCK CAMPER, RONALD'S solo camping routine incorporated tips and habits passed down from his father before his death six years ago. While he credited his basic camping skills to his outdoorsy father, he would have been surprised by any evidence that established proof the two had camped together more than twice and neither time with their mother or Harlan tagging along. His brother camped with their dad separately for reasons Ronald had never understood unless their father had been deploying a divide and conquer stratagem to get to the core of why neither of his sons even remotely relished getting into the back country as much as he did. Ronald giggled to himself as he couldn't imagine Harlan even trying to fake it. Ronald hadn't exactly possessed Daniel Boone sensibilities as a child either, but he had picked up acting almost as soon as he could walk, which had falsely extended their father's hope that he might make an outdoorsman out of his second son yet. That fizzled, and in dramatic fashion, once Ronald expressed his preference to accompany their mother to Miller Furniture in Gunnison, where he served as consultant while she pored over paint chips, wallpaper and carpet samples. At least at Miller's, Ronald's opinion was solicited and seemed to always be appreciated. The opposite was true whenever he attempted any activity with their dad. In the end, their father had been disappointed by the softer sides of both his boys, and embarrassingly, he got reminded of their preferences for any other pursuits with the start of each new camping or open hunting season.

Over the past twenty-five years since he'd abandoned teaching, Ronald accidentally-on-purpose became his own odd brand of outdoorsman. He'd returned to the Rockies to hide out and give his past the slip, but inside the first month living with his parents again, under their roof, he quickly realized he had placed himself on a path to insanity. As time went on, he firmly suspected that path had been lined and was being booby-trapped with stones his mother was still collecting to deliberately place in his way. His parents hadn't requested his return, didn't yet require the daily assistance Ronald would eventually justify his occupation by providing them and so they had probably assumed at first, this would only be temporary until Ronald could find his footing again. But by Christmas that first year, their second son had spiraled into depression and no amount of his parents' nagging could budge him out of his stupor. He put on 35 pounds from his mother's unhealthy cooking, which he supplemented with his not-so-secretive junk food snacking. Harlan had been summoned home from San Francisco to conduct a family intervention, but by this time, their mother's MS was advancing to the point she needed daily help with the basics. While he was there briefly, Harlan meal-planned a two-week rotation of healthy vegetarian recipes he'd been developing and left behind these rigid instructions as his prescription for better eating. Ronald took over the cooking, though Doctor Simpleman grilled himself side dishes of hamburger, elk steak, pork chops or chicken every night. Over the years, Ronald's unexpected tenancy gradually morphed into a godsend for June and Paul, but a clinical case of wicked co-dependency developed among the trio—as diagnosed by un-clinically certified Harlan. The surgeon mostly avoided the home front drama by refusing to retire. June's MS held her captive and soon required importing physical therapists and overnighting home care aids, which in turn, provided Ronald his respite. Escaping in the camper for two to three overnights at a time became his church and only salvation; so much so, he figured he'd probably taken over a hundred trips by now, since he camped pretty much all summer long every year—even more regularly now that both his parents were gone.

After parking his rig in a pullout off the gravel road that had carried him to this gloriously stunning grove of Ponderosas roughly two hours from his home base, Ronald set the emergency brake and in the order he always followed, he connected and turned the valve on the propane tank, unloaded the firewood he'd hauled from home and immediately built his campfire. Once that snapped, crackled and popped to life, Ronald climbed back into the camper to organize his provisions in preparation for his first camp cooked meal of the season. There were the dry goods like the Tupperware filled with Sanka, two bags of differently flavored Doritos, a few Hershey candy bars, a tub of creamy peanut butter, some apples, bananas and granola bars and a gallon of Mountain Dew split between two bottles all of which he displayed on the counter on both sides of the sink like a grocer merchandising his sales items. A few odds and ends like tuna fish, cans of pork and beans, bar soap and bug repellent, along with his shaving and first aid kits, he had pre-stowed in an easy access cupboard above the sink. From his portable cooler that he'd wedged against the toilet in the bathroom closet for transporting, he extracted a carton of eighteen free range eggs. These he'd cushioned with a loaf of bread and a bag of jet puffed marshmallows anticipating the bumpy, post winter roads he'd encounter, and certainly had on the way up to this spot. He lifted the carton lid to inspect for damages and was very pleased to see that not one of his brown beauties had cracked. From under a head of iceberg, two sticks of butter, a package of jumbo ballpark all beef hot dogs, a jug each of milk and OJ, Ronald's fingers snatched the family size pack of thick-sliced country style bacon at the bottom of the cooler that had ridden on top of the ice packs. He then carried the eggs and bacon back to the campfire under his arms with a pot and pan in each hand.

With the campfire smoking up what would have been a rather concerning plume had it been spotted by a forest service lookout later in the wildfire season, Ronald fried the entire package of bacon until it was crispy and left draining off to the side atop a double-fold of paper towels. He had to chuckle at the irony of frying bacon outdoors so as not to stink up the inside of the 1973 Mitchell "Low Boy" eight-foot camper that his father had purchased forty-one years ago. Doctor Simpleman had schooled him to never fry bacon inside the camper and right up to the year he passed, had stipulated this borrowing condition each time Ronald had asked to take the camper for a solo outing. By now—but even back then—there were so many indelible aromas swirling around inside that tin box, that bacon would have served as an air freshener.

Next, while waiting for water to come to a boil, he whipped up scrambled eggs for his arrival lunch that he gobbled down with his first raft of bacon. Only hours earlier, and decadently so, he'd poached himself eggs for breakfast with toast points for yolk dipping before hitting the road. On the grate of the fire ring, in an ancient pot with so many dents it appeared as though it might have been at one time used for target practice—and knowing his sharpshooter father, quite possibly it had—Ronald hard boiled all but three of the remaining eggs. The last three he'd save for frying, sunny side up, the following morning and he'd peel the rest for snacks over the next however many coming days. He would also ration the pre-cooked bacon for later consumption in his tuna fish and peanut butter sandwiches, which was his camping version of the triple decker club sandwich.

His arrival checklist, dishes and general tidying completed, Ronald split some firewood into kindling to keep his campfire going in the afternoon shade where the rays of sunshine weren't breaking through. He hadn't yet shed the outer of his two flannel layers, which was zipped and buttoned up to his neck behind the beard. Under this were the thermal long johns he generally lived in during his campouts. The functional front fly and nifty two-button back flap of the undergarment enabled him to tend to his biological needs without losing body heat. This mattered more this early in the season and at unserviced camp locations like this one, which only had a forest service outhouse about a hundred feet away. On other, lazier occasions, he'd plug into campground hook-ups and take advantage of their shower facilities—or, in emergencies, he could use the bathroom closet inside the camper that he maintained was only fit for a contortionist. If it meant avoiding the dirty task of having to pump and clean out the waste tank when he got back to town, then he would gladly make the early morning or late-night dashes to a nearby shitter. Ronald preferred not to drive the truck in the mountains with the water and waste tanks topped up anyway, as the added weight burned through gasoline and made the rig trickier to handle in loose gravel. He was already compensating for the weight of the spare propane tank he insisted on bringing simply because he couldn't stand being cold. If he got cold, he stayed cold, unless there were showers or hot springs in proximity. For his first campout of this new season, there would be no showers and even though the outhouse was near the trailhead leading to the hot springs he'd once frequented in his forties, at eleven miles away, he sadly could no longer reach them.

Sitting on the unfolded steps leading up to the camper door, he brushed his teeth, and as usual, drooled toothpaste into his beard, which meant he'd be smelling peppermint for the next hour or so. That was fine by him as he was about to head into the stinky camper for a nap. By this moment in his maturity, his beard was mostly as white as the toothpaste, so there was no risk of him looking like a total slob in front of the ground squirrels and sapsuckers that might later come calling. He'd long ago perfected this old man disguise of his, quite confident that even the new-fangled facial recognition technology he'd been hearing about would never confuse him with his younger, more reckless self. His altered appearance, he felt, could be plotted on a graph somewhere between the reference points of Charles Manson and the Unabomber—that is, after both had neglected their hygiene serving out their sentences in their separate penitentiaries. He'd also once read that as men aged and could no longer grow their family, their career, or a vegetable garden, they took to growing out whatever was left of their manes as the only continuing evidence of their virility. He had no idea if this ruse was working in his case, but his years in theater had taught him that the ultimate magic of stagecraft depended on where you were seated in the audience. This lesson likely accounted for why he maintained as much distance as possible from his past and prevented anyone he might once have known from sitting in the front row at his aging shitshow.

Inside the camper, the self-ordained mountain man unhooked and stowed the tabletop. Without the table, the inside of the metal box became an intimate sitting area, with two worn fabric-covered foam beds—if you could call them that—on either side of the narrow aisle. The illusion of spaciousness also depended on where you sat in this cozy theater-camper of the absurd. But at least inside, Ronald could tuck in his wings, let his dishevelled hair down and relax for a spell.

Just before lying down, he parted the cabana striped curtains above the mini sink and adjacent two-burner stove. This enabled him to access and slide open the single pane of glass in its badly worn track that hadn't latched properly since the 80s. This introduced a draft of fresher air creating a bit of a cross breeze. It also allowed more light in to better illuminate the wood-veneer paneling that was scratched with what looked like graffitied hieroglyphics etched in fingernail by primitive prisoners. Plugged into the camper's only working outlet that ran off the truck's battery and was positioned, pre-GFI code, to the immediate left of the sink, were a portable transistor radio and normally a flexible reading lamp that he'd just decided to swap out with his mobile flip phone, in case of an emergency, even though he'd lost cell service shortly after passing Judd Falls around forty miles back down the road.

The screen door was latched but the outer camper door was bungeed open so Ronald could hear the approach of vehicles or grizzly bears. He settled into a post-breakfast-for-lunch laydown on the foam mattress opposite the wall next to the custom-made igloo refrigerator wedged inside its cubby. The fridge didn't work all that well and constantly vibrated, loudly cycling off every so often while it was running. This seemed to always occur right after Ronald had incorporated its white noise into his drifting-off phase of sleep, thereby startling him wide awake again. Because of this, he tended to nap and sleep with his head as far away from it as he could get, astounded all the while that this original "little appliance that could" still kept his eggs and dairy chilled. Neither of the two mattress options was comfortable, as the foam had begun disintegrating around the time Jimmy Carter was in the White House, and each cut-to-measure rectangle was around six inches shorter than his height of six feet. This meant his knees were raised or he was curled in a fetal pose for daytime napping. He remedied this shortcoming at night by sandwiching the second mattress on top of the first, which raised him just enough that his socked feet could clear the partial wall frame and dangle in stale space.

Ronald closed his eyes and tried to inventory the new scents—beyond peppermint—that his sensitive nose was picking up on a breeze that was impossibly tasked with airing out the mustiness of this casket on wheels. Besides his own campfire smoke, ponderosa sap seemed the predominant aroma, though whiffs of barely unfurled aspen leaves and even a hint of wild rose could be detected around the edges of the blended profile. As for sounds, Ronald could hear either an agitated or lonely raven cawing in the distance, the breeze tinkling the aspen leaves like high octave piano keys, and the percussive Conundrum Creek plunging its steep and rocky course along the camper's right side. He'd left the camper window open on the creek side even though it was missing a screen and he looked forward to falling even deeper asleep to this symphonic accompaniment later, as long as the bugs held off once the sun had exited stage west.

After a twenty-minute inaugural snooze, Ronald lay there revelling in the laziness of the delicious high-mountain moment. He knew he could easily drift off again, but he resisted. He was fully capable of inventing things he could be doing, like chopping more wood, working his crossword puzzle book, or taking a short stroll up the trail. He could also start *The Last Testament of Oscar Wilde*, which was the first paperback in the little library of books he'd chosen for the summer camping season. He'd shoehorned the collection so tightly into a nook next to the paper-towel holder that the contents had no chance of tumbling out during transit. He'd stacked and shoved his firewood supply into the camper's miniscule shower space in the same no-shift manner. He'd already pulled the firewood outside, but was thinking he could use this time to clean out the cubicle, though he had no intention of showering inside the camper, since he hadn't filled the tank with water before leaving home and it would have never gotten warm enough no matter how much of his propane he threw under it.

He did none of the things he could be doing and instead resumed watch from his guard station in the lawn chair now fully spotlit by the sun, next to the fire he didn't need in that moment but stoked anyway. He peeled off his outer flannel and hoisted the under layer over his head and off his shoulders. It was impossible not to doze off again while sunbathing, and so he did. When he was stirred awake by the sound of tires on gravel, his private pocket of sunshine had migrated a few feet from his location. He sat up straight in his lawn chair, prepping for an encounter that sounded like it was about to come around the corner. He didn't have time to hoist his long johns onto both shoulders before a mint-green forest service pickup came into view. The ranger behind the wheel slowed the truck to an idling stop, bringing her window all the way down.

"Good day, camper," she said, raising her sunglasses into her auburn bangs.

"Heya," Ronald answered, without getting out of his lawn chair.

"I can see you've got your 2014 Back Country Permit on your rig. Thank you for your compliance. Just wanting to make sure you're self-contained and nothing is going into the creek."

"Self-contained and buttoned up," Ronald said with an appreciative smile. His long johns were the opposite of buttoned-up, both his white-haired pecs and down to his hair-concealed navel were exposed.

"Perfect. How long have you been in this spot? And have you observed anything or anybody doing anything, you know, anti-reg?" She paused, seeming to remember that she needed to use longhand with the public. "Against regulations?"

"Nope," Ronald said, threading his bare arms inside the sleeves of his long johns and hoisting his minimal wardrobe back onto his shrugging shoulders. "I just got up here today, and you're my first human sighting."

"Fine," the ranger said, noting his license plate number in an open logbook balanced on the console beside her. "Remember, your permit allows you to stay in one place for up to five days. Then you need to move on."

"Don't think my rations will last that long, so no problem there," he assured her.

The ranger flashed a smile and lowered her sunglasses. "Enjoy yourself. Stay safe."

And with that, her truck was in gear. She advanced another hundred feet, reversing direction at the turnaround near the outhouse, since County Road 317 didn't go any further than that. She raised a hand in acknowledgment as she passed his lawn chair for the second time before disappearing downhill around the bend.

This solitary human encounter underscored the reason Ronald timed most of his summer camping trips to occur during everybody else's work week. Rarely, an outing of his might spill over into part of a weekend if the circumstances were right—if, say, he'd been flirting with another lone male camper in a way that might build to a roll in the aspens. But that had been back when he was a decade or two younger. Anymore, when he camped, and at his cranky age, his excursions were confined to Mondays through Thursdays, and he stuck to himself. He had been encircled by mayhem-seeking yahoos in the past, so weekends during the summer had become strictly last resort. He didn't come to the mountains to be taunted or stalked, so he'd learned to avoid the alpha-wolf packs by getting the hell out of their habitats before their weekend prowls commenced.

His lawn chair had become uncomfortable, and when he stood up after sitting that long, he instantly needed to pee. He took three strides toward the closest ponderosa and marked his territory. The ranger had unfortunately gotten him thinking ahead to his departure and he'd barely arrived. He'd gotten a later start up the mountain this week than he'd intended, because he'd needed to see his dentist about a tooth that started troubling him and he couldn't get an appointment to be seen until Tuesday. Not wanting to drive puffed up on novocaine after the surprise root canal and wanting to be sure he was pain free before wandering too far away from his home medicine cabinet, Ronald had waited until Wednesday to head into the mountains. Given his usual Friday morning eviction rule, this was only going to be a two-nighter. Almost never did he think about packing up and leaving on the very same day he'd arrived, unless the site he'd chosen was infested with mosquitos, bears, or rednecks.

Post dinner, where the campsite cuisine had consisted of cut up hot dogs swimming in beans washed down with Mountain Dew, Ronald was feeling fuller of methane than a Jersey heifer. After reading his paperback for forty minutes fireside, until the last of the daylight had dimmed from the cloudless cyclorama overhead, he squished a pair of expertly browned marshmallows atop four pips of Hershey's milk chocolate sandwiched between a graham cracker he'd snapped in half. Fire waning and the yawns coming on, Ronald grabbed his headlamp and tooted his way to the outhouse with his rear flap unbuttoned so as not to imbue the fabric with a scent he'd be trapped with all night. Inside the shitter, he turned off the headlamp so as not to attract bugs. Certain his piss by now must be the same chartreuse color of the soda he'd been guzzling, he emptied his bladder of its carbonated contents. He let the door slap hard against the frame as he jogged a few strides away before gasping fresher air. He peered through the canopy of long needled ponderosa fronds and spotted the tail of the milky way in the southeastern sky. As the moon, which he expected to be full or close to it, hadn't yet cleared the hurdles that were the Rockies, Ronald sought out a clearing where he could stargaze unimpeded. Ambling up the trail a few hundred feet away from the outhouse and his camper, he reached an uphill meadow covered in June grass. Remembering his dad sometimes called this common bunchgrass by its botanical name, Koeleria, and he said that elk liked to browse on it in the spring as a good source of nutrition, Ronald wondered if Bruce had ever dined here and taken in the view of the night sky from this spot. Feeling wild and elk-like, he plucked a long blade of the stuff and clenched it in his teeth as he left the trail and selected the perfect spot where he could recline and survey the heavens. He switched off the headlamp to look up. He was already in the delicate two-armed slow-motion act of lowering his body onto the ground when he realized, with a tickle, that he hadn't fastened the rear flap of his long johns. He didn't have a free hand to tend to this now, so with a muffled giggle, he just sat his bare ass down on a clump of long grasses he'd bent backward with his body weight.

When he looked into the sky as he reclined, his eyes scanned a river of stars, some faint and others brighter and more tightly concentrated. This band stretched from one silhouetted mountain peak on his left to another mountain peak towering higher above him on his right side, like a tightrope he might have been able to traverse had he been airy-fairy enough. He couldn't recall ever seeing the Milky Way so clearly, up close, and brilliantly framed in by the mountains, at any previous point in his life. Since his cameras were back in the camper, and he feared the heavens would have shifted and the earth rotated off kilter by the time he retrieved one and scampered back to this depression in the Koeleria, he had to take it in with his photographic memory. He scanned from peak to peak, absorbing all the points of light, trying to expose the image so that when he shut his eyes, it could fix and develop on the insides of his lids. His unbreakable stare began to water turning that celestial river milky, and when at last he blinked his eyes shut, the Milky Way remained magically captured there—for all of two blissful seconds.

RONALD HAD JUST finished gobbling down the last of the fresh eggs sunny side up, as he waited for the morning sun to summit the ridge on the far side so it could warm his chilled bones. Just the exertion of setting up camp yesterday and cooking up enough bacon to best the Guiness Record for biggest batch ever fried above 10,000 feet, had left him exhausted. His first night of the campout, aside from the always awkward transition his body needed to make from mattress to a thin slice of foam, had been unremarkable except for a 2am snarly tussle between what—at least inside the camper—had sounded like two mountain lions but were probably just racoons or a pair of bent-out-of-shape chipmunks. The timpani tumbling of Conundrum Creek as it splashed off boulders in its rush past his camper had lulled him right back into high mountain sleep.

"Yo oh, yo oh! A camper's life for me!" Ronald's baritone voice barrelled through the woods and delightfully ricocheted back at him establishing the illusion in that moment that he had a whole chorus for company. He gave his ass crack a quick scratch and his finger grazed an ingrown hair or a bug bite or maybe just a pimple that seemed a little tender to the touch. He adjusted the way he was sitting so that the spot didn't rub as much on the lawn chair webbing. He crossed his unlaced, booted feet at the ankles, calculating how long it might take for the campfire to melt the rubber off his soles before the heat could reach his toes. He was in a chipper mood sipping on his second cup of Sanka. As his mind flipped through camping memories, he was still trying to figure out when and how he'd turned on to camping. If he could just pinpoint the influences and circumstances responsible for this flipflop-of-a-crush he had on nature, he could attribute credit where credit was due. One thing was sure. As he'd over-thought himself to sleep last night, he had comfortably moved beyond giving his father the flowers since his father had been too quick to lose hope his boys would ever become men.

They hadn't explicitly taught outdoor survivalist training at Stanford either, so his love of camping hadn't come from higher education. But tangentially, Ronald figured that if you could hunker down, endure a heavy course load, not succumb to the infinite smorgasbord of distractions offered up by the alluring California lifestyle, and still—only in your third year—begin pursuing a coterminal master of arts in English by analyzing Anglophone literary histories and theories—then, in actuality, you'd already mastered survival and dodged getting killed off by boredom. Honestly, he thought as finished his breakfast dishes and clipped his dish towel to the drying line with a clothespin, could a grizzly leave bigger scars than Chaucer, Shakespeare, Hemingway, and Steinbeck had?

So, how then, he wondered, could he have gone the first twenty-five years of his life, barely registering all the majesty that was out here? How had he gone from zero to sixty with a hobby that had by now become an annual necessity to spend every non-winter minute he could off the grid and under the stars? It certainly defied linear logic because he couldn't map the route between points A and B. This made him more curious and open to the notion that perhaps his harmonic alignment with nature might have been more deeply rooted in divinity than his ancestry. Then he thought—based on the minor revelations he'd experienced during each of the two times he had accidentally-on-purpose ingested LSD—that maybe he should explore these connections and mysteries further by looking into getting some shamanic guidance. Maybe peyote, magic mushrooms or ayahuasca could unlock his deeper vaults. He gave his sleepy head a shake as it had become too late in life for him to go trekking off to the Amazon.

Also contributing—however hedonistically—to Ronald's love for the backcountry was the discovery during one of his earliest solo outings that he wasn't the only one who became "amusement-park-thrill-level horny" at elevation. The four-decade-old truck camper parked behind him had been a-rockin' on more than several dozen occasions, which had nothing to do with road washouts or potholes and everything to do with what men got up to when subjected to rarefied atmosphere. Stargazing and smelling like smoke on your own were all well and rugged, but Ronald, in his day, had also enjoyed encountering other upright male members of his own species in the wild. Whatever pheromones he happened to be transmitting on the mountain breezes, it had not been uncommon in his rookie camping years for him to receive rutting-level attention.

Ronald was no baseball player, but he continued to wax nostalgically about a winning streak of seasons when he could score maybe three grand slams out of every ten trips he took into the back country ballpark—his own personal best and a darn decent average for his already aging bat—back when he was just getting into the game. Ronald scooted his lawn chair to the other side of the campfire to more directly absorb the thermal bounty of the finally rising sun. When he'd gotten up from the chair, he noted with some pride, that the sun wasn't the only orb that was rising to commemorate the legendary player he'd once been, as the shadow being cast by his tumescence beneath the crotch of his long johns continued to swell with promise that he might still step up to the plate with confidence for the right pitcher. And this changed his tune.

"Take me out to the ball game, take me out with the crowd . . ." he spontaneously serenaded the trees.

Even though he was well past his mate-attracting prime, this was still the habitual reason Ronald tended to either park his camper just offroad near popular trailheads, like he'd done yesterday. When he reserved a site in advance at a public campground, he gravitated toward those that had shower facilities as these were the equivalent of watering holes in Sub-Saharan climes and were ideally suited for attracting the beastliest and thirstiest of creatures.

Natural hot springs, and not the family destination splash pools with water slides, were his favorite spots on his well-traveled summer circuit. But as was the case here at Conundrum Creek, the good thermal pools were often only accessible by hiking in a fair distance. Of course, that had not been a deterrent holding him back in his younger, more agile billy goat years, but now that he was pushing seventy there was no way he'd be able to make the trek. Instead, he kept an eagle's eye out and his rabbit ears tuned to the sounds of crunching gravel, while his super-smeller bull elk nose was constantly sniffing the breeze for any lone buck that might start up or be coming back down the trail. June was still considered early in the short summer season in these parts and Ronald had driven past several patches of still-melting snow on his way up the mountain. The nights were likely too chilly for most hike-in tenters and the hike too long to lug firewood, so he expected most would hold off until July or August before trying to pitch nearer the hot springs.

As he sat there marinating in memories and campfire smoke, Ronald gathered his long beard into a ponytail and brought it to his nose. "Whew!" he exclaimed. He'd been on the mountain for less than twenty-four hours and already his nose was telling him it was time to wash up in the creek— from the neck up, at the very least. With a groan, he rocked into an upright position and headed for the camper. Inside, he snatched his fresh bar of Irish Spring and a frayed towel and headed for the glacial waters of the creek.

He hummed as he scrambled over rocks to reach a sunny spot with a deep back eddy at the creek edge. He unbuttoned and peeled down the top of his long underwear to his waist like a banana, liberating his arms one sleeve at a time. He braced himself for the icy water, then frantically splashed handful after handful of Conundrum Creek on his face and into his hair. He worked the green soap into a lather, growling like a grizzly bear the whole time so other animals would know he was there.

With the rocks starting to hurt his knees, he determined it was time to rinse his hair and beard. He dipped his head into the pool and was about to shake his hair underwater when one of the rocks he'd been gripping gave way. His upper body sort of torso-flopped into the eddy onto his bad shoulder, getting him wetter than he'd intended. The shock of the temperature bolted through him and out the other side as the suds swirled then got snatched by the current to race away from him downstream. Thinking the water wasn't all that bad as he became more used to it, he righted himself, heeled off his boots and pushed the long johns down to his ankles. Shaking his feet free one at a time, back into the eddy he stepped then instantly submerged, vigorously dispatching the bar of soap to the under bits he could reach, while holding the gulp of breath inside his shocked lungs. Unexpected bath complete, Ronald launched above the surface like a submarine fired Trident missile. He splashed out of the water and hollered a full-throated primal scream that sternly echoed back at him from the cliffs. He dried his limbs and chest, then wrapped his hair into the beehive of a towel tower looking like a housewife from the 50s (if that housewife had a beard and very hairy chest). He struggled to pull his long johns back up over wet legs and paused to scratch an itch between his butt cheeks. There was that bump or zit again, feeling more sensitive to him today than yesterday. He stepped back into his boots thinking he might try to get eyes on the spot using a mirror when he got back to the camper. He shuffled his way up the short trail so he wouldn't step out of his loose boots, forgetting all about his pimple when he saw the campfire that needed resuscitating. Another log added—this one cedar--he scooted his badly bent and banged up lawn chair into a wedge of sunshine and sat down to toast his goose-fleshed skin. He finger-combed his beard and flipped out his thinning hair, arranging it into an array on the chair back, where it could dry in the sun that was already warming his bare shoulders.

After a 15-minute warm up, he got up to clip his towel to the line and figured, while he was upright, he'd start the truck and let it idle a bit, just to remind the old engine what engines are supposed to do. But when he turned the key in the ignition, there was no sound. He tried again and then again, but he couldn't get the engine to turn over or to sputter or to whine.

Immediately suspecting a sparkplug issue, he released the latch on the hood, climbed out of the cab and stared inside. The truck had a V8 engine. The quasi-mechanic apprenticeship Ronald had received from Franco Cavaletti, Sr. during high school and for another year or so after graduation, had taught him eight cylinders meant each had a corresponding sparkplug. He'd need to check them all to determine which one (or ones) had cracked, or if maybe one of the electrodes had rounded and worn out and so was no longer making a connection. He'd need his socket wrench and other tools, which were stashed behind the driver's seat in a tangle of jumper cables he didn't remember ever having to use before.

He was three sparkplugs in before realizing the culprit was a cracked ceramic insulator with plug number four. Ronald didn't carry spare plugs, so he knew his boat was dead in the water. But since all he had was time, he thought he should check the remaining plugs while he had the tools in hand. By his eye, half of the eight plugs looked like they might have corroded electrodes, but he couldn't find his gap tool coin-thingy to test if all the rest of the connections were happening. He was stuck and 80% certain he held the reason in his left fist.

While he'd paid close attention to Franco Sr. at the auto-body shop when he was younger, Ronald was no mechanic. But he sure knew one—in the form of Franco Sr's son, Franco Jr. Problem was, Ronald didn't have cell service, and he was about sixty miles from town. He thought about coasting out of gear as far as he could get on the downgrade, but he didn't relish the thought of attempting this without power brakes. Surely somebody would eventually drive up, as the ranger had. He just needed to relax and enjoy his time until that happened. He was confident he could get a message back to town, and that when he did, his mechanic friend would be his Junior-on-the-spot, and speedy to his rescue.

Prompted by a rumble in his tummy, he wondered if it was too early in the day to break into his stash of hard-boiled eggs, maybe mixed in with some tuna fish. He assembled the table inside the camper in anticipation of an early lunch. A few bites into his sandwich, he reached for the box of Cheerios on the counter and carefully ripped the front cardboard panel along the folds. Pleased with how neatly he'd done it, he grabbed his cross-word pencil and printed out his SOS note in all capital letters on the blank side of the cereal box panel, which he would try to give to the driver of the next vehicle that ventured up his way:

> PLEASE DELIVER THIS NOTE AND CRACKED SPARK PLUG TO JUNIOR AT CB AUTO-BODY ON BELLEVIEW AVE IN CRESTED BUTTE. WENT CAMPING. ENGINE WON'T START. STUCK WITHOUT CELL SERVICE NEAR THE END OF COUNTRY ROAD #317 ROUGHLY 14 MILES BEYOND JUDD FALLS NEAR TRAIL HEAD TO CONUNDRUM. —RON

Next, he waited patiently like a fisherman for an elusive sucker. As it turned out, he didn't have to wait long for his first nibble. Ronald heard the blaring bass of an acid rock song pulsing through the ponderosas before he heard tires on gravel or saw the extended cab pick-up that sounded like it might be delivering the whole band to his camper door. The vehicle whizzed past in a Pig Pen dust cloud before Ronald could step into his unlaced hiking boots, gather his cereal box placard with the damaged sparkplug, and get out the door and down the step to wave the newcomer down.

Standing there in his long johns, he held the cardboard note to his forehead to block the sun from his eyes and waited to see if the truck would turn around. At the top of the road, one of the passengers jumped out and sprinted to the outhouse. Someone else, who Ronald didn't think was the driver, shouted, "Don't shit yourself!" The driver laughed as he revved his unmuffled engine.

Ronald began to tentatively walk up the road—intimidated, to be sure, but also motivated to arrange his rescue. Having not bothered to brush his hair after the creek plunge, he realized his crazed mountain man appearance probably looked more dishevelled than usual, every strand on his head amplified by the sun like one of those plug-in fiber optic lamps from the 80s. He could tell the driver had spotted him and was watching his approach from his side mirror, so he gave a friendly wave. The driver didn't wave back but instead laid on the horn, adding to the cacophony from the truck's multiple stereo speakers. He was hazing the passenger in the outhouse, but Ronald, too, was trembling.

Just as Ronald was about to reach the brake lights of the tailgate, the driver floored the accelerator, dispatching a spray of gravel at his legs.

"Whoa, whoa. Hey!" Ronald waved his arms as he took a quick wide step to the left, now detecting the smoke from some skunky marijuana mixed in with the truck's high-octane exhaust.

"Didn't see ya, old man," the twentysomething driver hollered out the open windows. Ronald knew he was lying but strode up to the driver's window with purpose. He needed to shout to be heard over the stereo volume that the jerk of a driver couldn't be bothered to lower.

"Good day, gents!" He made eye contact with each of the three clearly stoned men inside the extended cab. "My engine won't turn over and I wondered if you might be heading back into town at some point today."

"Sorry, Geezer," shouted the man from the backseat. "Truck's full. No room today." He sucked a giant toke from the joint passed over the shoulder of the passenger in front.

"I'm not looking for a lift," Ronald said. "I was wondering if you could take this note and the cracked sparkplug I've duct-taped inside and drop it off at my friend Junior's auto body shop in town."

The driver's attitude changed, and he turned down the volume. "We know Junior. You know Junior?" He seemed not quite able to comprehend how their friend and this mountain man could be connected.

Ronald nodded, wondering in turn how Junior and this truck full of stoners could be connected.

Just then, the door to the outhouse slapped shut like the sound of a bullet being fired and Ronald jumped, his nerves already on high alert. The relieved passenger loped back to the truck and climbed into the extended cab's back seat.

"Sure," the driver said. "We could get this to Junior sometime this afternoon when we get back to town. Just out joy-riding now."

"Wait, this dude knows Junior?" the outhouse user asked, trying to figure out what he'd missed while he was in the can.

Ronald handed the folded piece of cereal box to the driver. "Much appreciated," he said, relief washing over his blushed and bearded face. "You fellows have a good day."

He stepped away as the truck peeled out, displacing more road surface as it slid through a tight U-turn before barreling back down the hill. Ronald coughed on the dust, trying to wave it away with both hands.

Since he was already at the outhouse, and the tense encounter nearly had the effect of scaring the shit right out of him, it made sense to take care of business right then and there. When he stepped inside the dark brown painted closet, three smells hit him simultaneously: the mothball smell of a caged urinal cake nailed high on a 2x4, the foul, sulphuric stench of still steaming diarrhea he could make-out in the pit that he knew wasn't his, and the smoking end of a stubby joint that had been left burning perched atop the toilet paper dispenser. Sitting down to smother at least one of the offensive smells, Ronald picked up the joint, blew on the smoking end, and without trepidation, put the other end to his lips. He sucked in as he expelled out the contents of his bladder along with what he assumed had been last night's meal. He hadn't been keeping count but thought he must have inhaled a good six tokes before the joint began to burn his lips and fingers. He rubbed it out defacing a patch of graffiti he hadn't bothered to proofread but assumed it began with something entirely unoriginal like *here I sit all broken hearted . . .*

When he prepared to wipe, his cranium already beginning to feel lightheaded, he discovered only four squares of toilet paper had been left on the roll. Since the forest service only supplied one-ply and that was crepe paper at best, he turned his four squares into two-ply and cleaned his level best. On the last wipe, he grazed that ass pimple that had become so sensitive, he winced. Suspecting he'd caused it to bleed, he had to examine the toilet paper before tossing it on top of the diarrhea sundae, and there he saw it, a streak of dark blood. That was curious, his stoning brain tried to reason, but at least he'd managed to pop it, and so the healing could commence.

When he stood upright, he giggled. Ronald couldn't remember smoking pot since Stanford. As a freshman, he'd developed a late evening study break habit that consisted of getting quite high en route from his dorm room in Encina Hall to Memorial Court. Once there, he would put on a pantomime face and pose still as a statue, making believe he was the seventh of Rodin's *Burghers of Calais.* Since he normally dressed in brown anyway, and it was dusk or dark when he played this game of solitaire (if you didn't count the other burghers), Ronald appeared to be just another one of the famous bronzes. He would stand there frozen in place for ten, sometimes twenty minutes, just to see if anyone walking by noticed the extra statue. Of course, nobody ever noticed Ron Simpleman, whether he was stoned or not. He'd only started smoking Mary Jane back then to rebel and fit into the California scene, but as a scrawny, transplanted mountain teen, he just didn't. At least not at first, because he'd been trying too hard.

Back at his camper and not quite twenty minutes later, after catnapping like a tabby stretched out on his towel in the sun, Ronald was jostled awake by his stomach growling with the most horrendous case of the munchies. In short order, he devoured most of his trail mix, chased by three hard-boiled eggs, all but the last slice of his pre-cooked bacon and half a bag of nacho flavored Doritos—all washed down with belch-inducing gulps of Mountain Dew.

He was feeling fine but then he grew paranoid about everything all at once. Why was that zit on his ass bleeding? He sent his index finger on follow-up reconnaissance. There was still a little blood. Next time he was upright, he'd need to remember to check the bump with the mirror in the camper bathroom. Then he worried he had just consumed the very food he might have needed to rely on for long term survival if nobody came up the mountain to retrieve him. This got him second guessing his stupidity in sending the cracked sparkplug down the hill that might or might not have been the reason his truck wouldn't start. But now without it, the truck *certainly* wouldn't start. He got himself up off the ground and stumbled into the front seat and tried anyway. There was a click in the ignition followed by . . . nothing, of course. Because the truck was missing a spark plug!

He took a moment there, his arms and head on the steering wheel. Conundrum Creek continued rushing by, and Ronald followed his breathing, in and out, until he was able to think more clearly. Minutes later, egged on by abdominal pains he'd brought on himself by speed-snacking, he climbed out of the truck and walk-weaved five laps around the campfire trying to calm his tummy, quietly reminding his ping-ponging brain—altered or otherwise—that while he was stuck, he was still in paradise. He resuscitated the campfire that had mostly fizzled, grabbed his new crossword puzzle book from inside the camper that he'd purchased expressly for this camping season, and he placed a spare roll of toilet paper on the camper steps to remind himself to take it with him on his next visit to the outhouse. He repositioned the lawn chair in the last polka dots of afternoon sun and cracked open his puzzle book. He was only momentarily stumped by seventeen down: five letters, with the clue *V.P.* By the time it came to him, and he had filled in *B-I-D-E-N* with his pencil, he was starting to feel better.

The last of the day's sun sank behind the ridge of what he was pretty sure must be the backside of Copper Mountain. A glacial chill avalanched down its draws to tussle his flimsy hair. Ronald gathered the long strands together behind his neck and tucked it in a bundle, hunchback-like, under the collar of his long johns. He was already looking forward to a second showing by the Milky Way and maybe even spotting Venus and the full moon rise that would come later in the evening if he could stay awake long enough to witness it.

In the meantime, though his buzz from the pot was wearing off, his paranoia was still flaring strong. He feared his Cheerios box SOS and sparkplug had gone undelivered. He would not have been at all surprised to walk a quarter mile down the road and find it stuck in a bush—or, more likely, the stoner's pickup wrapped around a ponderosa trunk. Cannabis had been legalized in Colorado earlier in the year and at the time, Ronald hadn't expected it to change his life, but seeing someone behind the wheel smoking a joint had him reconsidering his own safety on the roads. That is, if he ever got himself back on the road.

He lifted a leg off the lawn chair webbing to release a quick series of hard-boiled egg farts. This propelled him to his feet to escape the sulphuric ass-ault. And since he was up anyway, he proceeded to chop the last of his firewood into smaller pieces that he'd begin to use more sparingly. He was already preparing to have to scavenge for more fuel if he was going to still be stuck up here tomorrow. He donned the outer layer of flannel and hoisted some jeans over his long johns.

Nervously nibbling on a cedar toothpick he'd separated from a piece of kindling, and with the last of his bonfires crackling inches from the worn soles of his antique hiking boots—not *antique* because he'd bought them vintage, but because the pair had belonged to his father before being handed down to him—Ronald was feeling bloated. While there was still enough daylight left to make his way back up to the outhouse without needing his head lamp, he decided to get up and give it a go. It wasn't until he was tucked back inside the stink box, squatting in the dark, that he remembered he'd used the last of the toilet paper and had forgotten to bring the roll he'd purposefully set out, with him. As he sat there, bracing himself for the unscheduled ice water bidet he'd need to take in Conundrum Creek in lieu of toilet paper, a short vibrating tone startled the shit right out of him and then kept repeating as somebody's cellphone screen lit up on the 2x4 cross brace next to his right thigh. The light illuminated a mosquito that had just landed on Ronald's forearm. He swatted the mosquito dead before picking up the cell phone that was way too fancy to be his, and especially if it had coverage that far up the mountain.

Ronald recognized it as a Blackberry model—the type of phone he knew President Obama used. The screen above the raised keyboard indicated an incoming call. Despite all the buttons on the gadget, it wasn't clear to him how to answer the thing. He began pushing buttons, and by luck, he was connected and could hear a frantic male voice.

"Hello? Hello?" the voice said.

Ronald raised the device to his ear. "Howdy," he said—as nonchalantly as he could, given that he was in an outhouse taking a dump.

"Oh, thank God!" the caller yelled in his ear. Ronald held the speaker further from his head. "Who's this?" the caller demanded.

"Who's *this?*" Ronald shot right back.

"Uh, you've answered my cell phone. I misplaced it someplace earlier today and I'm desperate to get it back."

As a teacher, Ronald had loved playing cat and mouse games with students—deploying clever traps and riddles, concealing secrets, springing surprises. It sounded like the caller didn't know where he had lost his phone, but Ronald had already guessed he must have be one of the headbangers from the truck he'd encountered earlier in the day.

"And where do you think you lost it?" Ronald queried unnecessarily.

The caller didn't like being toyed with. "If I knew that, dumbass," he said, "I would have retrieved it already!"

"No need to be rude, if you want your phone back."

"Look, whoever you are . . . man to man—" the caller paused a few seconds. "I have some photos and videos on that phone that can't fall into the wrong hands. I need you to tell me where you are and how I can get my phone back from you. I am willing to pay you, uh . . . say a hundred bucks if that's what this is about."

Ronald lowered his voice to a stern whisper. "That's not at all what this is about. It's about showing respect. You don't call someone a *dumbass* if they are holding what you want in their hands."

"Yeah, sorry. I am just a bit panicked. Let's start again. My name's Chad."

"Hello Chad. I'm Ron." His business in the stink hut completed with no toilet paper to finish the job, Ronald penguin-walked a few steps with his jeans bunched at his ankles and the back flap of his long johns down. He creaked the sprung door open, hopped outside the outhouse, and kept the door from loudly slapping shut with one hand, still holding the phone to his head with the other.

"Hey there, Ron," the caller said, his tone much softened. "It's a relief to meet you and 'sorry about the dumbass comment."

Ron took his feet out of the unlaced boots one at a time and then removed his jeans before stepping back into his boots. "Are you calling from Crested Butte?" he asked, hopefully. He had started to walk back toward his campfire, but the call reception was beginning to sound spotty, so he stopped moving and stood in the middle of the roadway.

"Yeah, sorta. I live in staff housing just outta town at CBMR. I am a lift mechanic working summer maintenance. I can drive into town right now to get the phone, though."

Ronald was warming to Chad and no longer felt like playing games; plus, he was anxious to use the working cell phone, while he had it, to contact Junior. He cut to the chase. "I should tell you, Chad. We saw each other earlier today, when you and your buddies drove into the mountains past my campsite. You left your phone in the outhouse. I just happened to be in the shitter when you phoned, or I wouldn't have seen or heard it."

"Ah, okay then. You must be that old guy with all the hair." He paused abruptly, catching himself. "*Older* guy."

Ronald laughed. "It's okay. I know I am old."

There was an uncomfortable chuckle on the other end of the call.

"The outhouse, huh? I barely even remember using one, but okay."

Ronald thought about lecturing the kid about how out of it everyone in the truck had seemed, and how someone could have gotten hurt or killed driving under the influence like that. Instead, he decided not to be *that* old man.

"Say," Chad said, "we dropped your note off to Junior, like you asked."

He seemed to be hoping to win points for that. "I think I heard Junior mention that he would be heading up after work. He should probably be on his way to you right now."

Ronald glanced to the starry heavens, so grateful to be hearing that news and touched to know that Junior might be on his way up the mountain—even after dark—to perform a rescue that could have waited until the morning. "That's wonderful! I had worried you and your friends might, you know, not follow through. Thanks for doing that."

"Yeah, so, uh . . . I guess we can both stop worrying now." The panic in the caller's voice was starting to subside. "We just need to make a plan to connect so I can get my phone off you," he quickly added.

"Well, if Junior's on his way to get my truck running again, I should be off this mountain and back to the Butte by sometime tomorrow morning, I expect. I could always give your phone to Junior to give to you, or—"

"Uh, I'd prefer to get it straight from you, if that's okay. Again, and you don't need to mention this to Junior, because it's embarrassing, but I have some sensitive stuff on my phone, and I, uh . . . well, I'd like to think I can trust you, Ron." The caller paused, possibly holding his breath.

Ronald was pleasantly surprised to have established this level of trust with a stranger likely a third his age. The development seemed even more remarkable since earlier in the day he'd misjudged this book's cover—in fact, the whole truckload of book covers. Stoned, irresponsible, and as out of it as they seemed, they still delivered his SOS to Crested Butte Auto Body which said something for their generation.

"Your phone's safe with me and I will look forward to delivering it back to you in person," he said.

Chad exhaled with pent-up force. "Great! How 'bout I call you on this phone around noon tomorrow, and we can make arrangements to meet up?"

"Sounds like a plan, Stan—I mean, Chad." Ronald guessed the kid wasn't old enough to know "Fifty Ways to Leave Your Lover."

"Paul Simon," Chad said. "Awesome."

"Have a good night," Ronald started to say when the call suddenly terminated, either because he'd lost cell service or Chad had jumped off before thinking to say *bye* or *good night*. The Blackberry screen went dark in his hand. Ronald withdrew a foot from his boot and balancing on the other, kicked the lowered jeans off one ankle, and then, reversed feet, to free the other. Now that he was expecting company, he needed to clean up and do some quick tidying. While he was standing in the middle of the road, headlights bounced around the corner, lighting up his bare dumbass like a Christmas tree. Exhibiting classic deer-like behavior, Ronald stood frozen a few seconds in those high beams before remembering to raise the flap of his long johns.

Junior had arrived on the scene, laughing his own ass off behind the wheel. He gave a friendly two-push honk of his horn and parked near the camper. Ronald met him at the open driver's door of his service truck. "What a treat to witness two full moons in the same night!" Junior exclaimed, climbing out of his rig, still laughing. He checked the sky and revised his moon forecast. "It was full when I was leaving town anyway, but I see it hasn't shown up here yet, but it's coming."

Embarrassed but relieved, Ronald stepped forward to receive a one-arm hug and back pat from his strappingly handsome mechanic friend. "Things are pretty relaxed up here," he offered by way of an explanation. "I was headed from the outhouse to the bidet." He gestured with a thumb in the direction of Conundrum Creek.

"Don't let me stop you," Junior said, ribbing him with his elbow. "I've got fried chicken from Slogar's after you finish washing up for dinner."

Enlivened, Ronald energetically popped inside the camper to grab his Irish Spring and snatched the towel from the clothespins on the line. He switched on his headlamp and bounded down to the creek. His knight in shining armor had arrived and his rescue was officially underway. That Junior, he was thinking, was way too thoughtful for a straight man. He heeled off his boots and peeled off the long johns. He'd brought dinner up that mountain, so he must not be in a rush to get home. That was curious, Ronald thought, with an ear-to-ear smile that nobody could see. But then, giddy and moving a bit too quickly for his age and the uneven terrain, he ran smack into a low arching branch that swatted him across the face, possibly knocking some sense into his noggin before he got unrealistically carried away with the fantasy he'd begun concocting.

Squatting as low as an old man could get, he splashed some ice-cold creek water and then directed the soap bar between his legs. He clenched his teeth together as the ache of the cold water ricocheted back and forth between his scrotum and his kidneys. As he scrubbed his bottom and man parts clean, he encountered that sensitive bump between his ass cheeks again and was able to determine by touch that if it were a pimple, it definitely hadn't drained. He thought about trying to pop it now to be done with it but worried, without seeing what he was squeezing, that it might be a boil—not that he'd ever had one before, but he'd heard how some of those infections could turn nasty. He decided it was best to leave it alone, and splash-rinsed away as much of the soap as he could stand, since the water wasn't getting any warmer.

A few yards away, his truck camper revved to a rumbling start, setting off a sustained sonic boom that echoed through the mountain silence. The engine reverberated a while before settling into a heavy idle that was punctuated by Junior's foot on the gas pedal every so often.

Ronald towel-blotted his body somewhat dry, but in his excitement to get back to his guest, he pulled his long johns on over numerous wet spots, and thought he probably looked like a leopard. He negotiated the rocks and followed the path toward the light of the campfire. "I'm a new man," he announced.

"You look like the same old man to me," Junior teased, standing at the fire he'd just stoked with the last of the firewood, Ronald's truck engine still running behind them. "By the way, the cracked plug you sent with your note was the culprit, so great job on your mechanical trouble-shooting skills."

"Well, I have nobody but your dad to thank for any car sense that I have managed to retain," Ronald said clasping his palms together in gratitude.

And I'll just add that you also had badly rounded electrodes on the other seven sparkplugs which likely kept your rig from starting properly. I just replaced them all."

"Just . . . *wow!*" Ronald exclaimed. "And you brought me dinner, too?" He knew he was fawning. He liked to tiptoe around the margins of flirtation with Junior from time to time, just to see if he could fluster his straight friend.

"Right!" Junior said, remembering. "Dinner is served!" Ronald's rescuer took a couple strides to the camper truck and reached in to turn off the ignition. He next went to his tow truck and grabbed two dinner boxes from an insulated tote bag. "We'll need to use your utensils or our fingers . . . up to you."

Ronald plucked an extra lawn chair from the storage hold on the side of his camper and unfolded it next to his, on what was currently the smoke-free side of the campfire. "Cutlery and paper towels on the way," he announced, climbing inside the camper to root around the drawers under the sink. He was happy to be eating outdoors, as he tended to become self-conscious anytime someone not accustomed to the aroma inside his camper climbed aboard. While in the camper, he cranked the only three working windows open even wider, in case . . . in case what? He didn't know. He pulled up his jeans over his long johns, inadvertently scratching the zit as he tugged the denim over his butt. He waited for the disproportionate amount of sting for a bump that small to subside, before emerging down the camper stairs with the items he'd gone into fetch.

"Slogar's famous fried chicken," Junior said, beaming. "Half a bird for you and the other half for me." He'd proven his odd friendship to Ronnie once again and this was deeply gratifying for Junior. He missed having his father in the world every day, especially now that he was having kids of his own. Hanging out with and doing things for Ronnie Simpleman was the next best thing. He'd learned in the five hard years since his dad's ski accident that you could approach grief in many ways. But this seemed the healthiest, since his dad always seemed to have a soft spot for Ronnie, too.

"I chose mac 'n' cheese for your side," Junior said, "thinking A. you're too skinny and B. you probably wouldn't like collard greens. But we can switch, as I'm happy either way."

Ronald accepted the box being offered to him. "You're happy either way? Is this your way of coming out to me as bi after all this time?" Ronald's tone was teasing as he handed Junior a fork and knife that he'd just burrito-wrapped in a double paper towel to make things seem fancier than they were.

Junior blushed, which was plain to see in the light cast by the campfire. "Sweet Sofie, my wife and the love of my life, as you know, is three months away from bringing our second daughter into this world. I think it's clear which side of the bread my butter's on, don't you?" Junior's eyebrows disappeared into his great curly hair.

Ronald was wearing a square-chinned grin but it was mostly obscured by his scraggly beard. He liberated the cardboard flaps of the takeout box, releasing the steam of civilization to the almost-orgasmic delight of his olfactory receptors. Inside the box was a container of coleslaw, a container of mac 'n' cheese, a leg, a thigh, a wing, and a breast.

"Where are my manners?" Ronald said, looking up from the buffet in a box. "May I offer you Mountain Dew or Sanka?"

It was Junior's turn to grin. "I brought Coors, because *it's the water up here.*" He parroted the beer company's slogan as he bounced back up, setting his box on the chair's webbing. He returned from his rig with a small igloo cooler tucked under one arm.

Ronald resisted making a face and graciously accepted the can after Junior had courteously popped the tab for him. Beer and wine had never done it for him, but he especially disliked beer from an aluminum can for reasons more to do with the leaching of toxic metals he'd read about than the taste, which he already didn't care for. "Cheers," he said, toasting his hero.

"Cheers, Pepperoni."

They began devouring their crispy, seasoned half birds, their silence only broken by *hmm* and *so good* as the crackling of the campfire carried them into a most pleasant evening.

"So. . ." Junior paused to chew and swallow. "You know that Sofie is the love of my life, but I've never asked: who was or is the love of your life, Ronnie?"

Ronald nearly choked on some wing meat that went down sideways and needed to be chased with a swig of Coors, though he would have preferred his by-now-flat Mountain Dew. He belched quite involuntarily. "Pardon me," he said, wiping his mouth and beard with the open paper towel he'd spread across his lap. "The love of my life?" It was as if he was on *Sixty Minutes* being interviewed by Junior. "That's easy. Mitchell Carson."

It was the first time he'd ever admitted or said it out loud.

"Whoa!" Junior yelped, slapping his thigh with one hand while holding a chicken thigh in midair with his other. "Mitch-ell Car-son," he repeated, articulating the syllables in both names so he'd remember this factoid. "Why haven't I heard this before now?"

"Uh," Ronald stammered. "We haven't ever really talked about or even acknowledged that I am gay. That's why." His intended bite of coleslaw tumbled off the fork and into his lap. He pinched what cabbage he could recover and tossed it on the fire.

"That isn't exactly breaking news, Ronnie."

"Well, you never heard it from me, is all I'm suggesting. Who did you hear it from?"

"My dad, I suppose, if I didn't figure it out on my own. It would have been when I was much younger, maybe a teenager, when he was explaining, you know, his version of the birds and the bees." He removed three quarters of the meat from his chicken leg in one chomp.

"His version?" Ronald asked even though he already had a hunch about what Junior might be alluding to. His hand nervously went behind his back to rub the spot above the pimple that had been bugging him.

"Yeah." Junior looked at Ronald over the chicken leg he was dismantling. "He told me the regular stuff. Then he made sure to tell me about the 'queer birds and the silly bees' so I was sure to get the whole picture."

Ronald sat there frozen for a second, pretending at first, that he was hearing this for the first time. He'd known Junior's father, better—or differently—than most. He remembered getting the exact same explanation in the front seat of Franco Cavaletti Sr.'s tow truck. Ronald didn't know if he could or should tell Junior this, about his dad, about the talks they'd had when Franco was teaching Ronald how to drive, and well—about life.

Junior swallowed a mouthful of chicken and then added, "I'm pretty sure that must have been when he offered up you and Harlan as examples of the 'queer birds.'" He paused. "Come to think of it, he might have told me Harlan was a silly bee. I'm not positive about that part, though."

Ronald issued an explosive burst of laughter. "Harlan is in a category all his own," he agreed. "Do you think your father told you about us so that you would keep away, just in case we tried to molest or convert you?" Again, his hand involuntarily reached for the tender spot around his sacrum.

Junior nearly choked on his chicken, laughing. "No," he answered firmly. "My dad insisted I always show you and your brother respect. He said that I should stick up for you because you were fine, decent people." He took a swig from his Coors can. "Though he might not have said *decent*. I may have just made that part up." He chuckled.

Ronald reached over and play-punched his buddy on the shoulder, deciding in that moment that he wasn't going to tell Junior about the 'queer birds talk' Franco, Sr. had given him once, too. Even though it had marked a critical turning point in Ronald's young life, he knew that Junior still got choked up when talking about his dad. Maybe he'd tell him someday. Ronald decided instead to steer the conversation in a different direction.

"Say, why aren't you racing back home to pamper the pregnant love of your life, anyway?"

"That's easy," Junior responded with his mouth full of collard greens. "My mother-in-law is visiting from Arvada. She's here to help Sofie repaint the nursery. I have a pass to stay out as late as I please."

"Ah, I see." Ronald didn't see, and didn't know why he'd responded like he did, but regardless, he was still flattered by Junior's presence and attention. Did this mean his mechanic friend was spending the night? He began to fret about sleeping arrangements and nervously, his lefthand started to fiddle with the waistband of his jeans behind his back, resisting the urge to scratch that bump in his ass crack that suddenly, itched like crazy.

Junior noticed. "Whatcha got going on back there, Ronnie? A mosquito bite or something?"

Embarrassed, Ronald put the box of chicken parts on the ground. "Or something," he answered, making a concerned face. "Earlier I thought it might have been an in-grown hair or a pimple at the top of my ass crack, but now it's itching and driving me to distraction."

"Well, let's have a look," Junior declared, putting his box of chicken on the ground, too.

"Right now?" Ronald protested, "In the middle of dinner?"

Junior nodded his head. "Drop 'em, Pepperoni!" He pointed both his index fingers at Ronald's jeans. "And I've already seen your ass once tonight, so just consider this a rerun."

Ronald hesitated out of modesty but was also relieved and confident he'd be smelling of Irish Spring back there. He turned to face away from his campsite company to unfasten and lower his jeans. When he had difficulty reaching the long johns flap buttons with his bad shoulder, he switched to his other, but Junior had already unfastened the flap.

"I can see where you've been scratching, and . . ." Ronald felt the mechanic's two hands part his butt cheeks. "Oh my," Junior said as he assessed the site by the light of the campfire. "I think you have a tick, Ronnie."

"A tick?" Ronald shrieked, taking a step forward.

"Maybe grab that headlamp of yours and a pair of tweezers, if you have that handy. Otherwise, I could try to get the bastard out with some long nose pliers from my toolbox."

"I'll get the headlamp and tweezers," Ronald replied, his blood pressure dropping like he was about to faint. He trotted toward the camper with his long johns' flap down and disappeared inside.

Unable to resist smiling at his friend's delicate predicament, Junior prepared his surgical area by rearranging the lawn chairs so that he could operate. When Ronald returned, Junior donned the headlamp and switched it on, instructing Ronald to face away from him, bend over and place one hand on the back of each lawn chair for support. Junior reached the tweezers to the campfire so that the flame could somewhat sterilize the ends of the tweezers.

"Now this may tickle. It could hurt. I really have no idea," Junior admitted as he placed his left hand on Ronald's fuzzy butt cheek to steady himself for the extraction.

"Just get it out, now that I know it's in there," Ronald demanded.

"I'll do my best," Junior offered, as he centered the tweezer prongs around the insect's exposed hind end. Ronald felt the hot ends of the tweezers and some pressure then Junior exclaimed, "Got it!" Ronald turned around to inspect the passenger he'd been carrying around the past twenty-four hours.

"That's disgusting. I think there are some alcohol pads in my first aid kit in the camper. Maybe we should disinfect the bite before it closes." With that Ronald headed back inside the camper.

Junior hollered after him, "and maybe bring back a small glass or container to drop this guy in, so we can have him checked out when we get back to town."

Ronald turned around at the top of the camper steps. "Who's the patient here?"

"We'll get you checked out too. Don't worry." Junior assured him. "It would suck if you came down with Rocky Mountain Spotted Fever or Lyme disease. Maybe get you on antibiotics just in case."

Ronald returned with the first aid kit and Junior swabbed the area for him, adding some Neosporin before covering the spot with a Band-Aid. "Good as new," he said, slapping Ronald's butt.

The men repositioned the chairs around the campfire to face each other and Junior asked if Ronald wanted anymore of his dinner.

"I'm stuffed," Ronald announced, trying to recompose himself after the indignity of putting his ass in Junior's face. "I'll have to save the rest for breakfast, unless I am following you down the mountain tonight."

"I'm about to break into my third brewski here, and I promised Sofie I wouldn't drive if I've been drinking. So, you're stuck with me for the night. Sorry if you were expecting someone else or had other plans, pardner." With a smirk, Junior scanned the desolation of their campsite where the campfire light merged into unquantifiable darkness.

Ronald straightened his posture in the lawn chair. This was a development he wished he'd seen coming, as he would have fussed all day sprucing up and airing out the camper. "That's great," he said. And it was—except his brain had just split along its longitudinal fissure and was hemorrhaging adrenalin-level panic into his bloodstream.

"Brought my own sleeping bag," Junior volunteered, in case Ronald thought they'd share a bed, or mattress, or whatever. "I've worked on that truck of yours a lot but not sure I've ever been inside the camper." He hopped up, crushing his second aluminum can by slamming it into his hip. Before Ronald could stop him, he'd taken the fold-down steps two at a time, opened the screen door and disappeared inside.

Ronald held his breath. This felt like a *Midnight Express* border guard inspection. Not that he had a speck of contraband, but still . . .

Junior emerged with a big toothy smile. "It's perfect! Gotta pee." He headed into the trees toward the creek, and Ronald finished his first beer in a series of hasty gulps. The second one went down much easier and with added anesthetic effect as the two told talked about everything and nothing.

FORTY-FIVE MINUTES LATER, the campfire had died down, and the two friends were inside the camper, laying on their backs in parallel on top of their sleeping bags with the narrow gulf created by the removed table between them. Ronald was in his one-piece long johns and Junior lounged in a sweatshirt with the sleeves cut off and boxer briefs. Both men stared at the ceiling, silently wondering if they could fall asleep with all the newly risen moonlight streaming through the dirty windows. Junior had apologized in advance in case he talked or yelled in his sleep—as Sofie had told him he frequently did. In turn, Ronald apologized for any farting that might transpire, blaming a recent hemorrhoid and his steady diet of hard-boiled eggs over the past 48 hours.

They'd been listening to Conundrum Creek tumbling past the camper and nothing else when a two-tone ping sounded inside the camper. The firefighter sprang to a sitting position like a jack-in-the-box, banging his head on the wall heating unit that should have never been installed there. "Fu-u-u-ck!" he wailed in the semi-darkness.

"It's not my phone," Ronald said. "Must be yours. I don't have cell service up here." Then he remembered he was safekeeping a phone that wasn't his—a phone that did have cell service.

"It's not mine," Junior said, staring at his phone. "I already texted Sofie and Madeline goodnight with that selfie of us I took while we were sitting at the campfire."

"I think I know what this is about," Ronald said, explaining the phone he'd found in the outhouse. "Belongs to a fellow named Chad. Says he knows you."

"I know Chad," Junior said. "He was a few grades behind me in school. He was with the guys that dropped your note and sparkplug by the shop."

That's when Ronald remembered something else Chad had told him—and without thinking about the confidence he was about to betray, maybe on account he was feeling a little buzzed off the beer, he just blurted it out. "He's worried about some images or videos on his phone falling into the wrong hands. I assured him his phone was safe with me and that I would get it to him sometime tomorrow."

"Images?" Junior asked with a mischievous grin, though he was still rubbing the sore spot on top of his head. "Let me see that phone!"

"I gave him my word—" Ronald started to protest, while simultaneously handing off the phone across the aisle. Though he'd been curious, he hadn't known how or where to find the photos on that fancy phone, so hadn't bothered snooping. But if Junior knew how to get to the treasure chest where these potentially incriminating images were stored, well, that was a different matter altogether, he was thinking.

"It's a text," Junior said when he opened the screen. "It says, 'good night, Ron. Look forward to meeting up tomorrow.' Well, isn't that sweet of Chad?" Junior observed, before navigating to a different screen and scrolling. "Chad, my man!" Junior hooted after finding Chad's cache of hidden selfies. Junior reached over to show Ronald—as he swiped through images of a naked man in various poses and stages of erection. "I hadn't ever given any thought to the notion that Chad might be packing, but I gotta say, that is one impressive schlong. Wouldn't you say, Ronnie?"

Ronald didn't know what to say. His split brain was now completely misfiring over the sudden awareness that he and Junior were side-by-side in his camper, looking at naked pictures of a man that stirred more than his curiosity.

Junior's voice crescendoed. "What's this? Houston, we have a video!" He held the phone in the space between them as they both watched Chad jacking off his instrument.

"Oh, my gods." The words fell out of Ronald's gaping mouth.

"Settle down, old man. Nothing *Brokeback*'s gonna be happening here between you and me."

Ronald guffawed. "I wasn't even thinking that, you dork!" But Junior's mock warning had more cinematic awareness than Ronald would have expected. When did Junior ever watch *Brokeback Mountain*, Ronald had to wonder?

"You're lying," Junior told him. "I can tell by your long johns, Ennis. I repeat, nothing's gonna happen."

But just then, something *did* happen. Chad ejaculated before two sets of astonished eyes.

Junior exhaled emphatically. "I think I need a cigarette," he said.

Ronald hit him in the face with his pillow. "Good night, Pervert."

"Good night, Pepperoni."

UNION CONGREGATIONAL CHURCH

January 2010

IN A MOMENT OF *DÉJÀ-VU*, RONALD FOUND HIMSELF looking across the closed casket bearing June Simpleman's body and into Harlan's unemotional eyes. He wondered if his brother felt anything at all, ever.

The pair had been the head pallbearers for their father's funeral in the same sanctuary seventeen months earlier. At that time, both Francos had been in the middle positions next to each of the Simpleman brothers, but Franco Sr. had since been killed in a tragic ski accident—just before Thanksgiving a few months back. And so now, a highly emotional Junior stood quaking shoulder to shoulder with Ronald, across from the former administrator from the Crested Butte Medical Center, who'd assumed Franco Sr.'s spot. Two of their father's hunting buddies, who also happened to be deacons and members of the Union Congregational Church, had been recruited by the pastor to carry the foot of June Simpleman's casket. These six plus the pastor led a somber and small delegation out of the sanctuary and down the steps of the historical church.

As the hearse pulled away, headed for Fairview Cemetery for the burial service scheduled at the top of the next hour, Junior put his arm around Ronald's shoulders and tried to squeeze the grief out of him. Still mourning the sudden loss of his own dad, the mechanic knew that words and flowers and tears didn't fix things, so he said nothing, hoping his hug and solid presence would help.

Harlan had disappeared, and Ronald didn't know where he had gone, but assumed he was settling accounts with the pastor in another part of the church. Their mother's decline had been precipitous before her husband had died. She'd had serial UTIs and pressure sores that her round-the-clock team of home nurses constantly struggled to stay on top of, and the advance of vascular and respiratory disease led to the development of a pulmonary embolism that labored her every breath. Her decades-long struggle with tremors, plus her difficulties with walking, coordination, and balance, had relegated her to a wheelchair for the last twenty-five years of her life. Setting the scene for the final act, Ronald had stood helplessly by as his mother experienced loss of appetite, an inability to swallow even her own saliva, and a severe dehydration that finally sapped her will to keep breathing. So, one quiet afternoon, she stopped.

Ronald's eyes flooded with tears that overflowed into a delta of rivulets that quickly disappeared among the reeds and tall grasses of his ten-year-old beard. Junior gave him a full-on man hug as the older man squeegeed his eye sockets with both fists and pulled himself together in the safety of Junior's embrace.

"We'll be back in this church for a much happier occasion come May," Ronald offered up, pulling out of the embrace to study the young mechanic's sad face. "I am looking forward to that, I can tell you." He pointed back inside the church. "Their god as my witness," he added.

"This may not be an appropriate time," Junior said, "but I wanted to ask you if you would consider being my best man, Ronnie."

Ronald's face registered shock. "Surely, you must have a friend your age—"

"There's nobody I trust more than you, Ronnie. All the friends my age are irresponsible and immature. They just want to turn everything into a booze party." He tilted his head to point back inside the church. "When I am up there, standing before my sweet Sofie, it would be the honor of my lifetime if you were standing there next to me."

A plump tear Ronald had managed to hold in reserve escaped his right eye right before he pulled Junior back into a hug. He whispered in the mechanic's ear, "The honor will be mine."

THE CASTRO

September 2004

THE BOX FAN WHINED ON OVERLOAD, CRANKED TO ITS highest setting. It was 96 degrees outside and at least 115 in his brother's apartment, on San Francisco's hottest day thus far that year. Ronald had been experimenting for the past hour and a half, trying to determine whether it was more advantageous to suck the outdoor heat in through the open second-floor windows of the eighty-four-year-old, rent-controlled brick building, or blow the stifling indoor heat outside.

He couldn't remember it ever getting this hot during the six-plus years that he'd attended Stanford in the 70s, but he was skinny back then and often went shirtless in shorts in his twenties. He was also more free spirit and not nearly as irritable or self-conscious about his body as he was now that he'd made it to fifty-seven. Even though he'd trimmed back down following his 'fat decade' when he'd first started living off his mother's homestyle cooking plus the junk food he consumed out of paranoia, certain a bounty hunter clutching an out-of-state extradition warrant in his fist was hot on his heels, he still felt fat. Along with the weight, he'd lost a chunk of his self-esteem, neither of which—in the seven years since—had made a comeback.

His experimentation with the fan was inconclusive. He'd already stripped down and was only wearing a red Polynesian sarong featuring a black Māori print that he'd wrapped and knotted at his waist after finding it in Harlan's bottom dresser drawer. Convinced his excessive body hair must be contributing an extra Fahrenheit degree or two, he was seriously tempted to shave it all off, but he didn't know where or who he'd be without his fur plus he didn't want to clog his brother's drain. He retrieved the giant pickle jar of sun tea he had set out on the balcony that morning, but it was too hot to drink, and he didn't have ice, since he'd chosen that morning, somehow oblivious to the forecasted heatwave, as a good opportunity to defrost Harlan's badly neglected freezer.

In February, the brothers had swapped living spaces—and lives—when Harlan needed to return to Crested Butte for his hip replacement surgery, which would be performed by their father. He had been rehabilitating at the family home in the seven months since the operation, which had gone as well as could be expected. Ronald had wanted to give San Francisco city living a try, thinking he couldn't shack up with his parents forever. Not only had he waltzed right into Harlan's apartment at 210 Church Street at the corner of Market and made himself completely at home—he also temporarily stepped into Harlan's part-time accounts receivable clerking position at XERO SUM, an accounting firm operating on Castro Street about an eighteen-minute walk away. The principles of the firm—trust fund brats and recent marketing graduates—were apparently obsessed with brand and insisted the company name always be written, printed, and advertised using all capital letters using an obscure font they took pride in resurrecting; this according to Harlan's twenty-minute orientation on his way out the door.

There wasn't much to the job. Ronald coded invoices on Mondays, Wednesdays, and Fridays, and got to boast that he worked in accounting, which seemed a whole lot more respectable than saying he didn't work at all. Harlan had said it was the "easiest gig in the world," and he had been right. The people Ronald worked with were so pleasant and welcoming that he looked forward to his workdays. Indeed, he wished this blistering hot day had been one of them, as XERO SUM had air conditioning.

It was at XERO SUM during that first week he'd started covering for Harlan in February, when Ronald reunited with James Wang, another part-timer who made guest appearances in the office whenever his health allowed. Parachuting back into the Bay Area, like Ronald was doing, after having been mostly away for the past thirty years, he just couldn't get his head around the chance of running into James for the third episode in his life, and at his brother's workplace. James was either really good at pretending he didn't recognize Ronald or maybe his long term memory was shot, because when Ronald had tried to fill in the blanks for him, James just smiled and said he'd take Ronald's word for it.

With Ronald's beard and long hair, plus all the changes to James's facial appearance on account of the retroviral meds he was on, it had taken some creative squinting on both their parts to detect any resemblance to the younger versions of themselves. Ronald reminded James that they'd last run into each other in the late 70s, at a Thanksgiving dinner party thrown by Harlan in his cramped Castro apartment. And that they'd first met when Ronald was a freshman at Stanford. "If you say so," James had replied, lacking the energy or interest in debating.

Over the next several weeks into spring, James began to open up more to Ronald. It was never clear what job function James performed at XERO SUM because on the random days he showed up, he spent most his time chatting with Ronald. That's how Ronald learned James considered himself busy these days between defying the odds—having lived HIV-positive since the mid- to late-80s—and managing his multitude of medications and doctor visits. He said he only worked a few hours a week to pay the bills. Ronald hadn't realized he needed a cause, but in record time, he'd made James his cause and for whatever reason, James humored him and seemed to appreciate, if not enjoy, Ronald's mother henning. For his part, Ronald just couldn't give up on his attempts to cure James' amnesia and there was the occasional breakthrough, like when Ronald told James he was pretty sure they'd first met during Ronald's freshman year, when he would sometimes drive downtown in the middle of the week to blow off steam at *The Gangway* on Larkin Street. Ronald even confessed he'd spent a several nights there ogling this hot Asian go-go dancer who went by the stage name of—

"Jimmy Wang!" the men had screamed in unison before erupting in raucous laughter that had a few of their colleagues peering over the tops of their cubicles. Thinking he might be making restorative progress and that the two of them might be reigniting more than old memories, Ronald went as far as to make the claim that he remembered becoming hypnotized watching Jimmy Wang wiggle and wrangle that ample egg roll in that jockstrap of his as he gyrated atop the bar. James claimed to be blushing but wasn't and said he held that egg roll negligently accountable for the HIV mess he found himself in now. In Ronald's version of that back-in-time story, it had been after one of James's high-cardio go-go shifts at *The Gangway* that Ronald had offered him a lift back to campus, where one thing led to another. James said he hated to disappoint him, but he didn't remember any of that, either.

Soon, they began spending many of their days off together, and several sleepover nights too, plutonic, at James insistence and Ronald's relief, alternating between Harlan's 210 Church Street apartment and James's loft at 295 Castro—a fourteen-minute walk apart. While Ronald owned a car and had driven his Volvo to San Francisco in February, Harlan had driven it back to Crested Butte just in time for his surgery. Once he had his new right hip, Harlan hadn't been able to drive for three months—and for reasons he never explained, he extended his rehabilitation in the Rockies for another four during which Ronald was left in San Francisco without his car. But the younger brother was enjoying the city and his freedom, out from under the parent's roof. He was in no rush to pull up stakes now that he was in what could loosely be considered the closest he'd ever come to being in a "relationship," and with James, whom he'd had history, whether James remembered it or not.

They would have hung out together today too, since neither of them were working, except James's place didn't have air conditioning either. Though they'd both already seen *Napolean Dynamite*, they'd discussed catching a repeat matinee as a way to cool off for a couple hours. In the end, neither of them could be coaxed into walking anywhere in this heat.

Ronald fussed with the box fan, angling and tilting it in different ways—even placing it in front of the open freezer door as the box thawed. He was miserable but also delighted, as it was slinky fun to sashay around in nothing but his sarong, singing the lines he could remember from a Michael Franks tune:

> Wear a sarong
> I can undo
> As soon as we're home
> Chez nous . . .

Ronald's whirling skirt was practically the only splash of color in Harlan's paper-white apartment. Yes, there was a sizeable coffee stain on the kitchen counter, but the kitchen cupboards, tile backsplash, floor, and appliances were all white. In the living room the wood floor diverged, only slightly, from the predominant white theme, with their father's faded Persian rug providing a mostly covered up landing pad for the overstuffed sofa and Harlan's recliner—both of which he'd camouflaged with bleached white chenille blankets.

Ronald knew his obsessive-compulsive brother meticulously kept these covers tightly tucked into and under the cushions. Once, when the sofa became untucked during one of James's companionship visits with benefits—consisting of side-by-side mutual masturbation while they gaped at an anime porno that James had on his Toshiba Satellite P25 laptop—Ronald realized why. The original upholstery, of unknown pattern or design, had been completely stripped away, and only the badly stained under-fabric remained. At the risk he and James might add new stains to the disgusting collection, not that they would be distinguishable from the others, Ronald became extra vigilant about re-tucking the washable throws when necessary from there on out.

Each of these pieces of sitting furniture were topped off by several white throw pillows of varying sizes. Matching teak coffee and side tables had somehow miraculously escaped a whitewashing paint brush. It was the same non-motif in the bedroom with the white floor-length curtains, a white down-filled bedspread pulled over white sheets and pillowcases with decorative white throws. The white hexagon-tiled bathroom featured what looked like linens lifted straight from a three-star hotel: white window and shower curtains, sets of matching towels, waste basket, soap dish, and toothbrush holder. There was also a clear glass container filled with white Q-tips and a larger one next to it filled with cotton balls. The entire apartment had been painted gloss white, with no art or photos hanging anywhere. There was not even a painted-over nail to suggest previous tenants might have decorated any differently. Apparently, Harlan couldn't risk either revealing his tastes or jeopardizing his security deposit. In any case, it was Ronald's duty to maintain and preserve this blank slate of an apartment until his brother recuperated and returned.

Looking back over the seven months of his unique sub-let tenancy, coupled with the bonus of getting to dabble as an actual working stiff in an office setting where he'd reconnected with James, Ronald was overall pleased with the sibling-swap experiment. It had certainly been an interesting time to live in the Bay Area. Before he'd reported to work at Xero Sum, before he had reconnected with James, and just days after Harlan had driven off in Ronald's gold-bronze Volvo (long ago nicknamed *Veruca*, after the second golden-ticket winner in *Willy Wonka and the Chocolate Factory*) San Francisco's mayor, Gavin Newsom declared the state's definition of marriage unconstitutional and discriminatory. Days before Valentine's Day, Newsom directed the city clerk to begin issuing marriage licenses to same-sex couples. Gobsmacked and suspicious this was some kind of early April Fool's joke, Ronald had hurried across the street to the J-Church MUNI stop on February 14th and rode the light rail nine minutes downtown to City Hall to see for himself what all the fuss was about.

When the train arrived and he stepped onto the platform and crossed the street, Ronald was enveloped and overwhelmed by the exuberant throngs of men and women that he encountered. The atmosphere was jubilant. Some percussionists were drumming, and a trumpet player embedded on one side of the crowd, could be heard jamming with other musicians a hundred yards away on the other side of the plaza. Ronald felt buoyant and humbled but more importantly, *optimistic*—perhaps for the first time in his closeted life. The movement of a people who had suffered unspeakable losses, who had been subjugated and persecuted for centuries too long . . . the power of gay people—*his* people should he choose to identify as such—appeared to have finally triumphed, at least on that patch of California real estate, and at least for that Valentine's Day.

As the crowd size swelled and its contagious enthusiasm reached fever pitch, Ronald had felt a tap on his left shoulder. Straining against the crowd's crushing grip, he turned around to receive a marriage proposal by some Jake, Jack, or Johnny on the spot (the crowd had gotten so loud that Ronald was sure he had misheard the guy's name when he introduced himself). The fellow—so desperate to be part of that historic day that he was prepared to marry anyone who said yes,—dropped down on his already grass stained one knee and asked for Ronald's hand. Astonished, Ronald considered the proposal as seriously as one could under the circumstances. The thirtysomething man was way beyond cute, with his tears of hopeful joy practically squirt-gunning from his big, beautiful blue eyes. But Ronald bashfully declined on the hunch that he would always be breaking this guy's heart.

Ronald tried to keep his eyes on—and was truly rooting for—the "would-be groom/bride," but he lost him in the sea of eager couples partying outside City Hall, referred to locally as the *People's Palace*, there to seek their licenses to marry the loves of their lives—or of the month, or of the moment. Ronald couldn't fathom that this same site had seen the assassinations of openly gay supervisor Harvey Milk and then-Mayor George Moscone merely 26 years earlier in 1978. Back then, and he was there in San Francisco that day, he had feared an open hunting season had just been declared for gays who were out of the closet in America. So, he'd stayed *in* for his short professional life and well into his adulthood. But all that changed on Valentine's Day 2004; the day hundreds of gays and lesbians got legally married, another man proposed marriage to him and the day that Ronald Paul Simpleman, officially and publicly decided to bust out of his closet—for the time being.

Not even days later, when reporting to work to begin the stint at XERO SUM, Ronald was back to acting like he was straight again—however unconvincingly—just not wanting to standout or be out, worried it could jeopardize things for Harlan. However, within the first five minutes and based on the reception he received, he suspected Harlan had likely already outed him to his boss and colleagues in advance of the Simpleman switcheroo. Then he re-met James, and any question about Ronald's sexual orientation was out the window.

While Harlan may have informed his employer that the younger brother temporarily replacing him was also gay, it wasn't clear to Ronald that Harlan had indicated to his employer when or even if he intended to return to his job. And so, after half the year had passed, James and everyone—including Ronald—had started to presume that perhaps Harlan had shuffled off for good. Ronald had been getting along so well with James and everyone else at work, he had been reticent to pressure his brother to beat a hasty return. He knew his brother was fifty-nine on the cusp of turning 60 and wouldn't keep working forever. But it wasn't until a recent phone call to Crested Butte, catching June alone in the house, that his mother let it slip that Harlan was thinking he might opt for an early retirement. This struck Ronald as curious, since his brother never had a career in the first place— not that Ronald could brag, since his teaching career had bottomed out after only seven-and-a-half years. But all of this uncertainty and tip-toeing around what Harlan would or wouldn't do next, created a big dilemma for Ronald, who had fit right into the culture at XERO SUM and had not once indicated to anyone—including James—that he would only be there temporarily—assuming that Harlan had already made these arrangements crystal clear with his work before leaving for his hip surgery.

At the start of their companionship with benefits, Ronald was pretty sure that whatever he was feeling for James couldn't be sustained, and James seemed so locked into the reality that Death was coming for him and was likely already slashing his path to hell with his scythe, that there had been no attention paid, no declarations made and no planning for a future between them. And it wasn't like either of them were keen to rush to the altar, just because Mayor Newsome had made it legal. Even that couldn't be sustained longer than the three weeks it took for the California Supreme Court (on March 11) to halt gay-free-for-all marriage licensing and vindictively annulled the more than four thousand same-sex couple licenses that had been issued in that brief time. That was the one-step-forward-and-one-yard-back California that Ronald remembered from his Stanford days, when protests and rallies never seemed to achieve anything durable.

So, thinking things wouldn't last because they never had, Ronald hadn't invested a lot of energy in sending down roots into the mishmash of sand, alluvial soils and landfill atop which San Francisco had been erected. He sensed his hall pass was either about to expire or get revoked, but then, he'd always felt that way at every stage of his life, perpetually waiting on somebody else to bring down the curtain along with the boom it was attached to, and with his luck, directly on top of his head.

Ronald had just placed a new LP on the stereo turntable to try to take his mind off the indoor and outdoor temperatures that had to have risen another several degrees, when Harlan phoned out of the blue.

"Hey, brother," Harlan said.

"Heya," Ronald replied.

"Just thought I'd let you know I am heading home this weekend."

The tonearm slipped from Ronald's fingers, bouncing the needle onto and across the vinyl, as blood flushed from his head and his face turned as white as his surroundings. "Oh yeah?"

"I hope that wasn't one of my records," Harlan said, sternly.

"Nope," Ronald replied with a roll of his eyes. "One of mine."

Harlan continued. "Problem is, Dad says I can't drive because of my new hip. He's willing to drive me in your car if you can bring him home when you come back here."

His surgery notwithstanding, Harlan was bouncing back to his old, inconsiderate self. He also relayed that he intended to return to his part-time position at XERO SUM on Monday. *So much for my going-away party,* Ronald thought, as he scrambled to figure out how he was going to break this news to James, and what in the hell he and his father would talk about on the long drive back to Crested Butte.

CRESTED BUTTE

December 1999

IF THE CIVILIZED WORLD WAS ENDING AT MIDNIGHT, AS computer geeks were predicting on this eve of the new millennium, then 53-year-old Ronald figured he needed to make plans and change a few habits. But he'd waited until the last minute to panic about this. His roommate-parents didn't have a computer and wouldn't have known how to use one, but they were always prepped for a blackout and accustomed to being cut off from civilization by drifting snow. Ronald had wanted to join the computer age and so regularly used one of the two internet stations at the Old Rock Community Library. But since mid-November, he'd had trouble finding a free station. Everybody else's Y2K panic seemed to have kicked in earlier.

On this New Year's Eve, the temperature outside had started out at −10 degrees when he climbed into his Volvo to head into town for more batteries, candles, and food. By the time he got back to his house three hours later—after encountering row after row of empty shelves at Clark's Market and Ace Hardware—the thermometer on the outside of the garage read 12 degrees. Smoke spewed a perfect white column out of the fireplace chimney, and Ronald reminded himself they probably had a good four cords of firewood stacked in the covered breezeway between the house and shed. Inside the front door, he smelled cookies as he wandered past the small herd of wicker reindeer with jingle-bell collars that had been grazing in the peony wallpapered hallway since Thanksgiving. A flocked ponderosa Christmas tree competed with the always festive Bruce the Elk for command of the great room, where his father sat in his brown leather recliner, reading about the acquisition of AMAX Mine by Phelps Dodge in the *Crested Butte News*.

"Store shelves are bare, I'm afraid," Ronald reported to his mother as she pulled a tray of snickerdoodles from the oven. "I snagged this carton of buttermilk that expired yesterday." He displayed the prize proudly. It wasn't as though he'd milked the cow himself, but he hoped his sacrifice would be enough to earn his mother's praise.

"Put it outside," she replied, taking a tray of baked cookies from the lowered range oven that had originally been built into the wall eighteen inches higher. "There's no room in the refrigerator."

Moving the built-in wall oven had been one of a dozen modifications made to the house so she could reach it from her wheelchair. "Looks like I'll be making muffins with buttermilk on New Year's Day," she said. "That is, if we survive past midnight," she joshed, believing neither men were listening—and they weren't, and certainly not expecting to garner any expression of gratitude from the unappreciative men in her life—and she didn't.

From the Grand Room and without lowering his newspaper, Paul bellowed a question to his wife, that he could have just as easily asked his son who was standing right there. "Did you tell Ron there was mail for him today?"

June looked first at the newspaper, then to their son, and shrugged her shoulders. "The envelope is on the table in the entryway," she told him.

So as not to disturb his father, Ronald tip-toed through the peonies to quietly retrieve his mail at the other end of the hallway. The return address indicated Seattle, but he'd recognized the handwriting and needed no other clues. It was from Mitch Carson, and before he liberated the flap, Ronald also predicted the contents would likely be another of Mitch's annual photo Christmas cards. The glossy card stock came out of the envelope with the message side facing him. Ronald flipped it around to study the delightfully artistic black and white composition featuring Mitch dressed up—Ronald ventured a guess—as Rudolph Valentino, maybe, in an Arabic sheik costume posed triumphantly inside the parted flaps of a nomadic Bedouin-looking tent. "Classic," Ronald commented in a whisper only audible to himself. He read the short note on the flipside as he returned to the kitchen: *To the world's greatest teacher, from the world's greatest . . .* and there, the word *lover* had been faintly hashed out and replaced, in block letters, with the replacement word, *student*. Blushing, Ronald roughly stuffed the photo card with its incriminating missive back inside its envelope, creasing the photo he'd want to keep but needed to hide. He tucked the evidence of his mail delivery, out of sight inside his back jean pocket.

"Ron, if you could get the ladder from the garage and start undecorating the top of the Christmas tree, I'll get to work on the bottom. Your father appears to have cement in his britches today."

"Sure, mom," Ronald said, having selectively heard that bit.

"And while you're up that ladder, can you dust, or—here's a thought— maybe finally take down the ornaments and garland from Bruce's antlers? On days when the sun is shining, all I can see up there are cobwebs."

"Sure, Mom." But Ronald couldn't leave it at that. "The world is probably ending at midnight, but the Simplemans will face their doom without cobwebs!"

"Nobody's touching Bruce!" his father wailed, protectively. "He's only hanging up there by a couple of cords that are probably fraying by now. Let him be!"

Ronald glanced at his mother and shrugged his shoulders.

"Thank you, Ronnie darling," she said, thinking this would overrule the surgeon's edict. But it didn't.

OURAY, COLORADO

September 1997

THERE WASN'T A HUE, SHADE, TINT, OR GRADATION OF gold that could hold a candle to the spectacularly gilded aspens that shimmered like sequins on every sun-kissed slope of the Rockies in mid-September. This was absolutely Ronald's favorite season. He quite contentedly lived outdoors from early-September until the first snowfall every year. With the pinnacle of color lasting no more than ten days, choosing the right week when planning his campouts was always a guessing game. But the mesmerizing sound of these leaves quaking in a breeze was always symphonic and rejuvenating inside Ronald's fifty-year-old ears—whether he'd found the apex of the senescence or not.

Navigating his dad's clunky camper truck southbound on US 50 through the towns of Gunnison and then Cimmaron, he turned left at Montrose onto US 550 South. Just before noon, with a triangle of his bologna-and-pickle sandwich dangling from his mouth, he used both hands on the steering wheel to veer left and then right into the town of Ouray. Population: 801.

Arranged in a twenty-four-block grid bisected by the Million Dollar Highway—which also doubled as its historic main street—the town had been established in the crotch of a valley in the 1870s when prospectors arrived seeking their fortunes. Of the thirty mines that popped up during the Gold Rush—none of which were still operating today—the Bachelor Syracuse Mine that Ronald had passed about four miles back had produced 1.5 million ounces of gold and another 4 million ounces of silver during its lifespan. He didn't need to wonder why those details stuck with him: he was his father's son and odd facts he'd picked up here and there occasionally shook loose and dropped out of his cranium. At the same time, numbers weren't his thing, so he was pleasantly surprised he remembered these otherwise useless mining statistics.

For right brain dominant, theater-minded Ronald, Ouray occupied what to him looked like the orchestra pit of a massive, convex amphitheater of towering granite peaks that encircled the town. He wasn't the only one to see it that way. The locals also referred to their mountain backdrop as the "Amphitheater." The odd part about traveling anywhere for Ronald, whether his dad accompanied him or not, was that he still heard his father's booming voice in the back of his head narrating the history of anywhere in the world he happened to be visiting. Take the history of the Bachelor Syracuse Mine, for example—the turn off for which the camper truck had just whizzed past—he was still recalling factoids about the place his father had spouted during every one of the half dozen trips the family had probably made through these parts when Ronald was a kid. The surgeon's skills at memorization were a parlor trick he polished to intimidate the lesser know-it-alls in his company. His youngest son understood this now, but growing up, Ronald had always marveled that his dad was some living brochure or a walking historical encyclopedia. He didn't know at the time that his dad would exhaustively research every travel destination in advance so he could regurgitate it later and seem like the ultimate authority on any subject matter. He was hearing that voice now as he was driving into Ouray: *The valley before you is part of the 150-mile-long San Juan Mountain chain of the Rockies that was formed by a volcanic explosion that occurred 27 million years ago—the largest eruption ever to occur on Earth.*

Ronald had needed to gently let down his Old Man and tour guide this time after Dr. Simpleman had offered to rearrange his surgery schedule to take this week off from the hospital so that he could accompany his son to Ouray. He'd even absent-mindedly suggested they could maybe do some target shooting together. But as exhilarating as his dad made gunplay sound, Ronald absolutely had to make this trip to Ouray alone, as he was meeting up with Mitch Carson.

Three months earlier, Mitch had Fed-Exed a loosely bound printout of his newest manuscript and had asked Ronald to critique it before the author started shopping it around to publishers. The instructions had been clear:

Ronald was to make grammatical corrections in red and write any notes or ideas in the margins of each page. Then Mitch would travel to Colorado to retrieve the markup and discuss the manuscript in person.

It was Ronald who suggested they meet in Ouray, since he would be heading there anyway as he always did this time of year to catch the start of leaf-changing season. Plus, he couldn't entertain or parade his former student in front of his roommate parents for the probing interrogation he feared he'd receive beforehand and after. He initially didn't think Mitch would show up, given how out of the way and difficult Ouray was to get to, but Mitch surprised him once again by announcing he would be driving up from Albuquerque with a friend named Sam. The two had apparently known each other going back to their university years together. As Ronald understood it, Mitch was flying from Seattle to Albuquerque, where Sam still lived, for a short visit, before heading into the mountains. Mitch hadn't said, but Ronald assumed that Sam might have also received a copy of the manuscript to critique. He expected to find out if this were true soon.

By design, Ronald was arriving in Ouray a day early to establish his handpicked and reserved campsite #032 at Amphitheater Campground. He'd stayed in the same campsite at least twice before, favoring its privacy, as it was hidden almost entirely by conifers and Gambel oaks. This and its proximity to the short trail that followed Portland Creek past Upper Cascade Falls to the Baby Bathtubs—so called for their naturally smooth, underwater indentations in the quartz-speckled granite—were among the campsite's biggest selling points for him. During summer campouts there, he liked to skinny-dip and sunbathe in the tubs in the late afternoons, after the families had likely cleared out.

The campground had a double outhouse but didn't have showers. Ronald didn't fuss about this since he could always book soaking time at one of the four commercially developed thermal hot spring resorts in the vicinity. His favorite of these was the Wiesbaden Hot Springs Lodge, about ten minutes away. He understood that the boys coming up from Albuquerque had booked their own accommodations there. Now, whether or not the pair would be sleeping together in the same bed, Ronald also looked forward to finding out. Not that he was nosy about such matters, but after being scorned by Mitch over a decade ago, he was just curious who—if not Ronald—might then warrant Mitch's affection. And yes, he had not gotten over that rejection.

Ronald had last seen Mitch Carson in San Francisco in 1986. In the strangest of developments and like a bolt out of the blue, Mitch had tracked down Harlan's phone number, apparently after remembering that his former high school teacher had a gay brother who lived in the Castro. Ronald could never figure out if Mitch had been trying to get to him through his brother, or if he was trying to get under his skin, by pursuing his brother. Harlan certainly hadn't understood the motivation behind the call, but hadn't wanted to appear rude either, so he gave the caller his coordinates and an invitation to crash on his couch. Harlan immediately, of course, placed a panicked call to his brother, indicating that he wasn't thrilled about this incoming invasion of his space by a stranger about whom he knew nothing. So, Ronald had dropped everything—which was nothing—jumped in the car and raced eighteen hours to San Francisco to take Mitch off—or *out* of—his brother's hands, depending on how the odd visit between the two gay men had or hadn't escalated. Ronald seemed to be apologizing to his brother ever since—though for what he'd never been sure, just as he'd never understood what, if anything, had transpired between his brother and Mitch before Ronald had pulled up to his brother's apartment building, nearly out of gas but full of questions that never entirely got answered.

By the time he finished fussing with his campsite prep, it was mid-afternoon and still much earlier in the day than when he usually headed up the short trail to reach the Baby Bathtubs. It was also autumn in the Rockies, he reasoned. Families had thinned out since their kids were already back in school. The prospects of running into other skinny-dippers this late in the camping season were greatly diminished by the chilly mountain temps. This also meant the creek water would have returned to its default setting of glacially cold, curtailing the chances that even naked bathing enthusiast Ronald would dare to dip a toe. He'd brought a ratty towel, just in case the sun cooperated.

As he'd predicted, there wasn't another soul on the trail nor at the Baby Bathtubs, but there were some reticent shafts of sunlight filtering through the upslope trees that seemed not yet ready to let go of what was left of the summer. Basking in it, Ronald could pretend the warmer season had stuck around for him too.

As he disrobed, Ronald was self-conscious about the remnants of belly fat he'd mostly shed but whose emotional weight he still carried. His mother's allegiance to cooking everything with Crisco and his own nasty junk food habit that he'd adopted to distract his nerves during the height of his post-teaching paranoia, had done a number on the scales and his already battered esteem. He wanted to think he was back to pretty much looking the same as he had the last time he'd seen Mitch Carson in the flesh eleven years ago, but he also wanted a chance to reveal something deeper than flesh—a glimpse inside his soul perhaps—that might cause Mitch to reevaluate the choices he'd made. Though he was fifty, he wasn't displaying any signs of graying, either on the crazy swoop of hair on his head, or on his torso, or in his pubes. He had tweezered the first white hair he'd spotted in his left eyebrow just a week earlier, fearing it was the advance scout of an invading force—but so far, reinforcements hadn't arrived.

He laid out his towel on the out of water flat boulder he'd chosen, or rather, the sun patch had selected for him. He pulled off his sweatshirt and dropped his jeans, stepping brief-less out of them. He squinted at the sun believing a quick, late season, tan-up would do wonders for his appearance, with the big reveal expected to occur sometime tomorrow, depending on what time the boys arrived from Albuquerque.

As he baked and daydreamed, Ronald was feeling pretty good about this reunion with Mitch Carson. He'd been all out nervous when he left the Butte, but the road—as hitting the road always did—had calmed his nerves and slayed most of his dragons. Still superficially stuck on his appearance, and flashing back to whatever had gotten him disqualified as boyfriend material twenty years earlier, and, of course, stewing about how Mitch would react when he saw him later today, stayed stuck at the top of his list of preoccupations. His fat phase notwithstanding and now in the rear view mirror, couldn't he almost boast that he hadn't changed all that much since the 70s, when he and Mitch had first begun their undefinable but doomed relationship? Sure, his head hair had started to thin, and his hairline was receding—albeit with the thankfully slow pace of a glacier. But such things were to be expected. Ever since childhood, Ronald had struggled with his hair that never fit into acceptable contemporary norms without daily and serious coercion. Back then, as now, it presented as wavy, unremarkably brown, and worn the only way it behaved, in a side part on the left. In fact, Ronald's hair made him look a little like Hermey, the elf who wanted to become a dentist in *Rudolph the Red-Nosed Reindeer*. Ronald had been a junior at Crested Butte High when that made-for-TV movie came out in 1964, and almost instantly, he became the target of a whole new phase of teasing and taunts that quickly culminated in his knighting with the new nickname of *Hermey Simpleman*. He hadn't minded all that much, since it had a nicer ring to it than *faggot*.

Now Mitch Carson's hair, on the other scalp, had showcased great diversity, as Ronald recalled while basking in the sun's warmth atop his rock bed, projecting images like Kodachrome slides on the screens of his eyelids. His student's variable hairstyles were like a trucker—in the sense that they were all over the map. When they'd first met, Mitch was working a Prince Valiant hairstyle—more in keeping with the Robert Wagner 1954 interpretation than the 1997 treatment by Stephen Moyer—which Ronald figured must have required a fair bit of daily maintenance, since no one's hair curled that way naturally. In 1983, cancer—and more directly, chemotherapy—did a cruel number on Mitch—not just with his hair (which he mostly lost), but with his face and frame, which looked gaunt and undernourished for nearly that whole year. That had been hard for Ronald to watch, even from the other side of Stevensville, where they had both been existing, if not truly living, at the time of Mitch's diagnosis. Both the younger man and his hair, ever resilient and youthful, bounced back from cancer. Mitch had transformed setbacks to advantages and barrelled into his second chance at life with a head-spinning, hair-tossing velocity and without Ronald, who he'd left behind, choking on his dust.

Ronald flipped onto his stomach to tan his backside while the sun cooperated, but his ever-analysing brain couldn't flip so easily. He was still stuck on Mitch Carson; possibly always would be. He eventually had needed to wrestle with and get pinned to the mat by the brute reality there wouldn't be a second round for their relationship. Cue the unhealthy eating, weight gain and self-flagellation.

With Mitch's first whopper of a novel, published only a year ago, and his second—the one he'd just recently asked his former English teacher and used-up paramour to read and critique—headed for bookstore shelves by the end of the year, Mitch's success seemed on a trajectory for the outer bands of the stratosphere. Left mortally bleeding on the launch pad, Ronald felt he'd been nothing more than a used up and jettisoned booster rocket.

For Mitch, as Ronald saw it, the very world seemed to have pried itself open and bent itself backwards, like a personal, briny, glistening oyster on a half shell for this pearl of a reborn man to gulp down whole at his leisure. The boy-teen-man he'd known all these years was going places where

Ronald wasn't allowed to go. And this—no matter how he shucked it—sucked, for Ronald.

He arched his back and sat up, dangling a toe and then his foot in the creek. He was truly happy for Mitch, and extremely proud, actually. His former English student and drama wonderkid had found his life's inspiration along with his passion for storytelling. And now, he was on his way to share that joy and success with his one-time teacher. Ronald's critical brain couldn't discount the specialness in that.

A DAY LATER, Mitchell and Sam were traveling from the opposite direction on the same US Highway 550, heading north from Albuquerque through Farmington and then from Durango to Silverton. They drove along the Uncompahgre River on the Million Dollar Highway before the eventual climb up and over the 11,000-foot Red Mountain Pass. Sam hadn't thought his car would make it, so Mitchell had rented a car at the Albuquerque International Sunport. Because of insurance, Mitch was the one driving when they stopped to pee at a rest area before beginning the ascent that would get them over the pass. Above the urinal, someone had written with a black Sharpie, *You don't have to be crazy to drive this road, but it helps.*

An hour and several death-beckoning-hairpin-turns-without-guardrails later, the pair of university buddies pulled off the road again to take pictures at a pullout with a billboard-sized carved wooden sign welcoming them to Ouray—the "Switzerland of America."

"Are you getting nervous to see him?" Sam asked, taking in the thin air which made the walls of his nostrils stick together.

Mitchell forced a short laugh and admitted to having butterflies but blamed them on the altitude. "I've warned you," he said. "Ronald is a quirky guy—an odd fellow in the truest sense."

"Yeah, yeah. You told me . . . a quirky guy with a big jackhammer."

Mitchell mock-shoved his buddy over the edge of the turnout but kept a solid grip on his shoulders when he did it.

A DEVIL OF an afternoon lightning and thunderstorm had delayed the arranged rendezvous at Ronald's Ampitheater campsite. Ronald had spent the past few hours inside his aluminum camper, counting seconds to ascertain the distance between lightning flashes and thunderclaps, grateful to be sitting atop four rubber tires. He'd re-read the last three chapters of Mitch's eco-thriller, marveling at the logistics and geographical territory the work had expertly covered. Ronald's brain was boggled by how this small-town author infiltrated what seemed like a very plausible underground world of environmental activism and eco-terrorism.

There was a quick series of raps on the metal siding outside of the camper door that startled Ronald into a more alert posture. "Hello," he shouted in a friendly, welcoming tone, thinking the boys must have arrived.

"Ron . . . is that you in there?"

Ronald popped his butt off the foam cushion and with two steps he flung the camper door open with a *thwack!* "In the flesh!" he announced, recognizing his visitor, standing there like a wet dog left out in the rain.

"Mr. Simpleman!" Mitchell said, while a smile stretched across his handsome, wet face. Rainwater guttered off both sides of his ballcap bill, and Ronald extended a hand up to get him out of the rain. Bumping his forehead on the upper frame of the doorway and cussing while he massaged it, Mitch shook off the wet chill and removed his ballcap revealing that he shaved his head now, apparently done with hair.

Then they were standing face to face for the first time in more than a decade. Neither knowing exactly what to say.

"Take off your jacket and stay a while," Ronald said, regaining his sense of hospitality. "Did you walk here?"

Stripping off the waterlogged, weather-inappropriate fleece and hanging it on a peg next to Ronald's flannel jacket, Mitchell explained that he'd left his rental car parked near the outhouses, and that it had taken him a while to figure out the map at the kiosk and find Ronald's camper.

"Where's your friend, Sam?" Ronald inquired.

"He's in the hotel room trying to recover his wits after the Million Dollar Highway," Mitchell said, opening his arms and stepping forward to hug his former teacher. "A road, by the way, that you couldn't pay me a million dollars to drive again!"

Ronald motioned for him to have a seat on the foam bench cushion at the table. "Care for a Sanka?"

Mitchell scoffed. "Are you still drinking that shit not-coffee? I'd take a bottled water or a juice if you have it."

Ronald opened the mini refrigerator door and displayed a single box of apple juice, which met with the visitor's approval.

"So, you're shaving your noggin these days," Ronald stated the obvious, sending a hand to his own head to needlessly demonstrate what he was referring to.

"Yeah," Mitch responded, sending his hands to squeegee away any rain the ballcap might not have diverted. "It's a throwback to my chemo days. I finally decided, I actually like this look on me."

"Well, it works, of course."

In the awkward pause that followed the compliment, Ronald reached for the annotated, three-ring bound manuscript that was leaning against the window opposite the table. Excited, he over-tossed it, causing it to skid across the Formica tabletop and into the author's lap.

"Whoa," Mitchell said. "That's my baby you're tossing around."

Ronald laughed awkwardly, visibly nervous to be alone in the author's company. Mitchell picked up on this and tried to lower the temperature of their first reunion in more than a decade. "You're looking good, Mr. Simpleman . . . you just don't change as you age. Unlike the rest of us."

Ronald suspected his visitor was lying through his orthodontically perfected teeth, but he liked to hear it, anyway. "You're looking very good, yourself. You've beefed up some more, I can see. It looks good." Ronald wasn't lying in the least. He was in fact intimidated by Mitchell's handsomeness. He supposed he always had been.

Mitchell fanned the pages of his manuscript. Seeing copious notes in the margins, he looked up and said, "Well?"

"Well," Ronald repeated. "This is indeed an *eco-thriller*, as you've called it. I'd never heard of that genre before, but I was engaged and enthralled. I was impressed by your grasp of the underworld of eco-terrorists. I had no idea where the story was heading and was surprised at least once in every chapter. The characters are strongly developed—loveable, even." He could have gone on, but his careful notes in the margins would fill in the blanks of his contemporaneous review.

Mitchell looked up from one of those notes he couldn't keep himself from reading to say, "Thank you for taking the time and having the interest." He closed the manuscript. "It's validating," he said as he reached across the small table to squeeze Ronald's forearm. "I'll look through your notes more carefully when I don't feel like I'm dripping wet." Then he switched topics, rather abruptly suggesting that was enough feedback on his book for now. "So, this is your secret lair, your hideaway, this camper?"

"It's my dad's. I'm borrowing it, so I can't be held responsible for the smells or the cleanliness; it's a hovel on wheels." Ronald brushed a layer of dust on the windowsill from where he could reach without getting up.

Mitchell grinned. "Bet you had lots of redneck sex in here, huh?"

Ronald blushed, which was not how he'd intended to answer the question. "I will neither confirm nor deny that accusation."

"THAT'S HOT!" Mitchell exclaimed, seeming to readjust himself under the table.

"You have to remember, young man, my equipment is now fifty years old." Ronald didn't know where this was going, but figured he needed to float a pre-emptive excuse just in case . . . of what? He wondered if perhaps he was misreading everything about this encounter.

"Oh, I remember your equipment, Mr. Simpleman. Every inch and every detail. Right down to that night crawler of a blue vein that runs the length of it." His voice had dropped to a whisper, and he raised his dark eyebrows suggestively. "I take it this table disappears, and this bench somehow folds into a bed platform?"

Ronald fidgeted. "I can see this is not your first camper."

"Do you remember what *my* penis looks like, Mr. Simpleman?" Mitchell asked, assuming he already knew the answer. "At every stage of its development?"

Ronald didn't answer. In that moment, even breathing seemed self-incriminating.

"Of course, you do," Mitchell said, "because you still have those naked photographs of me that I keep bugging you to give back." When Ronald didn't budge a muscle to retrieve a box or large envelope, Mitchell sensed another excuse was coming. "I don't suppose you remembered to bring them to this meet-up, did you?" Ronald flashed a sheepish smirk. Mitchell shook his head but didn't need to telegraph his disappointment as it had been anticipated, by both parties. "Anyway, maybe you'll have a chance to see it again. Plus, I can show you my new prosthetic testicle. It's a whopper!" Mitchell cupped his package under the Formica table. "Do you still have that old movie reel of porn outtakes you spliced together and showed me in your apartment that one time?"

"I suppose I do, yes."

"It would be something to watch that again with you one of these days,"

Mitchell said, before revising his wish. "But to get a copy made would be even better!"

"I'll have to hunt for that at some point." Ronald was tripping over memories that seemed to originate from another epoch.

"Where did you come across those clips in the first place? I don't remember you ever saying."

"I worked for these brothers once who ran an adult movie theater in San Fran. They had me edit out all the movie clips that showed men with their big rods. . . saying those grossly over-exaggerated appendages intimidated their clientele, who were likely lacking in that department." Ronald issued a half giggle.

"Anyway," Mitchell continued, not even subtly adjusting the erection he'd cultivated in his jeans, "there is this thermal pool at the lodge where we are staying . . . they call it the Vapor Cave. I plan to check it out later, if you want to drop over for a soak and suck."

Ronald was simultaneously relieved to be off the immediate hook and excited by the invitation. "I could really use the soak," he said. "It's hard to stay warm when you're camping and all."

Mitchell frowned, disappointed his former teacher hadn't jumped with joy about the sucking offer. "Great, then!" He looked at his white swatch. "Say, around four or five?"

"Let's make it five." Ronald figured that would give him more time to get his nerve up—or more time to chicken out. He didn't know what he wanted, since the least he'd been after was an invite to their lodge and a chance to make use of their thermal facilities. He was also curious about Mitch's traveling companion, Sam.

"Super," Mitchell said, putting his ballcap back on his head, which still smarted from when he'd bumped it entering the camper. "Hope I didn't dent the door frame with my hard head."

"How would you know?" Ronald asked in a way that could have had three meanings: he'd misjudged the door height since it was his first time entering the camper; his skull was so thick he hadn't felt the impact; or most obvious, that the camper was so beat up, you wouldn't know which dent was new. Ronald was certain he detected the erection in Mitchell's jeans when the visitor rose to leave. He quickly averted his eyes to the top of the door frame. "Watch your head," he warned, this time.

"Looking forward to seeing more of you at five, Mr. Simpleman."

Ronald stood there, as the camper door slapped shut. He parted the faded cabana striped curtains and watched Mitch Carson hop between rain puddles until he disappeared behind the trees that surrounded his Amphitheater campsite. He wasn't surprised or shocked by Mitch's innuendos and advances because the younger man had been that forward with him since the very beginning. He did worry, though, that this appointment at five could be a trap. He obsessed about it for the next hour, as the rain subsided and the last of the thunder rolled out of the wide end of the valley.

IT FELT EVEN more like a trap as he walked down a short pathway behind the main lodge. The weeping sides of the steep rock cliffs began to close in and narrow on both sides of him as he neared the entrance. Ronald ran his hand under the water flowing over the rockface on his right side to see if it was slimy, thermal, or cold. It was cold—likely runoff from the afternoon's thunder showers.

Ronald pulled open the thick wooden and slatted door that looked straight out of *The Flintstones*. Under the metal-roofed mineshaft entrance, he stepped over a metal rail threshold and into the mountain. (Or was it under the mountain? Or both?) The door cannonballed shut behind him with a bang so loud it nearly catapulted him into a long jump. He stood a moment in darkness that wasn't all that total, once his eyes began to adjust to it. A short distance away, at the end of a badly taped pair of uninsulated wires loosely looped over spikes that had been hammered at intervals into the slimy rock wall, he focused on a light bulb and sloshed his way toward it. His nostrils were rushed by sulphur, and the sounds of constant dripping beckoned him deeper into this steamy acoustic playground.

His first step was into water—which he wished he'd known, so that he could have stepped out of his unlaced hiking boots at the door. He did this now, setting his boots off to the side and curling his hairy naked toes around the uneven but mostly smooth river-rocked floor. He ventured half blind along the submerged pathway, finding the water only lukewarm, which would have been a disappointment if every step didn't tell him that it was getting warmer as he went farther. Now the interior walls of the shaft were slimy, cool, and glistening, like dripping icicles being strobed by the single lightbulb a short distance away in front of him. Ronald could not determine if he was alone inside the mountain, so he dispatched a diminished "Hel-lo" into the cavern where it echoed but wasn't answered.

Then he heard giggling.

"We're in here, Ron," issued out of the darkness to his left.

Feeling his way along the low ceiling, Ronald crouched halfway as the water became deeper and hotter and the air became dense with steam. His body blocked what little light the bulb behind him might have lent the space he was entering. Too late, it occurred to him to gather the bottom of the towel wrapped around his waist, as he crouched through the claustrophobic passageway. The tunnel's ceiling quickly ended, giving way to a slightly larger cavern beyond his outstretched fingers just as the water deepened to just above his kneecaps to soak the bottom portion of his hiked-up towel.

"Welcome to the Vapor Cave, Mr. Simpleman," said a familiar but faceless voice in the steamy darkness.

Ronald cleared his throat, trying to ascertain the size of the room via echolocation, as though he were suddenly a bat. "It doesn't seem very deep. Is this it?"

"How deep do you need?" asked a second, higher-pitched male voice, not even attempting to disguise the double-entendre.

Ronald decided he could give as good as he got. "Well, not as deep as Mother Spring up near Pagosa—that one happens to be the deepest geothermal hot springs on the planet, if you didn't know . . ." He paused, realizing he was parroting his father again. Apparently, he couldn't resist. "You can't swim in it, though. You'd be boiled alive!"

"I see you brought your towel," Mitchell said. "But there's no place to hang it."

"Here," said the second voice, which was nearing him through the steam, followed by the gurgling sounds of a trailing wake. "I'm Sam. I'm going to duck out for some fresh air."

Ronald surrendered his towel, though he couldn't see the hand in the dark that was reaching for it. That same hand missed the towel, grabbing and squeezing Ronald's manhood instead. "Whoa!" said the mystery voice. "There you are. You could hang your towel on that, I suppose."

Ronald giggled, clearing his throat so that this stranger could better judge where he was.

"Sorry about that," Sam said, before releasing his grip. But Ronald didn't think he was sorry at all. "Nice to meet you, Ronald."

"Uh, you too. Sam, I presume?"

"You two enjoy the cave, now." Sam carried the towel away, disappearing into the steam and out through the narrow passage. Seconds later, the sound of the door thudding shut resonated in the space.

Ronald was still standing, vulnerable and naked, in the thick vapor. Out of modesty, he lowered himself into the water. He squatted before he kneeled, driving the gravel into his kneecaps. The hot water lapped at his navel, and he hissed through pierced lips, sounding like a leaking tire. With outstretched arms, he sensed where the water was hottest—just beneath him—which led him to believe he may have been near the spring's source. He wondered whether this temperature was safe or even legal. As his surely reddened body adjusted to the water temperature and his lungs learned how to process steam without drowning, Ronald reached out to ascertain the size of the cavern. Finding the lower end of a submerged leg, he grabbed onto it, pulling himself through the pool in that direction.

"Your body will get used to the temperature," Mitchell said, "but I am here to advise you, *don't drink the water.*"

Ronald chuckled, instantly getting his former student's clever reference to the junior class play he had starred in back in 1978, when he brought down the house with his brilliant interpretation of Axel McGee from Woody Allen's play, *Don't Drink the Water.*

"Ah, sage advice from somebody who would know such things. Thank you." Ronald turned and sat his bare ass on the more naturally smoothed floor of the pool in that spot against the wall. "How many hot springs have we soaked in together?" Ronald was fond of statistics.

"At least half a dozen, maybe?" Mitch was guessing, though. He was not that much into numbers.

Ronald raised his hand out of the water. He examined it in the weird light cast by the solitary bare incandescent bulb that dangled like a hillbilly chandelier, just outside this steamier section of Vapor Cave.

"Let's see." Ronald counted hot springs on his fingers. "There's Lolo, Nimrod Warm Springs, Sleeping Child, Quinn's . . ." He paused to think and then added, "Lost Trail." He lifted his second hand out of the hot water to continue counting. "And then over in Idaho, there's Jerry Johnson Hot Springs, Red River Resort, plus . . . what were they called again? Soda something . . . no, Jemez! Jemez Hot Springs in New Mexico."

"Whoa, that's a lot of memories and wrinkled skin," Mitchell said. "And a lot of sex."

Ronald snickered, dropping both hands in a way that purposely sent a splash of water in Mitchell's face. "Your friend, Sam, didn't have to leave," he said.

"I asked him to," Mitchell confided. "I wanted a few moments alone. We haven't been naked together for what . . . a decade now?"

Ronald didn't know what to say but figured where this was heading. "I'm not sure how long I can stand this heat," he threw out as a countermeasure. For several reasons he couldn't grab onto because they were firing too quickly in his fight or flight state of wariness, Ronald was pretty sure that engaging in sex with Mitch would be a mistake, and possibly part of the trap he still wasn't convinced might get sprung on him at any second—possibly by Sam who may have stepped out to retrieve a camera to catch them in the act on film.

"Your body will get used to it," Mitchell assured him, threading his nearest hand between Ronald's thighs. Ronald squirmed, sitting more upright—a maneuver intended to relocate his swelling interest further out of reach. He'd physically responded to Sam's misplaced handshake, earlier, and this was only encouraging further mayhem.

"I'm a fifty-year-old troll that no amount of steam or darkness can conceal or enhance, I'm afraid," Ronald said. He doubted this disclaimer would work or dissuade either of them, but he felt obligated to put it out there.

"I don't know," Mitchell shot back. "In the camper this afternoon, you looked just the same to me as you always have."

"Maybe it's the altitude," Ronald suggested. "Plays tricks on your brain."

Mitchell scooted himself closer until the edges of their hips were touching. "Come on, Mr. Simpleman. For old time's sake." Ronald removed Mitchell's hand from his thigh, but Mitchell caught Ronald's hand instead, manipulating his fingers to wrap around his own erection. "See there? You still do it for me, Ron." Undetected, but predictably, Mitchell's other hand submarined around for the evidence he was after between his mentor's legs. "And I still do it for you."

Ronald didn't have to wonder why he was playing hard to get or why his defense mechanisms were sounding five alarms in his head. No doubt, he had broken the first principle of the Montana Educators Code of Ethics by taking the *Treats all students with love and affection* too far. But Mitch Carson had done worse: he'd broken his teacher's heart, which still seemed to Ronald to be the greater trespass.

Ronald's remorseful penance meted out over two decades had conditioned him to rebound, reform, and resist, to prevent this—whatever *this* was—from happening again, but then, it kept happening again. He'd folded in San Francisco. He'd floundered in Albuquerque. He'd failed in Missoula. Each time he'd promised himself he would be stronger the next time he faced Mitch Carson—that he would be the adult in the room who knew better and behaved. But that had been what landed him in his predicament to begin with. He *had* been the adult in the room. *That* was the problem.

Ronald also thought he'd moved beyond that frightening period of time when he'd been constantly looking over his shoulder, waiting to be turned in or caught and hauled off to prison. He didn't have the spine to resolve or move beyond the past. When it came to Mitch Carson, Ronald's pitiful avoidance tactics and flimsy denials that he still had feelings for the man didn't make for very convincing play-acting outside the theater of the absurd. Both men knew it, and one of them exploited it. The immediate, gripping issue (since Mitch hadn't withdrawn his hand) was that one of these men was manipulating the pronounced vulnerability of the other in the cruelest possible way, since their cat and mouse roles had reversed.

"Why don't you check out my fancy new prosthetic testicle," Mitchell suggested, manipulating his teacher's hand to cup his scrotum.

"How about you bring your friend, Sam, back in and—"

Ronald cut his nonsensical sentence short, realizing what it was suggesting. Mitchell released his grip, scooted away, and splashed to standing, before hastily navigating his way out of the Vapor Cave. Startled, Ronald covered his ears when the mineshaft door slapped against its waterlogged frame.

"You have a go," Mitch growled at Sam, who had been outside puffing on a joint. "He's asking for you."

PART II: 1998–1981

And then the justice,

In fair round belly

BUCHAREST, ROMANIA

October 1992

IT WASN'T THAT RONALD WAS A DYED-IN-THE-WOOL
Michael Jackson fan. But he'd become bored and family-fatigued in Bucharest, at the tail end of another expedition with his parents and brother. He'd been aching for a solo escapade where he could lose himself for a few hours, so he didn't think twice about splurging to see the thirty-four-year-old King of Pop live at the Bucharest *Stadionul National.* He purchased the last-minute ticket from a scalper outside the *Caru' cu bere* restaurant.

Harlan was disgusted by his younger brother's impulsivity, convinced that the ticket was a scam and that Ronald would get arrested at the gates. But hours later, Ronald lined up with 90,000 others. He'd been to operas and ballets before. He'd even attended an early Michael Franks concert in San Francisco with his brother during spring break in 1977. But never had he been to a stadium concert, or one that featured a superstar of Michael Jackson's caliber.

Still, he appreciated Harlan's skepticism. He'd never attended a ticketed event that didn't have a seat assignment, and his scalped ticket was marked DSP, which stood for *doar spațiu în picioare* and was Romanian for "standing room only"—not that Ronald knew that. After much confusion and the kindness of several dozen strangers who knew broken English, Ronald was swallowed whole by the masses on the stadium floor and transformed from a forty-five-year-old American into a thirty-something, emancipated Romanian compatriot.

Apparently, following twenty-four years of brutal, totalitarian oppression, twenty-three million Romanians needed to let off some steam. The

Gloved One seemed to know this, which was why he had chosen Bucharest to be the final stop of the first leg of his *Dangerous Tour*. It didn't matter that a day before the concert, standing on the main balcony at the Palace of Parliament, the superstar had addressed his legions of Romanian fans by mistakenly proclaiming "Hello Budapest!" causing a cacophony of gasps that rose into the air like rockets lifting off the grounds of Izvor Park. By the first chorus of "Wanna Be Startin' Somethin'," all had been forgiven with shouts and screams of "Trăiască Regele Pop! Trăiască Regele Pop!"

The Romanian Communist Party leader Nicolae Ceauşescu would have loved to have addressed the swarm of oppressed Romanians from that same palace balcony. But three years earlier, on Christmas Day, 1989, he'd been overthrown, and he and his wife Elena had been executed. That had been the culmination of the revolution against the last remaining hardline Communist regime in the Warsaw Pact. Three years later, visiting Romania was still considered risky, but Ronald and Harlan's father, Paul—ever the risk-taking explorer—had been eager and undeterred by State Department cautions. Already functionally wheelchair bound, June Simpleman had been jarred out of her living wits for four days, bouncing over the bombed-out cobblestone streets and sidewalks in Bucharest's Old Town, where their rooms at the Grand Hotel Continental were located. Distraught and heavily medicated on the final night of this ill-conceived adventure, and before the family was scheduled to return to Colorado, she was propped on a Matterhorn of pillows, staring off into space, while Harlan read to her *The English Patient*, newly published by Michael Ondaatje. Paul Simpleman silently stewed over whether this journey had perhaps been a challenge too far.

Ronald couldn't recall the exact moment he'd stuck out his tongue to accept the tab of acid from the cornrowed blonde who was gyrating a dervish next to—and sometimes against—him. She looked more and more like Bo Derek the deeper the LSD percolated into his capillaries. His best guess for the time of ingestion would have been during the short interlude and costume change between "Thriller" and "Billie Jean."

He'd accidentally-on-purpose done acid once before—in San Francisco in 1967—so he knew it was best to lean into the trip so that the train wouldn't leave the station without him. He felt momentarily nauseous during "Heal the World" but was soon uncontrollably weeping over the lyrics to "Man in the Mirror." He hallucinated that he was a marionette, involuntarily dancing with the moshing shoulder-to-clavicle crowd that threatened to squish the pulp right out of him.

Comically and perhaps tragically, the throng absolutely massacred what their fuzzy brains could remember of the choreography from the "Beat It" video, while MJ simultaneously entreated the entire stadium to do so. Shake-the-dice, step, step, step, step, pop right, pop left, double pelvic thrust . . .

Ronald tried to keep up with his adoptive clan of self-deputized backup dancers, but he was hopelessly clumsy and couldn't. Convinced his feet were no longer touching the stadium floor, and that he was being involuntarily levitated on a cloud of helium—was it being covertly pumped in?—he clutched a fistful of cornrow braids like reins in each of his hands, tethering himself to this misconstrued lifeline to reality. That seemed to trigger the much younger Bo Derek imitator's latent daddy issues, because she, in turn, misinterpreted his horsemanship as a come-on. A la *Dirty Dancing* (still the rage five years on), she began massaging his crotch with her upper thigh and pelvis, twirling around to grind her ass into his business. And when his nether region—completely disconnected from his other brain by then—began to visibly swell in response, she dropped to the astroturf and started rubbing her face against his denimed erection.

Nonstop, the audience-directed DMX stage lighting strobed, tilted, and rotated, lobbing multicolored geometrical shards that had Ronald trapped inside a giant kaleidoscope of sensory overload, above and below the belt. He experimented with this enriched and volatile euphoria, trying to hold off the nausea by closing and then opening his eyes, before deciding everything felt better and oddly *looked* better when his eyes were shut. His eyelids became twin IMAX projection screens as he metamorphized into a bullfrog squatting at the bottom of a pot of water he sensed might be coming to a boil. He delighted in seeing the thousands of bubbles coalesce about him before slipping up and away. He could hear them popping on the surface, but this was beyond his leap. He was feeling warmer and getting hotter.

Just then, a toilet bowl's worth of endorphins flushed from his cranium, racing to gush out his downspout in voluminous spurts. Ronald realized he had ejaculated inside his boxers, and as the wet spot expanded, Bo Derek clamped her teeth and jaws on the prize. Ronald screeched in excruciating pain, violently pushing her rug-burned cheeks and forehead down and away with the palms of both hands. She hinged backwards into a supine position on the turf, her legs bent at sharp, unnatural angles. She was instantly pounced on by one of the guys she'd come with, who seemed to have been waiting for her to become this incapacitated. The rest of her male friends created a colonnade around the happily dry-humping pair while holding her play-protesting girlfriends temporarily at bay, before everyone but Ronald piled on top of them.

The aged-out oddball was doubled over, convinced that he was bleeding from a penile amputation, and that the wet spot he was feeling and seeing must be blood, and not the semen he'd involuntarily surrendered. His dysphoria was neither helpful nor as fleeting as he needed it to be, but he was sure he had to separate himself from the situation and seek medical help.

The concert ended with stage pyrotechnics that absolutely blew the lens off the end of his kaleidoscope. Ronald abandoned his temporary friends, but his tripping continued as he exited the stadium and disappeared under the leafless northern red oak canopy of *Parcul National.* He stumbled to a stop in the shadows to piss on the trunk of a rubber tree and was relieved to learn he still had something to urinate from, though the earlier biting pain persisted. It was too dark to examine the damage, but Ronald was sure that the cornrowed wonder had broken the elasticized skin on the underside of his circumcision band. He wet two of his fingers with his tongue to see if the wound stung, but it didn't.

He gingerly tucked himself back inside his 501s. He stumbled along an Indian laurel-lined path toward a lake he could see in the distance; it bisected the park. Though a non-runner, he was effortlessly jogging now and veered a wide loping left at the water's edge toward the muffled sounds of honking horns. He thought he'd be able to hail a taxi to get back to his hotel, but hadn't considered that every cab in Romania would be chock-full of the thousands of other concertgoers who'd poured out of the stadium into the chilly Bucharest morning at the same time he had. After what felt like thirty infuriating minutes—in actuality, it was less than five—he lowered the arm that always ached on account of the high-school fencing accident. He staggered on, heading in the same direction as the traffic on his left, mostly sure this would deliver him to Old Town, where he'd encounter his family sound asleep in their hotel beds.

He stopped jogging and opted to skip for one full block along Bulevardul Basarabia, still feeling his helium-filled soles, then shot his right hand into the air and posed in the middle of a crosswalk like he was John Travolta in *Saturday Night Fever*. Ronald had arrived at the *Dangerous* concert venue with a windbreaker he'd borrowed from Harlan knotted about his waist. By the end of the first set break, he and the jacket—plus three-quarters of his common sense—had parted company. It was snatched away from him on an acid riptide—along with his hotel suite key he was now realizing and the forty US dollars he'd tucked inside a zippered breast pocket to pay for transit back to the hotel. He stopped and struggled to button his open shirt over his furry torso now that the evening had a sharp chill to it.

At that moment, the heavens over Bucharest began to sprinkle. He ducked under the circular portico of an expansive white mansion that fronted Strada Arhitect Dumtru Hârjeu just as the precipitation turned torrential. In seconds, the roof drains overflowed and a shimmering curtain of rain poured over the lip, seemingly encasing him inside a water column. It resembled the special effects deployed whenever Spock, Bones, and Captain Kirk got teleported on *Star Trek*. Ronald stood at attention, waiting to be dematerialized so that his energy could be put back together in his hotel bed—but nothing happened. Instead, the sensation overpowered his cerebral circuits, and he collapsed in slow motion, until he was sitting cross-legged like a blissed-out yogi in the middle of the carport.

The spaghetti tangle of synapses misfiring in his head convinced him he was in a bathroom shower, and so he decided to get naked. He began stripping off his wet clothing, including his Converse tennis shoes and socks, tossing everything far beyond the topiary shrubs that outlined the cobbled course. In the biggest shower of his lifetime, there was room to dance. He jigged. He waltzed and tangoed with imaginary partners. He leapt like a ballet dancer through the shower curtain and then back under cover. He was attempting his version of a very sloppy moonwalk when two white sedans with the blue letters *P O L I T I A* squealed into the semicircular driveway from opposite directions, flinging strobes of red and blue that reignited Ronald's kaleidoscope. When the shouting started, the hairy and ever-obedient yogi twirled into a seated position with his surrendering arms held high in the air.

The Romanian National Police officers emerged from their cars and Ronald in that moment corralled just enough sense to begin yelling, "American! American!" The next problem was that none of the three officers confronting the naked man spoke any English. Because it was clear there wasn't a gun anywhere on his person, unless it were somehow concealed inside him, the officers approached without their service weapons drawn. With two efficient clicks, the handcuffs went onto elevated wrists like bangles, and Ronald was pulled to his bare feet, his injured penis swaying nonchalantly side to side.

"*Unde sunt hainele tale? Unde sunt hainele tale?*" one officer repeated. Ronald was grinning ear to ear but clearly not comprehending the question, regardless of how many times it was asked. So, into the back of one of the police cars his nude body was fed.

Forty minutes later, at the Sector 4 police station, Ronald was given a flimsy flowery women's bathrobe, which he first put on backwards, unsure of how it was supposed to wrap around his backside. He sat unhandcuffed across from a desk in a private office, looking every bit like a dead ringer for Maxwell Q. Klinger from *M.A.S.H.*, a show which likely had never aired inside Ceaușescu's Romania. A sergeant who said his first name was Igor entered the room and shut the door. He must have been deputized or short-strawed as the officer on duty with the best command of English. But though Ronald was post-peak on his acid journey, he could not decipher what was being asked. He decided to lead his own interrogation by volunteering random information.

"Me?" he jabbed his index finger at the cleavage between his hairy pecs. "Ro-nald Sim-ple-man," he enunciated loudly.

The officer scanned his subject with the lackadaisical curiosity of an underpaid bureaucrat who'd rather be yanking out nose hairs than processing another crazed maniac hauled in off the street. "*Ai buletinul la ține?*" he said. "I-dent-i-fi-ca-tion?" The man in the borrowed woman's bathrobe kept smiling. Clearly, he had nothing else on his naked person, leaving the officer to wonder why he'd asked the ridiculous question in the first place. He pushed a blank sheet of paper and a ballpoint pen across the desktop. "*Scrie- ți numele,*" he said. "Write your name."

As the arrestee struggled to print out his full name in block letters— RONALD PAUL SIMPLEMAN—he began involuntarily whimpering. The psychedelic tentacles with their neon suckers that had wrapped his tripping mind in amusing, nonsensical knots began to untangle and recoil back into the recesses of his brain coral where they normally hid and remained dormant. His rapidly sobering focus now zeroed in on this new predicament, which would lead to his father finding out, and worse—his father being disappointed in him, yet again. With tear tracks creating subway maps on his cheeks, he looked imploringly into the policeman's spectacled dark eyes and decided to take a different tack.

"You know Michael Jackson?" Ronald asked the man sitting across from him in the windowless room. He began to sing. "They told him don't you come around here, don't wanna see your face, you better disappear . . ."

It was the officer's turn to start grinning as an explanation for the naked man's strange behavior seemed to formulate out of thin air. The career policeman finished the refrain, though off-key. "So beat it, just beat it!"

Ronald wiped his tears with two fists to his eye sockets. "I was at the concert. I think somebody—" He paused, suddenly quite vividly recalling who that somebody was. "She must have slipped me some, you know, LSD, when she kissed me on the mouth," he pointed to his extended tongue.

"Your passport?" the officer asked, removing his glasses. "Where is?" Ronald looked down, seeming to notice the flowery bathrobe for the first time. He opened both fabric panels wide, unintentionally flashing the policeman from the waist up.

"Not here," Ronald said. "In hotel room."

"Home? Where is?"

"Colorado . . . Rocky Mountains . . . Skiing . . . Alpine Adventure." Ronald sounded as though he was working for the tourism bureau.

The officer finished copying the family name he'd been given onto two sets of the official paperwork—the first being a duty logbook and the second being a smaller, elongated tablet page with a sheet of oversized carbon paper underneath. He signed his name, dated and loudly timestamped the tablet page with a pre-inked gadget before separating it. He copied numbers from that page into the larger logbook, then scooted it an arm's length across the desktop toward Ronald.

The long narrow page had a red lettered heading that Ronald could not read upside down. He rotated it using his thumb and middle finger. Beneath the crest depicting a yellow eagle with a cross in its beak, a sword clutched in one talon and a laurel branch in the other, was a scroll title that read *LEX ET HONOR*. It took him a few seconds, in his mental state, to decipher *Citare pentru Nuditate Publică*. The handwritten amount of 474.94 RON at the bottom of the page, he figured, was the fee he would need to come up with before being released. He glanced up from the page with a fresh look of panic, coaxing his brain to think . . .

"Think!" he commanded out loud, pounding his fist on the desktop, causing the officer to jump back defensively. Ronald instantly apologized in rudimentary sign language, showing the palms of both hands. "Grand Hotel Continental," he said, in a calmer voice.

"Your hotel?" the officer said. Ronald nodded and the officer reached under the desk for a giant phone book. He looked up the hotel and dialed the desk phone. He described the purpose of the call in Romanian before passing the army-green phone receiver to the man in the floral-patterned house coat.

"Yes, may I have the room of Harlan Simpleman?" Ronald inquired, spelling the last name. After three rings, his groggy father answered. They'd put him through to the wrong room.

"Dad, it's Ron," he said, reluctantly. "I'm having a bit of a challenge getting back to the hotel from the concert. May I speak to Harlan?"

Ronald's heart was thumping. He was sure the Senior Simplemans had intentionally left their adjoining room door ajar so they could hear when their youngest adult son returned from his night of concertgoing. Ronald's father sternly shouted out Harlan's name. Harlan picked up, and it took three attempts with the phone receiver clunking around in the cradle before his father managed to hang up his extension.

Ronald whispered loudly into the mouthpiece because people in sticky situations on TV did this when they were trying to be covert. "Harlan! Listen. Can you keep your voice low and find something to write with?" Harlan groaned and rustled around for a pen, and while waiting, Ronald muffled the phone against his chest and turned to the officer. "Do you take traveler's checks?"

"Cash only," came the reply in perfect English.

STEVENSVILLE, MONTANA

May 1989

RONALD'S PARENTS HAD BEEN DRIVING HIM TO THE brink of madness. And now he was driving himself to get at least two states away from them and their coordinated pressure campaign for a few days.

The strictly transactional surgeon had been relentlessly harping on Ronald to not throw away his Stanford education, since the surgeon had paid for it. June, the stay-at-home mom, had an inexhaustible list of probing questions she thought would help her youngest latch onto his passion and generate enough of an income to live elsewhere. She had been neither subtle nor the least bit apologetic. Mom knew best, and Mom conveniently chose to ignore all the caregiving Ronald was providing her, especially since her MS diagnosis.

Well, Mom doesn't know everything. Ronald repeated this mantra while tearing down the highway. He was making tracks to Stevensville, Montana—his first time back in five years. Veruca (his Volvo) had been acting up and Franco at Crested Butte Auto Body said he was waiting on a backorder of parts from Sweden. So, Ronald had commandeered his dad's hunting pickup and camper for this weeklong excursion "to clear his head," as he'd put it to his parents. Their tag-teaming had reached a breaking point and he figured they were smart enough to understand how they were driving him out of the house, either temporarily or for good. Ronald knew it looked odd, felt odd, smelt odd, and sounded odd for a forty-three-year-old man to be living back at home with his parents. He didn't need to be hit on the head with a two-by-four to get the message.

He was clearing out his head—not unlike someone trivially clearing out the holey underwear or socks from their dresser of drawers—and he was doing it the best way he knew how. The open road was the best medicine for helping him achieve the overhaul he believed he needed. The bonus was that he didn't need to wait on replacement parts from Sweden. When he had been a teacher, he'd felt independent—which was ironic, since he hadn't had much freedom to be himself in that rural town that he was heading back to for reasons that would make no sense to anybody else. Irony stacked on top of the trepidation he'd need to overcome in the next 900 miles if he was going to complete his mission, he was going *Back to the Future*—a brain-twister for the ages—to retrieve a relic he thought would help him better navigate the present.

True to form, Ronald had been over-playing his cassette of the latest Michael Franks album, *The Camera Never Lies*—which was apropos as the theme for his expedition. He played the title track the most, rewinding it so often, he'd already had to pull off the road twice when it got gobbled up by the tape deck and needed to be extracted then rewound using a pencil from the glove box.

> *And it should come as no surprise*
> *That the oppression's no accident*
> *We know the camera never lies*
> *No the camera never lies*

The reason why this song resonated so much with him was that Ronald fancied himself a talented photographer. Toying with still photography, dap-pling with filmmaking using his now-vintage ELMO Super 103T Super-8 movie camera, experimenting with a new Betamax video recorder, and not looking for work—to his parents' consternation—were how Ronald filled the balance of his life these days. He'd always had a variety of cameras—many of them antiques—collected during his travels or ordered by mail. Cameras, and more directly, the snapshots-in-time they produced, helped him catalogue the events of his ordinary, mundane life, as both a Simpleman and a simple man. But more than this, they gave him an inkling that he was possibly *good* at something. He often thought of the more thrilling life he might have been living now, had he pursued training and work as a cine-matographer or even a photojournalist. Whatever it was that had possessed him to become a high school teacher was maybe best explained by the adage *those who can, do; those who cannot, teach.*

Stuck behind a double semi carrying wood chips, the truck camper slipstreamed without rattling or shaking as much as when the brow of the camper was breaking the onrush by itself. Ronald's ears and nerves enjoyed the break. It was also nice to be able to play the music at a lower volume, since it no longer had to compete with the racket. Ronald rewound the cassette, just to hear and sing along with the refrain again.

> *Truth you can't disguise*
> *Just open up your eyes*
> *'Cause the camera never lies*

Coincidentally, it was a camera that lay behind this rushed mission and the reason Ronald was behind the wheel heading north to Montana like a crazed prospector seeking his fortune in gold, except the treasure Ronald sought was black, and if his hunch proved right, there was a better than 50/50 chance he'd strike it rich this time.

Until—and completely out of the blue—he'd managed to track Ronald down at his parent's house by phone this past Sunday, Mitch Carson had not been in touch in any meaningful way for over two and a half years. Not long after their last meet-up in San Francisco in '86, Mitch had dropped off the radar. As the months and then years ticked by, Ronald stubbornly refused to see this snub—if that's what that was—as a falling out or accept as evidence they were no longer on speaking terms. He just figured his former student had gotten himself into another relationship and had simply gone underground in love. And just like usual, the first thing Mitch did last Sunday was reach out, bruised and hurting after his most recent break-up, looking for solace from his mentor and former teacher. It was as if Mitch somehow knew he would be there, perpetually waiting for him in the wings, which of course his teacher was and always would be, because Ronald Simpleman was nothing if not hopelessly predicable and foolhardy optimistic that he would always be able to rekindle the extinguished.

When Mitch had phoned, the opener he'd given was that he was "just checking-in" but within a minute of niceties, he'd spilled the beans on what he vowed would be the final break-up he'd ever have with that cheating, doping, gay porn-starring, cheerleader ex-boyfriend of his and that he was off to Venezuela to lick his wounds and maybe do some acting/modeling. Mitch then indicated he'd probably bounce from there to Patagonia if his funds held out. Then he mumbled something promising, like he sincerely hoped he and Ronald could connect in person once Mitch returned stateside. "Oh," he'd remembered, right before hanging up, "And my parents are selling their house in Stevensville. The empty nesters are finally moving to Missoula, so it looks like my stash of Polaroids that I'd hidden inside the closet wall in my bedroom won't be something I'll ever be able to get back."

Having completely forgotten about Mitch's previously reported exploits with that polaroid camera, Ronald called his wandering mind back to the conversation and assured Mitch that his stash was probably hidden good as gone and that his secrets would always be safe with him. Mitch said "thanks," and something to the effect that he appreciated that and then the call terminated.

And that's why Ronald had been squeezing the steering wheel for the past fourteen hours until his knuckles had blanched white as the knight he intended to become, riding into Stevensville like he was, to win back the heart and save the dignity of his damsel—or rather *dude*—in distress. This was why Ronald did anything at all—because Mitch was quite possibly all that mattered.

Stevensville, Montana, pop. 979—a town Ronald swore he'd never step foot in again—for all its backwardness, foibles, sordid memories, and Wild West rodeo ways—was still the hallowed ground where Ronald's first and only collaboration with Cupid would ever come to pass. Mythology had it that this miniscule municipality marked the spot where Ronald the teacher, became accidentally-on-purpose smitten with Mitch the student. While true love might have been the intended aim and perhaps Mitch's young heart had been the target, the god of desire must have been hungover that day from a bacchanal the night before because the arrow from his quiver veered wildly nowhere near the bull's-eye. Not only had the Fates—Clotho, Lachesis and Atropos—who called all the shots, trampled the love that had sprouted there in Stevensville's weed patch, they'd first and fiendishly conjured up and nurtured a flower to grow there where nothing else could. Their creation, so radiantly rare that it bloomed only once every millennium, burst out of the sun-cracked soil with such marvelous technicolor ferocity dripping a nectar from its petals of promise whose scent only Ronald's predestined nose could detect. Mitch Carson couldn't see it, didn't smell it, even when Ronald pointed it out to him and rubbed his young nose in it.

To this day, Ronald had never figured out how something so beautiful could wither before his eyes into a life-sapped tumbleweed waiting for the next gust to whip up so it could roll the hell out of Dodge. But that was precisely how Mitch Carson had gotten away from him, like the roadrunner escaping Wile E. Coyote in the Looney Tunes cartoons, kicking up dust as he made the hastiest of exits.

Ronald's heart mimicked a fife and drum corps inside his chest as he left the highway to cross the Bitterroot River over what was known as the Stevensville Cut-off bridge. Relieved to be cloaked in truck-camper camouflage and not his Volvo as he slipped behind—for reasons he couldn't decode, was feeling like—enemy lines, he rounded the bend and rolled into town. Just past the Cenex gas station that had been a Conoco during Ronald's residency, laid out and suspended in a time before Montana even had statehood was the three-block, brick building-lined Main Street sagging at derelict attention. He checked his wristwatch at the only stop sign—the intersection of Main and Third Street—then hung a right, since he had a few minutes to kill before 11:00 a.m.

At Charlos Street, he turned left onto the gravel street, and as inconspicuously as he could, slowed down to pass the big white house, number 305, where his old upstairs apartment had been "home sour home" for seven-and-a-half arduous school years. He had not kept in touch with his elderly landlords and so had no intention of paying a courtesy visit now, and that's if they were still alive. In planning this touch-and-go mission, it had been his objective to slip in and out of Stevensville undetected inside thirty minutes. He turned left onto Fourth Street and eased the truck camper back onto pavement. He coasted to the stop sign at Main Street and didn't have to wait for an opening in Sunday morning traffic to cross over to the east side of town.

At Church Street, he hung a left and then a right onto East Third, slowing at College Street as he inventoried the half-full parking lot adjacent to the United Methodist Church—a two-story gray-and-white-trimmed historical building with a distinctive red bell tower cupola. Originally built to house the town's first elementary school in the 1880s, it had been renovated to serve as a church by the late 1920s. According to Stevensville lore, on Mother's Day—Ronald thought he remembered it was around 1940—neighbors across Pine Street had witnessed a bolt of lightning strike the bell tower, splitting its weathervane in two. The electricity was said to have traveled through the attic and onto the metal railing of the church balcony overlooking the sanctuary, before starting a fire that was extinguished by a church deacon.

The portico entrance with its six ionic columns and cupola-matching red doors had welcomed the congregation of the United Methodist Church since 1928, and, for as long as Ronald could remember, this congregation had included the Carson family. With Mitch now living in Seattle (but already landed or on his way to South America) and the two younger Carsons living their post-college lives married and raising dogs and kids of their own in Bozeman and Helena, Ronald had calibrated this mission on the stale intelligence that the parents had likely kept up with their Sunday tradition. His memory and his hunch were rewarded when he spotted their mint-green Volkswagen Rabbit in the third row of diagonal parking spots.

He checked his wristwatch. It was 10:50. He supposed the service would start at the top of the hour and last until noon, but having never attended church services in his life, he was just guessing. Then he spotted the 11 o'clock service time on the church reader board, below the scripture passage for that week: *For the wicked boasts of his heart's desire. And the greedy man curses and spurns the Lord. Psalms 10:3.*

Ronald let the shiver of that message bolt through his own body, fortunately without starting a fire. He accelerated up east Third, threading his father's camper top through a canyon of low-hanging cottonwoods. A loud thud made his head and shoulders cringe in the driver's seat, telegraphing that he'd clipped a branch. He checked the side mirrors but did not see any debris on the road.

The street then curved south, turning into Park Avenue. On his left, as his heart skipped several beats ahead of the truck, was Stevensville High School, the site of his assault on the foundational principles, ethics, and responsibilities of being an entrusted educator. Approaching the corner with Spring Street, Ronald spotted the *For Sale* sign in front of the two-story Carson family stone house. His gaze threaded through the tree trunks to surveil the address that sounded like it had been lifted from *Monopoly*: 215 Park Avenue. It was a stylish yet squatty, square-floorplan Craftsman home that had been designed to look heritage but wasn't. It had been in construction in 1975, the year that Ronald began teaching across the street. He'd never once been inside, though he was intimately familiar with its perimeter. As he edged past the home, he couldn't see any other vehicles parked outside, so he rested on this updated intelligence and exhaled the first in a series of heavy sighs—this one in relief.

Ronald parked the camper truck in the empty school parking lot using the same front row faculty spot he'd used for almost eight years. He shut off the overheated engine, unfastened his seatbelt, and sat there glancing intermittently between his wristwatch and the empty Carson driveway across Park Avenue. He had needed to relieve his bladder for the past hundred miles but had been too hopped up on adrenaline to pull his rig off the highway. He hadn't used the camper toilet since leaving Crested Butte, as it was a hassle finding a station where he could empty the tank. But since he no longer had a master key to the high school, his options for relieving himself were limited on a Sunday to either the camper or one of the bathrooms inside the Carson home, since that was where his mission was about to take him. The delectable notion of using the same toilet that Mitch had used for half his life seemed a heady though risky complication. But it would add brazen bonus points to the daringness of the operation if Ronald could leave a measure of his own essence behind as a calling card.

At a quarter past eleven, satisfied the elder Carsons were ensconced in their morning church service, Ronald left the cab of the truck and cut a diagonal path across Park Avenue. Cutting between two trees, he walked up the sidewalk. Purple and white pansies were packed into a half-dozen clay pots of different sizes positioned around the covered veranda porch that stretched the length of the front of the house. Ronald bounded up the four porch steps, taking two at a time. He rang the doorbell twice. When it wasn't answered, he knocked loudly on the wood frame of the screen door.

With his heart thumping, Ronald scanned the yard and what he could see of the neighboring houses. Then he made his move. He opened the wooden screen door and twisted the doorknob a quarter turn.

The door was unlocked—as he was nearly certain it would be, since nobody locked doors in Stevensville—and he opened it. He stepped inside, shutting the door behind him. He inhaled deeply, as though Mitchell's scent might be lingering still, some five years since the kid had last lived here. He gave a courtesy shout—"Hello?"—that wasn't answered.

Ronald's feet still hadn't left the entrance rug. His eyes widened as he took in everything, wishing he had more of a photographic memory and cursing that he hadn't thought to bring one of his cameras. He looked for a way into the basement, but the only staircase he could see led upstairs. With a few strides, he was through the dining room and into the kitchen. There, near the back door, he found what he'd been looking for: the set of stairs that would take him below.

He resisted turning on any lights so was careful in his descent, taking one painted wooden step at a time. He could sense with every fiber of his being and every receptor in his nostrils that he was entering Mitchell's underground lair. The daylit basement, as he quickly scrutinized it, consisted of a family room designated by a large rectangle of rust-colored shag carpet with bean bag chairs and a TV console, a shuffleboard that had been stencil painted onto the adjacent cement floor, a ping pong table, and a closed door. And next to that—and most critical for this bladder-strained burglar—a bathroom/laundry room.

Once inside, Ronald lifted the toilet seat, unfastened his jeans, and unleashed his kinked-up garden hose. Taking a long piss to remember all the times he'd tried to peep inside the half-underground window off his left shoulder, Ronald marked his territory, leaving a few drops on the rim that he didn't bother to wipe off, so that a certain returning alley cat might detect he'd been there. With the house for sale, this being discoverable seemed even more unlikely. Standing there with the washer and dryer to his right, Ronald deducted that Mitchell's bedroom must be on the other side of the wall he faced, based on Mitch's description of the bonus bedroom that he and his father had finished off in the basement.

Having come this far to retrieve what should be stashed within that wall, Ronald flushed—because he wasn't a heathen—and then lowered the toilet seat and lid to carry out the mission. He left the bathroom and rounded the corner to face the closed door. His fingers wrapped one at a time around a doorknob that Mitch's hand had to have opened and closed countless times. But when he tried to twist it, the door appeared locked. He jiggled it, but seeing the key cylinder, he sighed, not in relief, and leaned his torso against the door frame in defeat. When he did this, Ronald's trick right shoulder somehow pushed the door open. If it had been locked, the latch bolt hadn't engaged. Maybe it had never worked in the first place.

Ronald crossed the Rubicon into Mitchell's teenaged domain. A made double bed was positioned beneath one of the two windows that brought natural light into the subterranean corner. Ronald looked out of the windows that he had only previously peered into (after dark), and his memory circuit was completed. He quickly took note of the posters adhered by double-sided tape to the wood-paneled walls, and saw that some of them were promotional posters from Mitchell's world tour during the year after high school, when he'd travelled as a performer. There were also two heavier poster boards—one lime green and the other neon pink—that had been thumbtacked into the paneling. On these were illustrations of goofy cartoon cancer cells being obliterated to smithereens by handsomely drawn white blood cells, each with superhero capes unfurling behind them. Ronald assumed Mitchell had been the artist, and that the art must have helped him visualize the battlefield during his skirmish with cancer in '83 and '84.

He checked his wristwatch. It was 11:26. He felt a fresh rush of adrenaline.

He turned to stare down the closet, with its closed pair of bi-fold panels, which he quietly opened. He guessed where the toilet was positioned on the other side of the wall. He had to move some heavy boxes out of the way to see the white-painted back wall. He found what looked like a jigsaw cut-out in the plywood, about a foot above the floor. There, a capped black cast-iron branch of a sewer pipe encroached maybe a half inch into the closet at an angle.

Ronald knelt, and with his right hand fingers, he felt around the edge of the unframed and roughly finished oval opening in the plywood. The cutout seemed to have been filed or maybe sanded but not completely smoothed before it was painted. Under the pipe, the opening was larger than above, and Ronald could just get his hand inside, up to the wrist. His fingers worked like antennae, feeling around in the void.

There seemed to be nothing but spiderwebs, which he tried his best to ignore. He needed to approach this from a steeper angle and thought he'd have better luck with his left hand, so he adjusted his body to get his fingers further inside the opening. Not thinking to remove his wristwatch first, he forced his forearm partway into the slot until he thought he could shove it no further. He was able to touch the back of the bathroom wall on the other side of the 2 x 4 framing.

When he angled his fingers downward, he grazed something that shifted when he touched it. In his excitement, he shoved his forearm a half inch further in. He pinched a rigid corner of something not attached, moving independently. He worked the angle to secure a better grip and then began to extract his arm with the treasure, as if his appendage was part of a claw toy machine.

Then the face of his wristwatch snagged on the bottom of the pipe inside the wall. When he tried to ease it out, his arm became firmly wedged between the plywood and the pipe. In his panic, he yanked his hand completely free, ripping the flesh under his wrist, his fingers having let go of the small plastic box he'd located inside the wall, where he feared it had fallen flat-side down now out of reach. His right hand reflexively clamped onto his left wrist under the expandable watch band—a tourniquet in case the tear in his skin was as mortally serious as it felt. He lessened his grip to see if he was even bleeding and he was, but when he saw the time on the now-scratched face of his wristwatch, his panic accelerated.

He needed to get out of the house before the Carsons returned from church, but he couldn't leave without the relic he'd come for. He jammed his right hand back into the slot. It took him several tries to reach what he'd dropped—what Mitchell had deposited in this clever vault so many years ago. He was singularly focused on extracting the plastic cartridge, and so he missed the blood that was slowly dripping from his other wrist and onto the dark shag carpet.

With his thumb and index finger squeezing the half-inch-wide prize, he struggled to make his hand as flat as possible without letting go. It was like playing the battery-operated board game, *Operation*, but blindfolded. Only when he used his second index finger to steady a corner of the slowly emerging plastic packaging did he realize how much he was bleeding. With the Polaroid case successfully extracted, Ronald shoved it in his rear pocket and hustled to replace the boxes on top of the bloodied carpet. Mitch's bedroom was carpeted in the same rust hue as the rug on the family room floor, so a couple drops of blood didn't show . . . all that much . . . in the dark. He shut the closet doors and glanced at his wristwatch to confirm that he was running out of time. Squeezing the laceration on the underside of his injured wrist, he pulled the bedroom door shut and dashed into the bathroom to grab a handful of toilet paper to use as a pressure bandage.

Up the stairs and through the kitchen he darted, heading toward the front door, looking out all the windows to see that his escape route was clear. In a moment, he was outside, on the sidewalk. He turned around to appraise the house, as though he might be an interested buyer—a good alibi if any neighbors had been snooping on him. He then emerged from the trees along the property line and jogged back across Park Avenue to his camper truck, where, to his horror, he spotted a black-and-white Stevensville Police Department patrol car, which had pulled up alongside his rig in the otherwise empty lot.

As he tentatively approached, acting as casually as he could, Ronald tidied up his toilet paper wound dressing, trying to conceal the bloody mess with his left hand. Then he saw the sizeable cottonwood tree branch balanced on a corner of the camper.

"Good day, officer," Ronald crouched to look into the lowered window on the patrol car's passenger side. He held his hands out of sight below the window. "Good day, Officer," he greeted as nonchalantly as he could.

The officer made eye contact as the dispatcher came over the radio. "The license plate is clear," the dispatcher said. "Nothing outstanding. Copy?"

"Copy that. Thanks, Barb."

The policeman wrote *VOID* in block letters diagonally across the ticket he had started to issue. "There's no camping here, if that's what you had in mind," he advised rather sternly. "And if you're thinking of transporting that branch on the top of your rig, you're going to have to tie it down."

The officer, whose profile looked familiar, might have been Ronald's student once. But because the older man wanted to slink out of town as easily as he'd slunk in, he didn't mention it. "I'm just stretching my legs before heading over Lolo Pass," he said.

"Drive safe," the officer cautioned him, turning the key in the ignition of his squad car. "And mind that tree branch."

Ronald stepped back as the officer pulled away, heading down Park Avenue in the direction of Fourth Street. He unlocked the driver's door of the truck camper and climbed inside, remembering to extract the plastic Polaroid cartridge from his back pocket just in time to avoid sitting on it. He rolled down his driver's side window and then reached to roll down the opposite one. He sighed loudly this time, in astonished relief. He unwound the toilet paper and examined the wound that was still smarting but had stopped bleeding. With his thumb, he tried without luck to polish the scuff off his watch face. Another souvenir to commemorate this daring heist.

It was noon. Ronald supposed church would be letting out soon, but he wasn't about to leave his spot until he'd inventoried his purloined treasure. Leaning his forearms on the steering wheel, Ronald turned the plastic cartridge repeatedly, wondering if it contained what he thought it did. There was a hard side and a flimsier side that his fingers could push in—the original Polaroid film cards were spring-loaded. He pushed and dragged the first card to get it to emerge out of the slot. It was a solid piece of plastic, which Ronald remembered always ejected from the camera first, leaving the remaining photo cards ready to be exposed whenever a picture was taken. Through the cartridge window that had been revealed once the plastic protector card was removed, Ronald could see a white cardboard frame sur-rounding the black negative. He carefully pushed it out of the slot, holding his breath as he turned the card around.

The developed photo was a close-up of a young man's genitalia.

"Eureka!" Ronald shouted, pounding his fist on the steering wheel, not thinking of the damage to his wrist, which immediately started bleeding again. He reached for the glove box and withdrew a few leftover fast-food napkins. He pressed them to his wrist just as a mint-green Volkswagen Rabbit drove around the bend and into the driveway of the Carson house across the street.

Ronald decided to save the rest of the photos for when he stopped to camp for the night somewhere in the vicinity of Jerry Johnson Hot Springs, on the Idaho side of the border. Once the bleeding stopped, he fed the photo and the blank plastic cover back into the plastic cartridge, tucking it into a dashboard cubbyhole that already held two Michael Franks cassettes. That concluded his business in Stevensville. He took one last survey of the high school and one last glance at the Carson House before starting up the truck.

He put the gear in reverse and punched the accelerator. The Cotton-wood tree branch tumbled off the camper top, bounced on the hood and back toward him cracking the windshield with a horizontal line nearly as wide as the truck. He climbed out to clear the tree off the hood, his wrist dripping punctuation marks onto the pavement. He looked down, thinking his teaching career and blood sacrifice to Stevensville was at long last com-plete. He dragged the branch to lay it diagonally across his former parking spot, symbolically cancelling out any future business in this place, then Ronald headed back to Main Street, turned right and made the hastiest of tracks out of hick town.

THE CASTRO

April 1986

HARLAN WAS A WALKING ENIGMA AND EXTRAORDI-
narily complex for a Simpleman. It's not that he knew this about himself so
much as it was flagged at the water cooler by gossiping co-workers, scribbled in the clinical notes of a psychologist or three, highlighted on report
cards by elementary and high school teachers, and discussed by his concerned parents as a matter of pillow talk.

In addition to being a bookworm who easily devoured a novel or biog-
raphy a week, Harlan was a devout vegetarian, a borderline heliophobe who
was one shade darker than albino, the antithesis of sporty or outdoorsy,
functionally asexual, a 48 on the introversion scale, an INTP personality
type according to Myers Briggs, and a pacifist. He had little interest in
romance, positions of power, or leadership, and he simply didn't have the
stomach for activism due to his aversion to ever being the center of attention. He rarely took a stance even in his own defense and would choose the
white flag of surrender over self-preservation "six days a week and twice on
Sunday," according to an old saying his dad still overused. Harlan silently
judged but didn't rail against inequities. On principle, he seldom commented on political affairs his opinions would never change. He abhorred
small talk and so automatically declined most social invitations. When it
came to patronizing the arts, it was either ticketed, assigned seating—preferably on an aisle, to facilitate his escape (sometimes mid-performance)—or
he'd stay home, which was also fine by him.

So, when he'd received a telephone call fifteen minutes earlier from an exuberant "Mitchell Carson" saying he was a good friend of his brother's and in need of a sofa to sleep on for a couple nights, Harlan's brain crashed faster than his new Compaq Deskpro 386, which had been temperamental right out of the box. (The weighty upgrade from the TI 99/4A word processor he had been clinging to like a life preserver had been purchased for him by Tarcher, his publishing company, as part of his book advance. Its president, Jeremy Tarcher—married to ventriloquist Shari Lewis of Lamb Chop fame, and brother of novelist Judith Krantz—had needed to ensure that the rewrites and the final edit of Harlan's gourd-breaking vegetarian cookbook would be completed by the announced publication date, which was less than sixty days away).

Harlan pressed the disconnect button on his white Trimline. He counted to three in his head and then dialed his parents' home outside Crested Butte, which had been his brother's hideout since abruptly ditching his teaching career after the end of the previous school year.

"Hello, Mother. It's Harlan. How are you and Dad?"

"We're doing just fine, dear. How are you?"

Harlan—guarded and reticent—needed to get on and off any telephone call with the greatest possible expediency. No exceptions could be made for the woman who had carried, birthed, and raised him. "I'm fine, Mom, but I need to have a word with Ronald if he's around."

"Ronald!" his mother yelled, not covering the mouthpiece. "Ronald!" she yelled again, even louder. When Ronald did not respond, she said, "He must be outside, tinkering with his Volvo."

"You're probably right, Mom. Just have him call—"

"Ah! Here he is, dear. Just walked in, he did. Ronnie, it's your brother!"

In the pause, Harlan almost needed to remind himself what he was phoning about; so quickly could speaking with either of his parents cause the caboose of his thought-process to jump the track.

"Well, hello there, Harlan," Ronald sang in that chirpy, irritating way of his.

"Ronnie, listen. I have a situation. One of your former high school students just phoned me."

Ronald tripped through his mental rolodex. He'd taught nearly eight years' worth of students. "Oh, yeah?" he offered into the telephone, still having not solved the riddle.

Harlan prompted him. "Last name, Carson. First name—"

"*Mitchell*," the brothers said simultaneously—though Ronald only said *Mitch*, which was how he'd always known him. He felt like the wind had just gotten knocked out of him, but Harlan took his brother's pause as puzzlement. "Do you even remember him?"

That wins the Ridiculous Question of the Century Award, Ronald thought amid his sudden panic attack. He said, "What in the world did he want?" That wasn't the red-hot question he wanted answered but didn't dare ask: *What did he tell you?*

"He said he'd lost his wallet with his ID and credit card and needed a place to crash for two nights before his flight back to Albuquerque on Thursday. Said he'd remembered you saying you had a gay brother living in the Castro. Thanks for outing me, by the way." Harlan's tone became snooty-bitchy.

Ronald's brain scrambled to process everything he was being told. "Surely you told him your apartment was too small for company?"

"Had I been afforded ten seconds to come up with that lie, I might have."

"It's not a lie. So, does this mean Mitch Carson is coming over to your place to sleep, shower, shit, and shave?" He was incredulous. "And for two nights?" He faked a chuckle at his brother's predicament. "You should book yourself a room at the Hilton."

"And you should be the one to pay for it, giving out my private details like that," Harlan snapped back.

"It will be okay, Harlan. Mitch is a nice guy. He aspires to be a writer. You'll have that in common!"

"I'm not *aspiring*," Harlan corrected. "Must I remind you I'm being published in two months?"

"A cookbook," Ronald clarified, ever-so-slightly dampening his brother's slow-to-inflate ego. "A *vegetarian* cookbook," he modified his dig.

Ronald saw their mother trying her darndest to eavesdrop as she peeled potatoes over the kitchen sink. To stump her, he decided to employ more coded statements moving forward. "What's the weather like this time of year?"

"Why in the hell are you asking me that?" Harlan didn't have time to give a weather report.

Ronald realized he wasn't good at code so abandoned the ruse, but stretched the phone cord into the peony hallway and lowered his voice. "Would it help if I were there?"

"It would help if you used *your* credit card to book *your* former student his own room at the Hilton where everybody would be much more comfortable," Harlan suggested. "But yes, it would help a great deal if you were here. I am under deadline with the book, behind with my editing milestones and struggling to learn this new computer I'm supposed to be using. I don't have the time to entertain or—Zeus forbid—engage in mindless chitchat." Harlan had phoned to find an out, but he'd settle for a hand.

"I could leave here first thing in the morning, I guess," Ronald said. "Get there late tomorrow evening if I drive straight through." He'd made the drive more than a dozen times while attending Stanford.

At first, Harlan didn't respond. "Can you fly commuter just this once, Ronnie?" he implored. "Catch the 4:45 to Denver and arrive here before bedtime *tonight*?"

"How's this for a compromise: I could throw some things in a knapsack and leave here in the next few hours, arriving midafternoon tomorrow?" He watched his mother stop peeling. So much for using code, he realized too late.

"Fine. Drive safely." Harlan capitulated so quickly it caught Ronald by surprise. The older brother hung up so that there would be no further negotiation.

Then their mother started in. "Ronnie, you promised to help me put in the vegetable patch and flower gardens tomorrow." She was whining in that universal guilt-inducing Mom sort of way.

"The ground isn't even completely thawed out yet, Ma," Ronald replied, placing the wall phone back in its cradle. "You usually wait until after Memorial Day. I'll be back in two or three days. We can do it then. Harlan needs a hand."

"Well, why doesn't he just ask that student friend of yours to help him, if he's staying there anyway?" She sounded like a CIA agent caught covertly monitoring a wiretap.

Ronald had to smile at his mother's astuteness as he lumbered down the hallway toward his bedroom. In the throes of gathering a few clean items of clothing to stuff in his knapsack, he looked at what he had on, and decided he needed to change into something more suitable for a road trip. While his oversuspicious brain was already scrambling to decipher what Mitch Carson's motivation and intentions in reaching out to Harlan might be, he had to admit just getting out of the house and onto the road was the perfect anecdote to his months-long melancholy. A routine day of putzing around the house had just been transformed into a thrilling adventure behind the wheel of Veruca—his precious Volvo 244 DL—as they set out to christen their first road trip of spring together. And what good fortune, Ronald was thinking, having just had Franco down at Crested Butte Auto

Body rebuild the head gasket and overhaul the AC unit. Even without the monthly income, having bailed on his first and only teaching position, Ronald was glad to have been able to scrape enough cash together by selling some of his savings bonds so he could toss Franco the business. Just a few months earlier, the head mechanic and owner or the shop had mentioned to Ronald that times were tough, and he'd been feeling the winter financial pinch, what with needing to support his young family that centered around his son, a delightfully precocious three-year-old who was already the junior version of his pop's strapping self. Ronald would always harbor a soft spot for Franco Cavaletti because Franco Cavaletti had always been sweet on Ronald. From the time he'd taught Ronald how to drive, to the trial mechanic apprenticeship Franco provided Ronald after school when he was a young teen, to even letting a nothing-but-time-on-his-hands-Ronald shadow him at the shop to this day, as he tinkered on Ronald's Swedish import—the two shared an unusual bond.

Regardless of the tense circumstances that hastened the need for this sudden trip, Ronald was just excited to get Veruca back out on the open road. If he could get to his brother's place in time to steer the conversation away from anything incriminating, all the better.

PULLING AWAY FROM the house and not even halfway down the long driveway, Ronald's anxiety flipped into a palpitatingly high gear as he began to obsess over what exactly Harlan and Mitchell would find to talk about. The only topic they had in common was him!

His older brother hadn't been made privy to the scandalous chapter written out in flowery cursive between teacher and student. Ronald rarely bothered to keep his brother updated about his life, but the truth was that he hadn't confided in *anyone*. Mitch, on the other hand, might be capable of spilling the beans, possibly thinking Harlan already knew something about what had happened between them back in Stevensville.

Ronald's paranoia had not taken a break in ten years. Not once had he been lulled into believing he'd ever completely bury his whopper of a reckless past. Daily, all these years later, he still lived and breathed in fear, knowing there was always a chance his skeletons could spring out any second, like full-crazed jacks from an overwound box. Ronald pressed his foot on the accelerator and positioned ten fingers in a clamp-lock around the laced beige leather steering wheel cover. He mentally set his course for the Utah border and decided that from there he'd opt for the southern route, through Zion, Vegas, and then Bakersfield.

HARLAN HAD BEEN a dusting, vacuuming, tidying, and disinfecting Tasmanian Devil for the twenty-seven minutes that preceded the buzzer sounding in his second floor apartment. He identified with Tasmanian Devils, as he'd once bottle-fed enriched formula to an orphaned pup in a wildlife rehab centre on the outskirts of Hobart. The adorable and endangered creature had instantly become Harlan's spirit animal thanks to an Aboriginal woman from Wybalenna, who had explained to him that purininas were expert at establishing boundaries, keeping a low profile, and hiding in plain sight—traits Harlan felt described him to a T for Taz.

"Second floor, 2-0-5, end of the hall," Harlan said into the screened two-way talk box embedded slightly crooked in the white wall, before depressing a doorbell-like switch that unlocked the building's main door. He sucked in enough oxygen to fill two-and-a-half lungs and braced himself. He opened the door and stood in the arched threshold, half in and half out of his apartment, ironing the front panels of his white button-down shirt with his hands.

His guest crested the carpeted stairs and looked down the long hallway to the man who'd just waved. "Harlan?" he said with an outstretched hand as he approached. "Mitchell Carson. A supreme pleasure to finally meet you." The two started to shake hands but Mitchell used his to pull his host out of the doorway and into a quick hug. "I feel like I know you."

"Come in, come in," Harlan said, finding it awkward to hug a man wearing a backpack. He closed the apartment door and then led Mitchell down the hallway. He pointed to his left. "My bedroom." He gestured to his right. "Bathroom." When they reached the hallway's end, he motioned with both hands, sizing up his guest. "This is the living room. The sofa doesn't pull out into a bed, I'm sorry to say, but it should be long enough for you to stretch out comfortably." He pointed through the wide passageway. "The kitchen is through there."

Mitch hoisted the backpack off his shoulders and let it drop with a clunk to the worn wood parquet floor with a geometrical border inlay. "I can't tell you how much I appreciate your hospitality, Harlan. I promise not to be too much of a burden."

"It's no problem at all. Ronald has slept on that sofa plenty and never once complained. I'll pull out some sheets and pillows a little later when, you know, you're ready." Harlan clasped his hands together with a clap that startled his guest, who had just looked away to check out the bathroom.

"Sorry," Mitchell apologized. "I must still be a bit jumpy after getting— shall we say—relieved of my wallet in the Tenderloin this morning."

"Well, who wouldn't be?" Harlan sympathized while already doubting— on its face—a tale that seemed a tad too tall to be credible. "I hope you filed a police report about the mugging."

"I did," Mitchell lied, pulling a folded piece of official looking paper from his back pocket as a credibility earning prop. In fact, the paper was not a police report, but the receipt for his airfare back to Albuquerque. Mitchell didn't know why he'd just said that, except that he was embarrassed by what had happened and, on the spot, he'd just embellished the circumstances, so he wouldn't have to reveal how dumb he'd really been. He hadn't used the word *mugging*. Harlan did, but then Mitchell just went with it. He had been relieved of his wallet—this much was true—but from his own carelessness. He'd lost it as he rapidly extricated himself from circumstances he shouldn't have gotten himself into to begin with—especially during this dangerous day and age. He tucked the airline paperwork back in his pocket before quickly asking for a glass of water. He followed Harlan into the all-white kitchen saying, "Great place you have here."

"Rent-controlled . . . snug as a bug in a rug here for fourteen years now."

"Sweet," Mitchell said, looking around at the bare walls and seeing nothing personal to comment on. He carried the glass into the angled living room, gulping as he walked. He assessed the view outside the glass balcony door. "I need to get my bearings," he announced, trying to see around two giant rainbow flag banners attached to the streetlight just beyond the minuscule balcony. With the sun at its noon position in the sky, its rays streamed through the nylon flags, casting a slight stained-glass effect on the living room's white walls.

"Here," Harlan said, opening the balcony door. "I can orient you out here." He grabbed an oversized floppy straw hat from the closet; it looked like something one would win at a carnival by landing dimes into teacups and saucers. The two stepped outside, onto a balcony not much bigger than the floppy brim of the sun screening hat that Harlan kept by the door and had just donned. "That's Market Street on the left, and over here is Church

Street." He gestured, turning to the right. "Across the street is the Church Street Metro Stop. From there, you can get anywhere in the city."

Mitchell took it all in, noting the streetcar tracks embedded in the pavement and the overhead cables, which appeared anchored into the bricks of the apartment building another floor or so above their heads. A vertical, Art Deco neon sign with badly chipped blue paint spelled out SKYLINE in white block letters, with the *E* low enough for Mitchell to touch when he stretched his arm. "Does it still work?" he inquired, thinking what a cool feature that would be.

Harlan shook his head. "Not since I've been here." He paused, and then added, as if in consolation, "I think it would prevent you from sleeping in the living room if it did."

Just then, a sea-smelling breeze arrived, animating Mitchell's curly hair. He tilted his cleft chin upward and took a dramatic inhale through his perfectly sized nose. His youthful handsomeness and classically proportioned frame did not go unnoticed as it came into sunlit focus, but it seemed incongruous when crammed up against Harlan's slight paunch and balding pate. Sensing he was beginning to perspire, Harlan retreated inside the living room. In another two minutes, Mitchell followed. He started to shut the balcony door.

"You can leave it open," Harlan suggested, gesturing widely with open arms and somewhat of a graceful twist before he plopped down on his white blanket covered recliner. "Let some of that spring freshness indoors!"

"I can see you're theatrical, just like your brother," Mitchell said, smiling.

Harlan didn't know why he took offense to the comparison. "My brother and I are nothing alike, I can assure you."

"We'll see about that," Mitchell warned. He sounded presumptive, Harlan thought.

The sheer curtains ballooned into the living room on either side of Mitchell, who stood there like an archangel with gossamer wings. The illusion momentarily took Harlan's breath away. "Please," he said, fanning his face with his hand. "Make yourself at home."

Mitch plopped on the sofa opposite with his legs spread open as wide as you like. "So, you're the older brother." And with that, the interrogation began.

"By two years, one month, and seventeen days."

"And you both turned out gay." Mitchell was running through the things he'd been told.

"Apparently," Harlan answered somewhat conditionally. "It's not like we were Easter eggs that turned out pink instead of red due to a tablet mix-up at the Paas Factory—but yes, I identify as a homosexual. And I think that is what my brother feels he is—though he seldom wanders out of his closet to flaunt it."

"And you do?" Mitchell said. "Flaunt it, that is?"

Harlan shifted the weight from one butt cheek to the other. "I'm not the Grand Marshall of the Folsom Street Fair, but I will confess to having ridden on a Pride float or two in my younger days."

"Younger, as in last week?" Mitchell was flattering him. To Harlan, it seemed like maybe he was flirting. "I think you look fantastic for your age," he added, which Harlan, without further doubt, decided was flirting. "I see similarities between you and Ronald. But your brother's taller, though. I know he has always been taller than me and I'm five-ten, and I think I am a bit taller than you." He hopped to his feet. "Let's see!"

He urged Harlan up and out of his chair with an outstretched hand and Harlan complied. Mitchell took two strides forward, until he was standing an inch away from his host. His lips were even with the bridge of Harlan's nose. "Yep," Mitchell confirmed, but kept standing there, almost as if he were daring something to happen between them. Confused, Harlan took a step backward, knocking the wooden coffee table with the back of his calf.

Harlan decided to flip roles, and took over the questioning, to get his rump out of the hot seat. "Just what were you doing in the Tenderloin this morning, if you don't mind my asking?"

"Good question." Mitchell lowered himself back down on the sofa and had to concede he didn't have a great answer, though it was the truth. "I flew over from Albuquerque to, you know, check out the club scene. But when leaving the airport, I accidentally flirted with this sexy Euro-number on B.A.R.T." Mitchell paused, thinking it might be helpful to his story if he name-dropped an accomplice to the crime that wasn't a crime. "Lotár the Hungarian," he revealed. "Well, next thing I know, he invites me to his place. I abandon my better judgement and go with him. Long story short: it turns out he wasn't really my type. Or maybe I wasn't his. Anyway, though it was a cowardly move, I left this morning while he was sleeping, no doubt jetlagged after flying in from Budapest. What with my nerves shot and my internal compass all mixed up, I found myself wandering the Tenderloin."

This is where Mitchell dispensed with facts and improvised on Harlan's mugging scenario. "At the police station," he continued, "the desk officer asked if I knew anybody in the Bay Area to call. That's when I remembered Ronald telling me you lived in the Castro. Your last name is not very common." He inserted a short laugh. "Only one of you in the phonebook, it turns out. The officer let me use his desk phone and presto—here I am."

"That's true about the name. The majority of Simplemans live in Colorado. A few in Utah. Some in Missouri, maybe." Harlan was only remembering what he'd been told, since he didn't recall meeting blood relatives besides his grandparents, and they'd died early anyway. "I'm curious, though—how does one 'accidentally' flirt with somebody?"

It was a decent question if you didn't know Mitchell Carson, but his explanation made it sound innocent and wholesome and not the least bit manipulative. "Chalk it up to my gullible small-town rural ways, but I am just a friendly guy who makes eye contact and smiles too easily, I guess."

Harlan couldn't help but silently poke holes in the young man's façade of sincerity . He'd seen good-looking men like Mitchell before, the kind with too much swagger and confidence to pull off innocence, so he had reasons to doubt. "I can see how a pretty boy like you could get into a lot of trouble in a city as horny and testosterone charged as San Francisco. Coming from Albuquerque though, which is a decent size city with a university, you must know about AIDS, I'd assume.

Mitchell shifted on the sofa cushion. "I watch and read the news, so I guess I know what's publicly known—which isn't much at this point, is it? I know Rock Hudson died from it last October. But no one I know personally has gotten it or become sick yet."

Harlan was no authority, but as the elder of the two he felt obligated to deliver a cautionary message from someone who should know better but maybe didn't. "I guess I would say it's important to know your sexual partners, keep in contact with them, and use condoms for everything. At least until we know more."

"Condoms for *everything?*" Mitchell winced, remembering the clumsily dangerous hook-up he'd engaged in last night. "I gag on latex," he confessed not able to disguise the renewed panic that might be showing on his face. He'd started to realize, earlier that morning, that he might have screwed up by having sex with somebody he did not know. That was about the time he'd also discovered he'd lost or rather, forgotten his wallet.

"Better to gag than die from giving a blowjob, wouldn't you agree?" Harlan said.

There was a minute of silence, and then Harlan patted his palms on his thighs. "Do you need some cash?" He didn't know why he was asking this question, which only obligated him further. But it sounded like something his brother would have offered for this emergency.

Mitchell appeared to blush. "I would be immeasurably grateful for a meal ticket the next two days—until my return flight to Albuquerque. It's a big ask, but I promise I won't be a huge bother or eat all that much."

"Help yourself to anything in the fridge and cupboards. I'm not cut out for the nightclub and disco scene, but I would be happy to spot you forty or fifty bucks, so you get the chance to experience what you came here for."

Mitchell placed the palm of his right hand over his heart, still stewing that he may have taken on more than he bargained for when booking this spur-of-the-moment getaway. "I will mail you a personal check the second I get back to Albuquerque. Your brother, I'm sure, will vouch for me."

"He already has, as a matter of fact. He's on his way here as we speak—driving from Colorado, hoping to catch you before you leave." At first, Harlan's guest seemed astonished by this news, but then he rebounded.

"Bonus!" Mitchell exclaimed. "Two Simpleman Brothers for the price of one mugging! Must be my lucky day." Harlan smiled, getting up to retrieve his billfold and a set of spare keys.

RONALD FOLLOWED THE bypass route to get around Las Vegas, drafting behind a semi-truck that was already exceeding the posted speed limit in what seemed to be their shared race for the California border. Veruca hummed like a hive-bound queen bee as the odometer spun closer to the 150,000-mile mark that he expected to hit at some point on this trip. He always looked forward to the stretch of road through the Mojave Desert before it joined Interstate 40, but his late start meant it would be well after midnight before he crossed into California. He'd stop in the desert for some shuteye, but he also hoped to do some stargazing which should be optimal if the skies remained clear.

He had wondered at least once every other mile how things between Harlan and Mitchell were progressing. He hadn't told his brother anything about his former student, but he couldn't remember telling Mitchell anything about Harlan, either. Yet somehow Mitchell knew that Harlan lived in the Castro. Ronald banked on a hope that Mitchell wasn't the grudge-carrying, revenge-seeking type. It was possible, or he would have exposed him before now for what he'd done—or rather, for what he'd allowed to happen. Either way, Ronald preferred to keep his family out of this.

It was 12:47 in the morning when he crossed into California.

AROUND THE SAME time, Mitchell was weaving his way back to Harlan's apartment, after a night of blowing off steam at several gay bars and dance clubs along Polk Street, between Nob Hill and the Tenderloin.

He'd intentionally gone back to the Tenderloin on the lookout for Lotár, hoping to retrieve his wallet and downgrade his panic over their unprotected romp by learning that Lotár was healthy and not all that promiscuous. But the Hungarian was nowhere to be found. He was not at The Eagle—a notorious leather bar Mitchell had a feeling Lotár probably frequented. He was not at Club Uranus or in its raunchier backroom, The EndUp. And he was not at the I-Beam over on Haight Street, where a drag queen had talked him into sharing a cab so she could catch the last set of a concert by The Flaming Lips.

At one of these establishments (Mitchell had become too buzzed on comped drinks to remember which one) he'd pocketed a safe-sex kit, albeit a day late when the night before he'd been a condom short. The kit, shoved down the front of his jeans by one of the roller-skating Sisters of Perpetual Indulgence who had been making her rounds on eight wheels, consisted of a plastic baggie that contained lube in what looked like two ketchup packets, a tear-off strip of three condoms, and a printed list of dos and don'ts with a hotline number.

Mitchell didn't want to wake his host, and yet he hoped Harlan was still up. He wanted someone to talk to or make out with. He'd spent all evening curating that mood, and Harlan would fit the post-closing-time bill.

With his limited barhopping and cruising experience, Mitchell's go-to hunting technique had been to pick out weaker, less attractive men who had their own confidence issues or physical burdens to overcome. Whether it was depression, weight, age, a crooked nose, bad skin, or hair loss, these gave Mitchell a slight edge along with a boost of confidence. Sure, he had vanquished his cancers for now, but not without sustaining some hefty mental and physical battle scars that rendered him self-conscious for the first time in his life. To keep his high ground advantage, he needed to lower the bar on his conquests. This way, he could always dominate, as the closer-to-but-still-less-than-perfect specimen.

Stunned—having not scored a take-down at the bars this night, but refusing to accept his Darwinist predator-prey approach had let him down—Mitchell ambled back to the Church Street apartment building—licking his lips—sensing that Harlan might make a nice consolation prize. What with Harlan's advanced age, pudgy tummy, and balding head, he certainly met all the criteria. Mitchell not so quietly turned the key in the door and entered the apartment, which was darkened save for the one table lamp in the triangular living room. It had been left on, illuminating a stack of white sheets, a pillow, a fresh bath towel, and a washcloth.

He slipped off his shoes and tiptoed past Harlan's partially closed bedroom door, waiting for his eyes to adjust in the shadows. He didn't hear snoring. That didn't mean Harlan was awake, but he proceeded with setting the bait. He grabbed the towel and washcloth, and by the glow of a plug-in night light next to the sink, with the bathroom door open wide, he peeled off one clothing item after another, until he was gloriously naked. He calculated that Harlan's sightlines would be aligned perfectly; that is, if he were awake. Mitchell momentarily disappeared behind the white shower curtain and soaped and rinsed himself into an undefeatable erection. When he drew back the shower curtain, Harlan was standing in the bathroom doorway wearing only his checkered pajama bottoms.

"I was just checking to make sure you made it back safely," Harlan stuttered as Mitchell's hard-on sprung out from under the towel he'd confidently raised to see-saw dry his backside.

"Oh, hi there, Harlan." Mitchell tried to sound nonchalant as he continued the show and continued springing his trap. He saw in the dim lighting that his host had begun tenting inside his PJs. "I hope you don't mind my—"

"Boner?" Harlan said.

"Yes, that too." Mitchell grinned, making no attempt to cover up. He strode across the white tiled floor and grabbed Harlan by the crotch. "Seems like you've brought a sword to a pillow fight."

Harlan couldn't disguise the shock on his face and his own erection would have betrayed any protest he tried to mount anyway. A grin broke across his normally taciturn face when Mitchell didn't let go or loosen his grip. "I could invite you to my bed before I banish you to the couch, but I don't think I'm your type," he said, giving his guest what he thought was an escape hatch. But his house guest just growled, taking the self-deprecation as proof his host was positively devourable. That was the tell he was after.

"Lead the way," Mitchell commanded.

AFTER TURNING OFF the car, Ronald couldn't get comfortable enough to fall asleep behind the steering wheel, even when reclining in the driver's seat. He exited the vehicle, walked around Veruca's boxy hood, and got back in the car on the passenger's side. He moved the seat back as far as it would go, and when he reclined, it was horizontal paradise. A three-dimensional-looking Milky Way spanned the buggy windshield from side to side and after counting three shooting stars, Ronald drifted into a deep nap.

Half an hour later, his subconscious mind woke him out of a nightmare in which Mitch Carson was screwing his brother. Ronald promptly got back into the driver's seat and back on the road, to drive the dream out of his cranium, and the early morning wood out of his pants.

AFTER A BRIEF oral exchange, Mitchell grew impatient. He ached to cum after being deprived of the release twenty-four hours earlier. He suggested Harlan roll over and Harlan was already obediently in motion when he remembered the advice he'd given earlier. "You'll need to use a condom."

"And I have one," Mitchell exclaimed, bounding off to the bathroom to fish his safe-sex kit out of his jeans pocket. When he returned to bed, Harlan was on all fours, his fuzzy ass cheeks shaking in anticipation of the first penetrative sex he'd had since this AIDS scare had surfaced.

"You're big. I'm going to be tight. It's been a coon's age." Harlan rattled off his disclaimers.

Mitchell struggled with the first condom, putting it on inside out in the dark. The second one broke as he too eagerly stretched it down toward his base. "The third time's the charm," he mumbled out loud as he inflated the latex ballon with air. Then, without fanfare and with more aggression than may have been required or appreciated, he stormed past Harlan's well-guarded outer gate. Entrance gained, he wiggled to get further inside, completely tuning out his host's groaning objections.

"Wait, wait, wait!" Harlan said, clenching the life out of Mitchell's pulsating staff while he struggled to adjust and give the pain a minute to subside. But Mitchell couldn't wait and he rammed his rod past Harlan's prostate seven or eight thrusts before ejaculating inside the condom inside the ass of his teacher's brother. Harlan panted. Mitchell convulsed some and then pulled out more suddenly than he'd shoved in. "Whoa, whoa, whoa!" Harlan said, bearing down with every muscle and trying unsuccessfully to slow the withdrawal. Then he collapsed onto the white duvet like Bambi on a frozen pond.

"Thank you. I needed that," Mitchell declared with a modicum of gratitude, ignoring anything that Harlan might have needed from the exchange.

On the way out of his host's bedroom, his pushy apartment guest had the gall to add, "Your brother never let me do that to him. And you want to know something? I think I've wanted a piece of Simpleman tail since I was a kid!"

JUST BEFORE SUNRISE and maybe fifty minutes southeast of Bakersfield, an antelope loped over the barbwire fence in a single bound and crossed the two westbound lanes of Interstate 40, just seconds in front of Veruca's approaching bumper. Ronald had seen this *Wild Kingdom* moment unfolding from the corner of his eye and pumped the brakes so as not to skid. He couldn't tell if the animal had made it clear across the two lanes of morning traffic, but his heart continued to thump long after the close call. With another good five hours to cover, he stopped for gas and a stale muffin at the next exit that had services, trying to calm the anxiety that had been building up inside him since his brother's phone call.

HARLAN WOKE UP in a grouchy mood, his apartment still under siege by a visitor that now had something he could lord over him. Behind the closed door of his bathroom, he extracted the used condom out of the waste basket with the ends of two pinched fingers and held it and its milky contents up to the vanity light. His fascination was fleeting, so he dropped the evidence into the flushing toilet, hoping it wouldn't clog up the building's testy plumbing. Not caring if he awakened the satiated stranger snoring away on his sofa, he padded into the kitchen in his slippers to make his first morning cup of cardamon coffee. When Mitchell yawned demonstratively—no doubt for attention—Harlan met him in the living room.

"Good morning, Mitchell," he said firmly. "Listen, I'd appreciate it very much if you never mentioned to my brother what transpired between us last night." Mitchell held up his palms, indicating he wouldn't even think about it, but Harlan wasn't finished. "My brother, whether you know it or not, fell in love with you once. It would destroy him and our already tenuous relationship if he were to learn that I'd betrayed him in this way."

Mitchell's eyebrows arched into his bed hair. "You think what happened last night was a betrayal? I think it was organic and beautiful. I was just about to thank you again—"

Harlan cut him off mid-platitude. "I have a heavy day of manuscript editing ahead of me with a publisher breathing down my back, so I will be at the computer in my bedroom for most of the day. I expect Ronnie will arrive sometime around noon. Maybe the three of us can grab some Chinese later. Do I have your word that what happened between us will stay between us?"

"Uh, sure. You have my word, Harlan." Mitchell looked dejected but Harlan could tell it was for show by what Mitchell said next. "I was going to suggest we maybe have, you know, a round two this morning. But it sounds now like that is off the table?"

Pacifist Harlan could have punched him in the face.

"That is indeed off the table," Harlan said sternly. "Deadlines, I'm afraid."

"Oh, well. Them's the breaks, I guess. I think I blew through my supply of condoms last night anyway." Mitchell flopped his torso back down on the sofa bedding and pulled the sheet over his rejected self. There was a first time for everything, he was forced to concede, pivoting his young body a quarter turn toward the sofa, to try to fall back asleep.

MITCHELL WAS SUNNING shirtless in shorts on the balcony when the apartment buzzer sounded. Harlan had fallen asleep sitting at his computer desk in the middle of revising his step-by-step instructions on browning and deep-frying tofu.

Ronald had arrived, using his own key to access the building and apartment. The brothers exchanged almost impersonal quick hugs as Mitchell came inside from the balcony, looking beefier and more studly than Ronald remembered. "Careful out there," Ronald cautioned, pointing to Mitchell's abdomen. "You're sunburning your surgical scar."

Eyes still adjusting to the comparative dimness of the living, Mitchell glanced down at what looked like a red-hot zipper holding in all his guts. "Sort of the opposite of what I was hoping for," he admitted, and then opened his arms for an embrace.

In those youthful, muscled arms, Ronald Simpleman sensed the reactivation of everything he'd felt for the boy who'd become a man before his eyes. He hadn't gotten over him. Given the emotional jolt he experienced every time they reunited, perhaps he never would. "It's darn good to see you again, Mitch."

"Mr. Simpleman," his former student teased, not appreciating or respecting that the formal greeting came across as another twist of the guilt knife in Ronald's back. Ronald had worked to desensitize himself to this, but each time it made him wonder if Mitch was speaking out of habit or a retributive impulse. Feeling his brother's judgemental stare, Ronald pulled out of the lingering embrace.

In a congratulatory tone, Ronald said, "I see you two survived your first night as roommates"—though their awkward body language seemed to suggest the contrary. But there they were, the three of them, in the triangular living room, just looking at each other. "I need to empty my bladder," Ronald announced, to break the tension, before departing for the bathroom. Once the bathroom door shut, Mitchell mouthed the words to Harlan, *It will be okay.*

When Ronald emerged after a long and audible evacuation in the white-tiled bathroom, he suggested his legs could use a stretch and that he and Mitch could take a walk around the neighborhood and leave Harlan alone to work on his cookbook for an hour or two.

"Bring back Chinese takeout." Harlan directed. "Let's eat in tonight."

Mitchell pulled on a *UNM Go Lobos* t-shirt over his head, half tucking it into the band of his cherry-red and very short shorts. He laced up his matching Reebok tennis shoes. He was following the dress code of John, his on-again, off-again boyfriend (who happened to be on the Lobo Cheerleaders squad at the University of New Mexico) by wearing his left-behind clothes in mourning over their latest in a series of breakups.

Ronald left his knapsack next to the sofa, which raised the question about the evening's sleeping arrangements. But nothing was said, and nothing was decided.

Harlan, meanwhile, took the moment to pull his wits together. Even after Ronald and Mitch left the apartment, he heard them chatting all the way down the hallway. And he could still hear his brother's deep voice as they passed under the balcony, rounding the corner to head up Market Street.

"I'M GLAD WE are walking in this direction," Mitchell said, putting a hand on Ronald's trouble shoulder. "You don't need to show me Polk Street. I think I dipped my toes in every gay watering hole this side of Nob Hill last night."

"I would have suspected that after dark when the vampires came out, a young stud muffin like you might have been eaten—or might have been sucked—alive!"

"I ate loads of garlic at dinner and wore a crucifix, just to be sure." Despite his joke, Mitchell was still internally wrestling with the possibility that he'd already exposed himself to something far more ferocious than vampires. The thought of the unprotected sex he'd had with Lotár the Hungarian was enough to make his knees buckle, and not in a good way. Lotár had done to Mitchell what Mitchell had done to Harlan—only rougher, and without a rubber. "You can't be too careful with this AIDS thing going around," Mitchell said now—more to scold himself after the fact than to demonstrate common sense, which he had obviously lacked.

This did not illicit a response, and the two men walked half a city block before Ronald piped up. "It feels good to be stretching the ol' legs." He started to whistle a tune from the radio that had been stuck inside his head since he'd merged onto Interstate 5, west of Bakersfield.

"Dionne Warwick?"

"'That's What Friends Are For,'" Ronald confirmed. While is hadn't been intentional, Ronald elected to use this opening to explore whether his friendship still meant something to Mitchell. He walked sideways as he posed a question. "Was this trip of yours something that popped up at the last minute? I would have loved to have known ahead of time so I could have been here from the start. You know, for a longer visit and the chance to have more time together."

Warning bells began clanging inside Mitchell's slightly hungover head. In high school, he'd always been vigilant when it came to downplaying his teacher's attention and denying the accusations from his classmates, and even his parents, that he was Mr. Simpleman's pet student. To fend off the bullying and peer pressure, Mitchell had cowardly and callously brushed off his teacher in public, often joining in on the taunting and nasty rumor-spreading about the quirky, oddball faculty member. As Mitchell rationalized this now, it had been a matter of teen survival in that tiny town of cowboys with their country mouths full of crooked-teeth, but to this day, he felt ashamed by his behavior and wished he had been braver. But then, he might have been painted with the same tar brush as Mr. Simpleman and not only could that have gotten him killed, it nearly had during his sophomore year. Mitch Carson had had his own boogeymen to fight off and outsmart. He could spare not one of his self-preservation tactics defending anybody else.

Since he'd graduated high school and left his own Montana trauma behind, Mitch had found it easier to keep his former teacher at arm's length through neglect and silence. He didn't know how to be Ronald's friend now that he was an adult, when he still found it awkward and uncomfortable even being on a first-name basis.

"Totally spur of the moment," Mitchell answered at last, hoping to avoid further questions.

A shirtless, moustached, and nicely bearded muscle man in torn, knee-cap-exposing Levi 501s walked toward them on the sidewalk. Ronald watched Mitch's head pivot like a great horned owl to reciprocate the overt cruise he'd just received. In fact, Mitchell had been puffing his chest and slowing his pace for half a block. The muscle man, looking backward but continuing to walk forward, stumbled over his own feet.

Ronald had long ago accepted that men weren't tripping over their feet to get to *him*. He didn't have a face that turned heads or stopped traffic. But Mitch Carson had those assets in spades—Ronald had been tripping over his own feet to get in line for the man's affection since back when the man was a kid.

They crossed 16th Street after waiting for an F-Line streetcar to clear the intersection. Feeling road-weary and heart-wounded, Ronald switched into tour guide mode, just like his father always did. "We're coming up on Castro Street," he announced in megaphone mode. "We could stop at Café San Marcos or at the Twin Peaks Tavern if you're thirsty."

"Hair of the dog has never been an effective remedy for me. It's probably best I lay off drinking after last night. Unless you were suggesting a lemonade or tomato juice."

Ronald wanted to sympathize but also enjoyed this toned-down version of Mitch Carson. Maybe he could match Mitch's energy and even keep up with him for the first time in their mismatched relationship. "And here is the Castro Theatre, the last of the great movie palaces left in the city. It was built in the 1920s and seats 1,400. 800 downstairs and 600 in the balcony."

"Ah, the 1920s? Betcha Rudolph Valentino silent movies were shown in here, then."

"Possibly. The theater opened in 1922, and Valentino died in . . . what? 1926?"

"August 23." Mitchell fancied himself a budding Valentino authority ever since a medium at the New Mexico State Fair had done a reading and came to the opinion that Mitchell could well be the silent film star's reincarnation. From that five-dollar revelation from the spirit realm on, Mitchell had sought every book and magazine he could get his hands on, to learn everything he could about what might have been his previous life. Mitchell shielded his eyes from the sun as he studied the ornate plaster scrolling that arched over the elongated window another story above the marquis. "His most famous movie, *The Sheik*, came out in '21, a year before this theater opened. But *Blood and Sand* and *Beyond the Rocks* both came out in '22. *Monsieur Beaucaire* and *A Sainted Devil* were released in '24, then *The Eagle* came out in '25, followed by *The Son of the Sheik* in '26. But don't get me started!" Mitchell laughed.

"That's darn impressive," Ronald replied, his eyes wide, before veering back to the only line of questioning that mattered to him during this reconnaissance. "Are you dating anybody these days?"

"It's complicated, Ron." Mitchell stalled, scuffing his foot back and forth on the sidewalk, reluctant as ever to be idle. "After cancer and returning to university in Albuquerque I returned to working at that off-campus Burger King on Central Avenue—got my kicks on Route 66, you know. Next thing I know, I fell hard in love with one of my fast-food managers."

"Oh yeah? What's he like?" Ronald tried to sound interested instead of wounded.

Mitchell looked Ronald in the eyes to judge his sincerity before organizing his thoughts in a way so that he could deliver the short version. "His name's John. He's a year older than me—taller, athletic, built. Just all around gorgeous, really. And he's totally out of my league. He's on the UNM Lobos cheerleading squad." Mitchell paused to showcase the Lobos ensemble he was wearing. "I already had this suspicion and, you know, just crazy jealousy that he might be cheating on me when he travelled out of town for the away games. Turns out I was much more naïve than I realized at the time. That's what I mean when I say it's complicated."

"This story sounds familiar. Is it possible this is the same guy that you'd just broken up with when I visited you in Albuquerque a few years back?"

"More than possible," Mitchell said, embarrassed, even ashamed, to be telling the same sad broken heart story and to admit in the telling that he hadn't been able to move beyond this first love.

Wanting to break Mitchell's trance before losing him to a funk, Ronald said, "This is Dog Eared Books, by the way. They've promised Harlan they will prominently feature his vegetarian cookbook in this front window display."

Ronald sensed that Mitchell was hurting and felt an obligation to both listen and to care. But he also wanted to be the one to pick up the pieces and put his Humpty Dumpty back together again. "I interrupted," he said, apologetically. "Go ahead. Did something new happen between you and John?" He hoped he didn't sound hopeful.

Mitchell inflated his cheeks to exhale dramatically. "My best friend, Sam—he came over to our apartment while John was away in Las Cruces—the Lobos were playing New Mexico State for the Western Athletic Conference championship title, if I remember correctly. Sam pulls this videotape out of his book bag and says—'if you have a VCR, I think you should see this.'" Mitchell stopped on the sidewalk, lowering his head with eyes closed. Ronald stopped, too. Mitchell slowly raised his head, opening his eyes to stare straight ahead at nothing. "It was a gay porn movie called *The Cockeyed Eagle*. Co-starring my John, who goes by the stage name of Jason Ross!"

"You've got to be kidding!" Ronald said, while committing the movie title to memory.

"I wish I were, believe me. But that's not his only adult film. It's the only video that Sam could get his hands on, but there are others." Mitchell counted them out on his fingers. "Let's see . . . there's *Bedtime Stories*, *Headstruck*, *Fetish*, and Sam's favorite, *Stranded: Enemies and Lovers*."

"That's unreal," Ronald exclaimed. Thinking it would be impossible to recall all these titles later, he added, "What did you say his stage name was again?"

"Jason Ross," Mitchell supplied, already presuming Ronald would do some digging on his own. "It was a mortal blow, finding that out—so we broke up a few weeks ago, though, and this is interesting, John says he wants to start dating me again, and that his so-called acting days are behind him."

The pair crossed the rainbow painted crosswalks at 19th Street.

Ronald probed. "So, are you thinking about dating this guy again?"

"Yeah. I'm taking a break right now, but John's unique. He's my first post-cancer boyfriend—the first man to accept the surgically altered version of me." Mitchell patted his chest twice for affirmation and punctuation.

"He's got me following this bodybuilding regimen at the campus gym where the Lobo cheerleaders and football players all work out. That's been a good confidence builder for me. Besides, it's impossible to walk away from your first love."

Ronald didn't need to be convinced of that, since he was walking alongside his at that moment. It did sting to hear Mitch's declaration of love for another, but he latched onto the technicality that Mitch was taking a reflective break and seemed open to options. This could be an opening—even an opportunity—to pitch the plethora of benefits that came with dating a more mature man.

Ronald stopped Mitchell with his arm at 575 Castro Street, his feet framing the commemorative brass plaque embedded in the sidewalk. "This is the site of Castro Camera—the business that Harvey Milk opened in 1972." Mitchell's eyebrows revealed he was drawing a blank at the name. "Don't tell me you don't know who Harvey Milk was!" Ronald said. "Harvey Milk was the Mayor of Castro Street in the early 70s. He was an activist who pushed for gay rights, and he advocated for gay businesses and building up gay power. He was elected San Francisco City Supervisor in 1976—the first out and openly gay elected official in California."

"This sounds familiar," Mitchell said, encouraging his teacher to continue.

"Being a gay politician made him a target, and on November 27, 1978, Harvey was assassinated, along with the real mayor of San Francisco, George Moscone. They were shot dead in their City Hall offices by another supervisor, Dan White. I happened to have been on the grounds outside the building the morning it happened."

"Right!" Mitchell's lightbulb flashed on, finally. "The Twinkie Defense. I remember now. Wasn't he an ex-cop who blamed his outrage on eating too much junk food?"

"Yes. And that defense worked on the judge and jury. After being released from his short prison sentence, Dan White supposedly committed suicide. But people have their suspicions about that."

"Supposedly?" Mitchell scrunched his face into a question mark.

Ronald lobbed his arm over the back of Mitchell's broad shoulders and continued to walk them down the block. "It just seemed odd—and maybe a bit too convenient—that he would get away scot-free with murdering two public officials, be heralded as a hero for killing a fag and the liberal gay-loving mayor, and then just . . . kill himself." Mitchell allowed Ronald's arm to stay, as he was being guided, and the older man relished the contact as he continued. "I am not alone in thinking that his suicide may have been a coverup and that the guy is living under an assumed name, probably running a bed and breakfast in some little town up on the Oregon Coast."

"Sounds like a great premise for a novel," Mitchell said, getting on board with the conspiracy twist.

The pair crossed Castro at 19th Street and walked, arm over shoulder, in silent contemplation toward Kite Hill, which rose before them in the distance. That's when Ronald recalled a nifty nearby feature that he'd been introduced to during his time at Stanford. "You up for a little climb and a big thrill?"

"Sure!"

They quickened their pace to attack the elevation with gusto. Within two blocks, after zigzagging through the Noe Valley neighborhood, they reached the foot of the Seward Street Slides. Mitchell gazed up the winding, steep, and high-banked concrete channels. Ronald quickly sorted through a short stack of discarded cardboard pieces next to the sandbox landing pit at the bottom of the chutes, picking out two of the longest and handing one to Mitchell.

"Now, we climb some more!" he shouted with exuberance, leading the charge up the stairs parallel to the slides. Checking out the polished concrete channels reminded Mitchell of the giant humped metal slide that had been erected behind the Buttrey Suburban Shopping Center in Missoula, near where he'd grown up. There, they'd used burlap bags instead of cardboard.

Ronald was using the railing to pull himself up while Mitchell jogged past him athletically, taking the steps two, sometimes three at a time. Out of breath by the time they'd reached the top, Ronald realized it would have been wiser to avoid an activity that highlighted their age difference. His words rushed out between inhales. "If memory serves, the yellow track is the fastest. I'll take the red and we can race each other."

Mitchell accepted the challenge enthusiastically.

Ducking their heads to get under the trio of half-red, half-yellow painted pipe arches that heralded their adventure, the two grown men positioned their pieces of cardboard at the start of each concrete channel and then climbed aboard their magic carpets. Ronald curled the excess cardboard at his feet to grab it with both hands like a toboggan and the ever-attentive Mitchell mimicked his teacher.

"On your mark," Ronald said, still out of breath. "Get set . . . GO!"

After a couple of butt scootches, they were over the edge. The vertical race lasted all but five seconds. The thrill was short, and there had been no clear winner, but their laughter outlasted the ride. Mitchell threw his arms around Ronald and pulled him into what Ronald interpreted as an affectionate embrace. "Should we do it again?" Mitchell pleaded.

"You go," Ronald encouraged. "Try tossing a little sand under your cardboard this time." With that advice, Mitchell bounded back up the stairs and was back down again in a whoosh.

Deciding they'd worked up their appetites, they made a beeline for the Red Jade Chinese Restaurant, walking first down 18th Street before turning left on Church. Ronald pointed out the gay bars along the way—Moby Dick, The Badlands, the Men's Room, Francine's. Mitchell realized he'd missed this part of the gay strip when he'd gone hunting for his Hungarian in the Tenderloin the night before.

At the restaurant, which was directly across the street from the entrance to Harlan's apartment building, they placed their takeout order. Harlan and Ronald always ordered the same thing at the Red Jade—fried fish with sweet peppers for Ronald, Vegetarian Delight for Harlan, with an order of egg-fried rice to share. Mitchell selected the house special eggplant and an order of eggrolls. "Make those vegetarian eggrolls," he added, picking up that Harlan might be vegetarian, given the cookbook he was writing. He wanted to make a peace offering.

It was quiet in the restaurant while they waited for their order to be prepared, and Mitchell chose that moment to bring up a most delicate subject for him—one he'd tried unsuccessfully to broach before. "Ronald, I know I've asked you this, but in case I'm not able to fall out of love with my cheerleader and apparent porn star, I am maybe a little more sensitive about it." He swiveled his open legs around on his barstool to face the older man. "That series of nude photos and the video you took of me in Missoula . . . I really would like to get them and the negatives back from you." He saw Ronald squirm on his barstool. "And before you try and tell me you don't have them anymore—I know you better than to buy that."

"Well, now . . ." There was a tone of protest in Ronald's voice.

"Try to understand this from my perspective," Mitchell said, holding out his palms to layout his case and show that he had nothing up his sleeves. "I've taken this moral high ground with my boyfriend, John—or ex-boyfriend, whatever, you know, over his choice to parade naked on screen. It would make me the biggest hypocrite in America if he ever came across naked photos of me out there in the universe."

"I'll have a look again when I get back home, but you should know by now that I would never share any photos of you, even if I did have them." Ronald tried to assure him, but knew, all the while, exactly where he'd stashed his private collection. It included more evidence of their intimacy than Mitch Carson likely knew.

"Well, if you'd look again," Mitchell entreated, "I would be most relieved to have these destroyed or under my safekeeping." He reached out his right hand so they could shake on it. Ronald couldn't resist the chance to touch the object of his affection. He promised he'd have a look.

"Say, if you don't mind me asking," Ronald volleyed his next inquiry over the net of tension that seemed to have gotten strung up between them. Mitchell consented with his eyes. "Did anything ever happen between you and that backwoods-looking upperclassman who sat behind you in that American Literature class I taught during your sophomore year . . . you know, the kid that died in that gun accident?"

At first Mitchell faked drawing a blank. He knew exactly who his teacher was referring to but had mostly dulled the brunt of the trauma through therapy. "Stan Cockburn?"

"Yes. His name had slipped my memory."

"He raped me, Ron, in the back of his pick-up. That was the night he shot himself."

Ronald felt the wind rush out of his body at the same time the blood flushed from his brain.

"You were there?" Mitchell nodded. "Raped you . . . how?"

"He'd driven me out by the airport. We had just started messing around in the front seat and he suggested we climb into that canopy cover he had on the back of his truck; no mattress or foam pad, just a dirty blanket and at least the one gun." Mitchell sucked in a breath. "It started out okay. There was a little roughhousing, but then he overpowered me, forced his way inside me, held his greasy hand over my mouth and told me he'd kill me if I told anyone. *That's* how."

Ronald's eyes were stuck open large, and he couldn't get words to come out of his gaping mouth. He'd had a bad feeling about that Stan Cockburn. He'd heard and read things about him in the school records that he could have warned Mitch about but didn't. "I'm sorry, Mitch," he said, looking into eyes that contained a tear each that Mitch was refusing to let go.

The Red Jade hostess arrived at the bar, passing them two brown paper bags. "*Tài Xie xiè nǐ le,*" she said—which Ronald and Mitchell assumed must have been *thank you* in Mandarin.

THEIR THREE-WAY DINNER conversation was an awkward mess, with two of them trying to pretend that something that had happened, hadn't.

When Harlan excused himself from the table to retreat to his bedroom under the pretense that he needed to continue working on his cookbook, Ronald and Mitchell did the dishes, shoulder occasionally touching shoulder. Keeping their voices low so as not to disturb the vegetarian genius at work, they tended to their bedding arrangements for the evening's slumber party. Mitchell insisted Ronald take the couch, and he opted for the inch-thick foam exercise mat that Harlan had left out.

After Ronald's epic drive and Mitchell's night of clubbing, there was no need to negotiate lights out for an early bedtime. Having stripped down to nothing but the sheet he hoisted up to just below his navel, Mitchell lay on his back, waiting, hands behind his head and eyes wide open. Despite the disclaimer about an early bedtime, he'd assumed that he and Ronald would have sex, since they'd never avoided it before, but so far, neither of them made the move.

After twenty minutes, Mitchell started to doze off, but then felt a soft hand placed over his mouth and another hand slip under the sheet bunched up at his waist. He lay still as a statue, wanting to giggle or groan. In the dark, he couldn't be certain which Simpleman was making the moves on him. But when the back of Mitchell's hand brushed a very hairy chest, he reached with confidence for Ronald's erection.

"Say," Mitchell whispered in Ronald's left ear. "Do you know you are almost twice as large as your brother?" He squeezed for emphasis.

Ronald did know.

Harlan knew too.

ALBUQUERQUE, NEW MEXICO

September 1984

THERE WERE FEW THINGS RONALD LOVED MORE THAN a long, hot shower, and this one was feeling especially euphoric to him. For a man in the final years of his thirties, last night could not have been a more triumphant comeback.

Ronald was putting his self-sabotaged life back together. For the first time in several years, he sensed something positive and new. Mitch Carson had summoned him. He hadn't had to fabricate an excuse or dangle some fancy lure—like the return of the photos that Mitch often bugged him about—to draw the younger man into the open. Mitch was the one who'd made the overture and only for the second time since that first time when he'd been the conniving fifteen-year-old who made the moves on his teacher under the most tempestuous of circumstances. Mitch had come on strong back then but seemed to be pulling away ever since, that is, until he'd surprised Ronald with a telephone call a few weeks back. Of course, Ronald saw this call as an opening and a chance to train his bellows on the embers he'd kept glowing—like the sacred flame between Olympiads—just in case. Last evening's opening ceremony had been dazzling, rendering him love-dizzy. The pair had never spent a whole night together and Mitch hadn't pulled away when Ronald spooned him from behind. As Mitch drifted off in his arms, his back pressed against his teacher's hairy torso and emitting the most adorable low, rumbling snore, Ronald felt that this moment alone had vindicated his crazed dedication to lugging the Olympic torch for Mitch Carson all these years.

He felt so giddy and buoyant after a night of what he'd interpreted as lovemaking that it seemed like every skin cell was tingling and being tickled by the shower's conical spray. Then he realized—with a slight delay and a slap to his forehead—that the tingling could have been caused by Mitch's fancy, expensively scented soap bar he'd just placed back in the grate-lidded, ceramic dish, which was rendered in a crème de menthe shade that matched the shower curtain, the towels, the bath rugs, the waste basket, and the toothbrush holder in Mitch's off-campus apartment bathroom.

The last of the soap suds rinsed clean from his thick chest hair and raced down his equally hairy legs and between his hairy toes to disappear down the drain. Whiffs of the handsome fragrance delighted his nostrils. He didn't want this indulgence to end. He had never used conditioner on his hair—he never understood the point of it—but since the matching bottle was sitting on the sill of the frosted window next to the shampoo, and the hot water hadn't yet run out, he decided to give it a try.

While leaving the conditioner in his hair for the label-recommended five minutes, Ronald pondered his own immediate future, which seemed appropriate after spending half the previous night helping Mitchell sort his. It seemed premature to forecast blue skies ahead, he supposed, but could the storm clouds that had menaced his horizon these past many years be starting to dissipate? He didn't know why else he was feeling chipper, even hopeful again.

In the high-stakes poker game he'd been playing with Mitch, Ronald—the gambler with the most to lose—had always come up short, consistently pulling the wild card from a deck he hadn't stacked. His fellow gambler had also faced down the odds and assumed some modicum of risk, but unlike Ronald, he never seemed to go all in, waging his life, his reputation, and his career for a less than sure-fire bet.

At only twenty-two, Mitch was likely still too immature, inexperienced and self-focused and possibly would never see it this way, but from the start, he'd been playing and manipulating Ronald Simpleman to get what he wanted or needed from him in the moment. It would have taken a calculator to count the number of times Mitch had over played this card. For his part and from that same starting point, Ronald, who should have had the advantage of being sixteen years wiser, had been incapacitated by his love for the kid, and so would never be able to see their relationship dynamic as imbalanced, coping as he did with his own inexperience and emotional immaturity.

Mitchell could hear his former teacher whistling away in the shower and didn't have to wonder what had put him in such a jovial mood. He couldn't deny that even his own disposition had much improved since his mentor had arrived the previous afternoon to calm him down. After the overnight pep-talk, Mitchell was raring to get back in the game and on with his life.

Not that he knew better or had all the answers just because he was older, Ronald had always cut Mitch some generous slack. No doubt, the kid was heartbroken now over the breakup with his first boyfriend. In this, he and Ronald had something in common, even more so since Ronald's heart had been broken by Mitch who'd informed him not so many years ago, that he wasn't Mitch's boyfriend. In addition to being love-wounded, it sounded like Mitch wasn't getting good academic advice, wasn't sure he'd picked the right major to salvage his altitude-losing GPA, and that he was finding it next to impossible to focus on his course work while simultaneously pursuing a social and love life. Ronald hoped it helped Mitch to hear that he had struggled through college, too, and that in the larger scheme of things, university wouldn't matter much if Mitch pursued something he was passionate about and found work that gave him joy and satisfaction. Just like teaching had been for Ronald—until it wasn't.

Mr. Simpleman emerged from the bathroom holding his towel at his side, still dripping from his shower, almost looking like a steamy twenty-something Playgirl centerfold model. Mitchell squinted with one eye shut as he raised his two thumbs and index fingers to frame the perfect shot in his mind's eye. Perhaps if his teacher's head in the photograph was cropped below the neck, Mitch was thinking, to maximum the erotic and artistic mystery of the shot, this could enhance the impact of the photo when spread across a glossy double page with full color bleed. (Mitchell knew the jargon well, having been the editor of the 1980 edition of the Yellowjackets Yearbook). Mitchell was nodding his head with a dirty-smile approval. From the neck down, Ronald Simpleman could be mistaken for one hairy sexy fucker, if he didn't speak.

But then he spoke.

"I think I used every one of your many A-*ram*-is products in the shower just now," Ronald said.

"It's pronounced *A*ramis, with the accent on the first *a*." Mitchell felt obligated to correct his former teacher.

"Oh, as in René d'Herblay from *The Three Musketeers?*"

"Precisely." Mitchell did not mention that he'd never read the Alexandre Dumas novel even though it had been assigned reading for Mr. Simpleman's class.

"And believe it or not," Ronald said, "last night was my first night on a waterbed."

Mitchell found this hard to believe given what a throwback beatnik his teacher had always seemed to be. "You mean your first night *sleeping* on a waterbed? Or having *sex* on one?"

"Both," Ronald shouted. "And I liked both experiences on the high seas very much." He flashed that goofy, square-chinned grin of his, while posing with his towel to show off his post-shower hang, before pretending to dry his backside.

Mitchell had to suppress the urge to roll his eyes. Instead, he raised his torso off the waterbed, where he'd been daydreaming under the pair of John Travolta movie posters that he'd suspended from the ceiling. In keeping within his starving student budget, he'd mounted these cinematic souvenirs from *Staying Alive* and *Two of a Kind* atop clear vinyl sheeting that had been staple-gunned to wooden pine frames that he'd recycled from what had looked like a dismantled early summer greenhouse left at the curb a few blocks from his apartment. The posters—which had been illegally purloined from the Lobo Theater outdoor display case, which every UNM student knew could be easily sprung using a pocketknife—took on new meaning in this new, post-break up reality. Beyond just being mementos of the happier date nights, he'd enjoyed with his ex, but moving forward these movie posters would serve to remind Mitchell that he and John had *not* been two of a kind and that somehow, through the painful ordeal of their separation, Mitchell would not be discouraged. He was staying alive.

When the refracting motion of waterbed waves had calmed, he scooted his butt to the edge of the wooden frame and sat in wait with his bare legs open wide as Ronald expelled toothpaste in the bathroom sink. Still floating on cloud sixty-nine when he emerged from the bathroom, Ronald glided into the welcome wagon of muscular legs, which wrapped around him, pulling his fuzzy, Aramis-smelling abdomen against Mitchell's left ear.

Once the exclamation point pressing under his chin demanded more attention, Mitchell didn't hesitate in initiating round two—or was it three? There'd always been something special about Mr. Simpleman's boner. "Did your surgeon father circumcise you?" Mitchell asked, taking a break from his work, not considering that bringing up Ronald's father might dowse the heat of the fellatio for him.

But Ronald took the question in stride. "He's an orthopaedic surgeon, meaning he deals with knees, elbows, femurs, hip replacements . . . you know, the major bones."

Ronald spoke like an anatomy teacher standing next to a classroom skeleton. He had not been fishing for a compliment.

But Mitchell couldn't resist the opening. "I'd say your bone qualifies as major."

He picked up where he'd left off, nearly cross-eyed and spit polishing the smooth and pre-cum dripping glans with his lips and probing tip of his tongue. More than merely mushroom-shaped, the head of Ronald's boner was aerodynamic—more like the helmet on the jetpack-wearing rocket man he'd seen on TV last Friday night, flying the length of the coliseum during the opening ceremony at the Summer Olympics in Los Angeles. The fine art of Ronald's excision was most evident in the symmetry and uniformity of his circumcision collar. Ever so slightly puffy and a lovely shade of pink, his retracted and smartly tailored foreskin looked comfy as a turtleneck or ear warmer. Soft, Ronald hung—or more appropriately, swung—to the left.

Mitchell's favorite feature around the circumference of Ronald's penis was the quick-to-engorge bluish vein. Looking like a plump earthworm that had burrowed under the top layer of skin to escape a robin, it stretched the impressive length of his shaft from under his circumcision scar to the base of his pubic bone. This vein, only visible during arousal, when it took on the characteristics of a life-saving artery, kinked into a slight S-curve three-quarters of the way down (or up, depending on the examiner's perspective). But this deviation was mostly concealed by a canopy of untended pubic hair that today smelled like the Estée Lauder *Aramis* division. The added topography of this prominent vein gave Mitchell's tongue something to do and by the purring groans his attentive technique always elicited, he knew he was onto something.

And when Mr. Simpleman ejaculated, after minutes of oozing the sweetest, almost celery-flavored pre-cum, those hefty walnuts in his low-hanging, un-manscaped scrotum deployed the most spectacular hydraulics to eject a geyser's worth of life-giving spume. It clotted like cooling lava in his bark-dark chest hair and could be a devil to get completely cleaned up. It knocked the wind out of Mitchell to realize how much he missed this ritual—if not the man responsible. From the neck down, sex with Ronald Simpleman was still very satisfactory.

It was finally Mitchell's turn in the bathroom. He knew Ronald wanted to be shown around Albuquerque, as it was his first time in the Duke City, but car-less Mitchell needed to get the hell out of town. He would propose a day trip to Jemez Hot Springs, Soda Dam, Los Alamos, Santa Fe, and back. This would mitigate the possibility of running into someone he knew, to whom Ronald would need to be introduced. Mitchell did not want to have to explain him or their odd relationship.

Mitchell's parents had embarrassed him from time to time, each in their unique way, like parents do. But Mr. Simpleman embarrassed Mitchell constantly and from the beginning. Back when he was in high school, their clandestine extracurricular relationship had been a thrilling and terrifying balancing act. Mitchell knew without exaggeration that it could have gotten them both beaten, arrested or worse. Mitchell was embarrassed still and considered deploying a visiting-uncle-on-his-father's-side backstory to explain their current togetherness, should the need arise. Yet he and Ronald looked nothing alike and couldn't possibly pass as relations. This was a problem from a storytelling perspective but also a gigantic relief to Mitchell's ego. So, the next-best thing was to head out of town.

Thirty minutes later, Mitchell was back in the familiar passenger seat of Ronald's golden bronze Volvo 240 sedan, making the journey northwest into the Santa Fe National Forest up New Mexico State Highway 4. Mitchell had only been to Jemez Hot Springs and the Soda Dam once before and hadn't been behind the steering wheel that time either, so his navigational recall was hazy.

Ronald seemed happier than a free-wheeling pope out of frock on holiday, and certainly more relaxed and less high-strung than Mitchell could ever remember seeing him. The driver and passenger windows were down, and both occupants were shirtless—the driver in jeans, his passenger in white parachute pants. Piñon- and sagebrush-scented wind rushed in to animate Mitchell's curly brown hair and undo Ronald's receding, brownish comb-over. The two latest albums released by Michael Franks, *Passionfruit* and *Previously Unavailable*, took turns in the cassette player on full blast.

Some of Ronald's new favorites—like "Rainy Night in Tokyo" and "Lovesick Lizzie"—got rewound for second plays.

Ronald seemed in such an ironclad good mood that Mitchell thought it might be the right moment to bring up a sensitive subject again, seeing that Ronald had failed to bring him what he'd expressly requested when he'd invited his old teacher down for this visit. Since returning to university after being cleared of his cancer, Mitchell had been plagued with worry and second thoughts about a rash decision he'd made when there had been a chance that he might not survive his diagnosis. Knowing he was heading into a series of surgeries that would leave him altered or—in his frightened mind—disfigured, Mitchell had wanted to preserve, for his personal record, images of what he and his body looked like beforehand. Ronald had agreed to the assignment and wanted to be his photographer, thinking he too, would want to preserve his memories of Mitch on film, should something happen to him. Now that Mitchell was through the ordeal and looking, at least in clothes, like a picture of good health, he needed to get his hands on the photos or the negatives of him without clothes so that they never fell into the wrong hands.

"So, Ronald . . . what gives with the pictures of me you took that I keep bugging you about? You said you'd bring everything to me on this visit. And so far, what? Twenty-four hours in, you still haven't produced what I asked you for."

"What have I told you about ending a sentence with a preposition?" the driver asked, revealing a shit-eating grin.

"Come on, man. You promised me you would only develop those pictures when I asked you to, or if—" and Mitchell tripped on the notion . . . "if I didn't survive. I kept my end of the deal by beating cancer. Now you should keep yours by returning the undeveloped films. Unless you've developed them . . . or even worse, lost them!"

"Don't worry, Mitch. All the film is safe and secured. And as Michael Franks sings, 'Your secret's safe with me.' But you're right. I didn't bring them with me on this trip. I didn't forget. I was thinking instead maybe we could expand the collection with another shoot. Sort of a before and after cancer retrospective—especially since you are looking mighty fine and healthy these days."

Mitchell felt his face reddening with molten rage. "Ronald, listen. Those pictures, negatives, or canisters of raw film—whatever state they currently exist in, I would feel so much better if they were in my possession."

"So, you could destroy them, is my fear."

"What about the chance that something could happen to you? What if someone else found these images in your possession? Our secret, my involvement with you, would burst out into the open. That's *my* fear, Ronald." He turned sideways in the passenger seat to face the driver. "Honestly, this keeps me up at night. Look, I'm in university now, working my ass off in political science and learning languages. I might one day become a diplomat or an ambassador and, you know, maybe do important work to usher us out of this Cold War."

"Ah," Ronald lit up. "Just like Axel McGee in *Don't Drink the Water.*"

Mitchell couldn't help but break his tough guy stance and crack a smile, remembering the Woody Allen play he'd starred in his junior year. Ronald had directed him. But he shook off the memory. "If those photos got lost or leaked somehow, it would ruin me. I would never get the security clearance these types of jobs require. Plus, if I ever run for political office, they could surface during opposition research." The possibility of running for office had just occurred to him.

"Relax, Mitch. First, I intentionally cut off your head and didn't show your face for most of the shots we posed. Anything else captured in the images could belong to anyone. It's not like you were wearing a mugshot board around your neck with your name, height, and arrest date."

Mitchell considered Ronald's statement. "I appreciate that, and I am certain all the photos, including the money shot you filmed, are artistic and tasteful and that you wouldn't ever do anything to expose or compromise me."

The driver looked away from the road so the passenger could read his face when he said, "I would never do anything to hurt you, period."

Mitchell was embarrassed now, almost regretting that he'd brought it up. "I know that. It makes me nervous. That's all."

"You have nothing to be nervous or ashamed or even embarrassed about. You are a beautiful specimen of a man, and it gives me the greatest joy to capture the essence of your beauty. Whether it's on film or on stage, I only ever wanted to showcase the very best of you, Mitch . . . to show the world what I see in you."

Mitchell tried to hold his breath and his tongue for a whole minute, measuring the time between highway mile markers. Then he inhaled. "Sure, we can take some more pictures during this visit—maybe even at the hot springs, but I'll be the one behind the cameras this time. I'll take photos or Super 8 films of you, and don't worry. I'll be sure I cut off your head when I do. But mark my words, Mr. Simpleman . . ." He tapped the dashboard three times for emphasis. "One day I will be coming for all these pictures—yours and mine—and you won't be able to stop me from taking back every last one of them."

"You are one shrewd negotiator," the driver acknowledged. "But I like the idea. I like the idea very much," Ronald said, swiping his lower lip with the tip of his tongue as he drove.

"And just so you know," Mitch added. "I own the rights to my images. I looked it up in the law library. It's called the Right of Publicity. One of these days, you'll need to turn over what is rightfully mine."

"That's a deal, my friend."

"That's the law, Ronald."

MISSOULA, MONTANA
February 1983

MITCHELL CARSON TWIRLED THE LAMINATED HOS-pital bracelet around on his right wrist. Nothing during the past six weeks had gone particularly well for him. After a rushed surgical procedure in January that had occurred less than twenty-four hours after receiving a diagnosis he could have never imagined, the fit, twenty-one-year-young male, who weighed 178 pounds and stood five feet ten inches tall—when he wasn't doubled over retching his guts out in a hospital bed pan like he'd spent the previous night—was officially a cancer patient.

That initial surgery had robbed Mitchell of his right testicle that'd had the balls to turn cancerous on him. Follow up CAT scans revealed a much darker picture in the form of a considerably sized shadow a bit further north. As relayed to him by the visiting oncologist from Spokane who had read the dire scans, there appeared to be a growing tumor mass in his abdomen, currently the size of a deflated football, that would shortly begin to impinge on Mitchell's stomach, kidney, and liver functions if drastic actions weren't taken to slow the malignancy. Given the mass was deemed too large to remove surgically, the Montana cancer team at St. Patrick Hospital devised a rapid response plan they felt might shrink the tumor. They would attack the cancer with aggressive chemotherapy, Mitchell's first session of which, had been administered not long after sundown the night prior with the hope he would sleep through the worst of the side effects. He didn't, hence his retching.

The abridged diagnosis—after the drama dust had settled and all the scientific and medical terms got distilled down to something Mitchell and his family could wrap their heads around and pronounce—was that he was facing a foe that went by the name *intra-abdominal lymphoma.*

It had been a fluke that this cancer had been discovered in the first place. If it hadn't been for Mr. Simpleman, Mitchell might have ignored the signs altogether, such was the breakneck pace at which Mitchell had been sprinting through life ever since his much heralded (by him) departure from Stevensville two years earlier. Laying in that hospital bed now, feeling like shit from the toxic chemicals that had been pumped into his twenty-year-young body overnight, he had to concentrate to organize the head-spinning events of the past few weeks, trying to understand what was happening to him and make sense out of how he'd gotten there.

He'd traveled back to Stevensville by car from Albuquerque with his new best friend, Greg, who also attended UNM as part of the national student exchange program from Oregon State, just as Mitchell had arranged from the University of Montana. Greg, who owned his own car—a green olive colored Opal GT sport coupe—had driven the two of them three hundred miles out of his way to first drop Mitchell in Stevensville before cutting down to his folks' place near Corvallis. The two, who planned to return to UNM by taking the same route in reverse, had met during new exchange student orientation at the start of last semester and hit it off instantly, Mitchell stretching friendship a step further by secretly fostering a big gay crush on his straight new friend.

By Christmas Day, Mitchell was bored, ready and excited to link back up with Greg for their return to the University of New Mexico. Lost Trail Powder Mountain hadn't yet received enough snow to open for the season, which had spoiled Mitchell's plan to spend the remainder of his holidays out of the house and on the slopes. With almost another full week before he'd catch his ride back to Albuquerque, Mitchell was at a standstill, that is until he'd learned that his former high school English and drama teacher had returned to town early after spending Christmas with his folks and fizzling out with nothing to do in Colorado. Lucky for Mitchell, who beyond boredom, was pent up horny, he made a beeline across town telling his folks he was off to hang out with old high school friends.

Leaving his coat, boots, and clothes on the doormat inside his former teacher's apartment, Mitch and Ronald had immediately dispensed with formalities. The pair was naked in the darkened bedroom, going through the choreography of getting reacquainted, when the elder of the two cavorting contortionists cupped a handful of grossly mismatched nuts, and said, "While I have to admit the size of this one is damn impressive, I think you should see someone about it."

Now, whether this counted as Mr. Simpleman saving his life would be a subject for future debates. But Mitchell did see somebody—the Carson family doctor—the next day about his potential elephantiasis. No doubt the testicle had been tender, and Mitchell had wondered why it was the only one having a growth spurt. But there had been no indication that it wasn't natural or simply the result of racking himself on a table or desk corner. Besides, Mitchell hadn't minded how it gave him a conspicuously larger bulge in his shorts and jeans. Inside the doctor's examination room, however, stripping down for the second time in twelve hours which had seemed like such a simple, harmless errand to add to his holiday, Dr. Rockwell's touchy-feely probing revealed the opposite of harmless, and Mitchell had been booked for a rush radical inguinal orchiectomy of his right testicle the following afternoon in Missoula.

When he phoned Greg at his parent's home in Oregon to deliver the news, he started crying and then Greg started too, but before they'd hung up with little else to say and nothing that would change the situation, Greg insisted he was still heading out of his way to Stevensville to see him in the next couple of days before he continued on solo to New Mexico.

And true to his word and their friendship, Greg, did.

Not even a week later, Mitchell had been bounced back into the oncology ward at St. Patrick's where a parade of toxic metals and a punch bowl's worth of anti-nausea drugs that chased these, had been grand marshalled by his team to march through the IV and into his vein. CIS platinum, Vinblastine, and Bleomycin were on the A-Team that did the dirty toxic work while Reglan, Decadron, Compazine, Benadryl, attempted but completely failed—on a miserable scale—to keep the nausea at bay. Because Mitchell's youthful bravado had been mistaken for athleticism and sturdiness, the decision was to storm and overwhelm the cancer with an initial blast of heavy metals. Dosages of everything had been dialed up, and the horrendous side effects, not wanting to be outmaneuvered, gave as much as they took. Uncontrollable muscle spasms paralyzed Mitchell's body in a crescent shape he could not release on his own without more drugs sent in to relax his muscles. He went temporarily and functionally blind, only able to make out rough shadows of people entering and exiting his hospital room. Throughout the torture session of this first chemo session—officially the longest night of his life—he must have puked gallons followed by machine-gun heaving when there had been nothing but bile and what might be left of his riddled guts to expel.

By morning, his abdominal muscles aching, still blind and queasy, Mitchell was panicked and after his parents arrived, he wouldn't shut up about the impending loss of his hair. He insisted, upon discharge just before noon, that his frazzled parents drive him straight to a wig shop that his mother found listed in the Yellow Pages that was located out on Higgins Street near the railroad tracks. Inside the industrial warehouse establishment where his mother would later swear a whole different and illegal business must have been going on in the back behind a curtain, Mitchell couldn't see a thing. He could not tell the difference between a wig for a man and a wig for a woman, or between a wig and a poodle. Every rug and toupée the saleslady wedged over his still-intact head of hair felt like jute held together by chicken wire. Out of blindness, exhaustion, frustration, and fear, Mitchell began to cry—not even discreetly. His parents each lent an elbow and ushered their firstborn out to the station wagon.

As they left the Missoula city limits, streaking south along the Bitterroot River and passing through the town of Florence, a radio announcer broke in during the middle of a song to declare—in a voice that was sorrowful and gravelly—that Karen Carpenter had died. With a gasp but without uttering a word, Mitchell's father instinctively pulled the car off the highway and onto the shoulder and shut off the ignition. The three of them sat there, overlooking a wide bend in the Bitterroot, bawling their eyes out for what must have been a good twenty minutes.

No disrespect meant to Karen, but most of the tears the Carsons shed during that crying jag only marginally had anything to do with her. [Then, after this sentence, insert the following passage in the same paragraph] The Carsons had their connection to The Carpenters to be sure, and it was personal. Two years before the family had relocated to Stevensville once their new house had been built, they'd lived in Missoula where Mitch had attended kindergarten through sixth grade. To his budding ego's delight, Mitch had been plucked from his fourth grade Paxton Elementary music class as one of the fifteen students to make up the Missoula Children's Choir. The choir had been formed by lottery and talent scout from elementary schools across the city—expressly and exclusively—to perform the la-la-la chorus from the song, "Sing" on stage with the Carpenters when they appeared in concert at the Adams Field House on May 12, 1973. During the choir's only rehearsal and sound check with the famous sister-brother duo, Richard had gotten up off his piano bench and walked over to the choir. Placing his exalted hand on Mitch's head, he said to the choir's director, "we need to hear more volume from this one." For an eleven-year-old, star-struck, all-around-ham in front of any audience, and with performing aspirations of his own, this had been Mitch Carson's breakout moment. He had been the chosen one to sing louder than all the rest. And now, he'd been chosen again—this time by cancer, which was he and his parents had needed to take this moment.

With some measure of composure recovered, the wagon slowly edged back onto the highway, as snowflakes appeared in the air. The Carson Trio began fumbling its way through an impromptu repertoire, covering every *Carpenters* song the three of them could recall, for the rest of the disoriented drive home to Stevensville.

AFTER A WEEK of being back in the classroom following the holidays, Ronald was not himself and he knew it. Teaching for him, these past couple years since Mitch Carson had graduated and moved away, had lost its magic, but on top of this, Mitch had neither phoned him nor paid a visit to let him know how things had checked out at the doctor. It was on his way home that Thursday after school, that Ronald ran into Mitch's clearly upset mother at the Burnt Fork Grocery Store and got her to divulge what Mitch hadn't, that it was cancer and that he was back in the hospital. She then excused herself and went back out to the family station wagon where she sobbed behind the steering wheel before driving home without the groceries she'd gone there to buy.

Ronald stood frozen in the produce section of the grocery store, stunned.

A day later, he'd eagerly accepted the long-distance charges for a collect call that Mitch Carson had placed from the Marcus Daly Memorial Hospital in Hamilton. Mitch apologized for not letting him know sooner and said his mom had told him she ran into him at the grocery store. He then informed Ronald that he had been hospitalized again, and this time was being kept in isolation because the first chemo session evidently had killed the majority of his white blood cells. This seemed inconceivable to Ronald since the two of them had just frolicked together two weeks before, but he told Mitch he'd drive up to Hamilton right after school the next day, to at least so that he could give him a wave through the window of his isolation room.

The next morning, during his home period Intro to Theater class, he assigned a silent, in class reading of Tennessee Williams' *A Streetcar Named Desire*. He simply couldn't be expected to lecture under the circumstances. He was not in teacher shape and would use the weekend to get his own act together, if he could. As half his students read, while the other half pretended to but slept—it was an acting class after all—Ronald stared like a crazed mad man out the windows to the set of bleachers near the tennis courts. He had four more classes to get through before his day and teaching week were over, and amid his confusion and anger and all-around mental instability brought on by his new obsession over Mitch's situation, Ronald feared he might be on the verge or a nervous breakdown or worse. He could be irreparably slipping into a classification best generalized as temporary insanity, but then, what good would he be to himself or anybody else?

Ron Simpleman thought he knew what crazy was supposed to look like. At Stanford, he had once auditioned for the role of Stanley Kowalski in *Streetcar* by performing an unrelated monologue from *Equus* written for a mentally disturbed seventeen-year-old character named Alan Strang, who was erotically obsessed with horses. He and Harlan had seen the new-at-the-time and deliciously controversial play at the National Theatre in London the summer before, and Ronald had gotten a hold of the Peter Shaffer script via a Samuel French catalogue he'd consulted in the Cecil H. Green Library on campus.

He had needed to be strategic and cutthroat competitive during his final year in theater studies at Stanford if he was going to have a anything truly boast-worthy on his post-grad resume. The audition notice stipulated that actors perform a three-to-five-minute piece from a different play and be prepared to relate their scene and character choice to the role they hoped to play in *Streetcar*. Ronald had selected the *Equus* monologue because he wanted to showcase his range and his sensitivity to mental illness. He'd been called *crazy* plenty, but he didn't know anyone who had been institutionalized. "That's why they call it acting," he'd chant during his preparatory pep talks.

Had it been up to the tenured faculty professor overseeing that production—a man in his mid-fifties who Ronald sensed during the summer rep season, might have been incubating a small crush on him but maybe had just been too guarded or shy to show it—Ronald could have probably gotten himself cast as Stella, had he wanted that part badly enough. But then he learned the director was going to try something experiential, which was so very Stanford of him, and in an instant, any advantage Ronald might have deployed by, say, reciprocating a flirtation, got eliminated. The director had announced he would be turning over sole casting authority to a student coordinator.

Ronald would have done anything to play Stanley Kowalski that year. If he'd known about casting couches, he might have tossed his naked jay-bird self on the cushions, but he mistakenly assumed he had no sway with the student casting coordinator, as they had been fierce competitors for the same roles throughout their university careers, but he'd been wrong about that too. Ronald remembered two things from that audition: shrieking Alan Strang's line, "Mine! You're mine! I am yours and you are mine"; and the sting of not landing the part he wanted. The casting coordinator—also gay and also concealing his own secret crush on Ronald—had delivered the news with a smoldering smirk, choosing to cast him instead in the secondary role of Harold Mitchell. He'd known Ronald was dying to play Stanley, but he'd also observed Ronald kissing up to the director over that same summer rep season and wanted to teach Ronald a lesson about lifting his leg to urinate on the wrong tree.

Fast forward back to now. Ronald broke his stare out his classroom window and took a moment—as he faked writing something important in the open grade book on his desk—to appreciate the irony in that he too had become a director who'd wrestled with his infatuation for one of his students. Then there was also the poetry in coincidence, he supposed, that the object of Ronald's affections happened to be named Mitch, just as Harold Mitchell's nickname gets used in *Streetcar*. But there was tragic irony mixed into this too—the kind the Greeks and Shakespeare loved to employ—where the audience gets to plainly see the tragedy about to play out, long before the actors see it coming. With Mitch's cancer diagnosis, Ronald didn't know if he was one of the actors or relegated to the audience already suspecting how this drama might end.

From the minute Ronald learned that Mitch had cancer, all he'd wanted to shriek was "You're mine! I am yours and you are mine!" Ronald had never been able to tell Mitch this was how he truly felt about him—how he'd always felt—but it seemed urgent and imperative that Mitch knew this now, just in case . . . Ronald stopped himself from finishing the morbid thought. With the Carson family likely huddled protectively around their prodigal son, Ronald didn't know when he would get his chance, but he had to anticipate that he'd likely be shut out of Mitch's inner circle—not that he had ever been part of it. Mitch's mother, while always polite, had telegraphed that she was not thrilled by the special attentions Mr. Simpleman appeared to pay her gifted teenager. Ronald doubted he had appeased her when pulling her aside some years ago at a Foreign Language Club potluck to congratulate both parents for having nurtured Mitchell's creative side, as it had helped him stand out and above as a uniquely talented student with tremendous potential. Perhaps he'd been gushing, but Mitch was indeed special and worth elevating.

The mild-mannered, well-meaning, but still wary members of the Carson family weren't the only ones giving Ronald standoffish vibes. The entire time he'd been living in Montana, he'd been wide awake and aware that he didn't fit in and hadn't been accepted by the town. Neither had he achieved any social breakthroughs with any of his fellow faculty members who seemed more dedicated to ensuring he was treated like the outsider he was instead of welcomed. For years, Ronald had sacrificed everything to educate and inspire the dimwitted young rednecks that showed up in his classroom, hoping against almost insurmountable odds he'd uncover and have the chance to cultivate an occasional diamond in the rough. Mitch Carson had been one of those, rare as they come. But all the attention, opportunities, and encouragement he'd contributed toward Mitch's success, seemed to go unsung and unappreciated by his parents, the school, or even by Mitch. It seemed to make no difference that Mr. Simpleman never called in sick, even when he was under the weather and should have stayed home. He conformed with the school district policies and mostly adhered to the state's backwards curriculum. He did his duty and took his turns chaperoning their proms and homecoming dances. He had tolerated his student's ridiculous inabilities to act, memorize, create, or imagine any subject or scenario that they couldn't relate back to the only things they knew anything about which were fishing, hunting, and rodeos. There could be no misinterpretation about it. Ronald Simpleman had started out with more red marks against him than the report card belonging to the title-winning school idiot (if such a competition existed, which it didn't because Ronald figured it would have gotten decided in an eighty-three-student tie).

The unspoken demerits holding Ronald Simpleman back from ever being awarded teacher-, miracle worker- or even humanitarian-of-the-year, seemed to coalesce around a coral of rumors that had been interspersed with the known facts that he was single, male, and—most egregious of all—he had been sent there to teach high school English and drama to the local yokels—apparently the two most useless subjects the Wild West had ever heard of in them there parts. Ronald knew from Psychology 101 that people were generally uncomfortable with things they weren't any good at, so he'd made plenty of allowances for these country folk, even though they made not one for him. Had he been married, promised, engaged, or even remotely interested in dating a woman, Ronald suspected he wouldn't have been given a second look—stink-eyed, sideways or knowing. Had he been coaching one of the Yellowjackets sports teams, this, too, would have endeared and redeemed him for his quirky ways. He would have had cover even if the sports team hadn't been any good. He knew this because he'd seen it happen with the high school's special education coordinator—also male, also single—who had been savvy enough to get himself appointed the assistant coach of the losing junior-varsity football team. This breast-plate provided that single teacher all the protection he needed when—if the rumor was to be believed—he'd gotten one of the senior girls pregnant shortly before graduation last year.

The writing might as well have been carved on the *Welcome to Stevensville* sign at the edge of town, and if it already was, then Ronald had missed it, but after six school years, surviving twenty-four seasons of more weather than Ronald knew the skies were capable of stirring up and blowing around, and the countless snubs, he didn't need it spelled out for him. He was not welcome in Stevensville, Montana.

Weeks ago, heading into his seventh Christmas break, and with Mitch away attending university in New Mexico, he'd already been contemplating giving his notice to leave teaching in Montana by the end of this school year. But if Mitch was sticking around for his cancer treatments, maybe Ronald would stick around a while longer, too—though he was scared of what that might look and what could happen next. If Mitch survived, Ronald was sure he'd beat a path back to New Mexico to continue his university education, and then Ronald would still be stuck in Stevensville. If Mitch's cancer turned out to be incurable, Ronald would be shattered, of course—and he'd still be stuck in Stevensville. Even if Mitch experienced a near-death epiphany and finally realized that Ronald's love for him was his only cure and hope for salvation, they still couldn't make a relationship work in Stevensville. There was no hope for even a polishable silver lining to emerge from the tarnished scenarios laid out before him unless he changed his geography and got the hell out of Stevensville.

The end of class bell sounded, books thudded shut, and the room emptied out, giving Ronald five minutes to himself before the students for his next class, Greek Mythology, began filing into the classroom for their Friday dose of gods and goddesses. In this briefest of reprieves, a disturbing realization crept into Ronald's cranium that he could not keep out, that instantly triggered the most horrible guilt for thinking it in the first place. But if Mitch were not to survive this test, his trial by cancer, then Ronald—through the omission of evidence and the elimination of the only eyewitness—would automatically get sprung from the shackles of his most debilitating fear which was that he'd eventually get caught for what he'd done, or rather, for what he'd failed to stop from happening. Ronald hated his brain for even considering this morbid but oddly liberating scenario. Surely, Mitch the Lover would learn how to become Mitch the Fighter. He was going to pull through this battle, scarred perhaps, yet bounce back stronger and more beautiful than ever. And then what?

This former student of his who, on his own terms and not Ronald's, had never once played the victim card, had confessed to his teacher that he'd known he liked boys and had fooled around with a few since he was in 5th Grade, had not once seemed bothered, resentful, vindictive, or damaged by what had occurred between them. This teen burglar (now an adult) who'd pickpocketed his teacher's heart and who became more than a student and then more than a friend, had so far protected Ronald's biggest secret. But every day that Mitch Carson lived was a day Mitch's heart and mind could change or be changed by outside influences. What if a probing psychiatrist one day used regression therapy to get to the root cause of some yet-to-be-identified childhood trauma?

Not only did Ronald live in constant fear that sooner or later, he would be found out, but then he would be publicly ostracized, humiliated, and imprisoned. Or possibly hanged, this being Montana. And for what crime? For falling in love? For being unable to resist the charms of someone half his age? He could almost hear the judge's voice in his head: *You, Ronald Paul Simpleman, have been charged for committing unholy acts against nature with a minor. A big-time crime in Big Sky Country, in case you didn't know, punishable by life in prison or death. How do you plead?*

They'd have him on that one. These were facts he couldn't deny and charges he couldn't argue, the law being the law and all. *But first, let's meet the accused, the one who was supposed to have been the adult in the room; in fact, he was the only adult in the room.* What he and Mitchell had discovered together, quite organically and to his complete surprise, had felt both natural and beautiful, not the least bit criminal or coerced. It would be an uphill defense to try to prove who had seduced whom, and who had made the first move. It would be just as futile to try to establish who did or didn't resist. The crux of the case would be the indisputable sixteen-year age difference between them and that Mitch had barely turned sixteen years of age at the time of the crime. Plus, there would be the aggravating factor that Ronald had been a trusted authority figure—sure to sway the cowboy-booted jury of his peers. Nothing he said, no evidence he could reveal would hold the wheels of his defense on the axles of Wild West justice.

Class assembled, Mr. Simpleman divided the students into five discussion groups assigning each group the task of exploring a different relationship from mythology: Zeus and Ganymede; Achilles and Patroclus; Apollo and Hyacinthus; Hercules and Hylas; and Laius and Chrysippus—all of whom could be found in their assigned and state school board approved textbook for the class. The teacher dubiously expected that no group would raise the homosexual aspects to any or each of these relationships, but Mr. Simpleman knew he would not be the teacher—and not in Montana—to point out for his class what scholars had been saying about these same-sex pairs for centuries. Only a curious, student like Mitch Carson had been, would make this connection and ponder the possibilities objectively and intelligently.

With another of his classes engaged in a self-guided activity that didn't require him to actively lecture today, Ronald resumed his most reoccurring daydream of one day leaving Montana—which always came with the caveat—if he could make it out before the tipped-off authorities came to arrest him.

To prepare for the eventual reckoning, Ronald had spent an entire spring break a few years back researching Montana's criminal codes and reviewing related case law at the William J. Jameson Law Library on the University of Montana campus in Missoula. What he had discovered there, hunched over a microfiche viewer and sweating in a not-so-private cubicle, was that the State had been all over the map when it came to defining what constituted a criminal act. The age of consent had proved a prime example of shifting morals over time. While it had been eighteen years old for the last fifty years, it had been fifteen before that. And when Montana was becoming a state in 1885, it was only ten.

In Ronald's constant equity-seeking mind, the Territory and later the State of Montana had its share of explaining to do for having been all over the morality map with its criminal code. Based upon Victorian era laws brought over from England via the original thirteen colonies, the Wild West became a crude carbon copy of the plundering exploits happening elsewhere in the world at the time. It was clear to Ronald that it had been the men—always the men, having inherited the worst faults of their fathers—who discriminatorily and hypocritically rewrote the rules in favor of whatever suited them. Case in point: at the time Stevensville was settled, while it was legal for an adult man to have sex with a ten-year-old girl, it was a heinous crime against nature for a man to have sex with another man, never mind with a ten-year-old boy.

Mitch hadn't been ten, but that wasn't Ronald's point; neither was it his defense. When examining case law in the library, Ronald discovered a tranche of Montana history that had stuck with him ever since.

In 1865, the first session of the Montana territorial government adopted its criminal code, which included a law they'd lazily lifted from England, establishing sodomy as illegal and punishable with a sentence of five years to life. Only thirteen years later, in 1878, Montana Territory was home to one of the earliest reported sodomy cases in all of the United States. In *Territory vs. Mahaffey*, William Mahaffey was convicted of sodomy with a fourteen-year-old named William Cottrell, whom he called a "boy prostitute," and with whom Mahaffey had engaged in sexual relations more than once. The evidence produced against him had been hearsay and sparse, and the boy refused to corroborate the accusation. The conviction came down to the testimony of a hotel clerk who said he'd shown the two a single room.

In 1885, the same year Montana became the forty-first State, the definition of sodomy was legally refined to pertain to penetration only. Without penetration, the crime of sodomy would no longer be applied. Then in 1915, in *State vs. Guerin*, the Montana Supreme Court was tasked with deciding if fellatio should also be considered a "crime against nature," like sodomy. The decision was "of course it should be" and unanimous. In writing its decision, the supreme court stated:

> Every intelligent adult person understands fully what the ordinary course of nature demands or permits for the purpose of procreation, and that any departure from this course is against nature. It therefore seems to be trifling with our intelligence to say that copulation accomplished by use of the anus is against nature, whereas the same act accomplished by use of mouth is not. This view contravenes common sense.

In 1938, eight years before Ronald was born in Colorado, in what could be considered a small progressive step forward, a Montana man named Alexander Keckonen, who had been sentenced on circumstantial evidence to thirty-five years in prison for sodomy, appealed this decision with the Montana Supreme Court, and in a vote of 3–2, won his freedom. The judges in their decision acknowledged that while "the subject of sodomy was truly a loathsome one to many," in Keckonen's case, the jury seemed to have convicted him more on their abhorrence of the offense itself than on the facts of the case.

It was this man's story, above all the others Ronald had stumbled upon, that resonated the most with him, because it paralleled his own situation with Mitch the most closely. Keckonen was a colorful character with a checkered past. Born in Michigan and of Finnish descent, he'd been a marine who'd served in China in the 1920s but deserted from the military in 1926. He was caught, charged and served time as an inmate at Alcatraz. From there, he went to Utah, where he was arrested for burglary in 1931—a charge later dismissed—and then again for robbery in 1933. For the latter crime, he served five years at the Utah State Prison. When he was released, he was thirty-four, and he headed north, where he found work as a miner at the Anaconda Mine, in Butte, Montana. That's where and when he met a boy between the ages of sixteen and seventeen, near a hamburger joint.

Keckonen hadn't yet been paid by the mine, but he spotted a kid paying for his burger and he asked the teenager to buy him one, too. The boy did, agreeing to meet him there again the following day. When the two next met, Keckonen had been paid and so invited the boy back to his room, where he offered to pay the boy to be on the receiving end of anal sex. Once again, the boy was agreeable to his role and the compensation arrangement. The two began seeing each other almost daily for this purpose. When the boy's mother and stepfather began to take notice of the friendliness shown their boy by this miner, they became understandably concerned. They took extraordinary measures and moved their family twice to establish some distance. But each time, Keckonen moved across town too, so that he would be in the vicinity of the boy.

In the family's final relocation before giving up, Keckonen took an upstairs apartment in the same building above the parents and his teenaged lover. Both parents testified to having had separate conversations with Keckonen expressing their concerns about his interest in their boy. The stepfather said he confronted Keckonen and demanded he stop seeing the boy, but when the boy refused to stop seeing Keckonen, the stepfather realized any future protest would be futile and so stopped pursuing the matter.

A year on, at the teen's insistence, the stepfather went upstairs to invite Keckonen down to their apartment to join the family for Thanksgiving dinner. Some months later, when his parents traveled to Washington State to visit relatives, the boy, then eighteen, was supposed to be staying with his married sister in Butte. When he failed to show at his sister's place, she reported him missing. The police later located him in Keckonen's apartment, where they found the two of them asleep in separate beds. Both were hauled in and charged on the suspicion of having engaged in sodomy.

It was at that moment in his research that Ronald realized that this case wasn't just about the age of consent in Montana. What Keckonen and his eighteen-year-old friend had been doing, as legal consenting adults, was illegal in 1938, just as it was still illegal in 1983. Ronald noted that a decade ago—two years before he arrived in Stevensville—Montana's definition of sodomy had been revised again, this time to only pertain to people of the same sex. In essence, the state had legalized heterosexual anal and oral sex but maintained that these same acts were illegal and deviant when they occurred between same-sex individuals.

They weren't messing around in Montana. Ronald revised this observation as the class bell started ringing. The men *were* messing around. It's the courts that weren't. If he and Mitch got caught, Ronald would have been singled out for harsher punishment as the adult in an age-imbalanced same-sex situation. It would be curtains for his career and for him and who knew what would become of Mitch. That kept him nervous and perpetually looking into the wings and over his shoulder. In Montana, where the men are men and the sheep are nervous, Ronald counted himself among the sheep.

MITCHELL HAD BEEN cautioned not to scratch his skin on account of the chemo because it could leave dark and possibly permanent scars, but he hadn't been advised what to do to relieve the intolerable itching that came with half the drugs he was on, so he invented his own work arounds, like using the bed sheet or a hand towel to do the scratching. Every joint and bone of his skeleton ached in ways that Tylenol couldn't touch—like he'd just completed a decathlon. If it hadn't been for an experimental prescription for an abundant supply of THC pills—essentially marijuana—to combat the nausea, he would have skipped a few pages ahead in the plot and pulled his own damn hair out. Doubling up the dose of those "black beauties"—as he'd nicknamed them—kept him clinically stoned. It also gave him the munchies at a time when the mere thought of food made him too nauseous to snack.

AFTER ZIPPING TWENTY-FIVE minutes up the highway to Hamilton, Ronald was surprised to be greeted by name as he entered a hospital he'd never been to previously. The receptionist had been one of his students, and the female lead in his most regrettable of all the junior class productions he'd ever mounted, *The Green Pastures* a few years back. Seeing her—what was her name again? —made him question all over again what in the world had possessed him to stage that 1930 Pulitzer Prize-winning play by Marc Connelly, in rural Montana, and with the entire 43-member all-white cast of students in blackface.

Ronald walked down the short hallway as he had been directed and immediately found Mitchell's hospital room, marked QUARANTINE. He presented himself in the window and spotted a motionless and lumpy semi-colon shape on the bed under the sheet. It appeared to be turned away from him. It took several seconds for Ronald to detect the subtle rise and fall of the patient's breathing, but once he did, his own shoulders relaxed.

Realizing that Mitch had been captive in that room for a whole week and imagining the fright this must be giving him to have no germ- or cancer-fighting defenses, Ronald felt overwhelmed for Mitch. And this on top of the heap of his own helplessness, aggravated by a sense of time and vitality lost, Ronald's whole body sagged in defeat. Had he known earlier, he would have visited after school every day, instead of spending that time sitting in his Volvo in the faculty parking lot, kitty-corner from the Carson House, wondering why Mitch's bedroom light was never on.

Ronald saw no nurses or doctors walking down the wide hallway outside Mitchell's room, and the rooms on either side of his weren't currently occupied. Mitch had the ward to himself which must have compounded the isolation ten-fold. This was Ronald's first time inside any medical establishment since coming to Montana. For his own medical needs, he'd just phone his dad to work out a cause or remedy. And this may have only been his second or third time in Hamilton. Usually, when he got the itch to get out of Stevensville during the school year, he would make tracks for Missoula—aka the "Big Smoke," on account of the stink-belching Smurf-it-Stone pulp mill near downtown, on the banks of the Clark Fork River. It was bad enough that the nastiness from that industrial factory was being dumped into the river, but the aerial pollution often made its way up the Bitterroot Valley to cloak Stevensville in its putrid smog.

In Missoula, a much larger city of around 80,000, Ronald wasn't known—especially if he avoided the university area, where the chance of running into former students increased. Hamilton was twice as large as Stevensville, but the two towns, with their two high schools less than thirty minutes apart, shared a highway, a fierce school rivalry, and not much more. Fresh out of Stanford and casting about for a teaching gig anywhere in the Rockies, Ronald had considered Hamilton, but they weren't looking for a drama teacher at the time, and he could think of nothing less gratifying than only teaching English to a bunch of illiterate calf-ropers. In hindsight, he might have been happier in a town with a larger talent pool and a skosh more diversity, so he didn't have to put kids in blackface. But then he might not have met Mitch Carson.

For five minutes, he'd resisted tapping on the window to get the attention of the lone lump under the covers with a black bandana on his head. Ronald found himself delightfully riveted by this simple, uncomplicated chance to watch his angel sleeping. This wasn't spying, he justified. This was caring. He scanned the blinking equipment on the wall behind the bed, the IV stand, a quarter bag full of urine dangling in midair between the bed frame and the floor. From there, he followed the tangle of tubes and cords to where they disappeared under the sheet. Mitch wasn't acting. The set hadn't been staged for dramatic effect. Ronald couldn't direct how this tableau would resolve or end. This was scary and this was real.

Mitchell stirred, possibly aware he was being watched. The tails of IV and oxygen tubes and other cords monitoring his vitals began to stretch and slacken, like they were attached to the limbs and head of a marionette coming to life.

The patient turned his traitorous body toward the window with a view into the hallway. He opened his eyes just in time to catch what looked to him like his teacher fisting away a tear.

Red-nosed Ronald turned that fist into an open hand that gave a tentative wave hello. He tried to hide his unease by goofily transforming his face—a la Marcel Marceau—from crying Melpomene to laughing Thalia. Mitchell found this comical, but his appreciative laughter—though Ronald could barely hear it—turned into a rasp of coughing on the other side of the glass. Mitch at least looked happy to see him. This was the medicine that Ronald had come to the hospital seeking.

Mitchell reached for his dry-erase board and marker on the rolling side table that was cantilevered over his hospital bed. He wrote something and then he held it up toward the window. Ronald tilted his head to read the message.

GET ME OUT OF HERE!!!

Ronald started to laugh before comprehending whether Mitchell was being serious. He noticed a similar white board hanging on a chain below the window on his side of the glass. A blue dry-erase marker and an eraser were balanced on the windowsill. He wrote his reply.

SERIOUSLY?

Mitchell smiled, then nodded. Ronald erased his board and wrote:

WHERE WOULD WE GO?

Holding up the board, Ronald saw Mitchell was still smiling but his eyes had closed. Then the smile slowly disappeared. His head tilted to the right, but his eyes didn't reopen. Perhaps this was a sign that visiting hours were over. Ronald heard footsteps at the end of the hallway and saw a doctor or nurse approaching. As the gal got closer, Ronald recognized her at the same time he noticed the rival Hamilton Broncs school jersey she was wearing underneath her shortened lab coat, even though she'd graduated from Stevensville.

"Well, well," she said. "Katrina at the front desk told me you were here." Ronald smiled politely, trying to nonchalantly glance at her name badge, which was hanging backwards on the lanyard around her neck. "It's Martha, Mr. Simpleman . . . class of '79." Ronald's eyes grew larger to signal recognition, but he hadn't a clue who this big-breasted woman was. "I was in *Midsummer Night's Dream* with Mitch. We won the state championship with that one-act play."

"Right," Ronald confirmed. "Titania!"

"Well, I played Helena, but yes! It is so good to see you, Mr. Simpleman. We're taking good care of Mitch." Her quizzical eyes scanned down his torso to read the message on the white board he'd tucked under his crossed arms. "Is he still trying to bust out of here?"

Ronald blushed, nodding. "Any word on when he might be officially released?" He looked through the window at the inmate.

"That's gonna depend on his white blood cells. As I understand it, the first round of chemo he got in Missoula did a wipeout number on his whites. Without them, his body won't be able to fight off a common cold." She was wringing her hands, which Ronald knew was not a good sign. But then she added, "But his numbers are improving every day."

"I just ran into Mrs. Carson at the Burnt Fork in Stevensville yesterday and she said Mitch has his next round of chemo in Missoula at the end of the month."

"Sounds about right," Martha said. "He's currently getting a maintenance dose of a chemo drug called Bleomycin, just to keep his body in fighting mode. Hopefully, his system won't be shocked as much when he goes in for his next round." She pointed, drawing Ronald's attention to Mitch's latest message.

STOP TALKING ABOUT ME LIKE I'M NOT HERE!

Everybody laughed in that uneasy way you do when screaming or bawling is more appropriate.

"I'm just going in to check his IV and vitals," Martha said. "I'll leave the door open, and you can talk with him from the door. But don't cross the threshold, Mr. Simpleman." Her pre-emptively scolding tone suggested she was delighted to have their roles reversed. Now *she* was directing the play. She raised a face mask to cover her nose and mouth.

"Fresh air!" Mitchell's raspy and puny voice announced.

"Take it easy, Bottom. There are germs on the wind," Martha said in a playful tone, using Mitch's character's name from Midsummer.

"Heya, Ron," Mitchell said, trying to elevate his voice so it would reach the door. "Thanks for trekking down here to visit me." Martha paused when she realized the two of them were on a first-name basis. She wouldn't feel comfortable referring to any of her old teachers by their first names. She laughed to herself when she realized she didn't even *know* their first names.

"I ran into your mom after school yesterday at the Burnt Fork and she let me know you were here," Ronald said, in the teacher's voice he'd use to reach the numbskulls in the back of any classroom. (Mitch had always sat near the front). "Seems you've hit a rough patch," he added, but immediately regretted it. *The kid has cancer. It doesn't get any rougher than that.*

Martha pressed gently on the vein above the IV port on the top of Mitchell's hand. "Still tender?" she asked. Mitchell grimaced, nodding. "Those are the chemo drugs, honey. They'll strip your veins and can even collapse them. They'll find a new spot to poke you next once they have you back at St. Patrick's."

"Who says I'm going back to St. Patrick's?" Mitchell asked, even though he knew that's where he had to go next, and that he had no choice in the matter.

"Where else would you go, sweetie?" Martha had always loved flirting with her handsome and gregarious underclassman. "I hear Loverboy is playing Adams Field House in another week or so."

"Great! That's where I'll go instead."

"Yeah, in your plastic bubble, you might." Martha administered a dose of reality. "You're not going to be doing any crowds for a while."

"I'm sure if I called their tour manager and told them my sob story and that I was a huge Loverboy fan, they'd get me in for the publicity alone." Mitch used his hands to frame the headline: "Boy in Plastic Bubble Gets Final Wish."

"*Are* you a Loverboy fan?" Ronald asked from the threshold.

"No," Mitchell said. "But that's not the point."

Martha and Ronald both knew better than to argue with him. Mitchell might think he was dying, but that ending was far from conclusive, especially this early and after just one round of chemotherapy. Everyone seemed to recognize there was a benefit to a little levity.

"I suppose if you got seats backstage or even in a private box and wore a mask over your nose and mouth the whole time, you could get away with it," Martha said. Then she thought about her liability and added, "But you didn't hear that from me."

"I could look into getting the tickets if you really wanted to go," Ronald offered, trying to tamp down his enthusiasm in front of Martha. He would do anything to land an overnight getaway with Mitch—even a sick Mitch. But he needed to make this seem like it was not about his desires.

Mitchell nodded, making direct eye contact with Ronald, which the older man took as his marching orders to get Loverboy tickets. He wasn't even sure if he knew who this band (or group or singer) was. But like Mitch had said, that wasn't the point.

Martha put up her hands in surrender and said, "My work is done here. It's back to the white boards, men." She pulled the door closed. "Really nice seeing you, Mr. Simpleman."

"You as well, Martha," he said as she turned to walk away. "Take care of yourself. And keep taking good care of Mitch, too." She waved without turning around. She found it very odd that Mitchell would have kept in touch—in regular contact, it seemed—not just with one of his high school teachers, but with Mr. Simpleman, who had to be the oddest duck on Stevensville High's faculty.

When Ronald turned his gaze back through the viewing window, Mitchell had tented, either faking an erection or using his real one to raise the sheet in the vicinity of his crotch. The hospitalized devil arched both his eyebrows in a beckoning way and Ronald's mouth dropped open, no white board required to communicate his interest. He licked his lower lip.

The tug-of-tease began between them. Mitchell bit his lower lip and appeared to be stroking himself beneath the cotton pinnacle. Ronald had gone full mast himself, inside his polyester suit pants. The bottom of the window came to just below Ronald's chest, so his crotch was hidden, but Mitchell could tell what he was doing by the manner in which his right shoulder moved slowly up and down. Mitchell smiled. He loved being provocative with his fishing pole and Ronald Simpleman was such an easy fish, always volunteering to get hooked. Mitchell upped his game, lowering the sheet by paddling his feet. He hadn't been faking an erection, Ronald was delighted to see.

But in that moment, Ronald heard people around the corner at the end of the hallway. He was horrified to see who it was. He grabbed the white board and scribbled frantically, holding the message to the window.

IT'S YOUR DAD AND SISTER!

Ronald had erased the white board and was holding the blank slate below his belt in a concealing way when the two family members got within greeting range. "Mr. Carson . . . Molly," he said, with a regal and out of place bow of his head. Not a hand-shaker, Mr. Carson nodded back.

"Hey," Molly said, acknowledging a teacher she recognized but had never received instruction from. She was Mitch's younger sister by two years and more a sporty—not the grammar-focused drama—type.

"He's mostly sleeping," Ronald said, using a disappointed tone, as though they had gathered at a zoo and there was no activity in the primate cage. "I was just heading out."

He saw Mitch's sister looking at the white board. His erection down to half mast, he handed it to her, saying, "Maybe you'll have better luck."

He gave a quick nod and excused himself. It bothered him to have been caught red-handed. He knew what it must have looked like to Mitch's family. The two of them had been so careful and secretive for years. But now Ronald's concern for Mitch and his recovery was splayed out in the open.

It shouldn't have mattered—and it wouldn't have mattered, had they been in a larger city where no one else knew or cared about the details of your life. They were both adults at this point. Mitch could see and spend time with anybody he wanted. Ronald knew he could try to justify this until the Stevensville Yellowjackets beat the Hamilton Broncs at football—that is, until the cows came home. There just weren't any other faculty members driving thirty minutes to pay a hospital visit to a student they'd taught three years ago.

As he passed the reception desk, which was fortunately unattended, he looked down and noticed a dark wet spot on the crotch of his beige suit pants that the vest tails of his three-piece polyester leisure suit did not conceal. Just one more embarrassment on top of a heap of embarrassments. He strode through the main entrance doors and out to the safety of his Volvo. In the mostly empty parking lot, his supposedly one-of-a-kind car was parked right next to the crème-de-menthe-colored Carson family VW Rabbit.

ON THE VERY off chance that Mitch was going to be well enough in time or felt like using the concert as an excuse to get out of town to blow off some steam before his next round of chemo, Ronald had selfishly taken the first step. It was much easier than he thought to get tickets to the Loverboy concert, even at this late date. He'd had to pull a few strings and use his one contact at the University of Montana theater department to find the name of the fellow in charge of the Adams Field House. When he told the facility manager the slightly embellished story of his former high school student who was now in the fight for his life against cancer—adding that he'd been attending U of M before his diagnosis and that he was a superfan of Loverboy—the ramparts parted as easily as if he'd stretched out his arms and commanded "Open sesame!" It turned out the concert promoters didn't know how to sell the handful of box seats that they felt were too far back from the stage, so the university had been provided twenty-eight comped house tickets for faculty and VIPs. The facility manager said they had only been able to give away twenty of those, and half of those folks had no idea who Loverboy was. Mitch and Ronald would be sitting in a box normally used by football and basketball officials. There were six other spots in the box, but they hadn't yet been claimed. The concert was in two days.

Ronald shared the great news with Mitch by telephone, but must have caught him on a bad day, because Mitch didn't take it well, snapping back that he didn't even like Loverboy. Ronald felt horrible, thinking he had misunderstood or should have been more realistic and responsible, given the difficulty of Mitch's treatments. He also kicked himself for being surprised that Mitch was having a bad day. He probably hadn't had any good ones lately. Ronald seemed to be saying and thinking all the wrong things, so when the call ended abruptly, Ronald was relieved.

But Mitch phoned him back five minutes later, seemingly in a different frame of mind. He said he thought the concert was a brilliant idea. It gave them an excuse to go into the city together for an overnighter before his next round of chemo. Ronald liked this Mitch much better than the version from five minutes earlier.

IN A BRAZEN move, Ronald pulled Veruca right into the Carsons' driveway, and in broad daylight. He gave the horn a quick double honk. Within seconds, a face-masked Mitch and his mother were on the front porch. She gave a concerned wave to Mr. Simpleman and then smother-hugged her firstborn, who had to peel himself out of her arms to make his getaway. He had an orange bandana tied to his head and a knapsack on his back. He was carrying a large plastic yellow jug. Ronald saw its contents swishing as the Saturday morning sun shone through the container.

"What in the world is that?" he asked, after telescoping his arm to open the passenger door from the driver's seat.

"It's my piss. Want a swig?" Mitchell hopped into the car and stashed the jug on the floorboard of the back seat. Then he patted the dashboard. "Let's go!"

"Seatbelt," Ronald said. They both waved to Mrs. Carson, and the most recognizable car in town backed out and onto Spring Street. Ronald reached over to squeeze his passenger's thigh.

"Hey!" Mitchell said. "Not until we are out of town."

Ronald returned his careless hand to the steering wheel. "Explain the jug of urine, please."

"We're supposed to keep it cold," Mitchell responded.

"That's an instruction, not an explanation."

"Beats me," Mitchell said. "Maybe there are too many chemicals in my piss to flush it into the Bitterroot River."

"Tell that to Smurfit-Stone. And says who, anyway?" Ronald was happy to see Mitch in a sparring mood.

"The Environmental Protection Agency, for all I know." Then he got serious. "I'm supposed to collect it in between chemo sessions and bring it back for analysis."

"Bring it back where? The EPA field office?"

"The hospital, funny man."

"Is that where we need to go, then?" he asked. He braced himself in case his special arrangements needed to be cancelled.

"Eventually, yes." Mitchell stretched out his legs and seemed to be arching his pelvis for attention. Ronald, having been reprimanded once, resisted grabbing him until they'd crossed the Bitterroot River and turned onto Highway 93. "Did you remember your camera?" Mitch asked, since this had been his priority and the condition he'd negotiated and inserted into Ronald's overnight scheme. Mitchell wanted—make that *needed*—to capture for posterity what he looked like before the next onslaught of chemo and especially before his hair fell out completely. He was horrified by what he might look like after that, if he made it that far.

"I did. And I brought along an extra one plus the Super 8, too."

"Cool," Mitchell said, adjusting the arms of his movie-star sunglasses around the bandana to hook onto his ears. "I told my folks that you offered to take me and my urine to St. Patrick's tomorrow. They wanted me to tell you thank you, from them."

"Oh, did they, now?" Ronald was suspicious, assuming Mitch's parents weren't at all thrilled about this kidnapping.

"They're frazzled lately. This really does take one thing off their list. One or maybe both of them will head down to the hospital later in the day." Mitchell spoke toward the passenger window as he tracked the course of the Bitterroot, a river he and his dad had canoed many times together. The dark green almost black river ribboned around sandbars, veered close to the highway, and then disappeared behind stands of Cottonwood so thick that Lewis and Clark might have missed the river altogether, had they not been floating down it with Sacagawea, a few French fur trappers, and other members of their so-called Corps of Discovery.

Mitchell remembered from his father's recounting of local history that Lewis and Clark had renamed most aspects of their discoveries after themselves and egotistically so, wholly disregarding and erasing any native names they couldn't be bothered to learn or pronounce, names that had been used in this area by the Flathead, Lemhi Shoshone, Blackfoot and Nez Perce tribes since time immemorial. The Bitterroot River had been known as *Nexpúx'e*, named after the edible plant with the bitter tasting roots that grew along its banks. This just wouldn't do for Meriwether Lewis, who, upon spitting out a wad of the stuff from his mouth, renamed the plant and the river for what it was, a very unsavory bitter root that reminded him of tobacco. Contemporary botanists would later give the plant it's scientific name, *Lewisia rediviva*, named—not after any words the native tribes had used, but after Lewis, himself. Eighty years on, bitterroot would be officially named Montana's state flower in 1885.

Where the Lemhi Shoshone people had a name they had already been using for the nearby Clark Fork River, *Tum-sum-lech*, which translated into No Salmon, William Clark had to change it up, renaming the river after himself, as proof he'd been there, conquered that. His partner in trespassing exploration, Meriwether Lewis, had taken the "No Salmon" translation to mean there must be a treacherous downstream waterfall or intense rapids, over which salmon couldn't migrate. As a result of his misinterpretation and not knowing that salmon didn't exist east of the continental divide—having not yet crossed that mountainous barrier on his immediate left—he'd ordered the party to be on high alert, so they didn't float the whole expedition right over the edge of an abyss. But Mitchell knew you could float and paddle all the way to the Bitterroot's confluence with the Clark Fork River west of downtown Missoula before you encountered any elevation variance or significant rapids.

"Who names a kid Meriwether, anyway?" Mitchell said, distractedly.

"Pardon?" Ronald asked, having been daydreaming himself, thinking about when he was going to tell Mitch how he felt about him. He'd promised himself that this would be the weekend he finally expressed his feelings, getting some pronouncements off his hairy chest.

"Lewis and Clark, I mean. Clark's first name was William, but Meriwether? What kind of name is that for a boy?" Mitchell was fully engaged now. "Do you suppose Lewis and Clark were gay lovers?"

"I didn't grow up in this area, so I don't really know the history," Ronald admitted. "I suppose it's possible they were more intimately involved. Homosexuality as a last resort was and is common among explorers, sailors, miners, prisoners, and soldiers."

"Right? Lewis called Clark his friend and companion. After the expedition, he suffered from depression and mood swings. I guess he committed suicide shortly after he'd learned that William Clark had married a woman named Julia."

Ronald grinned. "You know the history better than I, and you raise important questions." He sounded like a teacher encouraging a student's curiosity.

"I'm not sure, but I don't think Meriwether Lewis ever married or had children."

"Perhaps you should write a book on this topic."

"And with a name like Meriwether, you can bet he was teased as a kid. He might as well have been named Gaywether. He was probably called that, too."

Ronald chuckled. "What's in a name, anyway? My last name's Simpleman, but I don't think that makes me simple."

"Yeah, where does a name like Simpleman come from anyway?" Mitchell was looking out the passenger window and thinking about his cancer again. There were periods, some as long as ten minutes, when he wasn't obsessed with the alien that kept expanding and contorting inside his abdomen. But whenever his mind managed to wander away, even temporarily, his fright always took him by the hand, leading him right back to the top-heavy reality that he might not pull through this. He vigorously rubbed his eyes before they had a chance to well up, so close to the surface was his emotional aquifer these days. His watery vision quickly focused on a passing rest area where he'd once given a blowjob to a trucker in his rig.

"It's a North American name," Ronald said, "and not that common. I think most people with that last name live in Colorado. A few in Utah. Some in Missouri."

Mitch didn't respond, maybe forgetting what the question had been, stuck on the resurfaced memory of the trucker.

"I assume Carson is English or Scottish," Ronald said, trying to restart the conversation.

"What? Uh, both," Mitchell said. "Comes from the Scottish English borderlands. There's even a crest."

"Well, apparently, Lynyrd Skynyrd wrote a song in the 70s called 'Simple Man,'" Ronald said, trying to even the score.

"Oh yeah?" Mitchell took the bait before remembering why he knew this song. "Why don't you sing me a few lines?"

Ronald cleared his throat. "Let's see," he said. "Baby, be a simple, be a simple man. Oh, be something you love and understand. Baby, be a simple kind of man."

Mitch had a sudden and traumatic flashback to Stan Cockburn and the assault that had transpired in the back of Stan's orange Toyota pick-up truck just over five years ago. He stammered, but eventually said, "'Simple Man' is two words. I don't think that counts."

"No?" Ronald smirked.

They rode on in silence for a good stretch of the highway. Mitchell had fixed his stare once again out the passenger window. His surveying eyes followed the ridge of a miles-long dirty snowbank that had been plowed to the side of the highway but still hadn't melted, while Ronald tried to summon the guts to say what he wanted to say, and try to take his relationship with Mitch to a new level.

Observing the slower speed limit through the town of Lolo, Ronald realized his passenger had fallen asleep, chin to his chest. It was a reprieve, since Ronald still hadn't come up with a way to introduce the subject that he wanted to discuss. It had been a strange and strained three years for Ronald since Mitch had graduated high school and left Stevensville. After four exhilarating years of observing his protégé five days out of every school week in class, during rehearsals and theater productions that always extended well after dark, and on the overnights the competitive drama team would take to display their acting chops in front of judges all over Montana—plus the clandestine visits paid to his apartment—Ronald had thought they were becoming closer, and that they had a thing going.

Ronald, the teacher and mentor, had grown much fonder and more desirous of the teen who was becoming a man in his final years at Stevensville High. He had assumed this relationship—and these feelings—were reciprocal, and that they could only expand and flourish once they were both adults and could get out of Stevensville. Around this same time though, Mitchell had become fixated on auditioning to become a singer and dancer with a touring troupe. He desperately saw this as his one-way ticket out of Big Sky Country and a chance to see the world for a year before beginning university. Mitch certainly had the talent and drive to go anywhere he wanted—nobody knew this better than Ronald, who'd spent the previous handful of years bolstering that unshakeable confidence. What kind of evil and self-serving person would he had to have been, to hold back his most promising student? Besides, it was only for a year.

When Mitch returned to Stevensville, after his year of singing and dancing and experiencing more of the world at age eighteen/nineteen than most Montanans experienced in their lifetimes, he had changed, while Mitch's absence had only made Ronald's heart grow fonder and obsessively so. While Ronald expected and wanted very much to pick up where the two had left off, Mitch acted disinterested, distracted, even disgusted once when Ronald tried to kiss him—something they'd never done previously. Then long summer short, when it started to feel like Mitch couldn't make his transition to university in Missoula (only thirty miles but a world away) happen any faster, he moved into his assigned dormitory room on the second floor of Aber Hall a week early, ostensibly, he'd told Ronald, to familiarize himself with the campus before classes started. Ronald was hurt by this because the hastened announcement seemed to come immediately on the heels of his suggestion that they spend the last week of summer together camping at a remote hot spring, before they both headed back to their respective schools.

As Mitch's first semester got underway, Ronald had at first persisted by telephone trying desperately to insert himself in Mitch's college life, coming up with excuses that would have him in Missoula for other reasons, but then insist on taking Mitch out to dinner or lunch or ice cream or a movie. Ronald was eventually made to know that he was pestering his former student who said he needed to concentrate on his courseload. But then the very next month, Mitch would be the one calling Ronald for sex, whenever his dormmate Chris announced he would be heading home to Bozeman to see his folks and his dog, so there had been those mixed signals, too.

The following semester and shortly before Mitch had shocked Ronald with the news that he would be transferring to UNM in Albuquerque, Ronald had been thinking he might suggest they share an off-campus apartment in Missoula while Mitch earned his degree at U of M. Ronald was even prepared to foot the rent. In his fantasy, they would travel the globe together during their summers out of school. Ronald would commute to Stevensville every school day, and when that became tedious, he'd find a teaching post in Missoula or even Frenchtown.

But Mitch was back home again, diminished and dozing right beside him in the passenger seat. Though now a cancer patient facing the biggest uphill challenge of his life at a time when most his defenses had gotten knocked down, Mitch was beginning to rebound after his week in isolation on a steady intravenous diet of antibiotics and anti-viral medications. It may not have been the best or proper time for Ronald to profess his feelings and desires, but if not now . . .

Mitchell stirred back to life when the Volvo's tires modulated to a higher pitch as the car crossed from pavement onto the grated bridge deck that spanned the Bitterroot River, entering Missoula's city limits. "Are we there yet?" he asked, coming out of his impromptu nap.

"Yes, sleepyhead." Ronald reached over to give Mitch's thigh a squeeze and to connect with the subject of his every thought.

"It's the drugs. My body is full of 'em. What happened to the sun?" He pushed the sunglasses to ride on top of the orange bandana pulled tight around his forehead and knotted in the back. Dark gray thunder clouds exaggerated the heights of the hills that surrounded the city and regularly trapped the pulp mill smog. The same valley depression, during the last ice age (around 14,000 years ago), kept filling with glacial meltwater to create an inland sea trapped behind ice dams. The dams eventually broke, dispatching catastrophic walls of water that raced down the river, scouring out the topography on its way to the real sea—the Pacific Ocean. Mitchell had hiked the Mount Jumbo Trail overlooking the University of Montana with his father a half-dozen times. He'd seen the engraved stone that indicated the highwater mark for Glacial Lake Missoula: 4,200 feet. His trained eye could make out a snow-dusted Mount Jumbo in the distance. There would be no hiking up there today—not as weak as he was feeling.

"Cloudy days are better for photography, especially for black-and-white captures."

"You're shooting in black and white?" Mitchell sounded disappointed.

"I brought along three cameras, so my bases are covered."

"There are actually four bases in baseball when you include home plate."

"This is why I shouldn't use sports metaphors," Ronald conceded. "In that case, I'll just have to sketch your portrait when we run out of film."

"You'll be lucky if you make it to third base, old man," Mitchell joshed. He was a budding master of the double-entendre, but these jabs were like bee stings for Ronald sometimes—like when Mitch referred to him as "Mr. Simpleman." Ronald took solace in the fact that he was no longer twice as old as Mitch, as he had been when they first met. Sometimes with Mitch, the stinger went deeper or got left behind in Ronald's thin skin to fester. But usually, the pinch or pain wore off in a matter of minutes with a little rubbing.

This was a big step they were taking, but Mitchell had needed to escape his doomsday world of stomach spasms and dry heaves before the chemo rollercoaster cranked up for another gravity-defying attempt at whipsawing the cancer right out of him—by centrifugal force if necessary. Mitchell cringed at the thought of sharing a motel room for the whole night, but he kept that on the inside. With his body functions out of whack on account of the drugs, he didn't know how he was going to manage sharing a bed and a bathroom. He and Ronald had never spent a whole night together, and never once slept when they were sleeping together. He had been used to getting all the purely physical sex he needed, usually under the cover of darkness, and then sneaking home or back into his dormitory room to sleep in his own bed under his own covers.

The Volvo coasted to a stop at the first intersection with a stoplight at Paxon Street. "I booked us a room at the Red Lion but I'm not sure if we can check in yet. We could try, or we could grab a bite, if you have an appetite."

"Not hungry, but we can stop if you are. I'd prefer to maybe do the photo shoot before I eat. That way I won't feel or look too bloated."

Ronald hadn't mentioned it, but he'd certainly noted that Mitch had lost weight. They hadn't gotten naked or even fooled around since the diagnosis—except through the hospital viewing window—and Ronald hadn't yet had the opportunity to check out Mitch's scrotum, now that it was reportedly down a team player. Mitch had said he'd been swimming and lifting weights at school, but he was afraid that all his efforts were going to be reversed as chemo and surgeries made a colossal mess out of his body.

"Let's try to check in first and maybe I'll grab a muffin or a sandwich. I'm thinking we could head out to Jacob's Island for the shoot if it doesn't start raining."

"Sounds like a plan. Funny, I was thinking Jacob's Island for this, too. It's like I can read your mind," Mitchell said.

Ronald so wished that were true.

THE COUNTRY MICE had been able to check into the big city motel when they arrived, but Ronald was disappointed the front desk clerk had assigned them to a room with two double beds when he'd specifically requested a room with one. For his part, Mitchell had been momentarily relieved when he saw the configuration. Ronald thought he should have had Mitch wait in the car while he checked them in, but Mitch said he needed to stretch his sore legs, as every joint in his body ached from all the drugs sloshing around in his system. He'd wandered into the lobby behind Ronald, and the clerk, assuming they must be traveling together on business, wanted to spare them the embarrassment of having to share a bed. Ronald, making a fuss once they'd arrived at the room, wanted to return to the front desk to get a new one. But Mitchell—depositing his jug of urine in the mini-fridge—convinced him to not bother, suggesting that the second bed gave them a place to throw their things.

Ronald busied himself organizing his various cameras while Mitch primped in the bathroom. When he emerged, he had removed the bandana from his head and had slicked back his dark hair using his sister's Dippity Do gel. In Ronald's eyes, he looked like a European model. "Let's do this before the rest of it falls out," Mitchell announced.

"You look amazing, Mitch. Stunning, really." Ronald raised the 35mm camera and focused for a shot of his favorite subject framed by the bathroom doorway. "Your hair looks great that way," he reassured him. "You don't need to wear bandanas." He took four more shots while Mitch adamantly disagreed with him.

Ronald wasn't usually one to gush. In fact, he didn't think he'd ever mentioned to Mitchell that he thought he was even decent looking. Ordinarily, this might have left Mitchell to wonder if maybe he wasn't attractive to Ronald—although he imagined his cancer added a certain tragic countenance to his appearance. But he wasn't working this new hairstyle to attract Ronald. What existed between them wasn't exactly chemistry—at least the way Mitchell saw it—and was not mutual. It was rather an arrangement born out of scarcity, necessity, desperation, and most of all, convenience.

Ronald was wishing Mitch felt better so that the two of them could have disappeared to some place more remote, but it wasn't the right time of year to get into the woods and Ronald had needed to take into consideration—almost as an afterthought—that Mitch had cancer, and that none of these circumstances were normal or made for the best of getaways, romantic of otherwise. In a perfect world, they could have stolen away to a hot spring somewhere, staged this photoshoot in nature, and—oh yeah, he thought to add to his perfect world scenario—Mitch wouldn't have this damn cancer getting in the way.

As Ronald packed the movie camera into his photography bag, he asked Mitch, "Have I ever mentioned Jerry Johnson Hot Springs to you?"

"I don't think so," Mitchell said, tapping his foot. Even though he felt his nausea coming back on, he was raring to go. Though he'd requested this, he wanted the photo shoot over with and in the can.

Ronald said no more, picking up on Mitch's impatience. The two made their way back to the parked car and commuted across town in silence. Ronald maneuvered Veruca into an Albertson's parking lot off Van Buren Street and drove around the back of the grocery store to get closer to the riverbank. He chose an empty spot near the trail bridge and parked.

Mitchell was out of the car with his knapsack hanging off one shoulder taking big sniffs of the river air before Ronald had unfastened his seatbelt. He'd felt queasy all day and with the dread of checking back into St. Patrick's for another assaulting round of toxic chemicals in the morning, his energy reserves were running low. He already doubted he would be able to make it through the whole concert that evening, if they went at all, and he hoped Ronald wouldn't be too disappointed by this.

Though neither had admitted it to each other, this was not the first time either of them had been over the river on that footbridge. Mitchell, who had been to Jacob's Island before, realized that Ronald must have been here, at least once, too. How else would he have known where to park?

For his part, Ronald seemed to have forgotten that Mitch had spent two semesters living on the nearby campus. Closeted or out, most gay students knew—or quickly found out—that Jacob's Island was a long-established and mostly top-secret cruising area. Locations such as this were whispered in clubs or mentioned in gay travel guidebooks like *Fodor's*, *Ferrari Guides*, or *Damron*. Bi and straight men—cowboys, businessmen, professors, football players, and even members of the Missoula Police Department—had followed the scent that would lead them across the same footbridge. But Mitchell hadn't required a travel guide or other cues. It hadn't taken him long to learn the cruising ropes as a freshman Grizzly at the University of Montana. Feeling worldly after touring the States and Europe as a singer and dancer, he had shed his naivety back then as easily as he peeled off his sweatshirt now, entering the tree cover with Ronald on the Kim Williams Trail. There was a skiff of snow on the ground, but it wasn't as cold as it looked, plus Mitchell felt like he was still running a temperature.

The sweatshirt off his model, was Ronald's signal to begin shooting. With a strained look on his face, he lifted the heavy camera bag off his bad right shoulder, cursing Shakespeare and *Twelfth Night* as he worked through the residual stab of pain he encountered daily. He'd start with the 35mm that had Kodachrome color film pre-loaded. Mitchell posed against tree trunks, sometimes looking away and other times staring into the lens like a predator. Hanging from its strap looped around his neck, Ronald swung the first camera out of the way and around to his backside. He took aim and snapped a few black and whites with the other camera. It was an older model camera, so he could tell them apart.

"Undo the top buttons of your jeans, why don't you?" the photographer lewdly suggested. Mitch didn't hesitate. This was old school to this seasoned model, who had never been bashful when it came to showing off. "But remember our agreement, Mr. Simpleman," he said, and the photographer faltered. "You don't develop these rolls of film until I tell you to—unless of course something happens to me. When I'm gone, I don't care what you do with these."

"Scout's honor," Ronald said, holding up three fingers before switching cameras.

Mitchell motioned Ronald to follow him as he started walking to a different location closer to the river. "That reminds me," Mitchell said, breaking his sequence of poses. "If something happens to me in the next weeks or months or however long this ordeal lasts, I'll need you to help me with something. Remember that Polaroid camera you gave me?"

"Of course I do."

"Well, I used it to take pictures of me, you know, naked. Some before pubic hair and some after, some with erections and some without."

"What did you do with them?"

"I fed them back inside the empty plastic cartridge they'd come in, plus another five photos from another cartridge, if that makes sense." Mitch scrunched up his face to see if Ronald was tracking his description.

"Clever. I wouldn't have thought of that. Makes a nifty storage system." Ronald was impressed.

"Well, I stashed this cartridge in my bedroom closet. When my dad and I finished my bedroom in the basement, he'd left this hole in the back of the closet wall where the neck of a sewer pipe sticks out—you know, in case a plumber needed to get inside the pipe to clear a clog or something like that."

Mitchell paused to admire in the distance a scattered assembly of boulders near the river's edge at the eastern tip of the island. He pointed in that direction. He was surprised not to have run into anybody lurking in the trees or cruising the trail, but he figured it must have been a slow day. He looked to his right and saw the arched roof of Adams Field House, where Loverboy was probably doing their soundcheck for that night's concert. In fact, when they walked out into the open, leaving the tree cover behind them, they heard it.

Mitchell went on. "Anyway, there was just enough space in the cutout for me to slip the Polaroid cartridge under the pipe and inside the wall. It's probably covered in cobwebs and spider droppings by now."

"I see," Ronald said, switching back to his camera with the color film. "That's good to know. I wouldn't mind seeing your Polaroid handiwork sometime, if you ever wanted to fish it out and bring it over. You know, Andy Warhol turned Polaroids into pop art."

Mitchell spotted a strange boulder a few steps into the river. It looked like a stone recliner, which gave him an idea for a pose. He tossed the sweatshirt he'd draped over his shoulders on top of his knapsack at the water's edge. He looked around. They were out in the open, but there was no one on either shore of the river. He undid the rest of the buttons on his jeans and pushed them down over his muscular legs, stepping out of them. "I should send my little cartridge to Andy to see if he could make something out of my Polaroids," Mitchell joked, standing in his nylon Jockey briefs while Ronald snapped away. With a leap that took more out of him than he anticipated, Mitchell was on the rock. He took off his Nike tennis shoes, tucking his half socks inside before lobbing the shoes onto shore next to his knapsack. "How's this?" he asked.

"Chilly but perfect!" Ronald was swelling with more than pride and had to adjust himself inside his own jeans. Mitchell gingerly reclined on the boulder, cursing its coldness. He began a series of poses trying to imitate what he'd seen in magazines, sending Ronald into a choreography of squats, shuffles, and extensions to get just the right angles. He switched back to the black-and-white camera, suddenly inspired to try an Herb Ritts approach. He fiddled with the F-stop and aperture settings and tried a few different special effects filters he snapped on the ends of the different lenses that he swapped out with great dexterity. But when he zoomed in for the close-ups, he saw that Mitchell was becoming erect, too, inside his briefs. The shadows this created on the nylon fabric were delicious and subliminal. Yet they left nothing to the imagination. Ronald was fully hard as he snapped away, which Mitchell could make out without needing to zoom in. Working even harder for the camera and the cameraman, the model experimented with arching his back, then standing on the rock like a Greek statue of Apollo. He lowered the band of his briefs to expose his pubic bush, then the base of his shaft. He held his undercover erection as he lowered himself back down to repose on his boulder.

Once again, Mitchell scanned both sides of the river, and the treeline of the island beyond his cameraman. Then he shed his briefs to pose in his birthday suit. Ronald didn't have to look down to know he had begun spotting in his own britches. He was instead focused on the bright red scar below Mitch's groin muscle that he could just make out under the recently shaved patch of pubic hair that looked like it was already starting to grow back. Mitch's erection reclined against his lower abdomen but cast its own shadow, which was even more impressive.

"If you're going to jack off, I'll switch to the Super-8 camera," Ronald said, encouragingly.

Mitchell thought about it and then began to touch himself in ways that signaled there would be no stopping. Ronald's hands plunged into his camera bag, and he quickly yelled, "Rolling!"

Mitchell bit his lower lip and went to work, shouting back, "Take your dick out, cameraman!" Ronald filmed with one hand and undid his jeans with the other. He could not believe his luck, or that Mitchell would go this far, allowing him to capture this act here in broad (though overcast) daylight. Mitchell played to the camera, narrowing his dark green eyes and exaggerating his facial expressions like he'd seen in porn movies—which he'd mostly viewed in Ronald's apartment on the mini-projector his teacher had balanced on his lap. Ronald moved in for a close-up on Mitch's ball sack to see if he could tell that only one testicle remained and got his shoes and feet wet in the process. He artistically focused instead on a mole to the left and above Mitchell's navel and then began to slowly pull back.

"I'm going to shoot," Mitchell said, right before he did. An impressive volume of semen hit his chest and stomach. Ronald went in for a close-up of the load and then intentionally blurred the focus as the camera panned up toward Mitchell's face. Ronald's feet were in the freezing water, and he still had his erection sticking out of the fly of his jeans, dripping milky strands of his own making into the Clark Fork. He backed onto the shore as Mitch hustled to get into his briefs before leaping back to land. He had just started dressing when two Labradors bounded out of the woods, racing for the water.

Ronald stashed the movie camera in the bag and tucked himself back inside his jeans just as a young family with a pre-schooler emerged into the opening, calling for their pets. Mitchell laughed as he put the last of his clothes on, but Ronald was terrified they'd been caught in the act. He exchanged pleasantries with the family and then the two naughty boys hightailed it back across the footbridge and into the car.

Mitchell reached his hand over the console to squeeze Ronald's thigh, and then the squeeze migrated to the wet spot. "We should get back to the motel to take care of that," he suggested.

"Grand idea," Ronald agreed. "We have just enough time for a little R & R before grabbing dinner and heading to the concert." He started the car and backed out of the parking spot.

"Look, Ronald, I don't want to disappoint you, but the concert isn't that big a deal for me. I am pretty wiped out and wouldn't mind just hanging out in the motel room tonight."

How could Ronald be disappointed when that was all he'd wanted from the beginning? The concert had been an excuse to spend some time with

Mitch and get him out of the house on a little adventure before he had to check back into the hospital. "You're right. Let's take it easy tonight," Ronald agreed. "We can pretend we're an average couple bored at home, rediscovering that sex is their favorite pastime."

Mitchell laughed but took umbrage at the term *couple*. "I don't know about the couple part of that scene . . . but we're both actors, right?"

It was Ronald's turn to laugh. That was precisely where he had wanted to steer the conversation. He *wanted* to discuss their relationship. He was still too chicken to bring it up, so he tossed out a non sequitur. "I have to say, that was an impressive amount of semen on one ball."

"Thanks," Mitchell said, blushing, while trying to re-tie the bandana on his head as Ronald weaved through traffic to get them back to the motel. "I'm worried that the next operation could leave me with a dry well—not that I have any interest in becoming a father."

"Any chance you might stay in Montana after your treatments and surgery . . . finish school here instead of zipping back to New Mexico?" Ronald couldn't have jammed more hope into his question. What he actually wanted to ask was *What about us?* But before Mitchell could answer, he tossed out another possibility. "I was thinking that if you were going back to New Mexico, I might make this my last semester teaching at Stevensville and maybe try to get on with a school district in Albuquerque."

Mitchell squirmed in the passenger seat. He needed to shut this down firmly. "At the moment, I'm busy falling in love with somebody else—his name is Greg—that, and beating this cancer."

"Greg?" Ronald blurted out.

"I met him at UNM. He drove me home to Stevensville for Christmas Break. He's from a town somewhere near Corvallis over in Oregon, originally." Mitchell stopped fussing with the bandana and shifted his butt so he could face the driver. "Greg's already returned to UNM without me and I'm hoping to get back there as soon as I can."

And then the question tumbled from Ron's quivering lips. "What about us? I was sort of thinking that you and I were boyfriends."

"I'm not your boyfriend, Ronald."

PART III: 1980–1976

And then the lover,

Sighing like furnace

YAKIMA, WASHINGTON

May 17, 1980

IT MIGHT HAVE HELPED IF RONALD FOUND AND USED his recently prescribed glasses which he'd either left at school or might be sitting on the dash in his car downstairs in the driveway. He'd been struggling for five minutes with an ancient roll of cellophane tape trying with his fingernail to find an edge he could peel back to wrap Mitch's graduation present. It would have helped if there had been a single decent light in his apartment but for a director usually obsessed with stage lighting, he preferred his hideout to be as dimly lit as possible. He had deep red and purple batik scarfs and sarongs he'd picked up in Java and elsewhere in Indonesia draped over every lampshade in the place. Similarly colored blankets and throws covered nearly every piece of beige tweed and floral-print furniture that had come with his furnished apartment. Ronald was uncertain of his own style, but from the moment he saw the mid-century rural apartment in the fall of 1974, he knew that these furnishings did not fit the bill. So, he modified them to better align with his undefinable sensibilities, as he did with everything. *Or almost everything*, he thought, cursing the roll of tape he couldn't tame.

He used to think that Mitch Carson could be modified and tamed, too. And all the gods in mythology—both Greek and Roman—could attest that Ronald had tried like Sisyphus nearly every day over the past five years to convince his student they would make great companions one day—as soon as Mitch came of age, of course. But so far, it hadn't worked. Ronald was self-punishingly aware of the risks he had taken, but even these seemed offset by the catastrophes he'd narrowly avoided, like the time the principal shared feedback with him—ostensibly received from parents, though he'd never been shown proof—questioning why Mitch Carson got the lead parts in every theatrical production. There had also been that incident at the Montana State drama competition, where a few other student cast members—Oberon, Titania, and Lysander, from their winning one-act excerpt from *Midsummer Night's Dream*—caught Mitch sneaking out of their teacher and director's motel room, on the eve of their travel day back home to Stevensville. All the improvisational training that Ronald and Mitch had worked on over the years saved both their butts that time. On the spot, Mitch had simply made up a story that Mr. Simpleman had been helping him with a university scholarship application. It had been another convincing performance, by all accounts.

Ronald gradually accepted that he needed to let go of any present hopes and desires—that Mitch needed to fledge the nest and accumulate some experiences on his own. He wasn't giving up on their future. His stubborn heart couldn't let Mitch get completely away. But every cold shoulder Ronald had received from the universe (and from Mitch himself, lately) seemed to indicate the time had come for him to break from his happily-ever-after fantasy and grapple, for a change, with the realities of their age difference and that Mitch was off to experience a world beyond Montana and Ronald's reach. In quiet moments of introspection that never lasted very long, Ronald also suspected he needed to address—in some meaningful way—his own ridiculous selfishness and possessiveness, if he was ever going to lure Mitch back to him. But he couldn't concentrate on any of that self-improvement mumbo-jumbo at the moment.

How was he to tackle the big stuff when the reality of this roll of tape was too much for him? He threw the spool in the wastebasket under the sink of the kitchenette and started rooting around the drawers for some string. Coming up empty, he remembered a ratty sweater of his he'd been holding onto even though it had been falling apart for years. He found it and carefully liberated a long strand of fuzzy, blue-colored yarn. He'd just tied the plain brown wrapping around his present together when he heard footsteps on the stairs outside his door, followed by Mitch's signature rap. The knock was unique to Mitch simply because Ronald had received no other visitors in the past four years—not even his landlords, as the stairs had become too physically challenging for them in their old age.

Mitchell spied Ronald at the dinette table through the normally curtained door window, so he showed himself inside. Ronald rose and the two embraced in a hug that lasted longer than the peremptory squeeze that usually preceded the removal of their clothing. This was not to be one of *those* visits and they both sensed it without needing to dwell on it. Mitch had appeared, at Ronald's summoning, to say goodbye.

"I can't believe you aren't staying for my big moment," Mitchell said, pulling out of the hug when it seemed Ronald wouldn't.

"My mother isn't doing well." It was the first time Ronald had lied to Mitch, and it was the same lie he'd given to the principal and superintendent. "I need to cut this school year a week short."

"But my graduation is in two days."

"I must hit the road, Mitch, just like you will in another few weeks. Here." Ronald twisted at the waist to retrieve the present off the tabletop. "This is for your journey."

He stared at the present as it transferred into Mitch's beautiful hands. He knew he couldn't look his student in the face, or he'd lose it emotionally. He was retaining each breath for longer than was necessary, trying to stave off the threat of waterworks. He intently studied Mitch untying each of the four string bows, memorizing the movements of his long fingers as they revealed the contents within—48 rolls of Kodak Kodachrome film.

When Mitchell looked up, Ronald did too. Two pairs of watery eyes— one olive-green, the other milk-chocolate brown—locked, and the two surrendered into another embrace that eventually evolved into rocking and then back-patting. This was a goodbye that neither of them had the grounding, maturity, or imagination to see coming. Ronald thought he had prepared for this moment, but he'd been wrong. He was a kinked-up mess on the inside. If he didn't get ulcers or hemorrhoids from this wrenching emotional distress, it would shock him. But he knew he needed to be the stronger of the two. He was the adult in the room and always had been. He needed to be the example to emulate, and he could not buckle. Not in front of Mitch, who was about to embark on the experience of his lifetime—not to mention launching into the lower stratosphere of adulthood.

The longer their embrace lasted, the more defiant and undisguisable Ronald's budding erection became, to the point that Mitch reached down to grab the outline in his jeans and command, "Down, boy!"

The two pulled apart. "It's involuntary," Ronald admitted. "It has a mind of its own around you," he added, with a tinge of pride. "Do you have time to, uh—"

"It's class night tonight," Mitch cut in with what seemed like a ready-made excuse. "I'm singing with a small group of my classmates, and we are meeting to rehearse our song one final time."

"I understand. What's the song?"

"'Our Last Song Together' by Neil Sedaka."

"I don't think I know it."

There and then, Mitchell sang his teacher the chorus, deploying his angelic, pitch-perfect tenor voice that Ronald had never heard him use for singing before now.

> This will be our last song together
> Words will only make us cry
> This will be our last song together
> There's no other way we can say goodbye.

A traitorous tear escaped Ronald's left eye, ignoring the all-points bulletin he'd dispatched to his body in advance of this fateful parting. "No words," he confessed as the two embraced one final time.

"I gotta get going," Mitchell stammered, pulling away. "Thank you for the film, Mr. Simpleman. I'm already looking forward to showing you the pictures I take!" He stepped toward the door.

"Wait," Ronald said, clumsily, not knowing why. "Break a leg tonight. You'll be amazing on stage, just as you have always been. You belong there, you know."

"Thanks again for everything, Mr. Simpleman." And Mitchell was out the door, and down the stairs.

Ronald stood in that spot, frozen as a statue with a hard-on, and for the first time since he was maybe six or seven years old, he unleashed a full-throated, ducts wide open, world-ending cry.

But his world did not end. He briefly thought he might sneak in the back door of the high school cafetorium just to watch Mitch perform at class night, but he'd already informed the superintendent he would be leaving town that afternoon. There was no sneaking in or around anything in a town as small as Stevensville. It was best, Ronald decided, that he shut down his apartment, pack his bags, and leave by sundown.

RONALD COULD NOT bear witness one minute longer. Just before six that Friday evening, he'd gotten out of town before the hellish conflagration of a lingering goodbye could consume and extinguish him. He was in no rush to get to Crested Butte and so had decided to take a circuitous route by heading first for Portland to take in the Oregon Coast before dropping down to visit and be consoled by his brother, Harlan, in San Francisco. In an emotionless zombie daze, he managed to make it over Lookout Pass, through the Idaho panhandle and to the outskirts of Spokane, where he checked into a smoky-smelling motel off the highway next to a Sambo's restaurant on Division Street. More than hungry or tired, Ronald stopped because he was sad. He ordered pancakes for dinner and somehow managed to fall asleep on a very uncomfortable bed in the middle of an episode of *Charlie's Angels* in which Kelly gets contacted by an attorney who says she may be the lost daughter of a millionaire.

When he awoke, he was disappointed to see that he'd only been asleep for forty-five minutes. He'd drifted off, smelling maple syrup in his hair or on his fingers, but had been too tired to wash it off. He knew he couldn't get back to sleep in what he now realized was a room he'd first dismissed as musty, but that now stunk to high hell of cigarette smoke that no amount of maple syrup could mask. He took a shower, left the key on the nightstand in the motel room, and climbed back into the bucket seat of his Volvo.

He drove another three hours, stopping for gas in Yakima. He'd been beating himself up over his decision to not stay for class night. He figured that even if it had run long, it must be over by now, as it was a quarter past eleven. *What's done is done*, he thought. Maybe he'd finally be able to fall asleep. He glided onto the shoulder of Highway 12, then turned right into the parking lot at the Red Apple Motel, because the two-story neon sign shaped like a red apple with green leaves and stem caught his eye, striking him as fresh and clean. He'd also cracked up at the tagline toward the bottom of the red apple; *Dial Phones*, it advertised. *How modern*, he thought as he parked Veruca under the canopy to inquire about getting a room.

The front desk clerk explained that the whole town was sold out, as the Class AA fast-pitch softball tournament was happening that weekend. But he had one room left, if Ronald didn't mind being in their honeymoon suite, oddly located on the ground floor next to the ice machine. With his shoulder starting to ache and the pancakes not sitting well on his stomach, Ronald needed a break from the road. For the past four hundred miles, he'd been trying to unwind from the very stressful school year, not to mention the relationship he thought he had with Mitch Carson, which seemed over, too. Ronald figured he needed to check in to check out of the self-punishing loop his brain seemed stuck in. So, he pulled out his billfold and said he'd pay for two nights. The employee looked at the wall clock and said, "Since you're checking in after midnight, I'll just charge you for one night. Check-out time is noon on Sunday."

Ronald knew that once he'd gotten sufficient rest and had mostly sorted out his strange emotions and separation anxiety, he'd be able to hit the road again. After all, he consoled himself, he wasn't expected by anybody anywhere, except maybe by Harlan, eventually, and that's if his older brother ever remembered he was coming. In other words, he had all the time in the world to get to wherever he wasn't really headed.

In the motel room door, he turned the key on the plastic red-apple-shaped key ring and turned on the overhead room light, the bulbs of which were red. Almost the whole room was red, from the carpeting to the velveteen wallpaper to the apple-shaped bed with the quilted bedspread to the basket of real—not wax—Washington apples. The pillows were covered in green pillowcases and arranged to look like the stem and leaves on the apple of the bed. The first smile in days stretched across Ronald's square-chinned face. This room was too kitsch for words, but at the same time, quite possibly the best spot in the world for him to begin his recalibration. He sank his teeth into an apple and held it in his mouth, slurping the juice to keep it from running down his chin, as he unpacked his leather shoulder bag and prepared for his delicious, Washington-red-apple sleep.

WHEN RONALD STIRRED, he was momentarily disoriented, unable to remember where he was. Through squinting eyes, he could make out the outline of his face and pelt-like torso reflected at him in the ceiling mirror, which he hadn't noticed in the darkened room when he climbed into the apple-shaped bed.

Through the gaps in the rubberized curtains, sunlight sent refracted bars of light into the room at steep angles. He checked his wrist but had taken his watch off at some point during the night and placed it on the nightstand. When he located it, he couldn't make out the time without his glasses, which he'd left on the table next to the basket of red apples.

Clue by clue, he was remembering where he was and how he'd gotten here. His morning erection was not a mystery, as he'd greeted each new day this way since he was a little kid. He flipped the sheet and blanket off his mid-section to appraise his penile prowess in the overhead mirror. "Well, good morning, sunshine," he said out loud to his most loyal companion—perhaps, sadly, his only companion. He thought about wanking off but needed to pee so fiercely that he nearly cramped his detrusor muscle getting to the bathroom in time. After a minute of mimicking Yosemite Falls, Ronald reunited with his glasses and checked the time. He couldn't believe it was just after one o'clock in the afternoon on Saturday, May 17, and that he had survived his first night after losing Mitchell Carson—an event he'd been certain would kill him.

Rather than climb back under the sheet and covers of the red-apple bed, Ronald tidied the linens and removed the browning apple core he'd left on the nightstand. Feeling indecisive and unmotivated, he returned to the bathroom to get rid of yesterday's pancakes. Then he took a long shower, because the water was hot, and the pressure was strong, which was how he liked it. Getting dressed, he inspected yesterday's white Jockey briefs and determined they were still wearable. Without a second thought, he stepped back into them. He swapped yesterday's shirt for a Murano touristy t-shirt from a trip the Simpleman family made to Venice two summers ago. He repacked his shoulder bag and dumped the remaining fresh apples from the basket into it.

He stepped out of the motel room to retrieve his well-used road atlas from the back seat pocket in the Volvo. He had two routes to choose from in his quest to reach the Oregon Coast from Yakima. Because he wanted to take in as much of that coast as he could, he decided to take Highway 12 so that he could link up with Highway 30 west to Astoria. That would allow him to travel the state's entire coast, from north to south. Already several decisions into his day, Ronald felt his tummy grumble. He'd worked up an appetite for something other than pancakes and apples.

Remembering that he had rented the motel room another night, he stopped by the front office to inquire about area restaurants. He was enthusiastically directed to the Minado Buffet around the corner on Front Street. The restaurant was surrounded on two sides by imposing solid walls of wooden apple orchard crates that were stacked ten boxes high. The scene reminded Ronald of the portion of the Great Wall the Simpleman Family had visited outside Beijing in '69.

He stood a minute inside the entrance to the restaurant before approaching the hostess station, waiting for his eyes to adjust from full sun to the darkened, apparently windowless establishment. Ronald had been shown to a table next to the 2,500-gallon freshwater fish aquarium—the largest in Washington State, according to the hostess who seated him. He hadn't eaten in a smorgasbord-style restaurant since he was a kid, when he'd begged his parents to visit Furr's Restaurant with each trip to Denver. As he surveyed the offerings beneath the sneeze guard, he was taken back in time. He overloaded his plate not once, but on three separate visits to the buffet line over the course of the next ninety minutes. He left the restaurant more stuffed than a Thanksgiving turkey. After the block-and-a-half walk back to his motel room, all he wanted to do was lay down for a nap.

WHEN RONALD NEXT awakened, to his time-warped amazement, it was once again dark outside. Having drifted off with his glasses still on, he checked his wristwatch and saw that it was half-past nine in the evening. He had a choice, he supposed, to stay or go. He could hit the road again, but not a big fan of driving in the dark, he got up and off the bed. He switched on the portable television set atop the dresser and grabbed an apple from the basket that had been replenished by the motel maid while he was out for lunch. He flipped the television dial past a baseball game, then past a static array of color bars. Finally, he arrived at a 1963 episode of *Mutual of Omaha's Wild Kingdom* with Marlin Perkins. He vaguely remembered seeing it before. Its title was "Winter in the Wild Kingdom."

He propped the pillows behind his back and leaned against the headboard. He watched intently as Marlin observed bobcats and badgers and foxes in the frozen woods of Wisconsin. Ronald chuckled to himself as he remembered teasing—taunting really—his older brother by calling him *Harlan Perkins*. Harlan despised animals and anything even remotely wild, so the nickname legitimately bugged him, which of course had delighted Ronald because it gave him something to lord over his older brother. Two years younger and his opposite in many ways, Ronald had never identified with his older brother, who seemed generally annoyed by his existence. He'd learned—through much trial and copious error—that teasing was a way to get his brother's attention. He still used the device today, always opening his visits and telephone calls with a joke or a jab, as if to say, "Hey, I'm here! Look at me!"

Ronald knew he remembered this episode because in the second segment it featured Marlin Perkins' sidekick, Jim Fowler, bulldogging an elk calf by jumping on its back in deep snow from a helicopter in the Colorado Rockies. Just then, the music changed dramatically, as the announcer called the play-by-play. "Jim jumps and misses but still manages to grab the young elk by its rear leg as it struggles to get away. Over its neck, Jim slips an orange neck band for tracking and clips an ear tag that directs whoever kills or captures the elk to report the tag and where the kill happened to the Colorado Game and Fish Department in Denver."

Watching the harassment of this wild creature, Ronald was triggered with thoughts of home. Specifically, of Bruce the Elk, mounted on the fireplace in the living room. How his father, or anyone, could kill something so regal and unthreatening had traumatized him as a child. It bothered him all over again now as he watched wildlife photographer, Dick Denny, show Jim how elk tagging was done properly. "Dick's really got his hands full now," the television narrator said, as another calf was chased down by the helicopter until Dick jumped out and tackled it. Ronald rolled his eyes, catching his reflection in the mirror on the ceiling. He got up to turn off the television and pee. Then he stripped naked and went under the covers so the mirror couldn't watch him anymore.

It was just after five in the morning when Ronald opened his eyes to catch an expectant sunrise beginning to reveal itself through the curtain gaps. "Enough messing around in this honeymoon room!" he announced to the mirror. It was time to hit the road. As he brushed his teeth, he realized he'd subconsciously held off traveling more than a day away from Stevensville, just in case he decided to race back to watch Mitch's graduation commencement.

The commencement was today. With a glob of toothpaste pooling on the edge of his chin, Ronald knew that he had a choice to make. Would he continue heading west to the coast, or speed eastward to demonstrate how much he cared for someone who didn't, couldn't, or wouldn't ever care for him, too? As much as Ronald felt his world ending, he knew he had to keep driving away from the heartbreak for it to eventually stop hurting so much.

Since the basket of apples was just sitting there, and since he figured that in some way, he'd already paid for them, he emptied the fruit into his shoulder bag, on top of the apples from the day before. He put the room key on the dresser next to the television set and left the room.

Outside, he tossed his bag into the back seat of the Volvo, and bid Yakima farewell, reluctantly signaling to turn westward onto Highway 12. He drove half an hour northwest, through apple orchards as far as his eyes could see, before the landscape dried out into desert, polka-dotted with sagebrush. He'd arrived in Yakima at night and so had missed how barren the geography was this side of the Columbia River and east of the Cascade Mountains.

A couple miles on the other side of the town of Naches, he'd been reaching into the back seat to retrieve an apple from his knapsack, when he missed the left turn that US Route 12 inexplicably took. He kept following the natural course of the pavement without realizing the road he was on had turned into State Highway 410. It wasn't until he'd detoured twenty miles out of his way along the Naches River near Nile that he realized his error and that he had been traveling north instead of west. He pulled off the road and checked his atlas, then turned around and doubled back.

It was a few minutes before eight in the morning when he next checked his wristwatch. Rimrock Lake was whizzing past on his left, according to the sign he'd just speed-read. He'd left the desert behind and climbed into the foothills of the Cascades. He gawked out of Veruca's windows at the size of the forest trees—mostly Douglas firs, with smatterings of ponderosas, hemlocks, whitebark pine, and aspen—as he passed an elevation marker of 4,500 feet and the clearcut slopes of the White Pass Ski Area.

He immediately started to lose elevation driving parallel along a forested valley below that had been carved by the snowmelt headwaters of the Clear Fork Cowlitz River. The peak of Mount Adams—or was it Mount St. Helens? he didn't know for sure without checking his atlas—was visible through the tree breaks and on a few of the highway bends, which followed the contours of the ridge he was slowly descending.

Ronald sprinted past an amber-colored caution sign, which warned of rocks for the next three miles. He had been riding the brakes but had just taken his foot off the pedal when the car lurched suddenly. He looked in the rear-view mirror to see if he had hit something, and when he glanced back through the windshield, he slammed his foot on the brake. The car fishtailed to a stop, leaving rubber on the road surface about fifteen feet short of a giant tree that had fallen across the highway.

With the car stopped, Ronald felt a rumbling that he at first thought was just his nerves. He turned off the Volvo's engine and violently cranked his window open to listen. Veruca continued to quiver audibly, leaving him to believe there was either an earthquake, or Gorbachev and the Soviet Union had sent their nuclear missiles to begin destroying America.

He unfastened his seat belt and stepped out of the car and onto the pavement. No traffic had arrived behind him, and no cars or trucks had arrived on the other side of the largest ponderosa he'd ever seen up close. There was a far-off rumbling that he thought might have been his imagination. But at the same time, the sky seemed to be darkening. He looked at his wristwatch. It was a few minutes past eight-thirty that morning. He reached inside the open window and turned on Veruca's hazard lights. With some effort, he climbed on top of the fallen tree trunk and hopped off the other side, jogging a few yards to a bend in the highway to see if he needed to warn oncoming traffic. From this new vantage point, he saw two other trees—one laying across the road and another at an angle so severe he didn't think a truck could get under it. He heard the thunderous sound of falling rocks now and fast-walked back to the first tree in the road. He climbed on top of the trunk to get a better view and from there, looking backward in the direction from which he'd traveled, he could see a voluminous cloud of dust about a quarter mile behind his Volvo; a cloud that obliterated any view of the highway on the other side. As it settled, Ronald was pretty sure he saw debris from a rockslide on the pavement in the distance behind his car.

He jumped in his car, turned it on, and then executed a sloppy two-point turn to drive cautiously back toward the rockslide to see if he might get his Volvo around it or up and over the debris field. He could see a sizeable divot in the hillside on his left where the mountain had let loose to tumble on the roadway that he could see up close was indeed now blocked and now in both directions. Ronald's heart was pumping so rapidly that he could feel its percussion in his extremities. Was he truly trapped here? No sooner had he asked the question when a sizeable boulder began to roll down the slope above him, leaving craters as it hopscotched across the pavement between Veruca and the rockslide, to plunge off the cliff on the other side.

Ronald threw the car in reverse to get out of the path of any other rocks that might come. Clearly, the mountainside was unstable. He turned the car around and headed back to the tree that had initially stopped his progress. He thought the sun must have slipped behind clouds, though the sky had been majestic blue and clear all morning. He stopped the car, straddling the no-passing center line, and got out to check on the sun.

It wasn't his imagination. The sky had darkened, and was getting darker, almost as though dusk was coming. The deep rumbling in the distance continued from somewhere on the other side of the valley below him. Was this thunder? Had the weather changed? Was there another rockslide just waiting to wipe him out? Satisfied that the trees were thick enough to offer him some protection, he got back in the car, leaving the driver door open. He started the engine again to see if he could tune in a radio station that might help him sort facts from the fiction his brain was busy inventing. All he could raise was static, so he gave up and turned off the car.

The strangest light surrounded him, filling the sliver of sky he could see in the gap between the treetops. It reminded him of the total solar eclipse that had occurred near the end of February the previous year. That was on a school day, just before classes began, and it was all his students could talk about for the rest of that day, making it pointless to teach. He hadn't heard anything about another eclipse, but then he received most news from his students, since he didn't have a TV or read newspapers much. His students could be counted on to share whatever their folks had discussed at the dining-room table. Summer vacation had always required Ronald to be more proactive with his news gathering—otherwise, he'd return in the fall to discover his students were better informed on world events than he could ever hope to be.

Ronald opened the back door and retrieved another apple from his knapsack, wondering if he'd eaten more apples in the past seventy-two hours than he had in the rest of his life. He leaned his butt against Veruca's front hood and gnawed his way around the red delicious apple core, chucking the remnant into the trees. Since the highway was blocked on both sides of his position, and no rescue was imminent, he figured he didn't need to duck behind a tree to urinate. He walked up to the tree that blocked his way and christened it, unleashing a four-foot stream and wagging his hose from side to side. When he turned back to the car, it appeared to him that it was snowing . . . in May. He held out his hand and became even more confused than he'd been up to that minute. It wasn't snow. It didn't melt and it was falling from the sky so thickly that he was driven to take cover back inside the car.

He rolled up the driver's side window, leaving an inch open at the top. He sat there calling on all his analytical skills to explain what was happening on the side of that mountain. It seemed too early in the season for forest fires. Plus, he didn't smell smoke.

Then he remembered Mitchell mentioning something a few months back about a Washington State volcano that might be waking up after a hundred years. Ronald reached into the back seat for his road atlas. He turned to the Washington State double-page spread and located Yakima, where he'd started his day. Using his finger, he traced his path up the wrong road to Nile which had cost him nearly an hour out of his planned travel. Had he not missed his turn, he might have made it out of these mountains before the trees came down and the rockslide happened. He traced US Route 12 past Rimrock Lake and the White Pass Ski Area. He paused, noting first Gilbert Peak and then Mount Adams, which appeared to be directly south of the ski hill—maybe thirty miles away, according to the page. Ronald had no idea if Adams was even volcanic.

He remembered learning that the iconic Mount Ranier near Seattle and Mount Hood near Portland were both volcanoes. He continued tracing the highway line on the page to where he guessed he must be stuck—near a place named Palisades on the map. It didn't look like a town, but maybe the name of a creek. As though he was looking through a viewfinder on his Super 8 movie camera, he pulled back his focus. That's when he pinpointed Mount St. Helens on the map.

Measuring with his fingertip and the ruler, he guessed he was about forty miles away to the northeast, give or take a nail. As with Mount Adams, he didn't know if Mount St. Helens was volcanic. In any case, there were three possibilities to explain the darkened sky and now this ash in the air. One, there might be a forest fire. Two, Gorbachev might have used his launch codes. And three, if there were volcanoes in the Cascades, one of them might be coming to life.

Ronald glanced up from the map he'd been studying to see that he couldn't see. The windshield had been entirely covered by the stuff falling from the sky. He turned the ignition and depressed the windshield wiper lever, letting the wipers go back and forth twice before shutting them off again. He heard the grit against the glass. The ash was so light it floated away in little clouds of dust. The hood of the car was covered. It was beginning to accumulate on the road surface, too, and on the puzzle-bark tree trunk laying across the roadway in front of him.

"What in the hell," he asked out loud, wondering if this was how Sodom and Gomorrah had ended. Was this brimstone or the start of a nuclear winter? He got out of the car and popped open his trunk to reveal the boxes of things he'd hastily packed but not labeled for his summer hiatus. Some ash landed on his lips and he couldn't resist tasting them. He didn't taste smoke, and he didn't taste sulphur. He had no idea what radiation would taste like or if it had a flavor at all, but he had the good sense not to swallow it, so he spit, except his projection was lackluster, and the loogey of saliva and particles didn't clear his square chin. He swiped the mess away with the back of his hand.

He liberated the flaps of three cardboard boxes before he found the one with his camera equipment. He fished out the Super 8 and a 35mm Nikon. With the ash falling, he started with the motion camera, walking around Veruca and pointing the camera to the sky and along the tree line, where the ash stood out against a darker background. When Ronald lowered the camera, it captured the footprints that he'd left in the inch or two of ash on the road surface. He took a few still shots of his car and the tree lying across the highway.

Suddenly, he worried about his exposure to this stuff. His mind flashed back to the bomb drills and warning films he'd been subjected to growing up in the 50s when he was in grade school and there was a very real possibility, or at least propaganda suggesting that bombs might start flying any second at the slightest provocation. He jumped back into the car, slamming the door shut, which sent a shiver of dust from the roof. It reminded him of the baby powder he'd apply to his students' amateurishly excessive stage makeup, to prevent it from deflecting the stage lights or running.

He tried the radio again. Nothing. He checked his watch. It was ten past ten in the morning. He nervously studied the atlas, trying to see if he was close enough to walk to the nearest town before it got any darker than it already was. Ronald wasn't completely devoid of wilderness sense, having grown up in the mountains the son of a hunting father plus he'd watched a lot of Wild Kingdom when he was a boy. But he still didn't know what this white stuff in the sky was. Would it coat his lungs or choke him if he tried to exert himself out in the open without protection? Even sitting in the car, he didn't feel safe—but he wagered he was better protected inside than he would be outside, so he stayed put. As he sat there, he heard the loud cracking and snapping of wood followed by a swoosh and a thud as another giant tree crashed down somewhere around him. He couldn't coax himself to go back outside to look. He'd take his chances where he sat trembling.

The windshield was already covered again. Ronald could barely make out the wipers tracks from the last time he'd cleared the portholes through which he peered into oblivion. As he fidgeted, trying to calm himself down, he tried getting an annoying piece of apple skin out from between his lower teeth. He looked through the console and glove compartment for a piece of string or thread or thick paper he might use as floss. He knew he wouldn't have actual dental floss, since the stuff only made his gums bleed.

In a folder with the registration for his vehicle, Ronald found a business card that he'd been given years ago by his auto-mechanic and friend, Franco Cavaletti. Using the rear-view mirror and Franco's card, Ronald liberated the piece of apple skin without drawing blood. One small victory in the middle of the apocalypse that seemed to be happening outside. He reclined the driver's seat. The side windows weren't completely covered but it seemed darker than before somehow, which was strange since it still wasn't even noon. Ronald closed his eyes and felt the grit that had gotten behind his eyelids. This sent him into a series of theatrical yawns as he tried to generate tears sufficient to flush his peepers. But the yawning also made him sleepy, and it wasn't a minute before Ronald had dozed off while the ash continued to accumulate outside the car.

A raven cawed its distress from an overhead branch, possibly trying to ascertain if it was alone in this strange new apocalyptic landscape. Ronald heard it as he slept, but it took him a few seconds to snap out of it, to rejoin the crisis in progress. He turned the key in the ignition without turning over the engine, trying to clean the windshield again. But now the weight on the glass was too much for the wiper arms to move. Under the ashen blanket that seemed to have covered everything, he sat there for a minute, maybe two, uncertain what to do.

He turned the ignition again to try the radio. Slowly spinning the tuner dial, he tripped over a brief signal—one syllable from a man's voice—that he could not find when he dialed back. The raven seemed to chuckle overhead—like something had gotten caught in its throat. Ronald, accepting that he wasn't totally alone, cracked open the door, careful not to let the dust or ash or nuclear fallout get inside. The oddity of the scene beckoned him out of the car.

There was no green left in his view. The trees had become as flocked as his mother's Christmas trees. The sky was mostly darkened, but the cloud cover seemed eerily backlit. He glanced at his wristwatch. It was noon. The ash was still falling. The raven swooped to a lower branch to monitor the alien that had emerged from the vehicle below him. It cawed again. Ronald called back in imitation, getting some of the ash flakes in his mouth. He went to the trunk and fished an old t-shirt out of one of the boxes. He ripped the shirt using his teeth, fashioning a facemask that he held over his nose and mouth, and tying the ends together behind his head.

He reached inside the driver door and retrieved his eyeglasses from the dashboard. With improved vision, he could make out the shape and size of the raven. Grateful the bird wasn't a vulture following the scent of death and hoping for roadkill, he had to wonder what this harbinger of odd tidings was making of him and this mid-May snowstorm that wasn't a snowstorm at all. Ronald's shoes were buried in a fluff of ash that had to be three or four inches deep and the slight rumble beneath his soles persisted. With the trunk still open and the ash still falling, Ronald fished out the long-handled ice scraper and temporarily cleaned all of Veruca's windows. He closed the trunk, taking the ice scraper back into the front seat with him—for self-defence, if need be.

He was thirsty. He reached to the floor of the passenger seat and felt around for his canteen, which he had filled with water from the bathtub tap in his motel room (since it hadn't fit under the tap at the vanity sink). The raven flew down, landing on the hood of the car, audaciously staring through the windshield at him as he took a swig from the canteen. The raven cawed. The ash made it look like it was wearing a beanie. Ronald grinned.

"Are you thirsty, guy?" he said as he rummaged through the center console for something that would hold a bit of water. He popped the gray lid off a black film canister, and carefully dispensed water into it from the canteen. With his left hand, he slowly rolled down the driver's side window. He transferred the lid from one hand to the other and gently reached out the window and around the front of the windshield to set the offering on top of the layer of soot.

The raven hopped a few steps backwards out of caution but didn't fly away. When Ronald withdrew his arm back into the car, the bird cocked its head to one side, trying to detect whether this was a trap. Ronald took another sip from the canteen in encouragement. To his surprise, the raven hopped forward, tested the water with its black beak, then grabbed the lid, spilling its contents before flying off with the plastic prize somewhere out of Ronald's line of sight.

"You ungrateful—" As he started to scold the thief, he heard a boulder begin tumbling down the mountain somewhere above him. He took in a gulp of breath and threw his arms over his head, crumpling low over the steering wheel to brace for the impact or the end. He heard the snapping of branches and trunks growing louder and then it stopped. There was silence.

He let the air out of his lungs. He watched the ash falling. Or was it soot? He wondered if ash and soot were the same thing. He wondered if there were other drivers and cars trapped on this highway. Trapped . . . or worse. He began speculating on his own chances for escape, survival, and rescue. He sweated under his modified t-shirt mask, and it was hard to breathe, so he untied it. He started to take inventory of his survival skills, the very exercise of which, under different circumstances, might have had him bursting out in dubious laughter, that is if he didn't believe his life might truly be on the line and that his rescue would be up to him.

He balanced the canteen on the dashboard then reached behind his seat for his knapsack, extracting his only sustenance. He counted as he lined up three apples on one side of the canteen and four apples on the other. The display on the dash looked dire, if he was being honest. He should have captured that damn raven, so he'd have something to eat when his apples ran out.

Over the course of the next hour or so, the windshield became covered again. He looked at his wristwatch. Mitchell's commencement and graduation ceremony must have been underway, though he couldn't remember the exact time it was supposed to begin. Had he not been so fragile and acutely stubborn, he could have been sitting on an uncomfortable folding chair in the Stevensville High School gymnasium right now instead of being stuck here in the middle of . . . whatever this was.

In hindsight, he realized he had unintentionally driven Mitch Carson away from him over the course of the last two years by smothering his paramour with attention, flattery, and showy theatrical opportunities, and in such a manipulative way, that they would have no choice but to spend time and grow closer together. Sitting there in his car now, isolated and insulated from everything but his own merciless judgements, he could almost pinpoint the exact moment he had miscalculated his strategy. Over the previous summer break, a slow-moving panic attack began to nibble away at his delusional belief that Mitch would, in time, come around to the realization that the two of them were meant for each other and therefore belonged together. Realizing he was almost out of time, Ronald dialed up the pressure campaign by selecting a serious dramatic play for the senior class production—Agatha Christie's *Ten Little Indians*—with Mitch cast in the hefty lead of Philip Lombard, a role so essential and pivotal to the plot that the actor portraying it would require equally hefty, hands-on direction, in order to pull it off. Not only would this force Mitch to work overtime under Ronald's tutelage, it would showcase to the community every virtue Mitch Carson not only possessed but exuded from every pore of his being.

This strategy had worked for Ronald before which gave him cause to try it again. It had been back in November 1978 when Mitch had been the runaway audience favorite as the lead actor in the junior class play. Ronald had cast him as Axel McGee in Woody Allen's *Don't Drink the Water*—setting the pair on a path of collaboration and intense mentoring. This had given Ronald cover to spend even more time with his protégé after school, after rehearsals reviewing his copious directorial notes and suggestions, and during out-of-town drama competitions. Ronald was not only chauffeur but chaperone to the traveling ensembles he'd delicately cast around Mitchell to support him in his variety of leading roles.

Mitch, in his *Ten Little Indians* role as Philip Lombard, made *The Missoulian* when an arts reviewer—a theater prof at the university who also moonlighted as a Big Sky arts critic and who was a quasi-colleague of Ronald's—traveled up the valley at Ronald's invitation to see the production. But mere weeks after the short run, the spotlight faded, and Mitch—oversaturated and eager to focus on other things—began to demonstrably pull away.

Becoming more desperate and aware of the diminishing sands in the hourglass, Ronald went for broke, announcing a first in SHS drama history: the drama class would mount three student-directed plays over a three-week period in early spring. He selected Mitch to direct *Tom Sawyer* giving his student director the challenge of staging the production in the round. This was something else that had never been attempted at Stevensville High; in Ravalli County, the only events that happened in the round were rodeos. Once again, through intense and round-the-clock mentoring, Mitch Carson—and by extension Ronald Simpleman—had been triumphant with the audiences and this time, earned a mention by the sportswriter of the *Stevensville Star* who had felt compelled to report on the physical stamina such an ambitious production must have required, adding that "if only the Yellow Jackets could show the same efforts on the field, they'd have a better shot at making it to regionals."

But then came the backlash and Mitch's pushback. Ronald had been made aware of the toll Mitch's involvement in drama had cost him, first by the principal and then by Mitch's parents, who had pulled him aside following the last performance of *Tom Sawyer* to inform him that the star student's other grades were suffering. When Mitch lost his spot on the honor roll, he rebelled. Having perhaps been primed by his parents to blame his extra-curricular activities, he dropped out of drama class and found any number of reasons to skip English. Ronald felt he had been cut off, receiving the brunt of his student's insurgence in the form of the silent treatment. He and Ronald hadn't had sex since Easter and there seemed no prayer compelling enough to bring about a second coming. Ronald had been used up and discarded.

Looking back, Mitch had probably felt like he was being buried under ash, Ronald thought, as he gazed toward the covered windshield that required another swipe of the wipers—and he began to posture and say hurtful things like he longed to perform in front of real audiences and that he couldn't wait to get out of Stevensville for good. Mitch had awkwardly expressed that it seemed like he was being smothered; that he couldn't wait to get out and away from Stevensville for good.

No matter how Ronald looked at it, he had been abandoned, and he was alone.

Especially now. He scanned his pantry of seven apples and a canteen. Though disoriented, he felt like it must be dinnertime somewhere. He selected one of the apples and ate, savoring each bite. This time, he reserved the core, just in case. Even without clearing a window, he could tell it was becoming darker outside. He wasn't sure he needed to urinate but felt safer doing it now while there was still some light, rather than later, when darkness might cue nocturnal beasts to start shopping around for their own dinners. He climbed out of the vehicle and stretched his arms and legs, looking around at the gray whiteness. It didn't seem like the ash was still falling, but his earlier footsteps had been covered up by subsequent accumulation. And either the rumbling vibration had stopped, or he had grown so used to it that he couldn't detect it any longer.

He walked to the downed tree he'd used as a urinal before, peeing the letters *S. O. S.* in the layer of ash. He didn't linger outside but got back in the Volvo and locked every door. He turned the ignition a quarter click to scan the radio and engage the windshield wipers, testing to see if new ash was still coming down, and it was, though not quite as much. He switched the radio to AM to see if this made any difference, but he was only getting static no matter which way he tuned the dial, until he detected a faint scratch. With the steadiness and dexterity of a surgeon's fingers, Ronald navigated the tuner dial back and forth until he stopped when intermittent words could be heard.

> . . .40,000-foot cloud . . . St. Helens . . . starting to evac-
> uate Toutle area . . . five-to-twelve-foot flash flood coming
> down from Twelve Mile . . . solid wall of logs . . . all the
> bridges, even Interstate 5 are going to be in jeopardy . . .
> confirmed there has been a pyroclastic flow . . .

"Holy shit!" Ronald exclaimed, dispatching spittle onto the steering wheel. He tried for the next five minutes to recover the radio signal but soon tired of the static. Mostly satisfied that—while stuck there on the side of that mountain with no way out—he was still a fair distance away from I-5 which sounded like it was in the path to take the brunt of it, what-ever *it* was, though it seemed clearer now that it must be Mt. St. Helens that was erupting. This explained the rumble and the ash. He turned off the ignition and reached for his road atlas to see if he could calculate the distance between his present position and the volcano. The lighting wasn't great, but it looked like it was more than thirty miles away when he used the distance scale and measured with the tip of his index finger to the general spot, he guessed he'd reached on the highway before encountering road-blocks. He cranked down the driver side window and repeated "holy shit," again, shaking his head in disbelief. Deciding he just needed to wait this out, he threaded his legs over the console and moved his butt onto the passenger seat. He knew that the passenger seat reclined further, and that he'd have more room for his legs without the steering column in the way. In the absence of rescuers or an activity or entertainment to stay awake for, he snatched his jacket from the back seat and covered his upper body. Then he took a little swig from the canteen to toast his bedtime.

RONALD SLIPPED FROM REM to light sleep. Then he sank into a deeper sleep, which is when the subconscious shenanigans started.

In his dream, he was flying in a machine resembling a helicopter and he and his pilot were chasing a herd of elk in deep snow across a clearing. The herd was racing for tree cover. The pilot swooped down, yelling at Ronald to "Jump! Jump now!" But Ronald was too scared to let go of the door frame, so the pilot jerked the chopper's steering wheel to the left, dumping Ronald out the open door.

Ronald fell. But it was more like floating through ash that had become snow. He tried to adjust his body in mid-flight, experimenting with his arms and legs as though they could be rudders. Instead of the elk calf he knew he was supposed to land on and tackle to the ground, Ronald saw he was descending off course. He was going to land on a bull elk with a rack of pointy antlers that could skewer him before he accomplished his task.

What was the task, anyway? Ronald's subconscious mind had plenty of time to wonder, as he was freefalling in syrupy slow motion. Just before making contact, Ronald deployed reverse rockets embedded in the heels of his special tennis shoes, so that he could softly touch down on the bull elk, legs spread wide to mount the beast's broad back. It lurched and leapt through the snow, none too happy to have a bulldogger on its back. Ronald wished he was wearing a mask like the lone ranger or a bank robber—so his subliminal mind fashioned him one from the t-shirt no longer on his back and instantly in his hand. In fact, he wasn't wearing any clothes at all now but riding bare on the elk's back. It was like a twisted scene straight out of *Equus*.

Each of Ronald's hands gripped an antler, pulling back as the elk snorted twin plumes of steam from nostrils large enough to stick a fist inside. "Whoa, boy," Ronald said before the elk skidded to a stop in the ash, tossing him over its rack and onto a hummock of ash-covered earth. Ronald spit ash out of his mouth and arched his back in agony as the irked elk took out his revenge on the dreamer's ass with an erection so long it seemed to cut the flow of air through Ronald's windpipe. The elk grunted and shoved, ramming deeper with each thrust as Ronald wailed at a pitch nobody would hear because it was a dream.

Blistering wet bursts of wild beast breath sandblasted the layers of skin off his shoulder blades as the elk settled into a rhythm that would get the job done. Entering into a more lucid phase, Ronald became aware that he was starting to slip out of the dream sequence, but he wasn't ready for it to end without knowing how it would end. He tried desperately to hang on allowing another few seconds for the very naughty dream to resolve.

Hot hydraulic juices injected his insides with a devilishly cozy euphoria Ronald didn't want to end . . .

But then something tapped the frame of his Volvo, and he was jolted awake.

A breeze must have cleared the soot from the windows of his vehicle and the light of a waxing crescent moon gave a spectral glow to the mysterious world outside his car. Ronald slowly turned his head from the windshield to the passenger window just beyond his right shoulder, and there, majestically awesome and patient, stood a completely ash-covered bull elk that had ambled onto the road from the upslope treeline. Either Ronald was still dreaming, or he was being haunted by the ghost of the elk named Bruce, whose bust hung on the Simpleman fireplace in Crested Butte. Ronald raised his hand to wipe the sleep from his eyes and the elk lifted its head, creating a small dust cloud that dissipated rapidly. The elk's hooved feet hadn't moved, and with his big brown eyes he stared at the row of Washington Red Delicious apples on top of Veruca's dashboard. Ronald very slowly reached for the window handle to lower the glass that separated man from beast, before remembering he hadn't rolled the window back up before dozing off, and that nothing separated them at all.

"Bruce?" he inquired, groggy but serious.

The elk snorted but didn't spook. He lowered his head and stuck his powdered muzzle through the opening, parting his jaws to show enough snow cubed teeth to build an igloo. As far as his rack of antlers would allow, the creature stretched his neck to chomp down on the closest apple before withdrawing it inside his massive maw, munching it into juice. The size of Ronald's brown eyes doubled in astonishment.

His voice cracked though he tried to sound calm. "Hi there, Bruce, I'm Ronald." The elk seemed to nod as he chewed, dispatching mini-ash puffs as his jaws clenched and relaxed. Ronald reached for the next apple and extended his hand out the window. Bruce didn't hesitate and the apple disappeared in a second from Ronald's palm.

Ronald brought his hand back inside the vehicle, adjusting the crotch of his jeans to better accommodate the feral hard-on he'd cultivated during his dream. It wasn't about to start flagging now, especially with the Bruce from his childhood amalgamating with the elk from his dream, the sum of which was standing there on four hooves in the flesh. Seeing no reason to wait around for another offering, Bruce stuck his nostrils back inside the window, sneeze-snorting a bit of snot onto the side of Ronald's cheek as he snatched the last apple on his side of the canteen.

"Attaboy," Ronald said, slowly raising his hand to stroke the elk's nose. This dropped a sizeable clump of ash onto his lap and this startled Bruce, who knocked the roof of the car with the tip of an antler. "It's okay, it's okay," Ronald softly whispered, eyeing the diminishing dashboard pantry. There were just three apples left. "How about some water, Bruce?" Ronald reached for the canteen and unscrewed the chained lid. He cupped his left hand, reaching it through the window, and slowly poured water into his palm. Bruce's giant eyes with their ash-laden lashes stared inquisitively as the water drained onto the pavement. His tongue emerged from what looked like talcum-powdered lips and lapped at Ronald's wet hand. It felt like warm sandpaper.

Ronald replenished the reservoir, and Bruce was much quicker this time. "I don't suppose you know what's going on out there, do you, Bruce?" Ronald spoke softly and made no sudden movements. A viscous drool of saliva water dangled from one side of the elk's mouth as Bruce seemed to look beyond the car and across the valley at something that only he could see. "How about another apple, big boy?" Ronald displayed the treat in his open and perhaps foolish hand. He was giving away the store and possibly his survival in exchange for this one, real, honest-to-goodness Marlin Perkins moment. He wanted to get out of the car. He wanted to stand next to Bruce, to size him up, to trot with him into the forest and far away from what could very well be a life-ending predicament for them both.

He grabbed the penultimate apple from the dashboard. Then he quietly pulled the handle and slowly opened the passenger door, displaying the apple to assure the elk that he intended no harm. "I only have two apples left," he said. Bruce took two elk steps backward as if to courteously provide Ronald room to emerge from the car, which Ronald did slowly raising to his full height as the mass of Bruce spasmed into several full body shakes that dislodged much of the ash he'd been carrying.

Ronald had to cover his eyes to avoid the gritty worst of it. When the cloud settled, he lowered the apple in his hand dejectedly. Bruce had vanished but could be heard crashing through the scrub brush off to the side of the moon-lit roadway. Ronald stood there and mournfully called out, "Bruce! Bruce, come back—you can have my last two apples and anything else that you want!"

The crashing sounds of the beast moving through the woods diminished until Bruce bugled one final goodbye and was gone. Ronald was once again alone on the side of the silent mountain, standing there dumbstruck with an erection like a north-pointing compass.

And unlike Bruce, it didn't seem to be going away anytime soon.

SAN FRANCISCO

November 27, 1978

RONALD SHOULD HAVE STUCK TO HIS REGULAR PLAN OF traveling to their parents' place for Thanksgiving instead of allowing himself to get talked into being the number nine at "Harlan's Vegetarian Thanksgiving Feast for a Party of Ten." This happened to also be the title of Harlan's first attempt at a vegetarian cookbook and since Ronald had been on a lifelong quest for new experiences and ways to get closer with his brother, he'd said he would be there to support the endeavor.

At Stevensville High, he'd just come off the fall production treadmill after mounting two performances of *Taming of the Shrew* featuring two live dogs (nobody knew why, not even Ronald). That had been a new experience, too—especially when the Corgi took a dump stage left, three lines into Petruchio's monologue in Act 2, Scene 1. By curtain call, there wasn't a character from Bianca to Biondello to Minola Baptista who hadn't stepped in it.

Ronald must have missed his brother's instructions and the overarching concept behind the dinner party during the brief, last-minute telephone invitation. He couldn't recall Harlan mentioning that he *wasn't* going to be one of the seated dinner guests whom Harlan had cast to be background models cunningly based on their visible ethnicities. Harlan had wanted not only to showcase the recipes and dishes he'd prepared but also to profile how diverse and cosmopolitan his close acquaintances were. He felt they were an ideal microcosm of the greater Bay Area.

Thick-skulled Ronald also hadn't picked up on the nuance of the word "participate" in Harlan's telephone invitation when he'd asked his brother to participate rather than just attend. This was a working invitation, as it turned out. Upon arrival, Ronald learned that he'd been slotted to be the cookbook and dinner party photographer, since Harlan was too cheap to hire a professional. Ronald always traveled with at least two cameras, which he'd use depending on his creative mood. So, he wasn't put out by this assignment. Nor was he bothered to be volun-told to be the evening's DJ—once Harlan realized he had forgotten music for the evening. Ronald was instructed to keep a steady rotation of Joan Armatrading, *Earth Wind & Fire*, and *Tangerine Dream* albums playing on the turntable throughout the evening. He was forbidden from playing Michael Franks, whose music Harlan thought was too sing-songy, and said would skew what he envisioned as a more energetic, festive mood. Ronald thought that eating nothing but soy and vegetables for Thanksgiving was more likely to bring down the mood (while also increasing bathroom visits). But he promised to adhere to his brother's wishes.

Ronald was introduced to the guests. Arriving first were two of Harlan's co-workers, who went out of their way to disclose to one and all that they weren't romantically involved: James (who was gay and Asian) and Monica (who wasn't gay or Asian but made it clear that she might be bi). Ronald was almost positive he'd met James during his time at Stanford, but when James failed to recognize him, Ronald spared him the embarrassment and made no attempt to restore his memory, since this level of uncertainty had him no longer trusting his own recollection either. Their arrival was followed by Monty and his adorable black boyfriend, Lamar, who wore the tightest black pants with white paint-on daisies, trousers that showcased everything cliché about the attributes of black men.

Next to arrive was the lesbian couple Harlan had advance promoted as the 'salt and pepper shakers' since the pair always dressed alike: short Susan, and her equally height-challenged girlfriend, Vivi. Crossing the threshold five minutes later were Jim and his Japanese boyfriend, Denis—who Jim appended with 'the Menace' the whole night long, thinking himself comically clever. And finally, Ronald met the late arrivers, French Canadian Bernard and his East Indian blind date, Ravi—whose ethnicity Harlan had absentmindedly failed to disclose to Bernard when he'd set them up. Bernard had made an association between Ravi and ravioli, so he could remember his date's name. This led to them being late for drinks and crudités after Bernard had wasted twenty-five minutes scanning the Balboa B.A.R.T. station for an Italian instead of an Indian.

It had been difficult to frame a Matterhorn-sized mound of charred Brussel sprouts on an oval platter as appetizing, but Ronald fiddled with the focus until the sprouts became background to Lamar's perfectly proportioned hand as he reached for the serving utensils. When the courses started coming out of the kitchen faster than he could document, Ronald bounced the record needle several notes into EWF's "Serpentine Fire" and hustled back to the table to snap at least six shots of each offering.

The polenta-tofu-sage terrine that Harlan had molded into the shape of a traditionally roasted turkey squatting on a wreath of sunflower sprouts cast such a menacing shadow across the table that half the dinner party appeared to be seated beyond the shade demarcation line during a solar eclipse. Ronald attempted to balance light and shadow by moving two floor lamps and tilting their shades to illuminate a few of the darker-skinned guests. The dinner party was looking like a pretentious meeting of the United Nations. But his lighting alteration earned a scowl from the chef, who under his breath in the kitchen reprimanded the photographer warning him this better not wreck the artistry of his meticulously curated tableau. Ronald had just started to reassure his brother that he could fix most exposures during post-processing, which he would skillfully address in the high school darkroom as soon as he returned to Stevensville—but then "Kissin' and Huggin'" ended abruptly, sending the needle on a free-wheeling skid into the raised center of the LP. Sporting a slick of sweat on his forehead, Ronald leapt from the kitchen to the stereo in the living-cum-dining room and was relieved to slap *Rubycon* on the turntable. He was grateful for its seventeen-minute-long tracks, one on either side of the album.

As Harlan's guests stuffed their gullets with all the root vegetables they could possibly cram in, Ronald lurked in the background, unobtrusively observing them through his zoomed-in lenses. From his position in one of two corners of the triangular shaped room he could wedge himself into, he took artsy snapshots between the guest's shoulders and focused food shots beyond their conversational hand gestures.

Framing one such impromptu shot, he zoomed in on the exquisitely handsome face of James, thinking, when he got back home, he might compare this with any snapshots he might still have in a shoebox at the back of his closet, leftover from his time at Stanford, in case one of them happened to include the James he thought he remembered, though he was beginning to recall that James had been a Jimmy. Eavesdropping all the while, Ronald heard Harlan showing off his impressive—for a white boy—command of Mandarin with this coworker of his who humored his attempt to converse. As the evening progressed, Ronald became less sure that this James could be that James he used to know, anymore. Ronald chalked it up to living in a small world of lookalikes. He wouldn't even mention this to Harlan later.

The after-dinner conversation took a darker turn as Harlan's guests tried to process the news coming out of Guyana. There had been a mass death of more than 900 people earlier in the week. Most of the victims had apparently been San Francisco residents before their church leader, Jim Jones, had moved his People's Temple to the South American jungle. The people around the crowded dinner table, with its cranberry-stained table-cloth, claimed to know people who knew people who likely knew some of those who had died from drinking the poisoned Kool-Aid. Monica got to take home the prize for having the most direct connection to one of the casualties when she piped up, informing the table that she'd spent a semester interning at the Leo Ryan for Congress campaign headquarters in San Bruno in 1972. The congressman had died, not from drinking Kool-Aid, but from the twenty-some bullets fired into his face and body by one of Jim Jones' devout followers as the congressman's plane, emergency-chartered to get him the hell out of Georgetown, had been ambushed on the runway as it taxied for takeoff.

Lamar, for one, had had enough of the jungle cult talk because it reminded him of his own Acadian voodoo roots. To change the subject, he reached inside the front of his waistband to extract a sizeable traveling bong, thereby addressing the presumption that had been burning the frontal lobe off Ronald's brain since the apparent stallion first arrived. He twisted the cap off the homemade contraption and filled the reservoir from his water glass.

"Anyone care to join me on the balcony?" he asked with his delightful gap-toothed smile.

"It's raining cats and more cats out there," Harlan piped up from the kitchen where he'd already begun removing dishes from the table. "It's okay with me if you toke inside." He was lying through his teeth, which didn't have any gaps between them. "The photographer, however, is instructed not to capture anything illegal on film." He wagged a warning finger at his brother through the kitchen passageway.

Once everyone had inhaled their way through two bowls and seemed sufficiently lit, Monty extracted two ropes of Zotz fizz candy from the pockets of his blazer, which had been hung over his chair back. One was apple-flavored, and the other blue raspberry. He extended a plastic snake of individually sealed exploding confections to the people around him.

"The object of this game," Lamar instructed, "is to be the last person to cum." Plastic crinkled around the table. "If your candy starts fizzing prematurely, you must raise your hand in surrender. Then you're out of the competition and we start spreading rumors about your inability to make it last. Ready? On your mark . . . get set . . . suck!"

Lamar clenched his Zotz candy between his front teeth, concealed by his luscious lips. He and Monty loved gaming this contest; they always wanted to boast that they were the last ones to cum. The trick was herding the saliva to the back of the throat and keeping the tongue from making contact. "It isn't rocket science," Lamar liked to say, after they'd played a few rounds. Hands began raising around the table, signaling the players' flagging status.

When the conversation began to wane as the tofu and bulghur expanded in cramping stomachs around the table, Harlan thanked everyone for being his guinea pigs (at least half of them wondered if that was what they'd just consumed). He tried to sound gracious as he suddenly remembered to pass around the mimeographed model-consent release forms he needed to legally be able to publish their photos in his cookbook. He policed the apartment door to extort the last of their signatures as his guests departed.

As Ronald reached in for the thank you and goodbye hug being offered to him by James, James whispered directly into Ronald's ear, "Do I already know you from someplace?

THE SIMPLEMAN BROTHERS spent the whole rainy next day putting the furniture back where it belonged, bleaching the stains out of the tablecloth and cleaning dishes, walls, rugs, pots, and pans. Just when Ronald felt it was time to plop his butt in the bucket seat of his Volvo to hydroplane and windshield-wiper his way through the saturated Bay Area and back up Interstate 80, Harlan cranked up the volume on the radio in his once again sparkling white-tiled kitchen so that his brother could hear the road report from the living room, where he was packing his bag.

"California authorities have shut down 100 miles of Interstate 80 this morning—including all of Donner Pass—as the biggest snowstorm of the season bears down on the Sierra Nevada," the announcer said. "Residents and travelers are urged to take shelter and stay off roads as forecasters call for up to ten feet of snow in some areas, as well as high winds. This is expected to snarl holiday weekend travel for thousands—"

"Are you hearing this?" Harlan hollered.

Ronald had heard it. He thought he'd have time to take the long way up the coast, if Crescent Pass at the California-Oregon border wasn't affected by this same winter system. He took a few strides into the kitchen.

"And Northern California is not going to be spared by this super storm," the announcer continued, "with chains currently mandatory for Crescent Pass between Crescent City and Grants Pass. OSP expects to close their stretch on the Oregon side before nightfall, as a precaution."

"Well, hell's bells," Ronald exclaimed.

Harlan's annoyed face revealed his realization that he would now have to share his small apartment for at least one more night. "We could do Red Jade takeout for dinner, I suppose."

IT HAD BEEN a good idea for Ronald to request a substitute teacher for Monday, because when Monday came, I-80 was still closed to all but essential travel. Four years into his teaching career, Ronald still didn't see his work as all that important, and so he didn't care that much about getting back. From his makeshift bed on the rectangular chunk of foam tucked behind the sofa, he propped himself up and waved Harlan off to work.

With the weather starting to improve in the Bay Area and the apartment still stale from the remnants of a vegetarian Thanksgiving, Ronald craved some fresh air. He thought he'd wander downtown to check out the early Christmas decorations and maybe visit the makeshift shrine that had been created to honor the People's Temple victims in Guyana. He'd just read about that memorial in *The Chronicle,* and it was apparently still growing on Civic Center Plaza outside City Hall.

Ronald took a leisurely shower in the apartment he had to himself for the first time in seventy-two hours. He thought he might stop by the House of Harlee at 538 Castro and see about getting his brother a new shower head. The City's notoriously hard water came from the Hetch Hetchy Reservoir, picking up plenty of grit and low-grade contaminants along its 160-mile course, and it plugged Harlan's nozzle with minerals like calcium and magnesium. Ronald knew this only because his brother constantly complained about it when he phoned home. Their father's response, from the bedroom extension, was always the same: "Why don't you move your picky ass back to the Rockies, then?"

Ronald selected a black umbrella from his brother's sizeable collection sticking out of the ornate holder that his brother had hauled back from Bangkok, positioned to the right of the door. The rain held off nearly all the way down Market Street, but it started to sprinkle by the time he rounded the corner at Polk Street and fixed his eyes on City Hall, that Beaux Arts architectural wonder with a dome even taller than the US Capitol in Washington, DC. Ronald scanned Civic Center Plaza to see if he could spot the shrine he'd read about. But the rain was no longer a sprinkle and seemed to have driven everyone but Ronald away. The precipitation intensified, becoming a downpour, which quickened Ronald's strides toward what he hoped might be the closest public entrance into City Hall, where he planned to seek refuge.

As he mounted the marble steps, he heard a distant siren that was quickly joined by others, and that seemed to be heading in the same direction: toward him. At the same time, sets of heavy doors slapped open on the landing above him, sounding like cannon rounds. Dozens of people began streaking through the doors in a panic, stumbling down the steps around him. Ronald lifted his umbrella arm as high as he could so as not to impale any of those charging his way.

"Turn back!" a woman shouted as she slammed into Ronald's shoulder, spinning him around.

"There's a shooter inside!" screamed another in passing.

A breaker in Ronald's brain tripped, just as a stranger who was probably around his age put his arm around his shoulders and steered him away from the building toward the nearest line of London plane trees that bordered the plaza on two sides. "I heard the mayor's been shot," the stranger said when the two paused at a tree trunk to catch their breath.

"Moscone?" Ronald inquired in disbelief.

"And—" The fellow choked on his words before delivering the worst part of his news with clarion enunciation. "Supervisor Harvey Milk, too." Ronald's eyes opened wide and simultaneously filled with tears. He couldn't respond. No sounds or air came out of him.

He'd met Harvey Milk once, at his store located at 575 Castro named Castro Camera. Harvey, with his ballsy New York City accent, had graciously given Ronald twenty percent off four bulk packages of Kodacolor film. On Harlan's recommendation and out of curiosity to see if he could meet the country's first open and out gay politician, Ronald had made it a point to stop in under the pretext of needing to replenish his film inventory. (Ronald already had more unexposed film than he could ever use.)

Under Ronald's umbrella and the bushy tree canopy that dripped mercilessly down on them, the pair of strangers huddled, loosely holding each other as the gravity of the situation sank in. It seemed every police car and ambulance in the Bay Area was descending on the two-block patch of civic real estate. People continued to flee past Ronald and the other man. About the time it occurred to him that they were still pretty much in the open, a line of police in riot gear began directing and pushing them and others back as they established a perimeter around the crime scene, which seemed to encompass all of City Hall.

THE NEXT MORNING, while it was still pitch-black and silent outside, Ronald awakened feeling hopeless and overwhelmed. He wanted to but couldn't stick around another day to attend that evening's candlelight march and memorial service for the two slain politicians. By no means an activist nor an emancipation seeker, Ronald hadn't been searching for a reason to come out of his own closet, but the brazen assassination of America's first gay politician seemed reason enough for him to add a deadbolt lock on the closet door he would continue hiding behind. Interstate 80 had reopened overnight, so before dawn, he decided to make tracks out of the Bay Area and drive somberly back to Stevensville, where he hoped to once again bury his head in the ever-shifting sands of his tenuous teaching post.

After sixteen hours on the road, navigating through high snow banked mountain passes and having managed to take a forty-minute nap at a rest stop near the Craters of the Moon National Monument, stiff and weary, Ronald perked up once he was on the homestretch. He knew he was returning to an even emptier-than-normal refrigerator, and so when he got close to home, he popped into the Burnt Fork on Main Street. As luck would have it, Mitch was working his after-school shift behind the meat counter, now that he was sixteen. Ronald hadn't shaved in two days and suspected he looked a rugged mess, but Mitch always acted so nervous and bothered each time they ran into each other in public that Ronald doubted his student would even notice his disheveled appearance.

"Oh, hey," Mitch said, looking up from the butcher bandsaw he was cleaning. "You haven't been in class this week."

Ronald gave the boy extra credit for noticing *that*. "I was stuck on the other side of a bad snowstorm. How was your Thanksgiving?"

"Ah, you know . . . too much food and too many grandparents." Mitch dropped his cleaning rag into the tub of soapy water. "Can I get you anything?" he asked, straightening his crisp, white apron that didn't have a speck of blood or guts anywhere on it—at least from what Ronald could see from the other side of the chest-high meat counter.

"I don't suppose you have any of those BBQ chickens left this late in the day?" Ronald said. After the vegetarian bacchanal, he was craving real meat something fierce.

"I just put the last one in the cooler. Do you want it cut up?" Mitch was already moving toward the walk-in at the end of the counter.

"Sure." Ronald appreciated how this would give them more time to chat. His eyes followed the curly dark-haired head as it disappeared behind the heavy refrigerator door, before popping right back out again. Mitch kept his back to the customer as he dissected the cooked bird into ten pieces on the butcher block.

"Were you in San Francisco, then?" It was just small talk for Mitch, like the store had trained him to do. He did not remember if his teacher had even mentioned where he was going for Thanksgiving.

"Well, yes," Ronald answered, surprised the kid would guess that. "Yes, I was."

The teenager swatted away a fly that had been buzzing near his face. "Nice," he said, somewhat automatically.

"Say, I was thinking about doing a Woody Allen comedy for the junior class play next spring."

"Oh yeah? Who's Woody Allen?"

It was a sincere question that might have rendered Ronald speechless had he been anyplace other than culture-sheltered Stevensville, but he didn't show his shock. "The play I'm thinking about is called *Don't Drink the Water*. It's a comedy in two acts."

"Cool," Mitchell said.

"I could show you the script if you wanted to drop by my place sometime." As Ronald said this, he feared Mitch would see right through him and realize this was just another attempt to get him to stop by.

"Yeah, maybe," Mitch responded. "I have this foreign language club thing on Thursday night. It's supposed to be a welcome party for Delia, the foreign language exchange student who's coming from LaPaz, Bolivia. She'll be staying with us in our home—in my bedroom, which means I have to go back to sharing a room with my little brother again." Mitch wrapped the cut-up chicken in white butcher paper. He scribbled the price on the top of the package with a green felt marker and tossed it on the counter. "I could maybe stop by your place after that. Or on Friday."

Ronald reached for the package, briefly brushing Mitch's withdrawing hand, and put it in his empty shopping cart. "Anytime sounds perfect," Ronald said. "No matter how late."

"Anything else I can get you?" Mitch looked ready to get back to cleaning the equipment.

"Nope. That'll do it. See you in class in the morning," Ronald said, waving goofily.

"See ya," Mitch said in a raised voice. His back was already turned as he hunched over the bandsaw.

Ronald added a quart of milk and a box of cornflakes to his cart, before checking out with Georgia, his white-haired landlady, whose part-time job was manning the cash register at the front of the store.

She had news for her tenant. "Vern thinks he discovered a leak in the roof while you were away. He says he had to move a bookcase away from the wall to get to it but doesn't think any of your things got damaged."

Ronald reflexively cringed at the thought of her husband going through his things, at the same time reminding himself that of course they had keys and the right to access to his apartment, as landlords. "Oh," he managed to get out, unsure what to say next.

"You let us know if you find any water damage. I don't think it was all that serious, personally, but then I didn't go up those stairs with my bad knees." Georgia always looked like she was fresh out of the beauty parlor, flashing her dentured smile as she tallied and bagged his few groceries. "On account?" she asked.

"I have cash today, Georgia," he said. "I should settle my account for the month, too." He smiled back at the gentle woman, who probably shouldn't still be working, but had turned it into her hobby. Her bony fingers walked through the S section of the indexed file card holder next to the cash register before extracting the Simpleman card with his November charges.

"Are you even eating, young man?" she lectured, displaying the card's face and the \$18.44 he owed.

Ronald chuckled, used to being categorized by his skinniness, paid his bill, and left. In another minute, he was pulling out of the Burnt Fork parking lot, heading south another six blocks to reach his apparently leaking stand-in for a home sweet home.

MITCH UNCHARACTERISTICALLY SLOUCHED at his desk during homeroom, staring out the yellow-framed windows toward the Yellowjackets tennis courts and sports fields. He knew he was dodging eye contact with his teacher, who had been harping on the *Importance of Being Earnest* for the past half hour, but the way Mr. Simpleman had this annoying habit that made it seem like he was lecturing only to him, made Mitch self-conscious and uneasy. The upperclassman fidgeting noisily behind him, whose name he'd recently learned was Stan Cockburn, all of a sudden kicked the leg of Mitch's chair before passing him a folded note that Mitch attempted to discreetly receive under his right armpit. Mitch waited a solid revolution of the minute hand on the wall above the chalkboard before unfolding the missive that read, *how 'bout we take us a drive after sundown tonight?* Mitch cryptically nodded his head without turning around, whether the body-hairy student with the gaudy pewter eagle-head necklace behind him had been paying attention or not.

For reasons unknown, this older student commuted from Phillipsburg each week, staying with a host family while attending classes. It seemed odd to Mitch, since Hamilton High was twenty-two miles closer to where he came from, but one thing everyone Mitch associated with could agree on was that the guy appeared too old to be a high-school student anyway. There were rumors that maybe he'd been held back to repeat a few grades, or that he was an undercover cop. But then for what purpose would a cop be undercover here, since nothing ever happened in Stevensville? Again, Mitch was startled by what he took to be a confirmation double-tap on his chair leg. If he was reading this correctly, that meant that he'd be picked up from the north high school parking lot for a drive in the country after dark. He shoved the note deep into his pants pocket, to be destroyed later when he got home, that's if he remembered before it got sent through the wash.

They'd done this once a few months before, he and this Stan, shortly after the start of the new school year. He fully expected the upperclassman would want to go further than the heavy petting they'd worked up to during the last drive, but Mitch didn't know what all that would entail beyond maybe dropping their pants this time, along with any leftover pretense of shyness or objection. The very prospect improved Mitchell's posture as he too wanted to go further down the country road than they'd ventured previously. They hadn't even taken their dicks out the last time, and Mitch was curious to see if Stan was as big as Mr. Simpleman, down there.

FROM THE HEAD of the classroom, where he leaned his polyester butt against the edge of his desk, Mr. Simpleman had, in fact, witnessed this not-so-covert transaction play out between the two students while struggling to present the dramatic ironies of Lady Bracknell's and Miss Prism's views on morality. Ronald didn't have a good feeling about it and may have been confusing concern with jealousy. From perusing the school's student records, he'd learned that this Cockburn character—whose devil dark eyes seemed spaced too close together—had been released from juvenile detention on the condition he finish high school. Ronald calculated that by this point, the kid must be close to turning twenty-one.

But that wasn't the most disturbing part of his story. Cockburn, it seemed, had been turned into the Granite County sheriff by a neighbor who'd repeatedly caught the energetic young man fornicating with his farm animals. Ronald felt he should say something to Mitch—and maybe he would when he came over to his apartment on Friday night to check out the playscript—but at the same time, didn't know how to divulge such sensitive information without violating the other student's privacy, not to mention jeopardizing the fresh start that his diploma could afford him. Cockburn, after all, had recently made the honor roll, to everyone's surprise. He displayed abundant charm and renewed promise.

These were the times when Ronald despised being a teacher. He was expected to make impossible on-the-spot decisions as if he knew what was best for all parties. Most days, he felt like an imposter and didn't have the first clue what he was doing. He lived in raw terror every minute of the school day, waiting for something to blow up in his face and end his career. He often thought his father, the orthopaedic surgeon, must approach his vocation in the same terrified way, since his patient's lives were on the line every time he reached for a scalpel. Chalk was Ronald's scalpel, and the blackboard was his OR.

ALREADY HEARING HARLAN'S nagging voice inside his head, Ronald used his free period to get a jump on developing the cookbook photos from the previous week's Thanksgiving dinner in the Castro.

The Stevensville High School darkroom was situated at the end of the hallway in a slightly enlarged, windowless closet with its own double entry and locked door adjacent to Mr. Kestler's chemistry lab. Ronald always checked first with the journalism teacher to ensure he wouldn't be interrupting by the aspiring student newspaper and yearbook photographers, who mostly used the darkroom for sleep and occasionally used it for masturbation—as he'd once discovered when the inner door had been left unsecured, and the red processing light switch hadn't been flicked on. In the dark, Ronald could barely make out the scrawny nerd who had scampered past him, fastening his pants and nearly knocking him down as he fled, before merging brilliantly into a sea of anonymity during a fortuitously timed class change. The culprit had left his own developer fluid in polka dots all over the counter; a mess that Mr. Simpleman had no trouble first sniffing, touching, sampling, then cleaning up after him.

Ronald locked the door and turned on the processing light that painted his hands and the room in deep sinful red. Robotically, he organized every item he would need to be able to locate in complete darkness in a half-circle array in front of him, including the film tank, cassette opener, film reel, water, thermometer, developer, stop bath, fixer, wetting agent, film cleaner, scissors, and the four rolls of film he'd carried in with him in his father's hand-me-down attaché case.

He turned off the overhead processing light and went to work in total darkness. He popped the plastic lids off the four film canisters and adeptly unlocked the film lids with the cassette opener. He extracted the exposed film from each canister, unwinding it and snipping off the attached ends with the long scissors. He clipped each of the strips to the darkroom's prestrung clotheslines. Then, working with one strip at a time, he fed the edge of the strip into the slit in the reel and aligned the spool teeth with the perforations running along the film's margins. He carefully wound each of the long strips around the four separate film spools. Next, he slipped each of these spools inside corresponding film tanks and fit the lids on each of the tanks. He flipped the red light switch on, so he could see, as he mixed water and film developer in a large beaker. He stuck a thermometer in the beaker and read the temperature. It was 68 degrees Fahrenheit, which he knew meant the optimal developing time would be between nine and ten minutes.

He lifted the lid and poured the mixture from the beaker into the integrated funnels of each tank, setting the glow-in-the-dark stopwatch, which he'd had permanently chained to the worktable after previous ones had gone missing. With all the lids secured, Ronald took two tanks in each hand. Holding the four together, he shook them for thirty seconds, like he was playing the maracas in a mariachi rendition of the Jarabe Tapatio. He placed the tanks in a line on the counter, waited twenty seconds, and then shook each tank for another ten seconds.

Watching the stopwatch, he tried to unwind his own stress from the internal spool that seemed wound so tightly it had been strangling him from the inside.

The long drives.

Jonestown.

Thanksgiving dinner.

Harvey Milk. George Moscone.

Missing two days of school.

Mitch and that strange Cockburn kid.

Harlan's cookbook and the fear these photos might not even turn out . . .

Ronald worried that he could be a candidate for a nervous breakdown, ulcers, or worse. He agitated each of the four film tanks, turning them upside-down and giving them another shake. His father used to swear his own vocation was either going to kill him, give him ulcers, or give him hemorrhoids—he joked that he didn't know which consequence would be worse. In the safety of darkness and the absence of external judgements, Ronald wondered if maybe his allegiance to an untenable work ethic might be hereditary.

He shook each of the film tanks again, more vigorously this time. When his overthinking brain was overrun by a burgeoning skepticism that he might have chosen the wrong career, all the spinning dishes began to fly off their sticks and shatter against the walls he imagined building up around him. Usually, the road cleared his head. But with the pressures of the photo shoot, Jonestown, and the political assassinations, this last road trip hadn't given him a second to calm his nerves before he had to face a whole different set of pressures at school.

With the fall class play in the rear-view mirror, Ronald hoped he could coast for the next few weeks till Christmas break, and at a much slower speed than he'd been trying to sustain. This semester hadn't exactly been a cakewalk for him, either. He'd endured scorn from the school principal for choosing *Between Time and Timbuktu* for the junior class production; the head of the school siding with the superintendent, both predicting that Kurt Vonnegut was going to sail over the heads of the students and the audience, which it probably did. But what was the point of art, if not to expand thinking? Ronald had defensively snapped back, refusing to back down from his choice, when rehearsals had already gotten underway. Then there was the night he returned to his car in the faculty lot to find it had been graffitied with shaving crème and the word FAG had been scrawled across his Volvo's windshield. To make a point, he'd driven Veruca straight down Main Street, which had been deserted as usual, to the coin-op car-wash next to the Conoco station, feeling every bit like Hester Prynne, with her letter *A*. At the very least, he was going to try not to take everything on as his personal responsibility or treat the truly petty things his students or fellow faculty members said as seriously as he did, which was his tendency. He also needed to grow a thicker skin and try to reframe teaching as just a job and stop pretending like it were some personal calling or crusade or that he was making one bit of difference in anybody's life or that he was even good at it. What business was it of his if the town was too ignorant to stomach Vonnegut or if one of his students happened to be an animal fucker? To each his own. Live and let live . . . blah, blah, blah. Or as the ancient Greeks would say: *bar, bar, bar.*

How else, where else, would I make a living if I quit teaching? he also wondered just as the stopwatch hit nine minutes. "I guess I'm a bona fide teacher," he said out loud—a self-affirmation in the dark, where nobody had witnessed or could challenge his candor. "No more pretending," he added.

Flicking on the red light, he uncapped each of the lids and dumped the developing liquid down the drain. He immediately filled each of the film tanks with stop bath and shook the canisters for thirty seconds, letting them sit for another four minutes before emptying the stop bath down the drain and refilling the tanks with fixer. It was getting close to the moment of truth. After another half minute, he emptied the fixer, removed the four reels from their tanks, and placed them in a bucket filled with wetting agent. He removed the reels from the bucket, unwound the film from the reels, and delighted in seeing four long strips of what looked like perfectly developed negatives that he proudly clipped to the clothesline to dry.

THE CARSON FAMILY supper ran long. They were having tacos and sopapillas in honor of Delia's first night with the family. Mitch's thighs nervously bounced under the Ethan Allen oak table. He'd been embarrassed by his mother's curious dinner choice—he wasn't even sure tacos were Bolivian. And he was in a foul mood, as it would be five months before he'd get his downstairs bedroom and privacy back. As the vice-president of the Stevensville High School Foreign Language Club, it had been his brainy idea to host a foreign exchange student, thinking his family might get awarded a boy he could turn into his new best friend. He never thought his parents would warm to it. But they had decided it would be a healthy cultural experience for the whole family, besides helping Mitch perfect his Spanish. *¡Que rico! ¡Que fantastico!* He rolled his eyes at some inane comment his younger brother had just made while their sister braided Delia's long black hair—at the dinner table. *¡Que bruta!*

As it had already been dark for over two hours, Mitch knew that Stan Cockburn would be parked in the high school parking lot, waiting for him in his custom orange Toyota pick-up with the canopy shell. He'd told him after class that he wouldn't be able to get away until after supper—if he could get away at all. Cockburn had said he'd wait until 8:30 and that he'd understand if they had to wait until next week. Now, Mitch was feeling the pinch of time to get to the high school before 8:30, which required ditching his family for teenage urges that would not be defeated. Delia was yawning, showing fatigue and other signs of culture shock—Mitch blamed the tacos.

"¿Estás cansado?" Mitch asked their guest. Delia sheepishly nodded. "We should let Delia have an early night. She must be exhausted," he layered it on thick, and the rest of his family played along, even though they didn't know what he'd asked her. Then, Mitch did something he'd never done before: he excused himself from the dinner table. "I'm going to run down to Kevin's place to play Pong," he announced. His father's eyes widened in surprise, before relaxing in capitulation, accepting that his teenager was of the age where he should start calling his own shots—which was precisely what he intended to do, with any luck, later on that night.

Mitch brushed his teeth in the main bathroom that he now had to share with his entire family. He ran a brush through his hair, thinking the world wasn't fair. Five months seemed an eternity to the sixteen-year-old. He bolted from the house, letting the screen door slap, knowing without seeing it, that his father's head had just jerked at the dining room table with his typical look of consternation. He sprinted like the devil was at his heels across Park Avenue and then jogged along the length of the high school, rounding the corner of the building so quickly that he slipped in the dewy grass. From there, in the far corner of the otherwise empty and dark parking lot, he spotted a patch of chrome reflecting a distant streetlight. His head swiveled like an owl's as he scanned the horizon for any signs of spies or tattletales. Seeing that the coast was clear, he walked quickly to the pickup, lifted the handle on the passenger door and pulled himself up and into the seat before pulling the door shut.

"Been waiting long?" the teen asked the driver, who looked like an adult. The last time Mitch had been in this pickup, he didn't remember it smelling quite so strongly of Old Spice, so perhaps tonight was a special occasion.

"Nah," Stan said, roughly slapping his right palm on Mitch's thigh, giving it a squeeze so firm that it nearly gave the teenager a charley horse. He turned the key in the ignition. Since he'd backed into the space, he set the gearshift and drove head-first out of it, keeping his headlights off for the moment. When he turned right onto Park Avenue, he turned on the lights and cranked the stereo system.

"You like Lynyrd Skynyrd?" he asked.

"I don't know yet," Mitch said, speaking loudly to be heard over the radio. "Is that who this is?"

"Yep. Song's called 'Simple Man.' It's my favorite on this album."

"Oh, like our English Lit teacher?" The driver didn't seem to get it. "Mr. *Simpleman?*"

"Hah. Yeah, I guess so." The driver half chuckled, his dimples showing next to those silly looking mutton-chop sideburns. His greased hair was parted on one side, swooping high across his forehead to the other hemi-sphere. A sedan—maybe an Oldsmobile Cutlas Supreme, by the look of its grill—headed toward them from the opposite direction. "Hey, get down," Stan ordered, pushing Mitch's back between the shoulder blades. With his head between his legs, Mitchell listened to the electric guitar music twanging in his ears and tried to make sense out of the lyrics, as the driver— who didn't have a bad voice—sang along.

And be a simple kind of man
Oh, be something you love and understand
Baby, be a simple kind of man
Oh, won't you do this for me, son, if you can?

Mitch sensed the pickup turning right, guessing they'd turned onto Pine Street and were heading for the Eastside Highway that would take them out of town into the country, just like they'd done once before.

"Okey-doke," Stan said. "The coast seems clear now. Sorry about that."

"It's okay," Mitch said, unfolding his torso and fishing with his right hand for a seatbelt he'd been too excited to remember when he'd first climbed in the truck.

"Seatbelt's busted," Stan said before turning the volume up even higher and wailing out the ending of the last chorus. "Lynyrd Skynyrd isn't the singer's name, by the way. Most people don't know that." Stan was trying to sound smarter than he was. "The singer is Ronnie Van Sant. He was killed last year with most of his band when their plane ran out of fuel and crashed in Mississippi."

Mitch turned to face the driver, with an open mouth, pretending to be shocked, pretending he cared about some rocker he'd never heard of before. "You're kidding!"

Stan shook his head no. "Sad day for the fans." He bit his lower lip, signaling to turn left at the Logan Lane Junction heading in the direction of Stevensville's small airport used mostly by those two-wing crop dusters. He shifted into third gear then let his shifting hand levitate to Mitch's lap, where it sought out the teen's crotch.

This broke the ice. Mitch stretched his left arm to begin massaging the driver's erection, which seemed readymade for the adventure at hand, and much stubbier than Mr. Simpleman's. At first, Mitch was too nervous—too much in his main head to mount much of a response from his little head. But by the time Stan turned right onto North Burnt Fork Road, the teenager was all in and throbbing inside his Wranglers. "Nice," the driver cooed, pressing his left leg against the steering wheel and undoing his fly as he drove. Mitch could smell the musk before the driver liberated himself from his briefs. The passenger scooted an inch, maybe two closer on the bench seat. He thought he might black out as he deeply inhaled the man scent.

"You can go ahead and put your mouth on it," Stan whispered with a directing tone. In the microsecond of hesitation that followed, Mitch's eyes met the driver's, before the latter's hand pressed down on the back of his head and neck. In a moment, Mitch's face had been planted bullseye on the protruding target. An out of control and pungent collision of *Old Spice* and something that smelled like milk that had soured occurred in Mitch's nose. He gagged before he could even open his mouth.

Recoiling, he knocked his head on the steering wheel before the upperclassman's meaty hand forced his skull back into his lap. "It's not a blow job if you don't open your mouth," he reprimanded. As this wasn't Mitch's first encounter with another boy's genitalia, he knew what to do, at least generally, and didn't require the heavy-handed coaching he was receiving. The musk was too strong. The radio was too loud. Stan's pubic hair was too smelly and seemed to be busting out from everywhere. The driving was erratic, and the gravel road wouldn't allow for a stellar performance.

But because it had been drilled into him—from piano and tap-dance recitals, years in the church junior choir, and a standout performance in *Paint Your Wagon* in eighth grade—that the show must go on under any circumstances, Mitch opened his mouth so wide that he nearly unhinged his jaw.

"Teeth!" the driver hollered, swerving to a jagged stop in the loose gravel. He turned off the engine and cut the headlights. "Let's climb into the back," he ordered more than suggested, before stuffing himself back inside his jeans—buttoning the top but leaving his fly open. Mitch straightened up and wiped his mouth, already gratified to have gone farther than their clumsy first attempt, when he'd been more nerves than hormones. He pulled the handle and jumped out of the rig, landing Adidas-first in a ditch that wasn't dry. Cursing under his breath, he climbed up the slippery bank.

Mitch's own erection made movement a challenge, but he arrived at the back of the canopy, his shoes squishing out muddy water, just as the tailgate creaked down and the hatch slapped open with a pop. "After you," the upperclassman said, suddenly all manners and a Cheshire grin. Mitch glanced up and down the dark road before climbing blindly inside the hold, where just enough moonlight illuminated the old and dirty flower-patterned bedspread that had been haphazardly deployed for the special occasion.

Stan climbed in after him, pulling the tailgate up. He tugged the canopy hatch closed but didn't latch it. A strong scent of gasoline—or maybe it was oil—now overpowered the Old Spice, and it was so dark Mitch couldn't see the palm of his hand that he was holding right in front of his face.

His heartbeats raced in the frantic buildup, while his britches were brutishly tugged open and his underwear shoved down by calloused hands that seemed perfectly able to see in the dark. He heard and felt the upperclassman panting rapidly on his neck and face. He sounded like maybe his nose was stuffed up.

Mitch felt what seemed like the handle of a shovel or an axe under the bedspread and he tried to scoot his body to a more comfortable position. That's when the upperclassman began to more roughly wrestle with him, using a force that suggested his mood was shifting. He was older and bigger, and his muscles were more developed making it no contest in the domination game. Mitchell took an elbow to the nose, which set off shooting stars on the inside of his squeezed eyelids. He could tell from the thud of the impact that his nose would start bleeding soon, like it used to when he'd been much younger. He sniffed twice, trying to vacuum back any blood—or any bit of his brain—tilting back his head just in case.

Mitch felt Stan's hot breath on his erection that involuntarily flexed in excitement and anticipation. Then the warm and wet sensation of Stan's mouth overwhelmed Mitch's ability to resist or hold back. When the head of his circumcised hard-on plunged past a gauntlet of wisdom teeth to the back of Stan's throat, Mitch launched into a spasm he and a thousand horses couldn't stop. He ejaculated as his hips rocketed off the shovel handle.

The upperclassman choked and spat while cursing a blue streak. "You little fucker!" he shouted inside the tin-walled box as Mitch lay on his back, still convulsing and hyperventilating. Stan spat again, this time sounding like he'd hocked out a loogie. The teenager knew he'd climaxed, and he knew what came out when he did, but he didn't understand why his classmate was acting so angry about it. Isn't this what they'd driven out there to do anyway? The older kid was on all fours above him, angrily pounding the canopy ceiling with a fist that sounded like a clap of thunder. Then he grabbed Mitch by one arm and a shoulder and flipped him on his stomach, holding him there on top of that shovel handle or whatever was poking him from under the dirty blanket, which—now that his nose was in it—had a different, putrid stench all its own. Mitch heard Stan fumbling with the lid of a container, before the lid flew out of his hand and clanged on a bare section of the truck bed not covered by the blanket.

"Fuck it!" Cockburn yelled as he greased his weapon. Suddenly, something else was poking Mitch, but from the backside. "Stop squirming, ya little shit!" Stan said gruffly, his lips touching then biting hard on Mitch's ear. Had he not been weaker and smaller, it would have been fight or flight for Mitch. The guy was trying to enter his butt.

"No! No!"

Mitchell tried to buck the suddenly crazed redneck off him. He felt teeth chomp into his shoulder as a hairy-knuckled, grease-stained hand covered his mouth to muffle the scream that only the aggressor figured would be coming next. After a few misaimed pokes, the upperclassman thrust his Vaseline lubed manhood with a most deliberate jab, then arched and leveraged his pelvis until he got himself completely inside Mitchell's virgin butthole, knocking the wind clean out of his victim.

Stan didn't pause five seconds before he began clumsily driving in and out of the kid, neither seeing nor caring about the tears trailing down his face and onto the badly stained bedspread. To Stan, he was just cavalierly fucking the shit out of another farm animal. He released the shoulder bite when the metallic taste of blood told him that he'd chomped down too hard. Mitchell whimpered, on the edge of blacking out. But he no longer struggled.

It was not that he'd gotten used to it, not that he was enjoying it, not that he had given in. Instead, he was gathering his courage and strength to fight the man off his back and out of his insides. He covertly worked a hand and then a forearm under the filthy bedspread, grasping the handle he'd felt earlier. A shovel or axe could be used as a weapon. But when his fingers traced the outline of a trigger guard, he realized that he had a far more dangerous weapon at his disposal. He'd had a gun safety training class and, in that instant, knew he'd been lying on top of a hunting rifle.

Ascertaining which end of the gun was which, Mitchell craned his neck, lifting his head as high off the pickup bed as he could. Then he simultaneously squeezed his butt cheeks and the trigger with every ounce he knew his life was worth. The rifle discharged a bullet through the back wall of the pickup cab, ricocheted off something, and shattered the windshield.

It sounded as though the rig had just been hit by a train. Thrown off balance just as he had been building to climax, Stan got knocked to one side as semen spurted from the head of his penis. His man seed sprayed everywhere, like his dick was a chicken who had just been decapitated. Mitch twisted around and dove headfirst through the unlatched canopy hatch like a trained dolphin sailing through a Hula-Hoop. He hoisted and fastened his jeans as he sprinted like a hellhound into the pitch-dark night through the stubbled alfalfa fields and back toward the shimmering lights of town.

The ferocity and volume of his attacker's threats and hollers had begun to fade with distance when Mitchell tripped on a rock and hurled out of sight into a ravine, where he skidded to a stop under a pile of spent tumbleweeds that had collected there. The bang of another rifle shot echoed in his ears as he scrambled along a dried-up creek bed he hoped was leading him in the right direction further from harm's way, especially if Cockburn was shooting at him or coming for him.

Twenty minutes, a half hour later, Mitch couldn't tell, but a crick in his left thigh and an ache in his side that felt like it was about to pry apart his rib cage brought him to a panting stop at the edge of town. He couldn't just show up at home pretending nothing had happened, given his shared bathroom and bedroom. So, he pinched the cramp in his side and jogged an extra five blocks to reach Mr. Simpleman's apartment.

Heaving for air at the bottom of the white stairs leading up to the apartment door, he tried to compose himself. His brain fielded a half dozen questions in a lightning round lasting less than a minute so he could get his story straight. What would he say? Should he try to act normal like nothing happened? Could he trust Mr. Simpleman with the truth? Would Stan kill him if he said something? Was he bleeding from his butt? What if Mr. Simpleman wasn't home? Was that last gunshot he heard aimed at him or—

Before he'd resolved his panic, had answers for his questions, or fully prepared what he was going to say, his fist—seemingly having grown tired of waiting for the teenager it was attached to— knocked on his teacher's apartment door.

AFTER SCARFING DOWN a TV dinner of meatloaf and mashed potatoes, Ronald, attired in a faded pair of Levi's and a white t-shirt with underarm stains, had been jotting down some casting notes as he skimmed a script for *Don't Drink the Water*. He had just dozed off when there was a rap at his door that bounced him wide awake. He hardly ever had visitors, and a glance at the digital clock on the kitchen counter told him that it was 8:30—too late for his elderly landlord to be climbing the rickety stairs that led to his attic apartment.

Carrying the yellow script with him, he went to the door. Through the pane of glass in the door's top half he saw that his visitor was Mitch Carson.

A smile of delight spread across his face. He hadn't expected Mitch to stop by until after his club commitment the next night.

"Well, this is a surprise—come in, come in," Ronald said, putting his free hand on Mitch's shoulder to guide him over the threshold. "Hey, you're shaking. Is it cold out there?"

Mitch's dark green eyes were big as silver dollar size pancakes and fancying himself a keen study of expressions and theatrical faces, Ronald could tell the teen was spooked.

"Can I get a glass of water?" the kid asked. His voice, normally a high tenor even after puberty, alternated between lower and higher registers.

"Of course," Ronald said, gesturing with an open hand. "Here, have a seat on the sofa." He turned to reach into the cupboard for a clean glass and held it under the running sink tap. "I thought your foreign language thing was tomorrow night."

He turned off the tap and telescoped his arm across the small living room space to deliver the requested glass of water. He switched on one a few floor lamps so that they could see each other better. That's when Ronald had a sudden intuition that something was very wrong here. Mitch certainly wasn't his normal fastidious self. The teen's chest was heaving, there was dried blood beneath his nose, his jeans were ripped at one knee and his Nike tennis shoes weren't even remotely white.

"My god, Mitch! Did something happen to you? It appeared his student had started to shake his head to signal *no*, but then he froze. "Listen," Ronald said, leaning forward to plant his bare elbows on his denim-covered knees. "We've had some pretty good chats lately. I hope by now you know you can trust me. If something's happened or someone's bugging you, I want to help you get to the bottom of it."

Mitch fidgeted, looking very uncomfortable. He finished the glass of water and then asked for some more. Ronald leaned closer to retrieve the empty glass, confirming the tear tracks that had wandered down his dirty, normally untroubled face. When Ronald turned his back to fill the water glass, Mitch rose to standing, shifting his weight back and forth from one leg to the other. "Could I use your bathroom?" His voice squeaked.

"Sure. You remember where it is?"

Mitch didn't answer, ducking down the short hall, quickly shutting the bathroom door behind him. Ronald saw the light come on from under the ill-fitting door his landlord had found, modified, and installed for him after his first year as a renter (the draw curtain that was originally there had made the bathroom too drafty). He heard water running in the bathroom sink. When the digital flip clock had tallied a good ten minutes, Ronald hollered in the direction of the bathroom, "Are you okay in there?" The door opened, and the bathroom light switched off.

Mitch emerged. "Now, that's you looking more like you," Ronald said, in his teacherly way, trying to reinforce the kid's confidence and hopefully help him overcome his reticence to speak. Mitch sat again on the sofa—almost in slow motion—and proceeded to iron with his palms the colorful silky fabrics that covered the saggy cushions. Ronald could tell the kid was all locked up inside. Probably struggling with teenage angst stuff. Maybe he'd gotten into a fight or was being bullied for being different, like Ronald had been—and mercilessly so—when he had been Mitch's age. Ronald doubted he'd have the key to unlock anything, given his own history of denial and—to a degree—his own victimhood, but he dove in anyway, since that's what teachers did. "Is there something you want to tell me or something you came here to talk about?"

Mitch sat there looking at his dirty tennis shoes. After a minute of thinking about it, he raised his head and asked, "I wonder if you could give me a ride home . . . to the high school, I mean?"

STEVENSVILLE, MONTANA

September 25, 1977

"HAPPY BELATED 15TH BIRTHDAY, MITCH," RONALD SAID to his Introduction to Literature student who'd shown up unannounced on the landing outside his apartment. "Come in, come in. How was your summer? How's the new job at the Burnt Fork? Take a load off and fill me in!" Ronald couldn't contain his enthusiasm. Mitch was laughing at him—probably thinking him a dork. But the teen—who had matured and filled out with a summer of hard labor in the woods—had been looking forward to this reunion, too.

"I had the best summer. It was a total blast. We did something different every day. Like stringing barbwire fences and tying these meshy plastic tube things around stakes to protect the tree seedlings we'd planted. And guess who my supervisor was?" Mitch didn't leave any time for Ronald to answer. "Mr. Luehr!" That was the accounting and business teacher from their high school. "He was so cool," Mitch added. "I'm taking Intro to Business Accounting from him this semester because we got along so well."

Ronald was taken aback, experiencing a flare-up of adolescent jealousy hearing that Mitch had grown closer to another faculty member over the summer. "That sounds like quite the experience," he said.

"What about you? What did you get up to?" Mitch was very polite.

Ronald suspected Mitch didn't actually care what he'd done or where he'd been, but in the spirit of exchange, he gave a quick rundown. "I spent some time with my brother in San Francisco. We went to a concert by a singer-songwriter named Michael Franks at the Great American Music Hall. Here, let me play you the album I bought! It's called *Sleeping Gypsy*."

Having not sat down yet, Ronald spun toward the stereo. The album was already on the turntable, since he'd been playing it nonstop. He turned the power on, and the volume dial up. He excitedly lowered the needle.

"That's cool," Mitch said, not paying attention, but then went on about his own summer. "Then we went to see my grandparents. They live in this little town in Iowa, but we got to visit the state capital in Des Moines. So, that was cool. And let's see, I guess that's pretty much it." Then he remembered. "Oh! And last weekend at the Burnt Fork, I was put in charge of the dairy case, and I clean up the meat department after the butcher goes home at five."

"You've taken on quite a lot of responsibility since I last saw you," Ronald said in a congratulatory tone.

"Well, I'm growing up, I guess." Mitch rolled his eyes with chagrin as he said it.

"You look taller to me, and more developed. Like you put on some muscle over the summer." Ronald sat down on the sofa next to his student, instead of in the stuffed and silk-covered chair across from him. He could smell the anti-perspirant he imagined the teenager sprayed liberally under his arms. He had probably sprouted nice patches of hair there.

"It was hard work, for sure," Mitchell explained. "And Mr. Luehr was always teasing and challenging me to be the fastest and, you know, the first to get things done. He'd race me to the top of a hill or dare me to leap over a creek that was maybe too wide for my legs. But I always showed him!"

"I assume there were other students you knew from school who were on your work crew," Ronald said. He was curious but he was also trying to change the subject from the kid's newfound fascination with his colleague—who was an athletically tall and very good-looking married man.

"Yeah, there were a few kids I already knew or had at least seen around school. But half of our crew came from Hamilton. There was even this one gal from Missoula who got dropped off by one of her parents each morning at the ranger station. She was pretty."

Ronald sensed that Mitch was sharing this last detail as a fact, rather than an indication of his romantic interest. "It's really nice to finally have you in one of my classes," he said, awkwardly changing the subject.

"Yeah," Mitch shrugged. "Mr. Luehr says I have talent as a writer and that I should pursue that. He had me write the crew reports at the end of each workday."

"I see," Ronald said. He did not like the adulation he heard in Mitch's recounting of his summer-long bonding with another male teacher. He needed to work harder. Ronald desperately wanted to be the cool teacher that Mitch idolized and hopped over logs and streams to impress.

"This is a cool song. I like it."

Ronald was pleased to be introducing Mitch to the slow, jazzy music of Michael Franks. After that summer's concert in San Fran, Franks had become his favorite singer, songwriter, and storyteller. "It's called 'In the Eye of the Storm,'" Ronald said, reciting from memory the lyrics that spoke to him so personally:

> We glide on these streams
> Just postponing our dreams
> The love that's inside us
> How come it divides us

Then he said, "Say, I wanted to suggest you consider joining drama club this semester. I've already had some opportunities to work with you—you know, in a theatrical way, like back when you played Abraham Lincoln in that Bicentennial cavalcade and we had to use spirit gum to put that itchy beard on your face."

"Yeah, it took forever to get that cement off my face!"

Ronald chuckled. "Or when you were still in middle school and had that big role in *Paint Your Wagon*. What was the song you sang again?"

"'They Call the Wind Mariah,'" Mitchell answered without taking a second to think. It had been a big moment for him, and he'd basked in the applause.

"I think with some more experience and a little coaching—they call it *directing* in the theater," he clarified, "I can see loads of potential in you."

"Thanks. It is one of my interests, for sure. But right now, Mr. Luehr thinks I should focus on writing."

"That's fine," Ronald said, before biting his lip. He didn't think it was fine, but that was beside the point. He needed to expand Mitch's thinking. "There is writing in plays and musicals and operas. Writing forms the basis for all these performing art forms."

"That's cool," Mitch said. "What kinds of things happen in drama club?"

"Well," Ronald said, grateful for the opening. "We work a lot to develop skills in something called *improvisation*. Do you know what that is?"

"Maybe," Mitch suggested, "but how about you tell me what it means to you, first."

Clever, Ronald thought. He had to give the kid extra credit for thinking on his feet in tossing the question back at him. He'd build on that. He shifted his butt to sit sideways on the sofa facing Mitch. "Acting isn't just about pretending to be someone you're not. It's not all about memorizing lines from a script and delivering them on stage in a way that is believable to the audience. It's also about developing the skills to react to other actors. It's how you respond to their lines and their mannerisms with actions that are your own, that you sometimes have to come up with on the fly. It's about how you think on your feet, how well you know your own character, and how you respond when something goes wrong."

"When something goes wrong?"

"You know, like when someone forgets or messes up their lines. You have to know the story and what is supposed to happen in the scene, so that no matter what happens, you can keep the story moving along. A good actor knows the play and his role within it. He knows and understands his lines. He—or she—is constantly looking for and taking cues and clues from others, including the audience, and deciding, on the spot, what to do with that feedback. This takes a special awareness and an ability to improvise, or make something up, right on the spot. Improvisation means reacting to things happening around you, in a believable way, if that makes sense."

"I think so. Can we try it?" Mitch straightened his posture.

This caught Ronald by surprise, in the most pleasant way. "Right now? Sure!" He launched off the sofa. "I will set the scene and then we will act it out. Stand up."

Mitch hopped to his feet and Ronald sized up his emerging favorite student and saw that he had grown taller over the summer. Ronald still bested him, just not by that much anymore. "Okay. We are in England, and we are strangers who don't know each other." Mitch nodded. "We've both purchased tickets for the train from London to Dublin, but we discover onboard that we were both assigned the same seat number. Got it?"

"Maybe," Mitch said. He looked unsure.

"Okay, so I have set the scene. I have told you where the action takes place. So, let's jump in. You come from that side of the living room." Ronald pointed. "And I'll come from the door to my apartment. The sofa is where our seat is assigned, and we meet each other there. Okay?"

"Sure," Mitch said, turning to take his place near the hallway that led to the rest of Mr. Simpleman's apartment.

"And . . . *action!*" Ronald said from the apartment door. The two moved toward the sofa. Ronald tipped his head to acknowledge Mitch, who had his head down, looking at an imaginary ticket in his hand. This brought a satisfactory grin to Ronald's face. Mitch looked from the ticket to the sofa, and then back at the ticket, before starting to sit down.

"Excuse me, but I believe that is my seat," Ronald said, pointing to where Mitch sat.

"I just checked my ticket, and it says this seat was assigned to me," Mitchell said, in an overly dismissive way. "Your ticket must be wrong." He opened an imaginary newspaper and began to scan imaginary headlines. Ronald was thoroughly impressed by the character Mitch was creating.

"May I see your ticket?" Ronald asked.

"Only if I can see yours," Mitch shot back, raising only one of his eyebrows before a mischievous grin overtook his cute face. Ronald had to look away out of embarrassment . . . and, in a way, defeat. Mitch was excellent at this improvisation game. Sticking to the scenario he'd laid out, Ronald pantomimed pulling a ticket out of his trousers, holding it out for examination. Mitch did the same, and with their two hands touching, fingers pinching make-believe tickets, Mitch said, "Obviously there has been a mistake. Tell you what. Seeing that you are much older than me, you take this seat. I can stand."

Ronald broke character, grinning. "All the way to Dublin?" He tried to recover but ended up nodding his head. Then he called, "Scene! Alrighty then. You really impressed me there." He put a hand on Mitch's shoulder. "How about you set the next scene?"

Mitchell soaked in the praise. This was how he had felt after delivering (from memory) the Gettysburg Address the previous year, or after hitting the final high note in that *Paint Your Wagon* ballad.

The kid's a bit of a ham for attention, Ronald thought. That was good. It would serve him well on stage. Mitch took a few steps back from the sofa and raised both hands to his face, seemingly erasing the last character from his mental Etch A Sketch so he could create a new one.

"Okay, here's the scene," Mitch said. "We don't know each other, but we both get into an elevator. We push buttons for different floors but then the elevator jerks to a stop and loses power. We're stuck inside, in the dark. Your kitchen is the elevator. Ready?"

"Sure." Ronald moved his feet onto the linoleum.

"And . . . *action!*" Mitch said, walking into the kitchen space and pressing an imagined button on a made-up panel. He looked up and away as Ronald got into the elevator, pushing his own button. The two faced the living room, staring straight ahead as the imaginary elevator doors closed. Mitchell made a mechanical noise, suggesting the elevator had just stopped. He looked overhead at the light he imagined flickering before it went out completely, leaving them in faked darkness.

"Ah, shit," Mitch exclaimed.

"Language," the teacher couldn't help saying, before stepping back into his character. "I'm sure the power will come on in a second or two."

"What if it doesn't?" Mitch scraped his foot back and forth on the floor. "What if we're stuck and nobody knows we are in here? What if we die in here?" He leapt several pages ahead in the evolving script in his mind to build up tension.

"We're not going to die in here," Ronald said. "Nobody dies in an elevator."

"People, and children especially, die in elevators all the time!" Mitch insisted.

Ronald almost smiled at the teenager's singling out of children as being particularly at risk, but then childhood was probably still the cohort he identified with, even when he was play acting somebody older. "I'm sure the fire department has already been notified, and rescuers must be on the way."

"But what if they aren't? I'm too young to die. There are too many things I haven't done! Too many experiences I haven't had yet."

God, the kid was so good. "Experiences like . . . what, for example?" Ronald asked.

Mitch hesitated, thinking. Then, suddenly, he came out with it. "I'm still a virgin!" he said, suddenly admitting one of his character's vulnerabilities. "And I've never given another guy a blow job."

Ah, there's the old Mitch, Ronald thought, flashing back to the crank phone calls and their revelatory moment together on the bleachers at the tennis courts that had taken place just before summer break. He tried to stay in character. "And these things you haven't experienced yet—they're important to you?"

"Well, duh!" Mitch's character snapped back at him, sounding every vowel and syllable like the teenager he was. No make-believe required there.

Ronald paused as his character had a consequentially dramatic decision to make. This wasn't his improvisation. He hadn't set the scene. He wasn't the director. That's not how improvisation worked. He stayed in character. "Well, I am a man . . . and if we're going to die, I can't really help you with your virginity, but . . ."

Mitch dropped to his knees, his face level with the actual button and zipper of Mr. Simpleman's pants, feverishly determined to finish the scene.

STEVENSVILLE HIGH SCHOOL

May Day 1977

RONALD HAD A VAST BODY OF EXPERIENCE BEING ON the receiving end of crank phone calls. But this one stood out as different—more sensitive, somehow. That's why he hadn't hung up right away.

For the life of him, he didn't recognize the voice. To determine which of Stevensville's less than one thousand residents this caller could be, he would need more clues than he was getting. The caller was a younger-sounding male, so if Ronald subtracted what he assumed had to be half of the town's population that was female, he still had roughly 500 men to choose from, and deducting another couple hundred from this figure that represented males either too old or too young, then he felt he could be getting somewhere. The caller's command of vocabulary seemed above average, and his grammar was correct. For instance, he didn't just say *seen* instead of *saw* when he said he'd spotted Ronald at the Burnt Fork Grocery the other day. The accent was remarkably devoid of Montana's unique brand of Western twang and slang, which the young teacher had had trouble adjusting to when first assigned to this remote outpost nearly three years ago.

At first, he didn't think this caller could be one of his students because he didn't recognize the voice and he was picking up on a level of maturity and confidence that seemed beyond the reach of most high schoolers he knew. This caller seemed to have a functional command of word order, pronoun agreement, and the use of connectors to form more complex sentences. If he had been one of Ronald's English students, he would have been singled out by now as top of the class—an academic distinction so far only achieved by a handful of thick-spectacled girls, in Ronald's experience. The caller spoke in a whisper and so Ronald thought he must not have wanted to be overheard. That probably meant there were others around. So, the caller was taking a significant risk. But then, the caller revealed he was an SHS student, so the list of suspects narrowed drastically.

"Some of the kids at school say you're gay," the caller said.

Ronald paused, his pulse racing. "What do *you* think?"

"How would I know?" the kid shot back, raising his voice above the whisper.

"Do you think *you* might be gay?" Ronald flipped the table, expecting the caller to hang up.

There was silence on the line. Ronald thought he heard a clock ticking in the background. The caller stammered, "If you really want to know, meet me at the high school baseball diamond and I'll tell you there."

"Tell me what?" Ronald asked.

The caller cleared his throat into the receiver. "What else they've been saying about you."

"Look, you obviously know who I am, but I don't know who you are."

"Come to the baseball field right now and you'll find out." The caller sounded more pleading than ominous.

"It will take me ten minutes—"

The line went dead. Ronald stood there listening to the dial tone before deciding what he would do next. It was Sunday. A school night. Maybe he should just stay home. The caller hadn't sounded like an adult and had referred to what kids at school were saying about him. Chances were high that the caller was that one student in a gang of hillbilly hoodlums who had drawn the short straw, tasked with the phone call that would set their redneck trap. He wasn't about to hand them a victory in their end-of-the-school-year caper to bag a fag. He placed the phone in its cradle and went to take a shower before going to bed early.

RONALD AVOIDED SPENDING too much time in the faculty lounge on account of the cigarette smoke that his nose sometimes picked up clear across the other side of the school, but there he was before the first class of the day, gathered around a small black-and-white television on the yellowed Formica countertop, shoulder to shoulder with a gaggle of his colleagues, listening to an ABC reporter deliver the grim details of an airline accident. Two 747s had collided on a foggy runway in Tenerife in the Canary Islands just a few days earlier. Five hundred and eighty-three people were dead. Ronald didn't mention that he'd been to Tenerife because he didn't want to sound like he was bragging, but he'd flown in and out of that same airport. The less the other teachers knew about him, the better he could maintain his trademark aloofness and distinguished air of mystery. Gods forbid he disclose something that revealed anything he might have in common with any of them, though he doubted Tenerife would be a common denominator anyway.

The bell rang, and the principal came over the intercom with his daily announcements. Class rings and yearbooks could be picked up in the school library starting at noon. There was a pep rally at 2 p.m. for the Yellowjackets track team, which was heading off to Bozeman to compete in the state finals. The principal then said something about cleaning out lockers, but that part of his message came out garbled, and Ronald figured it didn't apply to him.

He left the faculty lounge and joined in the migration of students clogging the hallway as they headed to their first classes. Not much rose above the stench of Brut aftershave and cherry lip gloss, but Ronald's sensitive nose could cut through the olfactory pollution like a Coast Guard ice breaker when it came to seeking the scents of young male body odor.

He had always been curious about his over-developed olfactory epithelium—which had been his father's way of putting it. As a teen, he had tried to research the topic in his dad's medical journals and encyclopedias. He read enough to know he wasn't a freak. Super smellers like him went on to have fabulous careers in wine, cheese, and perfumery. He'd opted to become a high-school teacher and so had fallen short of ever being able to use his talent for financial gain. But he dabbled in hobby sniffing. The hallways always presented the biggest challenge to his ethmoidal cells, as they needed to sort through the Brut aftershave, the Right Guard anti-perspirant, the girls in various stages of menstruation, the perfumes, the hairsprays—not to mention the janitor's bleach.

He hadn't proven this scientifically—didn't even know how he would go about it—but he believed his nose could distinguish scents from the different stages of male development, specifically pre- and post-pubescent. He liked the almost portmanteau nature of that word—pubescent—a simple combination of pube, the slang for pubic, with the word scent. There was the milky virgin version he knew how to recognize and avoid, since it wasn't all that appealing and led to nothing but underage mayhem and unnecessary drama. There was a faint but distinct essence he could pick up around actively pubescent boys when their sweat gets broken down by bacteria on the skin to give it a characteristic odor. Then there was his favourite of the smells—the scent of confidence as he liked to distinguish it—exuded in the developmental phase when advanced teens began casting about their pheromone-like androgens, willy-nilly on the winds. These distinctive chemical messages converted into steroidal signals were broadcast like beacons that would beckon his nose straight to their sources, where he would then gather the evidence needed to prove his olfactory hypothesis statistically. And finally, there was the everyday, common stink of those who had made it to adulthood—like his male colleagues in the faculty lounge. Men ready to conquer and repopulate the earth. Ronald had little interest in these smells, nor in the men who off-gassed them, because he was one of them and to him, that seemed and smelled boring.

His keen olfactory sense didn't make him a pervert, more like an aroma voyeur or smell connoisseur. His outward behavior was rarely influenced by what his nostrils took in and he had never felt compelled to act on any of these scent impulses. This hobby, his gift and his research were only for self-gratification and self-edification. He was very clear and strict about this with himself and always stayed well within the established moral guardrails. He had no choice in the matter if he was to survive here—and not just because this was rural Montana but because rural Montana was no different than rural anywhere. Country folk just had their noses in everybody else's business. He knew how his fetish would appear if discovered and scrutinized by others. The opprobrium alone—never mind the lynching or incarceration to follow—would be more than he could bear, regardless of whether he'd ever laid a finger on a teen just by the way he smelled. (For the record, he had not.)

Today's scent gathering was being hijacked by Ronald's quest to discover the identity of the young male who'd phoned his apartment the previous evening. While he sniffed, he scanned the mob in the hallways like a prison guard looking for a more-than-casual glance. He should have been walking against the student traffic so that he could study their suspicious looking faces given that every one of them had something they were hiding. When classes broke for lunch, he'd try to invent an excuse to be walking from the opposite direction.

His first class of the day was his easiest. English Literature was an opportunity for students from the upper classes to slouch and sleepwalk into an easy *A*, as they pretended to read strategically opened books that concealed their shut eyes. Ronald would stare without blinking at the wall clock above the chalk boards, waiting to see how many minutes passed before a single page got turned. There were mornings when his eyes would water and cross before this occurred. Sometimes, he'd knock the stapler off his desk just to wake the class up.

Today, he spent a few minutes studying each of the seventeen teenage boys in his homeroom for a sign any of them might have been the crank caller. It was like taking a very special roll call.

Steven was the only male senior on the honor roll. Ronald wouldn't have minded learning that he had been his Sunday night caller. But Steven's voice was crazy deep, and he had a maturity that made Ronald wonder if he'd been held back a grade at some point. His smell—which Ronald could often pick up from his teacher's desk—only emphasized that possibility.

Ronald scanned the rank and file . . . William with the puka shell necklace, was a *no* since his hot and heavy romance with Martha the head cheerleader was renowned. There was another Steven, who also had a puka shell necklace—not to mention a bright-eyed smile when he wasn't asleep behind his *Moby Dick*. He could be a possibility, and a pleasant one at that, but *no*. There was the preacher's son, Daniel, who was a *no* on account of his drunken behavior with his hands inappropriately all over his mousy female date at the prom last month. (Ronald had been a chaperone.) Brent was a definite *no* as the kid had already signed on to join the army after graduation even with his lisp, which the previous night's caller did not possess. He supposed that Terry was a possibility with his large white teeth that had been orthodontically corrected during Ronald's tenure. But something told him this kid had other things on his mind than dialing crank calls. Jerry was the mortician's son and looked like a dark-haired Ken doll. He was likely taking over his father's funeral home and just didn't strike Ronald as the type who was all that much into the live ones.

Ronald looked at the wall clock. He momentarily abandoned his perpetrator review and decided to knock the stapler off his desk instead. The boys in this first class of the day were all graduating in a matter of weeks. Ronald's developing hunch was that the kid on the phone had time on his hands, time to set his snare and time to patiently wait for his prey to put a paw in it. The caller wasn't graduating soon and so would more likely be sticking around or was maybe just stuck in general looking either for trouble out of boredom or a life preserver to save him from drowning in a sea of self-loathing. Ronald more than remembered these feelings from when he was a teen. He decided he should be looking for someone who reminded him of himself when he was that age. In that case, he realized, he needed to observe underclassmen. He had an Intro to Writing class following lunch, but that seemed too long to wait before resuming his investigation. This gave him an idea.

Ronald knew he would find Coach Blankenburg in the faculty lounge at 10:45 sucking the tar out of his Viceroy before his 11 a.m. freshman and sophomore PE class. Ronald had a break from eleven to noon on Mondays,

Wednesdays, and Fridays, and once before had gotten the coach's permission to use the therapy whirlpool on the men's side of the gymnasium changing rooms so he could treat his bum shoulder. If he could time his soak to linger long enough to catch the frosh and sophs returning to the locker room at the end of P.E., he'd be in a great position to spring a trap of his own.

As Ronald had anticipated, the coach was sitting on the counter in the lounge, and they gave each other a chin-tilt acknowledgment.

"Say, coach. I wanted to see if the whirlpool was up and running today."

The coach held his drag, analyzing the drama teacher. "That Shake-speare shoulder of yours acting up again, is it?"

Ronald smiled, nodding. "*Twelfth Night*—you have a good memory. It's an old swordplay injury." He massaged his right shoulder like a prop.

"I'll flip the heat and jets on when I get back to the gym," the coach said. "I'll have the class outside playing flag football for the period, so you'll have the change room to yourself."

"Thanks, coach. My shoulder appreciates it." Ronald turned to leave the lounge before he had to contend with a real nicotine headache on top of the faked pain from his long-ago shoulder injury.

He killed some time sorting the photographs he'd taken during a dress rehearsal of *Annie Get Your Gun*, which had been the senior class production he'd directed last month. When he saw it was a quarter past the hour, he closed his classroom and made his way down the silent and empty halls to the gymnasium. He knew it would be bursting with scent.

He had walked past a student he knew, Mitch Carson, and one he didn't know, but whose name he thought might be Tom. Both freshmen were in their gym shorts and t-shirts, dry mopping the large lobby between the gymnasium and what the school called its "cafetorium." Large enough to store a blimp, it was an arch-roofed part of the complex. It had a curtained proscenium stage whose audience area also doubled as the school cafeteria. Ronald wanted to think he'd caught the eye of the one student he knew only from working with him on a bicentennial variety show sponsored by the town's chapter of the Montana District Kiwanis Club the year prior. This student hadn't yet been in any of Ronald's classes or productions, but he knew it was only a matter of time.

As the odd and out-of-place-looking teacher loped through the double doors into the gymnasium with a rolled-up towel under one arm, he casu-ally glanced back and saw Mitch Carson glance quickly away. Ronald made a mental note to pay more attention to him in his investigation. This student could not yet be ruled out.

He pushed open the door to the men's change room and was hit in the face by a humid, pungent assault on his senses, experienced foremost inside his tingling and delighted nostrils. His glasses steamed up and he squinted, adjusting to the dim lighting. Through a maze of benches and lockers, he heard the gurgling, motorized sounds of the whirlpool spa that the coach had left running for him in the corner, across from the showers. He unrolled his towel and placed his swimming shorts on top of it. Loosening his tie before unbuttoning his shirt, Ronald surveyed the space. He wished he could leave his eyeballs behind after his spa.

He peeled off his t-shirt to reveal to nobody the dark, lush carpet of pit-to-pit, nipples-to-navel hair that adorned every ridge and contour of his torso, arms, and legs. This distinguishing characteristic was the only flash of real masculinity he could display since debuting as a human Chia Pet toward the end of his puberty. He had other unique attributes, of course, but these were not so easy to show off in polite settings. He unfastened his belt, unzipped his pants, and let them crumple to his ankles. He stepped out of his loafers and withdrew his black-socked feet through the pant openings. He swapped out his tighty-whities for the bathing suit briefs he'd brought along.

He loosely folded his clothes in a pile on the wooden bench and then climbed the step stool to test the water temperature with one hairy leg and then the other. He lowered the rest of his body into the whirling waters, holding his breath until he could relax to savor the exhale. He'd forgotten to remove his eyeglasses, which comically steamed to opaqueness, as if a silent movie cinematographer had smeared Vaseline across a camera lens to create a dream sequence. Ronald removed them and held them underwater so the temperatures could equalize, before putting them back on his face without realizing how ridiculous it made him look, taking a spa with spectacles.

He'd need his glasses to make out the faces of the underclassmen for whom he'd devised this ruse. It would allow him to inspect them when they returned from their flag-football playing. Ronald hadn't minded flag football when he was their age. He'd always marveled at the ways the colorful streamers dangled and flapped spectacularly with the slightest velocity. And he of course appreciated any activity where he didn't get sacked, bloodied, or tackled.

The fifteen-minute end-of-class warning bell rang, jarring Ronald from his olfactory overload and soaking stupor. He planned to slightly overstay this session so that he could catch and be caught by the returning students. So, when a vanguard of aspiring jocks filed into the change room—stuttering in their steps when they noticed one of their teachers, hairy forearms propped up on each side of the stainless-steel whirlpool tub like he was riding a bobsled at the Innsbruck Winter Olympics—Ronald was in his element and couldn't help but grin.

Coach Blankenburg entered the scene and flashed Ronald a surprised look. He'd probably expected the interloper would have splashed and dashed before he had brought his class of impressionable youngsters back in from the field. Ronald twisted his grin into a look of apology but couldn't move a submarined muscle now, because his periscope had become engorged and otherwise engaged. Chlorinated bubbles popped and stung his eyes behind glasses that had fogged up again.

"Hey, Mr. Simpleman," one of the dumber junior-varsity football players called out, liberating himself from his athletic supporter that was de rigueur for the class uniform regardless of the activity. He headed for the showers, muttering only slightly under his breath, "We could have used you on our *fag* football team."

"Hey!" Coach Blankenburg hollered after him. "Watch your language!"

Ronald raised an eyebrow, eliminating that smart-mouthed rabble-rouser—whatever his name was—from his suspect list. Ronald's crank caller had been softer spoken and sensitive. A few jock straps sling-shotted over his sweating head, and one landed on the rim of the tub, inches from his fingers. He resisted the urge to snatch it and instead tried to identify the teen who'd just shouted, "Hey, that's mine!"

It was Mitch Carson, taking tentative steps toward the whirlpool, cupping his genitals in both hands.

"Sorry about that," the curly-haired student apologized in a diminutive whisper as he retrieved his gear. Ronald could tell the kid's gaze was fixed on his hairy chest, not his eyes. One of Ronald's pectoral muscles spasmed. It was involuntary, but to the student it might have appeared deliberate, as though his teacher had winked his eye. Mitch blushed, turning on his heel to return to a locker; his white butt cheeks offset by tan lines that Ronald found curious, given that it was only the first of May and there was still a skiff of snow on the ground.

Ronald understood he'd crossed a line and had no business still being there, but in this testosterone-fueled predicament, staying put and submerged was the decent thing to do. He could have vanished without a trace before the class had returned from the field, just as the coach had probably expected he would, but that would have defeated his purpose in being front-row at the wide, un-curtained entrance to the white-tiled shower room. In his defense, he had climbed into and sat in the whirlpool trough-like contraption with his back to the showers. He could make out, however, in the reflection off the stainless-steel wall guard he faced, a tangle of appendages moving in and out of the steam, providing Ronald's ever-improving photographic memory a deck of flashcard references he catalogued by decimal system and filed away in his fantasy library like a dirty Dewey. He tried to casually clear the inside of his lenses with a nonchalant wipe of a slow-moving index finger, but they kept steaming right back up again.

All but gagging in the dense fog of aerosol anti-perspirant, Ronald waited until he heard the last locker door slam shut, before quickly extracting his wrinkled self from the chlorine soup that had nearly bleached him. He half toweled off in haste and hustled back into his clingy polyester three-piece suit before striding back to his classroom at the opposite end of the sprawling high school where he gobbled down the bologna sandwich, he'd brought from home.

BEFORE DRIVING HOME from school, Ronald wanted to test a theory he had been formulating all afternoon—that his mystery caller had to be none other than Mitch Carson. Ronald stopped by the admin office on his way to his car to transfer some grades from his attendance and grade book to the student records that were kept in filing cabinets behind the principal's desk. He'd made a practice of adding a few grades each day so that he would be caught up and done before the last day of classes, which was only two-and-a-half weeks away.

There was a file cabinet for each class year, and the files were alphabetized by last name. The records for Ronald's students were mostly in the top two file cabinets—though he had a few sophomores and even some freshmen in his Intro to Writing class. With the principal out of his office and at the front counter helping the secretary out with the task of matching class rings and yearbooks to those who had lined up to retrieve what they'd pre-ordered, Ronald bent down to extract the Carson folder from the bottom drawer.

He reviewed the contents of the thin file. He was happy to see that Mitch's grades were decent and that he excelled in English and had been on the junior high journalism roster in middle school. He scanned the comments left by Mitch's junior high teachers and was not surprised to see him described as "thoughtful, highly creative and sometimes sensitive." Another teacher recorded, "Mitch is clever and adept at diplomacy and resolving conflicts." His music teacher wrote that "Young Mitchell is someone who shows great interest and little fear in performing," specifically noting his eighth-grade performance in the role of Steve Bullnack in the junior high production of *Paint Your Wagon.* "Mitch's standout solo, 'They Call the Wind Maria,' really brought the house down."

An English teacher wrote that "his grammar and writing are actually very good, and he has a keen sense of humor and a very pleasing personality." A social studies teacher felt it necessary to record that he felt Mitch may have been working too rapidly, that "there seems to be an urgency on his part, to finish quickly so that he can join the other early finishers in the reading area at the back of the class." "His work is always in on time and complete," wrote another, "but I think his haste tends to make him a bit careless."

Ronald was more interested in the impressions of Mitch's current teachers, now that his freshman year was nearly over. But high school teachers only recorded letter grades with an occasional smiley face or exclamation point when a student stood out from his or her peers; the paperwork format left little room to elaborate. Mitch Carson had received both in his first year; a smiley from his freshman typing teacher and two exclamation points—one upside down before the grade and the other right side up following the *A* that had already been recorded by his Spanish teacher, Zona Hedley.

Everything Ronald had read bolstered his working theory.

HE'D GREETED HIS landlord, Georgia, with a wave in the direction of where he spotted her sitting on the front porch when he pulled up. She'd shouted back at him—just before he ducked behind a hedge of lilac bushes at the corner of the house—that there had been no letters or packages delivered for him today. He climbed the stairs to his apartment and stopped to water a pot of what would become pink geraniums on the landing. They were finally showing signs of reconstitution following the harsh winter they'd had to endure in the Bitterroot Valley that year. He sat the antique metal watering can back in the open where it could continue collecting rainwater.

He turned the key in the doorknob to his apartment and forced the warped wooden door with its gingham-curtained window open into the linoleum kitchenette space. Inside, he heeled off his loafers and put down the recycled denim bookbag that had been made for him in home economics by a quiet tomboy named Ramona a few years back. Before she graduated, he'd talked her into playing the only female role in *The Mouse That Roared.* This brave casting move had transformed a timid, overly religious gal into perhaps the most popular girl in her class at the time. Ronald had grown concerned that by providing her this opportunity, he'd helped her incubate an oversized ego that led to unintended consequences when she seemed to have developed an infatuation with her director. He hadn't wanted to encourage this attraction nor discourage her just-go-for-it spirit, but he did have to sit her down after one particularly punishing rehearsal to tell her that, if she was trying to flirt with him, she'd lost the plot and needed to redirect her energies back into her character onstage.

In the end, Ronald heard that Ramona turned out to be a born-again Pentecostal lesbian, but before graduating high school, she'd stitched him this nifty and sturdy bookbag out of several pairs of old jeans that she'd convinced him and other teachers to donate. He'd used the bag ever since.

Putting two frozen Swanson pot pies on the counter to thaw, Ronald set his toaster oven to *bake*. He bought these flaky meat-filled morsels every time they went on sale at Burnt Fork Grocery (four for a dollar) and sometimes he could scarf four of them in a single sitting. His teacher's salary ($14,537) only stretched so far, and Ronald was proud of his ability to economize. His toaster oven only had room to cook two pies at a time, and tonight he was feeling lazy and not all that hungry, so it was a bonus to have saved half a buck.

He'd known all afternoon that he'd spent too long in the whirlpool because he smelled like a urinal cake and the hot water had robbed him of his energy—though he had no plans for this evening, anyway. He relished school nights like this when he didn't have a rehearsal or performance, either of which easily doubled the length of a teaching day without commensurately enhancing his take home salary.

He had his legs crossed at the ankle and propped on a foot stool as he rubbed his exposed, post-dinner belly. This time of year, he'd automatically shed his polyester leisure suits, unbutton his dress shirt or strip down to his underwear briefs the moment he arrived home from school. The built-up heat inside his stuffy attic apartment—with its one window wedged stuck in its sill that couldn't be forced open—meant that when he was home, he often left the screenless apartment door ajar which let in bugs he had to tolerate. He couldn't imagine surviving without a cross breeze during the heat of summer and was grateful his landlords didn't charge him rent for June through August when he wasn't there. Today was only the second of May, but he already needed to fan his face using a shamrock green script he'd selected from a stack of Samuel French playscripts he'd been perusing for the following year.

The phone on the wall began ringing. With an anticipatory groan, Ronald leveraged his butt out of the easy chair to answer it. Maybe it was his caller from the previous evening. The hot pink sarong he'd covered the chair with stuck to the sweat on his backside as he crossed the small kitchen trailing it behind him.

He hadn't even had the chance to say hello when the soft tenor voice on the other end said, "You didn't show up last night. Why?"

"Well, hello there," Ronald said, instantly seized by mixed feelings over being given this second chance. He hadn't entirely solved the mystery of the caller's identity, so he was grateful to collect more clues. But fearing where this could lead, he felt himself on tenterhooks. The caller's question hung in the ether, unanswered. "I didn't think you were serious," Ronald offered in response.

"I was there," the young caller said.

"Were you by yourself?" He'd been suspicious of a trap sprung by a pack of pranksters.

"Of course I was by myself," the caller said, sounding exasperated. But that was followed by a boast. "I ended up jacking off on the pitcher's mound when you stood me up. My cum's probably still there in the dirt. You could check it out."

"Ah, well, then all's not lost," Ronald replied, sarcastically.

"But I didn't want to jack off by myself," the caller whispered.

Ronald grinned but paused. Then he said, "What do you think about when you masturbate?"

"Mostly, I guess I think about seeing you naked."

Once again, Ronald paused. He had neither the courage to shut this down nor the words to steer the conversation in a different direction.

"Is that a possibility?" the young man asked, sounding more sheepish now.

"May I ask how old you are?"

"Uh, old enough to make jizz come out of my dick."

That set off alarms, but for some reason, "impressive" was the word that came out of Ronald's mouth before he'd had a chance to yank it back. He hadn't meant to say that. He shouldn't have said it. And yet, he was impressed because if this caller was who he thought it was, then he was impressed that somebody as young as Mitch Carson appeared to be, had mastered masturbation to the extent he could boast about his ejaculation. That impressed him.

"I bet you can make lots of sperm come out," the caller said, tauntingly. "I'd like to see that sometime."

In what seemed like a non sequitur, Ronald asked, "Do you drive?"

"Uh, I get around," the caller fired back, sounding impatient. He had to be a kid then. Ronald had asked because students in Montana could get a driver's license at age fourteen but couldn't drive at night until they turned sixteen. The caller went on. "So, you going to show up this time?"

"The baseball diamond?"

"Sure."

Ronald needed to slow this down. "I'd be more comfortable if we talked first. Could we do that?"

"We're talking now, aren't we?"

"In *person*." There was silence on the phone, but the kid didn't hang up. He must have been thinking. "Tell you what," he said. "Why don't we meet in the tennis court bleachers? We can sit and, you know, talk first."

"Okay. I'll be there in five minutes." And the telephone line clicked to dial tone.

Ronald's goal was to establish rapport and trust. He was not interested in what the boy claimed to be after. He only wanted to solve the mystery, provide support—maybe give a little advice and useful direction. *That's what teachers do*, he reminded himself as he hunted around his closet for something to wear that didn't, ironically, make him look like a teacher. He poked his head from his bedroom into the hallway and could see through the window that dusk was mostly over, prompting him to grab a windbreaker.

Two years at this short commute and Ronald was convinced that if he had to, he could probably drive from his apartment to the high school blindfolded with his steering arm tied behind his back. He parked in his regular spot in the faculty section of the northeast parking lot and turned off his engine and headlights. He figured his car's distinctive boxy profile would have been detected from the bleachers with the naked eye, if that was where his curiosity-seeker was lurking in wait. He climbed out of the car, locked it—already accustomed to student pranksters—looked around, and then quickly began walking past the parked school buses and along the backside of the school.

His pulse quickened to match the cadence of his stride as he left the glow of the high school and parking lot floodlights. He'd never been to the school's sports fields at night when there wasn't a football or baseball game underway. He neared the wide pedestrian and service bridge that would carry him over the full flowing irrigation ditch to reach the tennis courts he could see from his classroom, and whatever else lay beyond in the pitch-black darkness.

Cloud cover kept the moon from doing its job, but Ronald could feel the mosquitos accomplishing theirs; he swatted his bare forearm as he crossed the bridge. He squinted toward the bleachers, trying to see if he could make out anyone there waiting for him. Drawing closer, he spotted the silhouette of somebody rising to a sitting position from where he must have been reclined on the bench. Ronald was still struggling with his night vision, but it seemed that the person was alone and maybe this wasn't an ambush.

He cautiously climbed over the first three rows of bleachers and approached the figure on the fourth row, who slowly withdrew the hood of his sweatshirt.

"Well, hello there, Mitch," Ronald said. He did not reveal the slightest twinge of shock, because he wasn't shocked. Mitch Carson had reached the top of his shortlist of possible crank-callers. But since he'd been brave enough to show up, Ronald thought the calls may not have been crank calls at all.

"Hello, Mr. Simpleman." Mitch said. "Thank you for showing up." He was polite, but too young to reach out for a handshake. His teacher took a seat on the wooden bench about three feet away. Mitch said, "Were you wearing a swimsuit in the whirlpool today?"

Ronald grinned. The kid was direct. "Yes."

"Cool. I was just wondering." Mitch's hands were deep inside his pants pockets.

"You just live across the street from the school, don't you?" Ronald asked, already knowing the answer.

"Yep. And you live on Charlos Street, above the Rileys, right?" Mitchell seemed to be talking to his feet.

Ronald chuckled. "How did you know that?"

"Small town. Plus, I know the Rileys. They've promised me a part-time job at the Burnt Fork as soon as I'm old enough." Mitch looked up and across the tennis courts toward the school buildings. "I mean, I'm old enough this summer, but my dad has me working this Youth Conservation Corps job with the Forest Service."

"After you turn sixteen, you mean?" Ronald asked.

"Yeah." Mitch gently kicked a piece of gravel off the bleachers with the point of his shoe. "Thanks for meeting me this time."

"I'm happy to talk anytime about anything that's on your mind," Ronald said. Mitch went back to staring at his tennis shoes. "Do you have questions you wanted to ask me?"

Mitch pulled the hood of his sweatshirt back onto his head. Without looking up, he asked, so softly that Ronald could barely hear, "Are you a homo, like the other kids say you are?"

Ronald was relieved to be starting with this inquiry so they could get to the heart of the matter that had precipitated this rendezvous. The kid was just fifteen so regardless of any impulses either of them might be feeling, talking about it was all Ronald could allow them to do at this point. "I guess that depends on what you and the other kids mean by *homo*. We're all homo sapiens, after all."

"The other homo," Mitch said, in a tone that indicated he wasn't there to play word games.

"Ah, you must mean *homosexual*, then. If so, then the answer is yes. How do you feel about that? Does it bother you to know that I am a homosexual?"

Mitch shrugged. "I guess not. I mean, the reason I asked you to meet me here was because I thought . . . I hoped . . . I wanted to find out, that's all." He went back to staring at his feet.

"Do you think you might be a homo, then too?" Ronald whispered.

"Sapien? Sure." Mitch revealed a grin on the half of his face that was visible under the hoodie.

"Smart aleck. That's what you are!" Ronald couldn't resist giving the kid a friendly shove—but perhaps should have—because now he'd made contact.

"Is it wrong?" Mitch asked. "You know, if you're the other kind of homo, like you say you are?"

"No," Ronald said quickly, at the risk of sounding defensive. "It's *not* wrong. In fact, it is completely natural to like, uh, to be attracted to other boys."

"You're not a boy."

That was obvious, Ronald knew. "But I was once. Believe it or not, I probably had the same thoughts, questions, and desires that you are having and feeling right now."

Mitch continued scuffing his tennis shoe on the plank of bleacher beneath their feet but didn't respond otherwise.

Even as a new teacher, Ronald felt he was good at seeking common ground—finding appropriate levels to engage with students at any age. He didn't have many freshmen in his classes, so Mitch was younger than most his other students. But he and Mitch already shared some previous history together. He'd helped Mitch with his Abe Lincoln make-up and a year or two earlier, he'd offered some advice on gestures and body language for the whole cast of 'Paint Your Wagon' when Mitch was still in middle school, though Ronald doubted he would even remember that. "Do you want to tell me what you're thinking or feeling?"

"You mean right now?"

"Well, I meant in general. What type of interests do you have? What are you curious about? Are there things you want to know about my experience as a gay man—which, by the way, is the more common and modern way of referring to a homosexual?" Ronald knew he was asking too many questions and being teacherly, but he hoped one of these prompts might be a way to get to whatever was bugging the kid.

But Mitch's silence and now foot-tapping on the bleachers suggested he was overwhelmed. Ronald decided to focus his questions. "Has your dad or your mom talked with you about the birds and the bees? You know—about sex and how sex happens?"

"Sort of but not really," Mitch finally responded. "They got me this set of books that is supposed to explain things."

"Have you read them? Looked through them, maybe?"

"I looked at pictures and read some stuff, sure. I know how sex is supposed to work with a girl, but that's not my situation."

"Maybe you want to know about how sex is supposed to work with another boy?"

"Not so much with boys, really." Mitch looked up and over at the teacher. "Trust me, I've tried stuff with boys my age, and they don't have a clue. You asked me what I'm curious about and what my interests are—" Mitch paused, straightened up, and pulled back the sweatshirt hood. It seemed to Ronald like he was trying to look and act more mature than he was. "I'm interested in someone older who knows what they're doing—you know, somebody like you. So that I don't waste my time."

Ronald needed to but didn't want to discourage this come-on, now that Mitch was opening up to him. Ronald the teacher wanted to hold the keys to whatever doors this fifteen-year-old wanted to unlock and look inside. But Ronald the man, aside from ethical limitations and with full awareness of the boundaries, was terrified by the consequences of caving in to his own impulses—desires that were likely just as scrambled as the boy's—half his age—in this tender and delicate moment. Something Archibald Cox once said, popped into Ronald's brain in the middle of this deliberation. Cox said he always maintained a 'naïve belief that right will prevail in the end.' But what was the wrong way to handle Mitch's advances, and what was the right? At a minimum, Ronald needed to slow this down until he figured that part out.

"Okay, then. That gives us a starting point."

"Cool," Mitch exclaimed, leaning back on the bench behind them and launching his crotch into greater prominence. "You wanna touch it?" He'd banished all his pretend shyness that must have been for show. "I wanna touch yours," he confessed, staring into Ronald's lap.

Ronald knew he had to suppress what he was feeling so as not to reveal even a smidgeon of intrigue over the proposition. But he also needed to give the kid some hope they might eventually get somewhere, give him something to hang on to, so that the trust they were establishing could hold. "Not here, and not yet," he said, his own voice cracking as he laid down the law. "You remind me of myself when I was your age. I've enjoyed this conversation. I hope we can become friends after we are better acquainted and get to know more about each other."

"What else do you want to know? I have a hard-on in my jeans right now!" Mitchell was stammering, not taking rejection well. He squeezed the denim on both sides of his erection in a show-and-tell way. "See?"

Ronald couldn't help looking, and that was another mistake to add to his growing list of transgressions. And the list wasn't the only thing that was growing. "Look," he said. "Let's plan for you to come to my apartment sometime after summer vacation. We can continue this conversation there and then. But this stays between you and me. Nobody else ever needs to know what we've talked about, okay?"

He stood to leave, and that was mistake number . . . he'd lost count. Like a lightning bolt out of nowhere, Mitch grabbed at the outline of the man's full-grown interest. Ronald let the kid's grip linger milliseconds longer than he should have, and the squeeze produced a dark wet spot that was visible, even in the dark, on his mostly completely faded jeans.

"And on that note," he said, removing the boy's hand from his crotch and turning it over to shake hands, "I'm pleased to have had this conversation with you, Mitch. I want to be a good teacher, and someone you can trust. I want you to feel comfortable coming to me with any questions or trouble you might experience. Most importantly, I look forward to continuing our little talk at my place in the future." He almost made another mistake by adding *when you've at least turned sixteen*. Instead, he asked, "When's your birthday, by the way?"

"August 16."

Ronald chiselled the date on the front of his brain and turned, saying, "I'll see you at school and nobody will ever know we've had this conversation or learn what we've talked about. You have my word, Mitch. Your secret is safe with me, and I hope my secret is safe with you."

Looking dejected, the kid nodded reluctantly. "Same," he said, before bolting off the bleachers and running away into the darkness.

Ronald stood there—stunned and throbbing in his britches—and watched as Mitch leapt over the irrigation ditch like a gazelle and disappeared around the corner of the high school building.

PART IV: 1975–1954

Then the whining school-boy,

with his satchel

STANFORD UNIVERSITY

June 16, 1974

ON THE GRASS FLOOR OF THE FROST AMPHITHEATER IN full sun, Ronald tried to come up with three academic achievements he was proud to hang his cap and gown on—to prove that the past seven years had been worth the struggle and his father's money. Sweating there in a polyester leisure suit under his black and cardinal-red graduation regalia, he already and quite literally had his thinking cap on and so he started rewinding his brain back through his university years in search of his three achievements.

Three might be a stretch, he was thinking after just a minute had elapsed. Then he supposed he could count his twin BAs in the English honors program and in theater and performance studies, which he had just topped off this past year by earning his Master of Arts degree in English education. The master's could have counted as his number three, but lazily naming his degrees individually wasn't enough of a challenge, so he counted them together as a single achievement in order to make the task even harder.

Ronald had maintained a 3.3 GPA throughout, despite a myriad of distractions, detours, and sometimes apathy. So, that could be considered his second academic achievement. He'd bested Harlan who had dropped out of UC Berkeley some twenty credits shy of completing his BA in Asian studies, choosing instead to study Mandarin in situ by living in Guangzhou for the past three-and-a-half years. Graduating from university, when his older brother hadn't, was Ronald's third academic achievement.

He regularly issued these self-pop-quizzes not so much to pass the time but to ensure that each minute of his allotted time on earth was cerebrally productive—contributing, however marginally, to his evolution and forward momentum. He'd discovered in his twenty-eight years of keen observation that humans spent more of their lives waiting for someone or something to happen to them than they did living up to their full (if brief) potential.

In this current moment of reflection and account taking—while everyone else clapped along to the Cardinal marching band's rendition of "Come Join the Band" and awaited the arrival of the commencement speaker—Ronald took on a new challenge which was to spot his parents in the stands. Even before the band had finished their rousing number, he'd succumbed to eye strain and abandoned his search for his folks as a futile waste of time. He was now thinking about his brother Harlan, likely back in his Castro apartment stewing because he had been one of the 3,000 people who had wanted to attend Stanford's 83rd Annual Commencement but couldn't get tickets when the identity of the commencement speaker had been revealed three weeks earlier. Ronald had offered to let Harlan dress up in his gown and pose as himself, since he was making such a stink about it. But as usual, Harlan chose pouting over victory.

Ronald hadn't appreciated at first what a big deal the featured commencement speaker was because he hadn't been paying much (if any) attention to the news while he buckled down on getting his master's degree. In their astute political wisdom, the Stanford faculty and student senates had selected special prosecutor Archibald Cox to deliver the commencement address to poke the school's accusatory finger in Nixon's eye. Cox had been fired by Nixon the year before, during what became known as the Saturday Night Massacre. With Nixon's impeachment hearings already underway, and the grandstands bursting with anti-Nixon sentiments, Cox earned a resounding standing ovation when he said, "I have a sort of naïve belief that right will prevail in the end." Ronald had his own collection of naïve beliefs—about himself and the world around him—and so this declaration resonated with him.

He vowed to carry Cox's hope forward.

IN HIS FIRST years at Stanford, Ronald—a Rocky Mountain transplant, a romantic, and an idealist—had been swept up in student activism. That seemed to be a non-negotiable prerequisite for attendance there in the late 60s early 70s. He cut his teeth in various movements by attending any number of protests and rallies demanding civil rights, women's rights, and, much later, gay rights. He had this chicken-out setting on his commitment dial allowing him to always slip away just before things turned disobedient or violent. He couldn't gamble away his free-ride, parent-paid tuition, by making headlines in the Bay that might find their way back to the Rockies. He took cautionary stands against US involvement in Laos and then Vietnam, and he was particularly proud of his stamina, which lasted the entire nine-day sit-in at the Applied Electronics Library in April of '69, when he and around 400 fellow students demanded an end to classified military research on the Stanford campus.

This cause hadn't been particularly important to him, but he had developed a crush on a tall and handsome Chinese American student named Jimmy, who, when he even noticed Ronald existed, encouraged Ronald to tag along with him and his disgruntled band of rovers as they tried to force the university to capitulate. On the evening of December 1, that same year, Ronald and Jimmy had reported to the second-floor lounge in front of a Quasar television set with around a hundred other male students between the ages of eighteen and twenty-six, who were also studying at Stanford and living in Encina Hall. They had gathered to learn their fates during a nationally televised first-draft lottery that picked at random those men who would be forced to enlist and would be sent to fight in Vietnam.

In the most-watched television event since the moon landing in July of the year before, you could hear hearts racing as the host cranked the cylindrical plexiglass container with its 366 blue capsules, each containing a number representing a date in the calendar year including February 29. Several numbers were drawn before the first man in the lounge gasped the word *FUCK* when the number corresponding to his birthday was drawn and announced by the host. Ronald's number, 283, because he'd been born on the 283rd day of the year, had not been announced that evening, but Jimmy's had been—though, as a Chinese man first and an American man second, he said he'd be damned if he took up arms against his fellow Asians.

Like California wildfires whipped up by Santa Ana winds, word had spread that student draft deferrals were being offered to full-time undergraduates and graduate students. This had been Ronald's argument when negotiating with his father to finance some measure of a graduate program to keep him from getting drafted. The surgeon and his check book complied. Since the US military at the time both despised and banned gays from serving, there were others in the lounge that night—including Jimmy who claimed to be gay since birth—who planned to stage their spontaneous comings-out by each offering to give the draft officer head during their induction appointments. Soon, others all over the Stanford campus started to claim they were homosexual even when they weren't, which made for a very confusing time to be a real, closeted gay man at Stanford looking for a meaningful connection.

Jimmy didn't need to fake it. For years, he had made insane money moonlighting as a go-go dancer at the Gangway, in the Castro. As Jimmy's hanger-on friend, Ronald invented an excuse to see and be seen around the gay nightspots, regularly driving Jimmy to and from the city, so he didn't have to take Caltrain, which stopped running at midnight most weeknights. Personally, Ronald hadn't yet been ready to come out, though his older brother Harlan supposedly had and years ago according to him, though he hadn't informed the family. Ronald had never been entirely sure of the timing or extent of Harlan's sexual emancipation because he'd always behaved like a snooty celibate priest, but after learning his own lottery number had been selected, Harlan swished his way out of the draft-office door and straight onto a Pan Am plane to China in search of other pursuits.

At Stanford, Ronald's on-again off-again social life had been resuscitated inside the theater and performing arts productions during his undergraduate years especially. His English studies curriculum had been the boring cakewalk he imagined it would be, but Ronald loved and felt loved by the kooky band of thespians, who didn't take university life the least bit seriously. Practically waltzing across the quad from his dorm room at Encina Hall before and after rehearsals at the Memorial Auditorium, Ronald exhibited an extra bounce in his already spring-coiled step whenever he was involved in a production.

He didn't always have to be acting to get that loopy theater high, either, as stagecraft, sound, lighting, props and other behind the scenes tasks thrilled him equally. But his giant, head-swelling acting moment had transpired— and expired—in his third year, when he'd received critical praise from the *Stanford Daily* arts reporter for his role as Harold Mitchell in *A Streetcar Named Desire*. He'd taken a close-up photo of a quote from the review and had it enlarged and framed: "The perpendicularity with which Ron Simpleman undertakes the duplicitous role of Mitch is at once unsettling and positively arresting." Ronald had pretended to be embarrassed by this, since none of the other actors from the production had been singled out by the reviewer. He felt an imposter besides, given he had basically mimicked Karl Malden's performance from the 1951 movie, for which Karl had earned the Oscar for Best Supporting Actor. Since he was a kid, Ronald had this uncanny gift for mimicry and memorization. He could look at a page of script from a play in his first readthrough, with maybe a second glance for brush-up, but then have his lines and entrances and exits committed for the remainder of the rehearsal and production schedule. Ronald never spent much time on-book, so he avoided the stress of other actors when the dread moment came to go off-book. By then, Ronald couldn't even say where his script had ended up, though a good guess would always be in Giselle's crammed glove compartment.

His other Stanford productions included Lillian Hellman's *The Children's Hour*, for which he'd worked on the set's dark and almost Brutalist design, with elements carved out of Styrofoam that were painted to look like steel and ornate marble and built atop a turntable, so the production could be performed in the round. He understudied but never got to perform the role of Krupp in William Saroyan's *The Time of Your Life* which had introduced him to another of his favorite quotes, which he'd also photographed, enlarged, and framed: "In the time of your life, live—so that in that wondrous time you shall not add to the misery and sorrow of the world, but smile to the infinite delight and mystery of it."

He'd worked costumes and makeup for the repertory production of *Androcles and the Lion*, which showcased an attractive grad-student actress named Susan Weaver, with whom Ronald had struck up a cozy yet brief friendship during the thirty minutes it took to apply makeup each night of the two-weekend long Piggot Theater run. This make-up design entailed not just her face, but her bare shoulders and cleavage, which required a foundation bronzer so as not to bounce stage lights into the audience when she started to perspire there, under the hot lights. Once Ronald told Susan he was gay, she never once fussed when the make-up sponge in his fingers did its deep dives down her front. Their chats sometimes turned into no holds barred debates during the nightly application of her make-up and covered the gamut of politics, both traditional and sexual, nearly as effectively as the bronzer concealed her freckles and moles. Susan chuckled every time Ronald insisted on covering up the smallpox vaccine scar on her left deltoid, insisting the vaccine wasn't around during the time of the Roman Empire. The two shared and sometimes invented childhood stories with embellished shock value, and they even came up with the perfect stage names in case they ever became good at acting and famous for it. Ronald's was Salvatore, and Susan's was Sigourney. The run ended and the two theater chums never saw each other in person again, but then Ronald eventually saw Sigourney on screen.

WHEN HARLAN FIRST floated the notion that he might move to China to study the country's languages, Ronald had whole heartedly encouraged his brother's flight of fancy. But in this brotherly encouragement, Ronald had a secret agenda. After four years, he'd outgrown dorm life at Encina Hall on Stanford's campus and the prospect of moving a mile away into graduate housing in Escondido Village was as off-putting as it was stifling. Ronald was absolutely convinced that unless he moved off campus, the living conditions would stunt his intellectual growth. So, Ronald began angling for a way he might take over Harlan's rent-controlled lease on his Castro District apartment during the period his brother was planning to be away immersing himself in the People's Republic. To Ronald's shock, Harlan went for it, because Harlan had an agenda too; he didn't want to lose his rent-controlled lease.

Knowing he would be heading straight into grad school in his efforts to continue dodging the draft, and because commencement coincided with the same weekend that he would be taking over Harlan's apartment, Ronald had waved off their parents' insistence that they attend his undergrad commencement ceremony. He'd made them a deal—on top of the deal that they would continue financing his ever higher academic pursuits—that they could be in attendance when he graduated with his master's or doctorate. When they'd asked how long that might take, Ronald's response was, about as long as the Vietnam conscription stayed in place, and then everyone shook on it.

During those grad school years to follow, he never once minded the hour-long commute to campus in each direction, merrily whistling behind the padded steering wheel of his very first car—a used crème-colored Volkswagen Beetle he'd named Giselle—that he'd acquired at the start of his second undergrad year at Stanford for $800 cash. Giselle could have been a stand-in for the car in *Herbie the Love Bug*, if Ronald had added the number *53* in collegiate lettering to the hood and doors—which he'd seriously considered. Ronald had named his car a year before that movie came out and so was tickled to learn that Herbie's love interest in the film was also a *Giselle*, though she had been a Lancia Scorpion. Alternatively, a BART monthly transit pass would have cost him $11, and so Ronald calculated that by the time he finished grad school, Giselle was going to save him at least 124 bucks, if you didn't include the gas and motor oil. Of course, Giselle turned out to be one thirsty beast, what with an oil crisis that led to the OPEC embargo. So, Ronald needed to find work, and fast, preferably with an employer that paid him in gas tokens.

Desperately, he'd answered an ad in the *Bay Area Reporter* and landed a night job cutting and splicing adult films for an enterprising—not to mention dirty minded—pair of brothers. Before researching and writing his thesis had started to interfere with work, Ronald regularly stood in as the projectionist at their adult theater in the Tenderloin. While this occupation and Ronald's employment didn't last more than four months while the theater morphed into more of a strip club, Ronald did manage to amass a sizeable collection of celluloid outtakes that he broomed and dustpanned off the editing room floor; clips he was allowed to keep in lieu of being paid a decent wage. And the brothers had been adamant about the sequences they wanted excised from the films they featured when they gave Ronald his snipping orders. They weren't about to start losing patrons they feared could be made to feel inadequate in the penile department if they were constantly bombarded with close-ups of cocks with frankly untenable proportions. Fine by Ronald.

Meanwhile and work aside, Ronald threw himself at this strange, exhilarating new independence that rushed up with arms wide open to squeeze his virulent dining hall and vending machine dependencies right out of him, like puss from a pimple. He'd never lived alone before. He'd had roommates since birth—sharing a bedroom first with Harlan in their parents' house, and then sleeping, showering, and shitting in tight quarters with three different dormitory roommates as an undergrad. Ronald reveled in his freedom and gluttonously overdosed on all things Castro (The District, not Fidel).

His old Stanford acquaintance, Jimmy, sometimes crashed at his place on Friday or Saturday night so he could perform well into the early morning hours as "Jimmy Wang," in bars and clubs that were always popping up like pre-Easter daffodils. Ronald had been to them all—Moby Dick, the Men's Room, Badlands, Francine's, Buzzby's, the Stud, Pilsner Inn, the Eagle, and the Pendulum. He once attended three grand openings in a single week—cruising his rocks off from the Tenderloin to Twin Peaks.

Ronald wore his sideburns long and his gym shorts short back then. He embraced the code, learning to dress—or more accurately, *undress*—so that he looked like every other Castro clone, running errands shirtless on the street during the daytime, wearing denim jeans without a belt and three-stripe Adidas tennis shoes with or without socks. Ronald became adept as a quick-change artist, too—unbuttoning or removing his shirts, turning a tank top into a headband—which helped him on Polk Street just as it had in the theater. He slipped almost effortlessly into Harlan's left-behind wraparound assless leather chaps, which he could never imagine his brother wearing, but that Ronald front-laced over his jeans with a leather cord that suggestively incarcerated his bulge with the lift of a sub-midriff bustier.

He learned to accessorize any ensemble with a light-blue bandana tucked into the right rear pocket of his jeans and a mustard-colored bandana, rolled just phallically enough that it would jut out of a front pocket of his jeans. Worn in tandem, these kerchiefs advertised to anyone and everyone in possession of a Castro decoder ring that Ronald was a 69er (light blue) with over eight inches (mustard yellow).

The problem with the ever-evolving hanky code was that electricity didn't appear to have been invented in half the clubs in town. The lighting was so poor around most dancefloor fringes—not to mention the back-rooms—that it became tricky to distinguish between light and dark blue. Dark blue would have incorrectly telegraphed that Ronald was after anal sex. And more than once his mustard hanky had been mistaken for yellow, leading water-sports lovers to think he might be into their piss. When the code got lost in translation and he'd invited someone back to his apartment who was hankering for more than oral, Ronald usually got tagged the odd top out, given his prod worthy attribute. He was functionally capable of being the driver and doing the deed, but his brain quickly got in the way—unless he'd gotten stoned first, which could alleviate his tendency to overthink about feces.

But as so often happens with fads and fascinations, particularly under artificially boosted indulgence, Ronald's rocket ship flamed out before achieving orbit, spectacularly breaking up into charred and scuffed bits as this unqualified astro-NOT re-entered the atmosphere and splashed down in a post-graduate, adulthood reality. The gig was up. Captain Simpleman simply wasn't cut out for gay outer spaces.

RONALD REALIZED ALMOST too late and two months before graduation that he needed to buckle down and apply himself. His goal and deadline, if he had any hope of becoming a professional educator in the real world, was to finish and defend his thesis he'd titled *Teaching the Queer Birds and the Silly Bees*—a concept he'd ripped off from Franco Cavaletti, his older, auto-mechanic friend and mentor back home in the Butte. Ronald wasn't kidding himself or goofing around anymore. He suspected teaching would take far more bravery than becoming an astronaut, so he buckled down and went for broke on his thesis. At last, he started to believe he was prepared for the challenges, intensity, zigs and zags that would come with teaching, his chosen vocation. Around this same time, Ronald came to terms with who he was and who he wasn't. He'd burned himself out on the gay lifestyle amusement park he'd been indulging and living in and he had a feeling—that just like Stanford, The Castro was about to eject him too—not because he wasn't tall enough to ride the rides, but, as it turned out, because he just wasn't all that sexual. Ronald squarely recognized and understood he needed to get himself out of the city. He gave himself permission to stop pretending at something he would never become any good at. The time had come in his maturation to get himself a real adult life, preferably in the middle of nowhere, that better suited his native inclination to cleverly blend in rather than stupidly stand out.

AND SO, CONCURRENT with this commencement day, June 16, 1974, Ronald's eviction time had come with Harlan's return stateside. This brought with it a whole new suite of brotherly incompatibility, more than evident after only one overlap week of cohabitation on Church Street. Harlan's apartment wasn't big enough to share and San Francisco, it turned out, would also not be nearly large enough for the two of them to coexist in either. For this and other limiting factors—like the sunsetting of his parents' tuition, room and board paying agreement—today's graduation ceremony couldn't come soon enough for Ronald.

From the elevated stage, decked out in his red trimmed black gown with its hood and sleeve linings in royal blue, after being handed his diploma and having the golden tassel on his cap ceremoniously moved from side of the mortarboard to the other, Ronald took a moment. He took in a gasp of astonishment, squinting his brown eyes in the California sun. There they were. He'd just spotted his parents, Paul and June, who appeared to be wiping tears of pride off their cheeks in the stands off his stage left. He wondered how it was even possible that he had made them proud without bankrupting them in the drawn-out process. But he went with the fantasy of make believing, in that moment, that perhaps he had done just fine by them.

HUMAN BE-IN, SAN FRANCISCO

January 14, 1967

GUESSING IT MIGHT ONE DAY BE CONSIDERED VINTAGE and just in case he ever broke down and decided to finally hang something on his bare apartment walls, Harlan carefully unrolled the poster on the dining-room table, pinning each of its curling corners down with a bean bag from the Cornhole game they'd played when they were kids, and which, for some reason, Harlan still possessed. He had been the Crested Butte Junior High FUN GAMES two-time-champion, after all. "Think of this as my going-away party," he said. "I don't want to go by myself."

Ronald stared at the illustrated photograph of a swami with his third eye drawn in the middle of his forehead, surrounded by psychedelic scroll lettering that spelled out the details of what promised to be an event not to be missed. He recited the rest of the poster's contents aloud.

> Human Be-in . . . A Gathering of the Tribes . . . January 14, 1967 . . . 1 to 5 p.m. . . . FREE . . . Bring Food to Share . . . Bring Flowers, Families, Incense, Animals, Beads, Costumes, Feathers, Bells, Cymbals, Flags . . . Timothy Leary . . . Richard Albert . . . Dick Gregory . . . Allen Ginsberg . . . Jerry Rubin . . . Many Others . . . ALL OF SAN FRANCISCO's ROCK BANDS . . . including Santana and the Steve Miller Band . . . Golden Gate Park Polo Fields . . . San Francisco.

Ronald looked at his brother. "Wait. That's today!" He realized he'd been hoodwinked into arriving two days early, ostensibly to get an orientation on the apartment and neighborhood, when Harlan just didn't want to attend, what purported to be a massively crowded event, solo. Always happy to go-along-for-the-ride-Ronald, enthusiastically agreed to go, plus he would be happy helping his brother decide what to pack and take with him for his four-month exploration of China, Indonesia, and India on no fixed itinerary. Harlan just smiled and not-so-innocently shrugged his shoulders. "'So happy you are here, brother," he said, sounding almost sincere.

Ronald would have arrived six months earlier, had it been up to him. He and their parents had been quarreling over his indecisiveness regarding which university to attend and which major to pursue. For much of the year and a half since graduating high school, Ronald had suffered from motivation deficit disorder—a clinical sounding term coined by his impatient father—spinning his wheels but getting nowhere.

It was not that he'd done *nothing*. He'd spent the two summers camping and hiking to out-of-the-way thermal hot springs, and he'd dedicated last winter to shadowing Franco Cavaletti at the Crested Butte Auto Body Shop. It was supposed to have been something like a mechanic apprenticeship arrangement. But Ronald knew, even if Franco didn't, that he wasn't cut out to become a mechanic. He wasn't even getting paid, beyond the occasional twenty-dollar bill Franco slipped him on a Friday afternoon before closing. He'd just liked hanging out with Franco, who treated him like a son. Plus, he enjoyed the camaraderie of the other grease monkeys, who gave him a hard time for not having a half-dozen girlfriends by now.

Riding on a stuffy aluminum coach that had motored him from Colorado, a thousand miles through Utah and Nevada, and finally into California, Ronald hadn't been able to sleep or get comfortable, trying his twisted pretzel best to contort his six-foot frame on a pair of seats he had mostly to himself. Though he was already well-traveled from trips he'd taken with his folks and brother, this was Ronald's first foray on his own. He snapped photos and filmed the occasional segment of his journey across the desert—a region which, as a mountain boy, intrigued him immensely. As he daydreamed out the window at the barrenness of the landscape, he embodied the character and bravado of *Lawrence of Arabia*, the work of cinema he and his mother had considered their favorite back when he was still in high school. His indefatigable brain couldn't get over his great luck. Yes, he was going to miss his mom. But he was also about to become a temporary sub-letter in downtown San Francisco before starting his first semester at Stanford University. *How adult is that* he kept asking himself over and over. Ronald had brought with him two large suitcases that were packed to bursting with his clothes, the Super 8 camera he'd received for high school graduation, his records, his books, and everything else he hadn't sold or given away during the Annual Union Congregational Holiday Rummage Sale. Deposited at the Transbay bus terminal just after midnight, stiff with his bad shoulder that seemed stuck in a cramp he couldn't release, Harlan had been there impatiently waiting for his brother's traffic-delayed arrival.

"Are you trying to grow a moustache or something?" Harlan asked. It sounded like an insult, or at least a judgement. He'd always been envious of his younger brother's virile ability to sprout hair when and where it was needed most. Harlan, by comparison, was nearly hairless as a Sphynx cat, and always had been, to the detriment of his maturation and abilities to keep up with the male Joneses of the world.

Ronald wasn't self-conscious by nature, but insecurities always flared up in the presence of his older brother, whose approval he yearned for, and whose acceptance always seemed an arm's length beyond his reach—though Ronald had long arms. He said, "It's a peace caterpillar, you dope! Everyone who can is growing one. And women are refusing to shave their legs on Stanford's campus. I read all about it in *LIFE Magazine*. You should really get with the program."

"No thank you," Harlan shot back. "Especially if there are anti-war gorilla women running amuck!" It wasn't a funny comeback, but Ronald flashed his brother a quick smile for effort. Harlan went on. "But in the spirit of getting with the program and needing to get out more, I hope you will accompany me to my going-away party at Golden Gate Park this afternoon."

"I don't like crowds, but I guess I could go," Ronald said. "That is, if I get to bring my movie camera."

"What do you even know about crowds, coming from Crested Butte?" his brother asked incredulously. "But you've got yourself a deal. You can bring your damn movie camera, but don't embarrass me."

HARLAN HELD RONALD'S damn movie camera as he hopped over the chain-link fence along with the thousands of others who were pouring onto the patchouli and smoke-filled Polo Fields at Golden Gate Park.

Ronald thought he could make out a Maypole poking out of the crowd in the distance, maybe halfway to the small stage. "That's where I want to be," he said, pointing. "You know, to get the best shots of the stage." It was as if he thought he was Alfred Hitchcock himself, about to film a sequel to his horror film, *The Birds*, which was also shot in San Francisco.

"Stay out of trouble," the older brother warned. Ronald noted, with a tinge of disassociation, that this might have been the first time Harlan had looked out for him in their lives. "That bearded fellow climbing onto the stage looks like it could be Allen Ginsberg—the poet, in case you didn't know," Harlan hollered after him. Ronald gave an upward jerk of his chin in acknowledgment before being swallowed whole by the hippie sardine packed crowd.

Ronald found San Francisco to be pleasantly warm and sunny for January, while Crested Butte, he knew from the phone call home to let his folks know he'd arrived safely, was immobilized under a foot and a half of snow. Taking a cue from the other shirtless audience members—mostly males but a few females—and streaming the intoxicating essence of a cavalcade of body odors into his delighted nostrils, Ronald pinched his movie camera between his knees as he unbuttoned the large flower-patterned shirt that Franco and the mechanics had gotten him as a gag gift when he announced he would be heading to California for school. They probably never imagined he would wear it, but Harlan had convinced him it was the perfect costume for a gathering like the Human Be-in.

He hesitated for a moment, having locked eyes with a handsome, long-haired hippy who was maybe a few years older. Then, without breaking his stare, he seductively peeled the blousy shirt off each shoulder, before rolling and stuffing it into his back jeans pocket. Ronald was new at flirting, but he had long been proud to show off the dark plush fur that hourglassed above and below his sternum before dividing around both sides of his navel and merging into the thicket of pubic hair that was just visible above the layered waistlines of his faded pink briefs and well-worn blue jeans. He'd spent hours studying hairy men in magazines and was grateful that his body hair pattern was distributed perfectly—not connecting with his underarm hair and not creeping over his shoulders or around his ribcage to taint his naturally follicle-barren backside. The hippie approached him as Ronald retrieved his movie camera from between his knees. When he glanced back up, the two were standing nose to nose and sandaled toes to sneaker toes.

"My name's Mac," the handsome hippie with miniature silk daisies tied into his hair said. His voice was so low it made Ronald imagine that he must have gargantuan testicles. He was pinned so closely against the guy, that he just might find out.

"I'm Ron—" he started to say when Mac palmed his crotch with a Herculean squeeze and suctioned his mouth on Ronald's, extending his tongue beyond the wisdom teeth to plant a dot of LSD in the fertile garden of Ronald's salivary glands.

"Enjoy the trip," Mac said, looking over the bridge of his lowered, purple-lensed sunglasses. "Find me later if you want more." The hippie batted his long eyelashes, smiling through eyes that looked brown, the narrow rings of color outlining his giant pupils like dark chocolate on the outside of a Milk Dud. Then, as if by magic, the hippie was suctioned back into the crowd, just as the chanting began from the stage. Most everyone surrounding Ronald at the Maypole joined in like a sea of robots whose power switches had just been flipped on.

> Hare Krsna, Hare Krsna, Krsna, Krisna, Hare Hare
> Hare Rāma, Hare Rāma, Rāma Rāma, Hare Hare.

Ronald commandeered a patch of grass at the base of the Maypole. Steadying himself with his back to the pole, he began to film. The chanting started to fade just as the speakers on the stage blasted the trumpeted introduction to "Dancing in the Streets" by Martha & the Vandellas.

> Calling out around the world,
> Are you ready for a brand-new beat?

The vast sea of humans on the Polo Fields transformed into a giant amoeba with arms and legs and flags and streamers flagellating in the marijuana-laced air. The Maypole sprang to life with an interweaving ceiling that twisted lower until two cloth ribbons lashed across Ronald's bare chest from different directions, snugging him to the pole. Other ribbons followed and he had to raise the camera above his head to keep filming. Ribbons immobilized his thighs and then his calves. He'd been focused on a man in a striped long-sleeve shirt, who was dancing solo in the distance on the roof of his van. Then his eyes and camera trained on the fingers of strangers pointing to a skydiver who was descending onto the field to the left of the stage. He zoomed in, following the skydiver until the cloth of his parachute became the newest toy to amuse the Human Be-in amoeba. The daredevil was celebrated—hoisted onto shoulders by a dozen pairs of the strongest arms closest to his landing site. All the while, Martha and the Vandellas anthemed on . . .

> An invitation across the nation
> A chance for folks to meet
> There'll be laughin', singin', music swingin'
> Dancin' in the street

A trio of nymphs joined hands to skip and dance around their sacrificial filmmaker on the Maypole as Allen Ginsberg moved onto the stage to take the microphone. He recited some event-pertinent passages from *Howl*— one of his most famous works, according to one of the nymphs who filled Ronald in. He zoomed the lens as close as he could while Ginsberg testified.

> I saw the best minds of my generation destroyed
>   by madness, starving hysterical naked,
> dragging themselves through the negro streets at
>   dawn looking for an angry fix,
> angelheaded hipsters burning for the ancient
>   heavenly connection to the starry dynamo in
>   the machinery of night,
> who poverty and tatters and hollow-eyed and
>   high sat up smoking in the supernatural
>   darkness of cold-water flats floating across
>   the tops of cities contemplating jazz . . .

The crowd had gone silent in meditation, contemplation, and prayer. No doubt there were several dozen who had already blacked out while Ginsberg sang his spoken-word gospel. At the same time, Ronald's smuggled acid began to kick in with soft, lurching convulsions that tickled his innards. He kept the camera steady and rolling, thanks to the Maypole ribbons that were holding him upright. The nymphs no longer tended their captive and seemed to have forgotten Ronald bound up there. Each of them had frozen in a different statue pose, staring and gesturing to the heavens, as Ginsberg continued to howl.

> . . . who were expelled from the academies for
>   crazy & publishing obscene odes on the
>   windows of the skull,
> who cowered in unshaven rooms in underwear,
>   burning their money in wastebaskets and
>   listening to the Terror through the wall,
> who got busted in their pubic beards returning
>   through Laredo with a belt of marijuana for
>   New York,
> who ate fire in paint hotels or drank turpentine
>   in Paradise Alley, death, or purgatoried their
>   torsos night after night
> with dreams, with drugs, with waking nightmares,
>   alcohol and cock and endless balls . . .

Ronald was seeing lots of things by that point—mostly prisms of color and strobing lights, plus one elephant he guessed must be Dumbo because it was flying. He also thought he spotted Mac, his most lovely hippie, in the distance. But when he tried to zoom in on him with his camera, his vision went completely out of focus. Ronald felt like he was spinning, or like the pole he had been lashed to had begun to rotate like the spindle of a giant turntable. He was feeling pleasantly dizzy, instead of the sick kind, and he began giggling, unable to stop.

Then the nymphs broke their poses and squatted one behind the other in front of him until all he could make out was the girl in front of him hypnotically gesticulating her arms in trance-inducing movements. As she did, her arms appeared to multiply. In a flashback, he was in Thailand again with his family, witnessing the Thousand-Hand Bodhisattva Dance. Bangled arms and hennaed hands began appearing out of nowhere and everywhere. A giggle got caught in Ronald's esophagus when one of the more opportunistic pairs of hands devised an opening in the braided May Pole ribbons not so coincidentally around the level of his crotch. Without making physical contact, the other two nymphs, with their thousand arms each, directed the energies of the universe below the belt of their sacrificial subject, who wasn't even wearing a belt. Bansuri flute music spewed from the stage as a thousand puffs of marijuana smoke spun into a tornado that encircled Ronald's stoned face.

It wasn't just the temperature or the nymphs' spiritual fortunes that were rising in supplication to their gods—Ronald's denimed phallus was somehow gaining prominence in their ritual. His boner became an obvious and sacred organ for bliss and a lingam worshipped by the nymph attendants and their lookers-on. Ronald clamped his eyes shut and squirmed as though he was being tickled to death and the friction this created inside his jeans induced a euphoria his brain could not restrain. He lifted his heavy eyelids and there was beautiful Mac standing three feet away, his left hand cupping his own crotch in solidarity. For the second time, Ronald's eyes locked with Mac's, as the long-haired voyeur waxed and polished his lower lip with a luscious tongue that glistened like diamonds in the slowly dimming sunlight.

Ronald's touch receptors and nerve endings piled into the go-cart with him to begin the impossibly steep funicular climb to what sure felt like a climax. He captured a breath in a single gulp and locked it in his lungs, refusing to expel. *Stop it. Don't!* he coached his acid-tripping libido. He clamped his eyes closed and in that lights-out instant, the expanding circle of his *bija* darkened the denim. The nymphs tumbled backwards on their keisters as if by the force of a blast, their eyes rolling into their craniums as they each turned into rainbow-colored pillars of salt.

Mac gathered a fistful of his luxurious, daisy-accessorized hair and tucked it behind a diamond-pierced ear as he took a step forward to Ronald's rescue from his multi-colored tethering. With a solid press of Mac's groin pinning his butterfly specimen in place and concealing from view any spermatozoic evidence of the random milking just committed, he untangled and detached the spent and shirtless filmmaker from the May Pole. Extracting the flower-patterned shirt from the back pocket of Ronald's jeans, he fashioned an apron by knotting the long sleeves around the back. Then the two men balanced forces against each other, arms crossing over collar bones.

An announcer took to the stage and approached the microphone, holding up the arm of a boy child in one hand and a cutout peace sign on the end of a long pole in the other, saying, "If the parents of this child are here, please come and take him."

And that was the last thing Ronald could remember hearing, though the Super 8 movie camera dangling at the end of his arm continued to film the trampled grass of the Polo Fields until its batteries ran dry.

AFTER OBSERVING THE setting sun en masse, as the announcer had implored them to do, the crowd began dispersing. Harlan looked high and low for his very high brother. After ten impatient minutes without success, he figured it would be good for Ronald to learn to find his way back to his new home.

The next morning, when he was awakened pre-dawn by the high-pitched alarm and rattle of his glow-in-the-dark bedside Timex, Harlan peeked out into the living room and thought he could make out two bodies splayed oppositely, appendages pointing in more directions than a weathervane in a hurricane. He hoped that one of them was his brother. Later, still unable to rouse either of them, he left a note on ruled paper, using all capital letters, warning his younger brother to SAFEGUARD THIS APARTMENT AND MY THINGS, OR ELSE—and then called himself a taxi to the airport.

GUNNISON HIGH SCHOOL

September 1962

AFTER BEING MESMERIZED BY A FILMSTRIP HE'D watched in his sophomore English class, Ron became convinced that he had been reincarnated not just from William Shakespeare's time, but from the Bard's village. He must have been both a contemporary and a friend to Will, because he seemed to know a lot more things about him than his teacher and classmates didn't.

Over summer vacation, he had renewed *The Complete Works of Shakespeare* four times. It was a navy-blue covered volume so thick, he counted it as a workout every time he picked it up or put it down. The librarian hadn't minded, since nobody else had checked out the monster in years. Ron became so engrossed with everything having anything to do with Shakespeare that his parents grew concerned.

They were simultaneously disappointed to observe that, just like his older brother before him, Ronnie was not exhibiting the least bit of interest in girls. He was instead fixated on an Elizabethan playwright who delighted in creating female roles so that male actors could dress up in women's clothes to play the female characters in his far-fetched plays. Ron's father was having none of it. He scrubbed his hands of parental responsibility when neither of the two boys he'd sired became a man's man. It was easier to blame their mother.

It was just weeks ago—during the Union Congregational Church's Summer Vacation Bible School, which Ronnie had protested he was too old to be attending—that he experienced an epiphany. While all the other good little Christian-pretending kids were making crosses out of burnt wooden matches and uncooked macaroni, Ron worked industriously alone in a corner. Over the course of four scripture-interspersed days, he constructed, from memory, a near-perfect replica of the Globe Theater out of Fudgsicle sticks he'd started saving on St. Patrick's Day, having no idea at the time what he was going to do with them. To save face with the pastor, who was called upon to pick a winner from the camp's art projects, Ron claimed his creation was a rendering of a medieval church. He didn't see this as a sin or a lie, since the Globe looked like the type of place where he would have been happy to worship (and he'd likely done so if there was any truth to his reincarnation hunch). For his work, he was awarded a copy of the King James Bible—which was appropriate, since it was possible that he might have met King James around the same time he was palling around with William Shakespeare.

Three weeks into the new school year, when the drama teacher at Gunnison High announced he would be directing a student production of *Twelfth Night*, Ron was over *the fickle and inconstant moon* and thinking *thus die I, thus, thus, thus*, if he didn't get a part. He also faced a quandary. He was turning sixteen in another month, which meant he could get his driver's license. But after rehearsals, he wouldn't be able to drive the twenty-seven miles back home from Gunnison—since Crested Butte's census of youngsters had become too small to support its own high school—at night without an adult in the car. (He also didn't have a car, but that seemed beside the point). He decided he would try out first and deal with transportation later. In the meantime, he would need to brush up on his *Twelfth Night*.

Harlan had been part of the last graduating class at Crested Butte High School. That had been in 1960, before the school was repurposed as an elementary school. It was the same year the Crested Butte Ski Area opened, but this wasn't forecast to increase year-round population for at least another decade. The ski hill was forecast, however, to make Harlan and Ronnie's dad—the only orthopaedic surgeon on the Western Slope—a very busy and rich Simpleman.

Ron had started bussing to Gunnison schools in the sixth grade, so he'd grown used to the commute. He had trained himself to read on the bus without getting carsick, and that's how he mostly avoided the antics, pranks, and bullying that got crammed into that forty-five-minute ride in each direction. His secret weapon was to find another bookworm—preferably a girl—as his bus partner. He would use that person like a human shield, providing he could get them to believe that he didn't get sick reading on the bus as long as he sat next to the window. This ruse came in handy a week after *Twelfth Night* tryouts, when, to his delight, he learned he'd been cast as Sebastian. That meant he had plenty of lines to memorize.

That's also when he began riding the bus in both directions with Taunia, another student from Crested Butte whom he'd known since kindergarten. She'd been cast as his identical twin Viola, even though he didn't think the two of them looked all that much alike. The drama teacher had assured them that once Viola began masquerading as Cesario in Act 1, Scene 4, the audience wouldn't be able to tell them apart. Ron was skeptical, but this was the least of his worries, since he was already hyperventilating over the epic, twenty-two-line monologue that he would need to memorize and pull off in Act 4, Scene 3, shortly after a sword fight.

FOR AT LEAST twenty minutes, Ron had been waiting for his father like a doofus at the four-way-stop in downtown Crested Butte. According to an arrangement that had worked just fine for the first five weeks of the new school year, Paul Simpleman was supposed to retrieve his teenager from that spot on his way home from the hospital. But today he was a no-show. Car after car stopped at the intersection before continuing to wherever they were heading. Some of the drivers recognized the teenager in the sweater vest and waved to him. But none of them were his father.

Then the town tow truck, driven by Franco Cavaletti, pulled up to a stop. A thirty-year-old who sometimes went to their church, Franco had a toothy Hollywood smile and a crewcut that was so dark brown it was practically black. He tooted his horn twice and motioned Ron to the open passenger-side window. Ron stepped onto the running board and stuck his face and nose inside the cab, inhaling a giant whiff of man world that nearly made him faint and fall backwards onto the curb.

"Heya, Mr. Cavaletti!" Ron not only knew the tow truck driver's last name but had memorized many of the trademarks about his homegrown idol, like his dimples and the cleft in his chin or how his eyebrows almost but not quite grew together. He'd gleaned these details during the top-secret investigative work he'd conducted over the past few years when the Simpleman Family sat across or behind the Cavalettis whenever Franco drove his parents to church on the odd Sunday they attended.

"It's Ronnie, right? I sometimes get you and your older brother confused."

Ron nodded. "That happens all the time, even though we look nothing alike."

"I suppose you're waiting for your dad, huh?" Franco glanced in his side mirror to see if he was holding up traffic. It was Crested Butte, so he wasn't. He twisted his thick neck to look back at the kid hanging off the side of his rig. "He's tied up at the hospital with an emergency. I just hauled a mangled car from the accident to the wrecking yard. Totaled." He said, looking dead serious.

"Wow," Ron said—but not in response to the news of yet another car crash on the mountainous roads surrounding the town. His dad was always bringing home the gruesome details to gross out he and Harlan. Ronnie scanned the dashboard, with its various red and green nobs and levers, grinning like he'd been dropped into a toy store. Or—since he was now a teen with more diverse and sophisticated interests—like he'd been given free rein in the literature and Shakespeare section on the second floor of the Old Rock Library.

"What do you say we grab some milkshakes? You can call your mom from Slogar's and let her know I'm going to give you a lift home and that your dad's gonna be late for supper."

"Sure," Ron shouted back without hesitation, his voice a bit too loud for the confined space inside the cab.

Franco's eyes flashed wide as he recoiled in an exaggerated fashion, pretending to be astonished by the kid's enthusiasm. "Well, hop in!" he commanded with a stern smile, as if to say *What are you waiting for?* Ron had to balance on the running board so he could leverage open the heavy door whose hinges howled as he pulled on the handle. He maneuvered the book bag off his shoulders and tossed it on the seat between them.

"We're only going a block," Franco said, "but buckle up, Buckwheat!"

"Buckwheat?" Ronnie scrunched up his face.

"You know! *Our Gang? The Little Rascals?*"

But Ron didn't know. Probably because it wasn't related to Will Shakespeare. "It's the nickname my Pop calls me," Franco said, and then Ron had the warmest feeling in his belly. He was happy to be called *Buckwheat* if that was how someone else referred to his idol from church. He reached for the seatbelt buckle.

"What's your favorite milkshake flavor?"

Ron didn't have to think about it. "Caramel."

"Mine too!" Franco wailed, slapping his big hand on Ron's thigh.

FIVE MINUTES LATER and tucked into a red vinyl upholstered booth in the front window at Slogar's, Franco slipped Ronnie a dime across the chrome-rimmed table so he could call his mom from the payphone next to the restrooms.

Afterward, happy to have checked in with his mom who had started worrying, Ron bounded back to the table thinking the vinyl from the seat should still be warm since he'd only been away a few seconds. The mismatched pair slurped their shakes and got to know things about each other. Franco had heard of Shakespeare but couldn't elaborate. Ron expressed his fondness for cars and said how he couldn't wait to get his driver's license in another few weeks. He dreamed about the day when he could drive himself to and from high school in Gunnison like other kids he knew.

Franco said he could hang out at the body shop anytime if he wanted to learn more about cars, displaying his dimples as he sucked the last of the caramel syrup from the bottom of the glass. Franco left a five-dollar bill on top of the check the waitress had written when she delivered their shakes and then suggested they should get going. "Time is money," he said quickly patting his hand loudly, two times on the table, as if to mean chop, chop.

It had started getting dark, which gave Franco an excuse to light up the tow truck like a Christmas Tree. Ron thought this was the coolest thing. Franco knew that would impress him, so he grinned as he fit his greasy looking ballcap back over his crewcut.

"You gonna get your dad to teach you to drive, huh?" Franco asked, revving the tow truck's diesel engine, practically rumbling the giggles right out of Ron.

"He's too busy."

"What about your older brother, then?"

"He moved away to California before summer started," Ron said without the slightest bit of sadness or longing. He was enjoying having a whole bedroom and the occasionally focused attention of their parents all to himself. It wasn't like his brother was dead or anything, so what did he have to be sad about? And it wasn't like the two of them were close or buddies— not since Harlan had decided to shut him out, way back when Ron was still in elementary school and Harlan was finishing junior high.

"Maybe your folks'll let me teach you," Franco suggested, lifting his dark eyebrows almost to the rim of the ballcap he'd turned backwards to drive. "It will be good practice for me for when I have a kid of my own one of these years."

"Oh yeah?" Ron asked, remembering to fasten his seat belt. "That would be fantastic if you had the time to teach me."

"I can make the time . . . after school, on weekends. The only time I couldn't do it would be Sundays, when my own folks are usually nagging me to drive them to church. But even after church could work, sometimes, too." Franco eased the rig out of the parking lot. He and his wife had been trying to get pregnant since their wedding ten years ago, but it hadn't happened yet, and he had grown discouraged.

Ron couldn't believe his good fortune. He would be the coolest kid in school once he could boast that he was getting driving lessons from Franco. He was already starting to work out this new fame in his head and how he would show it off. Maybe he'd learn to drive this tow truck and become a mechanic like Franco, too, one day. It was almost exciting enough to get him to forget about Shakespeare for five minutes. Almost.

"I'm going to be in a play by William Shakespeare. It's called *Twelfth Night*," he blurted out.

"That's cool," Franco replied, wondering if maybe his driving school offer hadn't landed properly with the kid. He'd expected a little more excitement, was all. "Is it a love story, like *Romeo and Juliet?*"

"No-o-o!" Ron chuckled uncomfortably. "Nothing gross like that."

Franco looked over at his passenger and smiled. "Do you even like girls yet, Buckwheat?"

There was that warm feeling in his gut again. Ron very much liked the sound of this new nickname and how it made him feel a special bond with Franco, someone he looked up to as the perfect specimen of what a man was supposed to look and act like.

"They're okay," he admitted, sounding less than enthusiastic. "Do you know this girl Taunia Thompson?"

"Is she your age?"

"Same grade as me."

Franco made a thinking face, moving his lips to one side. "She's a Crested Buttian?" he asked, referring to how locals were distinguishing themselves these days from the residents of Gunnison, Aspen, or even Snowmass. When Ron nodded, it came to him. "Chuck and Darlene's oldest daughter?"

"I guess so." The teen didn't really know many parents' names.

Franco asked the next legitimate question. "Is she your girlfriend, then?"

"No-o-o!" Ron said so forcefully that he launched a bit of spit onto the dashboard. Embarrassed, he reached to wipe it off with the sleeve of his shirt before going on. "Sorry. Taunia's going to play the role of Viola, who's supposed to be my identical twin in *Twelfth Night*. I don't think we look anything alike."

"Do you at least get to kiss her in the play?" Franco asked. Clearly, he knew nothing about *Twelfth Night*.

"Eeew!" Ron shrieked. "No! She's supposed to be my character's sister. But here's the interesting part," Ron set up the shocker. "Her character starts dressing as a man halfway through the play and begins going by the name *Cesario*."

Franco was trying to follow the kid's explanation because he was clearly excited about this play, but it just wasn't something Franco knew anything about. "Do you at least get to kiss Cesario in the play then?" he asked his passenger. Seeming like he was no longer grossed out, Ron just sat there with a guilty grin on his peach-fuzzed face. When he didn't answer, Marco said, "Because there would be nothing wrong with two guys kissing, you know."

Ron did not know that, as a matter of fact. He tried to take it in responsibly. "What do you mean?" He found himself suddenly unable to look at the driver.

"Let's put it this way," Franco said. "I assume your dad has had the talk with you. You know, about the birds and the bees."

"What about them?" Ron asked, looking out the passenger window at the strands of barbwire sagging between the fence posts as the truck bounced along on the gravel country road.

"I mean about sex and how everything works . . . you know . . . down there," he reached across the seat and pointed to the bump in the high-riding polyester pants the teen was wearing. Ron couldn't help but stiffen up, clenching every sixteen-year-old muscle he had

"Yes, he showed me some medical books once."

"So, he told you about the birds and the bees, but I'll bet he didn't tell you about the queer birds and the silly bees, did he?"

Ron giggled. He knew the word *queer* because he'd been called that at least twice every school year for as far back as he could recall. "No. I would have remembered that part if he did. There was no talk of queer birds."

Franco took his foot off the gas pedal and the tow truck slowed, before pulling off the road onto a patch of graded gravel, where the plows usually piled up the snow during winter. He shifted into neutral and pulled the parking brake located between them. He turned until he was mostly facing his passenger. Ron's heart in that moment was trying to spring out of his ribcage. Ten seconds passed.

"Do you want to try driving for a little bit, Buckwheat?" Franco asked.

The imprisoned breath Ron had been holding blasted out of his lungs and mouth like a cannonball. "Yes!" he said nearly exploding out of his seatbelt, spittle hitting the dashboard again.

"Let's switch places," Franco said. "This can be your first lesson." They both unfastened their seatbelts. "Here," Franco said, helping Ron lean forward with a gentle push on his closest shoulder. "I'll slip under you. You pass over me." In a comical moment, they both got hung up on the emergency brake but eventually succeeded in switching spots. Franco fastened his seatbelt and Ron copied him, pumping up his chest before gripping both hands around the steering wheel, just to get the feel of it.

"Okay, Buckwheat," Franco said, using hand motions for brakes suggesting a pause, "before we go too crazy, I just wanted to finish our chat about the queer birds and the silly bees. It's important. My dad screwed it up and maybe your dad did, too. Most dads get it wrong, to be honest."

"What do you mean?" Ron had suspected that his dad didn't know the full story or had been keeping something from him, when they'd had the talk about sex a few years back.

"Well," Franco began. "What I mean is that there are lots of different kinds of birds—"

"Duh. Everyone knows that!"

"What I meant is that there are boy birds who like other boy birds. And there are girl honeybees that prefer the company of other girl honeybees." Franco could see Ronnie's eyes growing large as pie plates. "And some boy birds like both girl and boy birds the same."

"And it's the same with the honeybees?" Ron asked. Somehow, he wanted this clarified so that he could grasp the concept.

"That's right. And here is the thing that most dads don't tell their children . . . all of this is completely natural. It is part of the design of nature."

Ron felt a cool wash of calm come over him. His hands let go of the steering wheel and he clasped them in his lap, turning to his driving instructor. "And these are called queer birds and silly bees?" he asked, with the innocence of all heaven's angels combined. He wanted to get this right, because he sensed it applied to him. Franco began nodding from the passenger seat, as the most perfect and reassuring smile slowly stretched across his handsome face.

Ron Simpleman knew he was a queer bird in that moment. And being a queer bird was something completely natural to be, he repeated silently to himself.

"Can I tell you something, Mr. Cavaletti?"

"Sure, Buckwheat," he said, squaring his shoulders to more directly face the driver, who hadn't started driving yet. "Just one condition though," he negotiated. "You have to stop calling me Mr. Cavaletti. That's my dad's name. Just call me Franco. Deal?" he reached out his hand to shake on it. Ron grasped it firm, just as his dad had taught him to do.

Letting go and leaning back against the door, Franco whispered across the seat. "You can tell me anything, Ronnie."

Ron sucked in a giant inhale. "I'm pretty sure I'm a queer bird," he admitted for the first time to anybody.

"Me too," Franco said, without hesitation. "But I am even queerer than you, Buckwheat."

"How's that?"

Franco cleared his throat. "Because I'm a queer bird who likes boy birds *and* girl birds."

"At the same time?" Ron's voice leapt to a falsetto register.

Franco let out a rifle shot of laughter. "Well, so far, no. Not at the same time. But there's a first time for everything, I suppose." This last statement was more to himself than the kid.

Ron thought about what he wanted to say next. "You were right about my dad. He didn't get the talk right. He didn't tell me anything about the queer birds and the silly bees."

"Most dads don't. That's a real problem for the world."

"How so, Franco?" Ron straightened in his seat behind the wheel.

"It's sort of the faults of the fathers that there is so much hate in this world of ours, Buckwheat." Franco turned his baseball cap around, so it faced the regular direction. "You know, instead of teaching their kids that people are different and that everyone is beautiful and that every type of person needs to be respected and loved and that it doesn't matter how they act, who they love, what color their skin is, or the language they speak, our dads—they lie to us, just like their fathers lied to them. This is what I mean when I say it's the faults of our fathers that humans don't just get along—if that makes any sense to you."

Ron wasn't confused in the least. It made all the sense in the world to him now.

Brushing the long sleeves of his baseball shirt high up on his dark hairy forearms, Franco said, "Now, let me teach you how to shift gears."

PART V: 1953–1946

At first the infant,

Mewling and puking in the nurse's arms

CRESTED BUTTE

April 1958

RONNIE HATED IT WHENEVER HARLAN WAS LEFT IN charge of him because his older brother always treated him like a science project. Ronnie was twelve years old now. He could take care of himself. Harlan was so dumb he didn't even know how to heat up a can of pork and beans. Ronnie figured he'd probably starve to death before his parents returned from the doctor convention they were attending in Denver.

Another example of how stupid his brother was: when their father killed an elk and had his head turned into a trophy, Harlan was the one who suggested they name it *Bruce*. Their mom had asked at the time whether Bruce wouldn't be a better name for a moose. Harlan said he thought it *was* a moose! That's how dumb he was. His little brother teased him for six months after that, calling him *Harlan Perkins*, since he was so bad at knowing animals.

They'd only lived in their new house for five years and everyone was still getting used to it. Though Harlan had just turned fifteen, the boys still had to share a bedroom, because their father had not been willing to give up his home doctor office, which was always locked. Their shared bedroom was where Harlan conducted his science experiments—like it was his personal laboratory or something. The brighter younger brother had figured out what Harlan was doing beneath the blankets on his twin bed across the room and under the window, but he mostly pretended to sleep through it.

But this night—a Friday, and the first of the two nights they'd been left alone, with the expectation that they'd be on their best behavior—Ron could no longer pretend to ignore his brother after the lights went out.

Harlan needed an assistant and accomplice for a new experiment he'd been curious to try.

Harlan whispered a challenge through the stale air from his side of the almost pitch-black bedroom. "Truth or dare?"

Ronnie acted like he hadn't heard the challenge. But that only made Harlan repeat it louder. "Truth or dare?" he practically yelled.

"I don't want to play your stupid game, Harlan!"

"Shut up, Hermey, and play!"

Ever since the boys had seen *Rudolph the Red-Nosed Reindeer*, which had come out last Christmas, Harlan had relentlessly teased Ronald for having a hairstyle that made him look just like Hermey, the elf who wanted to become a dentist. Their parents had driven them to Gunnison in the middle of a blizzard to see it, the night before the night before Christmas. (Since he was ten, Ronnie had taken issue with the term *Christmas Eve*. If this was supposed to mean the night *before* Christmas Day, why did the word *Eve* come *after* Christmas?)

"Dare," he said now, trying to speed up the process. Maybe he could be made to do something silly and then they could both go to sleep.

This caught Harlan off guard. Normal people chose *truth* first, because that was the chicken's way out. He should have known little Ronnie wasn't normal. After all, he'd been intending to prove how abnormal and queer his little brother was with the night's experiment, which he'd been cooking up for days.

"I dare you to come over here and put your mouth on my penis," Harlan blurted out in the darkness.

That was a different sort of dare, and a lot more than Ronnie had been expecting. But it seemed quick and simple enough—so he pulled off the blankets, walked the three steps between their beds, and bent over his brother. Harlan hadn't removed his own blankets yet—he was slightly shocked his brother wasn't putting up more of a stink about the dare.

"Well, whatcha waiting for?" Ronnie stammered. "I'm sleepy!"

A corner of the flying blanket whipped him in the face, making one of his eyes water. Rubbing the sting out of it with the heel of his hand, Ronnie folded at the waist and tried to make sense of the topography of his brother's body in the dark with just one peeper. It took a couple of head bobs to find the subject of the dare, but when he did locate it with one of his nostrils, he opened his mouth and put his brother's pokey thing inside.

It didn't smell or taste like anything special. So, at first, Ronnie didn't see the point. He figured he'd satisfied the dare and now it was his turn. He abruptly stopped what he'd been doing and returned to his own bed, leaving Harlan huffing and insisting it didn't count because his brother hadn't done it long enough. But that's not how the game was played, and little Ronnie knew it, because he was smarter than his brother.

"Truth or dare," he challenged from his side of the room.

"Truth," Harlan said, chickening out like a normal person.

"Why is it, do you think, that your willie is so much smaller than mine, when you're supposed to be three years older than me?"

"Who says it is, you idiot?" Harlan snapped back, making use of his little brother's left-behind saliva and stroking himself.

"Well, I was just on it, and it's way smaller, so there," Ronnie answered. "You're supposed to tell the truth anyway. Unless you wanna change your mind and do a dare instead."

There wasn't a ready answer as Harlan absorbed the jab and weighed his next move. "Okay, smartass. Dare, then."

Ronnie was ready for this. "With the bedroom light turned on and the blankets off, stroke your willie until you make it throw up."

Harlan considered the challenge and wanted to know more about the terms. "While you watch me, I suppose?"

"Duh!" the younger brother said before erupting in giggles. He got out of bed and flicked the switch. His brother shielded his eyes with his arm and groaned so loud he sounded like a lion. Ronnie stood there, at the side of his brother's bed, and stared at the slobbery, glistening little boner his brother had. "I'm waiting!" he said, tapping one foot like he'd seen his mother do in the kitchen. Harlan began to move the skin up and down with his thumb and forefinger.

"How do you even know about making the willie throw up," he said, as he stroked. "You're only twelve!"

"I heard Mom talking to Dad about your wet dreams. She told him you were having them every night and asked him if there was something wrong with you."

"Shut up so I can concentrate," his brother barked, closing his eyes and conjuring up God knows what in his imagination. Ronnie bit his upper lip and tried not to smile—because this was funny and he wanted to laugh. He knew about willies throwing up because he could make his do this anytime he wanted and didn't think it was that big of a deal. His older brother, though, made it seem like the hardest thing he'd ever been asked to do—worse than having to mow the lawn, given the sweat Ronnie could see on his brother's forehead.

His brother's breathing changed, and he varied the speed of his hand before sucking in a breath and then letting it burst out into the bedroom as a trickle of milk leaked out the end of his baby boner. Ronnie folded his hands in front of his own erection and said, "Good. Now we're even. I'm sleepy." He returned to his own bed, slapping off the light switch on the way.

Harlan lay there heaving melodramatically in the darkness. Little Ronnie knew what being melodramatic meant too, because their dad was always telling him not to be so. Harlan sighed, saying, "Good game. We're even now"—as if there had been unsettled business between them. Ronnie lay there thinking about the difference in the size of their willies, knowing the two weren't even at all.

THE FOLLOWING MORNING, Harlan was up before his brother and had placed a short stack of magazines on the kitchen counter. When Ronnie walked into the kitchen to reach for the box of Cocoa Puffs, he noticed the stack with a woman in a swimsuit in the pool and a cartoon bunny rabbit laying on the diving board above her. "What's this?" he asked Harlan.

"They're *Playboy* magazines, you idiot! Look inside and you'll see what I mean."

Ronnie opened the magazine, and his eyes doubled in size. Harlan doubled over in laughter. "Dad gave them to me, a few years ago. Maybe when I was your age. He told me to hide them from you and Mom, but I got bored with 'em. You can have them now. But you must keep them hidden from Mom. Promise?"

"Sure!" Ronnie said, scooping up the stack and trundling off to their bedroom, forgetting all about his Cocoa Puffs. It didn't take him fifteen minutes to see that all the pictures were of women not wearing any tops. What wasn't in any of the fourteen issues—and Ronnie had checked twice—were any pictures of men. No wonder his brother had gotten bored.

He put the stack of magazines in his knapsack, sandwiched between his colored pencils case and a *Superman* comic book. He had an idea.

OVER THE COURSE of the next few weeks, entrepreneurial Ronnie selected a different boy from his school and told him to meet up in the baseball field after school. There, in the abandoned dugout, Ronnie would extract one of the magazines from his knapsack and make the other boy the deal of the century.

"You show me your boner, and I'll show you mine, and you get to keep this *Playboy* magazine," he'd say with all the polish of a used-car salesman. Then he'd add, with a shake of their hands, "But this is our secret. And your secret's safe with me."

UNION CONGREGATIONAL CHURCH

October 1953

RONNIE WAS A SEVEN-YEAR-OLD WITH A COWLICK HE couldn't tame no matter how much of his dad's Brylcreem he slathered on it. He sat there wedged in the front pew between his girdle-wearing mom and second grandma, both of whom were dressed in black, from their heads to their toes. Ronnie's first grandma was his mom's mom, who he visited much more often. Spare tissues were tucked everywhere there was an elastic wrist or waistband to hold them in place. Ronnie's second grandpa, who was on his dad's side of the family, was laid out and wearing a blue suit in the casket without a lid, right there in front of them, with bouquets of stinky lilies on either side of him.

Ronnie hadn't liked this grandpa. But he sensed his dad didn't like him much either, so he didn't feel compelled to pretend. He loved his second grandma, though—and not just because she'd just slipped him a red-and-white-striped peppermint candy.

There weren't all that many people in the church. Harlan and their dad sat in the pew opposite them, with the other men, who were waiting to carry second grandpa away in his box. Ronnie couldn't understand how Harlan could be considered one of them, sitting there in his Easter suit. He was such a weakling, and he couldn't lift anything anyways.

There hadn't been any talking or singing so far, which Ronnie also found strange, since that was all that happened in church the other times he'd been there. His second grandma leaned over him, practically squishing him with her breasts, to whisper in his mother's ear, which was adorned with one of her favorite peony clip-on earrings. She hadn't been able to find the mate, so she'd spent an extra five minutes getting ready—fussing with her hair so that it swooped to cover her naked ear. Ronnie knew where the earring had gone, because he was the one who had taken it, just for fun. He flushed with the thrill of remembering how it felt to try on. He hadn't expected her to notice it was gone. He'd have to remember to put it back when she wasn't looking.

"June, I just want to say I'm sorry," his second grandma whispered, with a hand shielding her mouth. Her lipstick hadn't quite filled in all the cracks in her lips, Ronnie noticed.

"For what, Margaret?" his mom whispered back.

"Your husband—my son—well, I don't have to tell you, but he's a bit of an asshole."

"Margaret!" Ronnie's mom hissed. "We're in church."

"I blame his father, cramped inside that box right there," Grandma said, pointing with her arthritic finger. She looked to Ronnie like she must spend her days just rocking in her chair, cracking those knuckles from sunup to sundown. "He abused your husband as a child. I don't know if he ever told you that." As she spoke, a piece of spittle landed on Ronnie's cheek. He wiped it away. It counted as girl germs, even if it was coming from his second grandma. She was technically a girl, he supposed.

Ronnie's mom shifted, then scooted closer. The girdle she had on was killing her almost as much as the news her mother-in-law insisted on delivering before the start of her father-in-law's funeral. "Abused him?" she whispered back. "How?"

"Sexually," Grandma said, perhaps louder than was necessary. Ronnie knew the first part of that complicated word and wondered if it meant what he thought it did. "It's the fault of his father, that Paul turned out the way he did. Just like it's going to be Paul's fault that your boys turn out . . ."

She stopped herself. June Simpleman clasped her hands in her lap and stared straight ahead, her own lipstick-outlined mouth pursed and protruding in deep thought. The organist launched into a toned-down and abbreviated version of "Autumn Leaves"—a song made famous by French singer Edith Piaf as "Les Feuilles Mortes," a few years earlier.

Just as the pastor began walking down the aisle toward Ronnie's dead second grandpa, who seemed to be blocking his way, June leaned in and whispered, "Isn't it the faults of all the fathers who came before us, Margaret?"

Ronnie's second grandma nodded in silent affirmation as her grandson noisily sucked the hell out of his peppermint candy.

GUNNISON VALLEY HOSPITAL

October 10, 1946

RONALD PAUL SIMPLEMAN MARKED HIS DEBUT AT 7:38 p.m., kicking and wailing up quite the full-throated tantrum as he hogged center stage on the sparsely decorated set of a rural delivery room.

In the throes of a fierce blizzard—the first of the season—that had already closed Highway 135 behind his frantic freewheeling and fish-tailing parents, with their almost three-year old wedged between them in the front seat of the Chrysler New Yorker, their second child—who had just been swatted on the bum by a grouchy nurse who'd been called in from home to assist with the delivery—was making it clarion clear to everyone within earshot in all of Gunnison County that, not only had he arrived on the scene, but he was not the least bit happy about the part he was expected to play.

"When we are born we cry
that we are come to this great stage of fools."
—William Shakespeare, *King Lear*

ABOUT THE AUTHOR

MICHAEL SCOTT CURNES IS THE AUTHOR OF *SIMPLEMAN* and five previously published and award-winning works of fiction. All but one of his novels, were set in rural America where he was born and raised in the Pacific Northwest. His writing has appeared in *The Globe and Mail*, the *Times Colonist*, and in two published anthologies: *Writing the West Coast* and *Living Artfully (Reflections from the Far West Coast)*.

His debut novel, *VAL*, was published in 1996 by Brownell and Carroll. Inkwater Press published his next three novels, ***For the Love of Mother*** [Fiction Prize Winner at the 2011 Green Book Awards in San Francisco]; ***Coping with Ash*** [Fiction Prize Winner in the 2017 New Apple Book Awards and Bronze Medal Prize in the Independent Book Publishers Awards]; followed by ***Wicked Ninnish*** [Fiction Prize Winner in the 2020 Royal Dragonfly Book Awards]. In 2022, his eco-thriller, ***To Pay Paul*** was also published by Down Wind Press [2022 Royal Dragonfly triple prize winner for Best Fiction, Best LGBTQ Fiction and Best Environmental Fiction].

Simpleman is his sixth novel.

Michael is living his best life alongside his soulmate and husband—Bernard—on Vancouver Island in Victoria, British Columbia. Michael is a member of the Writers' Union of Canada.